EPILOG

EPILOG

AND OTHER STORIES

The Complete Short Fiction of
Clifford D. Simak,
Volume Fourteen

Introduction by David W. Wixon

OPEN ROAD
INTEGRATED MEDIA
NEW YORK

"Lulu" © 1957 by Galaxy Publishing Corp. © 1985 by Clifford D. Simak. Originally published in *Galaxy Science Fiction*, v. 14, no. 2, June 1957. Reprinted by permission of the Estate of Clifford D. Simak.

"Smoke Killer" © 1944 by Real Adventures Publishing Co., Inc. © 1972 by Clifford D. Simak. Originally published in *Lariat Story Magazine*, v. 14, no. 1, May 1944. Reprinted by permission of the Estate of Clifford D. Simak.

"Shadow Show" © 1953 by Fantasy House, Inc. © 1981 by Clifford D. Simak. Originally published in *The Magazine of Fantasy & Science Fiction*, v. 5, no. 5, November 1953. Reprinted by permission of the Estate of Clifford D. Simak.

"Epilog" © 1973 by Random House, Inc. © 2001 by Clifford D. Simak. Originally published in *Astounding: The John W. Campbell Memorial Anthology*, ed. by Harry Harrison, 1973. Reprinted by permission of the Estate of Clifford D. Simak.

"A Bomb for No. 10 Downing" © 1942 by Better Publications, Inc. © 1970 by Clifford D. Simak. Originally appeared in *Sky Fighters*, v. 27, no. 3, September 1942. Reprinted by permission of the Estate of Clifford D. Simak.

"Limiting Factor" © 1949 by Better Publications, Inc. © 1977 by Clifford D. Simak. Originally published in *Startling Stories*, v. 20, no. 2, November 1949. Reprinted by permission of the Estate of Clifford D. Simak.

"Masquerade" © 1941 by Street & Smith Publications, Inc. © 1969 by Clifford D. Simak. Originally published in *Astounding Science Fiction*, v. 27, no. 1, March 1941. Reprinted by permission of the Estate of Clifford D. Simak.

"The Fence" © 1952 by Space Publications, Inc. © 1980 by Clifford D. Simak. Originally published in *Space Science Fiction*, v. 1, no. 2, September, 1952. Reprinted by permission of the Estate of Clifford D. Simak.

"Rule 18" © 1938 by Street & Smith Publications, Inc. © 1966 by Clifford D. Simak. Originally published in *Astounding Science-Fiction*, v. 21, no. 5, July 1938. Reprinted by permission of the Estate of Clifford D. Simak.

"Mr. Meek Plays Polo" © 1944 by Love Romances Publishing Co., Inc. © 1972 by Clifford D. Simak. Originally published in *Planet Stories*, v. 2, no. 8, Fall 1944. Reprinted by permission of the Estate of Clifford D. Simak.

"The World That Couldn't Be" © 1957 by Galaxy Publishing Corp. © 1985 by Clifford D. Simak. Originally published in *Galaxy Science Fiction*, v. 15, no. 3, January 1958. Reprinted by permission of the Estate of Clifford D. Simak.

Introduction © 2023 by David W. Wixon

ISBN: 978-1-5040-8312-6

This edition published in 2023 by Open Road Integrated Media, Inc.
180 Maiden Lane
New York, NY 10038
www.openroadmedia.com

CONTENTS

INTRODUCTION:
CLIFFORD D. SIMAK:
THE MEMORY OF MAN

"This series [the City *stories] . . . was filled with the gentleness and the kindness and the courage that I thought were needed in the world. . . . I made the dogs and robots the kind of people I would like to live with. And the vital point is this: that they must be dogs or robots, because people were not that kind of folks'."*

—*Clifford D. Simak, as quoted by Sam Moskowitz, science fiction historian, in* Seekers of Tomorrow

Clifford D. Simak's book *City*—perhaps the best known of all his works —became immediately notable in its time for its development of a "future history" in which dogs attained intelligence, robots became independent beings . . . and mankind vanished from the Earth. And before the end of the *City* stories (I am including "Epilog," which appears later in this volume, in that canon), even the dogs are gone.

A large portion of Cliff Simak's science fiction stories—perhaps one-quarter of them—featured, or at least mentioned, robots. (In fact, even one of Cliff's western short stories, "Barb Wire Brings

Bullets!" (see volume six of this series, *The Complete Short Fiction of Clifford D. Simak*) actually used the word "robot"—not as a reference to the creatures we now think of as "surrogate humans," but in a probably unthinking and anachronistic use of the word to demonstrate a wounded man's inability to think. . . .)

Although Cliff Simak wrote a lot of stories that featured or mentioned robots, he did not make them all the same sort of creature. Readers generally remember those of his robots who were portrayed as a better sort of human, uncorrupted by the baser sort of instincts and needs of the human race—"the kind of being that a human should be, but very seldom is." In other Simak stories, robots were little better than machines, mere mechanisms lacking personality.

The body of the typical Simak robot represents a triumph of human technology; but Cliff Simak very often housed in those bodies the souls of gentle, naïve, childlike people—creating, perhaps, a synthesis that could alleviate mankind's fear of technology, by creating an appropriate balance of man and technology. This is particularly striking in the cases of the many robots Cliff portrayed as having an interest in religion (such as the robot in the novel *Time and Again*, who charged all of humanity with having disregarded its own Commandments, or the robots in *Project Pope* and *A Choice of Gods*, who set up their own religious organizations because humans seemed no longer interested in doing so), or the other robots shown as happy-go-lucky beings whose interests never extended beyond their work or the simplest of pleasures, as in the short story "Installment Plan" (see volume one).

On the other hand, there was Nellie, in the story "Ogre" (see volume one), who literally beat a human being to death! (Nellie is also the only one of Simak's robots to which he gave a female name, and for which he used the pronoun "she."

The stories that, with their interstitial materials, make up the book *City* have many threads; and one of the longest, and most important, is the biography of the robot Jenkins. (There is another robot of that name in a different Simak story, but that is not the same character.)

As it happened, Jenkins did not appear at all in most of the early *City* stories. But if Jenkins "lived" (can robots be said to live?), he lived a long, long life; and he evolved through the course of the book. Until, by the time of "Epilog," the very last of the stories, Jenkins seems to be the only animate being living on Earth (aside from the mice for which he feels a certain fondness).

Jenkins spent much of his long life trying to take care, first, of the Websters, the members of the human family he served when he was just a colorless mechanical butler. Later, when the humans left Earth and the last Webster went to his eternal sleep, Jenkins took over the Websters' duty of guiding the civilization of the intelligent dogs. And when those, too, were gone, all he had left was the memory of having been "proud to be a Webster." But he also realized that he had lived too long; he was not able to forget all that had happened and all the sadness it contained.

Long before people and dogs abandoned Earth, Jenkins had begun taking on human characteristics. He had a metal body that never wore out, and yet he sat in chairs—in fact, he liked to rock; and when engaged in thought, he developed a habit of rubbing his chin . . .

In fact, the question might be raised whether Jenkins himself had become another of the tragedies and failures that followed, one after another, through the course of the book. He bound himself to the Webster family and to Webster House and the Earth; and then he put his faith in the dogs after concluding that humans were a failure . . . only to see them, too, follow the fate of the humans. Did Jenkins replay in his life the rise and fall of the Websters . . . and all humans?

And then the past came back to find Jenkins, when some of the other robots who had once lived on Earth returned to see what had happened in the time since they had left. One of those was Andrew, who appears in the story "The Trouble with Ants," volume thirteen. Upon learning that dogs had largely forgotten Men, Andrew tells a dog: "I suppose Jenkins kept you afraid of men. For Jenkins was a smart one. He knew that you must start afresh. He knew that you must not carry the memory of Man as a dead weight on your necks."

"And we," Andrew continued, "are nothing more than the memory of Man."

In Cliff Simak's very first novel, *Cosmic Engineers*, one of the Engineers, robots found by men on a far planet, contrasts his fellows with humans, saying ". . . we are not driven by restless imagination . . . imagination that will not let one rest until all has been explained."

Robots in Simak stories were created to work. They knew it, and they were happy—if they could be thought of as "happy." And is that the problem with the humans in *City*? Is the problem that led to the end of humans on Earth the fact that they did not know, or had forgotten—or even never had—a purpose, a job? (See the contrast, in the short story "I Am Crying All Inside" (see volume one), between the last robots left on Earth and the degraded humans they took care of.)

"He was doing for a Webster once again," Jenkins realizes in "Hobbies" (see volume eleven). "A warm peace came upon him, the close and intimate peacefulness of the old days when he had trotted, happy as a terrier, on his many errands.

"For he was doing for a Webster once again."

Jenkins, at that point, was able to savor his oldest memories. But in the end, memories of mankind did not last, and did no one any good.

David W. Wixon

LULU

The spaceship was a robot, and a robot can be too human, making it a danger—particularly when it thinks it is in love. "Lulu," she was called, and some readers have found her intriguing; but I myself am irritated by such irrationality, which I find insulting to womankind. And I also found myself remembering Hal in the movie 2001: A Space Odyssey. And that in turn led me to think about all those Frankenstein stories, as well as all the other stories about technology gone awry.

"Lulu" originally appeared in Galaxy Science Fiction, *in the June 1957 issue.*

—dww

The machine was a lulu.

That's what we called her: Lulu.

And that was our big mistake.

Not the only one we made, of course, but it was the first, and maybe if we hadn't called her Lulu, it might have been all right.

Technically, Lulu was a PER, a Planetary Exploration Robot. She was a combination spaceship/base of operations/synthesizer/analyzer/communicator. And other things besides. Too many other things besides. That was the trouble with her.

Actually, there was no reason for us to go along with Lulu. As a matter of fact, it probably would have been a good deal better if we hadn't. She could have done the planet-checking without any supervision. But there were rules which said a robot of her class must be attended by no fewer than three humans. And, naturally, there was some prejudice against turning loose, all by itself, a robot that had taken almost twenty years to build and had cost ten billion dollars.

To give her her due, she was an all-but-living wonder. She was loaded with sensors that dug more information out of a planet in an hour than a full human survey crew could have gotten in a month. Not only could she get the data, but she correlated it and coded it and put it on the tape, then messaged the information back to Earth Center without a pause for breath.

Without a pause for breath, of course—she was just a dumb machine.

Did I say dumb?

She wasn't in any single sense. She could even talk to us. She could and did. She talked all the blessed time. And she listened to every word we said. She read over our shoulders and kibitzed on our poker. There were times we'd willingly have killed her, except you can't kill a robot—that is, a self-maintaining one. Anyhow, she cost ten billion dollars and was the only thing that could bring us back to Earth.

She took good care of us. That no one could deny. She synthesized our food and cooked it and served our meals to us. She saw that the temperature and humidity were just the way they should be. She washed and pressed our clothes and she doctored us if we had need of it, like the time Ben got the sniffles and she whipped up a bottle of some sort of gook that cured him overnight.

There were just the three of us—Jimmy Robins, our communications man; Ben Parris, a robotic trouble-shooter; and myself, an interpreter—which, incidentally, had nothing to do with languages.

We called her Lulu and we never should have done that. After this, no one is ever going to hang a name on any of those long-haired robots; they'll just have to get along with numbers. When Earth Center hears what happened to us, they'll probably make it a capital offense to repeat our mistake.

But the thing, I think, that really lit the candles was that Jimmy had poetry in his soul. It was pretty awful poetry and about the only thing that could be said of it was that it sometimes rhymed. Not always even that. But he worked at it so hard and earnestly that neither Ben nor I at first had the heart to tell him. It would have done no good even if we had. There probably would have been no way of stopping him short of strangulation.

We should have strangled him.

And landing on Honeymoon didn't help, of course.

But that was out of our control. It was the third planet on our assignment sheet and it was our job to land there—or, rather, it was Lulu's job. We just tagged along.

The planet wasn't called Honeymoon to start with. It just had a charting designation. But we weren't there more than a day or two before we hung the label on it.

I'm no prude, but I refuse to describe Honeymoon. I wouldn't be surprised at all if Earth Center by now has placed our report under lock and key. It you are curious, though, you might write and ask them for the exploratory data on ER56-94. It wouldn't hurt to ask. They can't do more than say no.

Lulu did a bang-up job on Honeymoon and I beat out my brains running the tapes through the playback mechanism after Lulu had put them on the transmitter to be messaged back to Earth. As an interpreter, I was supposed to make some sense—some human sense, I mean—out of the goings-on of any planet that we checked. And don't imagine for a moment that the phrase *goings-on* is just idle terminology in the case of Honeymoon.

The reports are analyzed as soon as they reach Earth Center. But there are, after all, some advantages to arriving at an independent evaluation in the field.

I'm afraid I wasn't too much help. My evaluation report boiled down essentially to the equivalent of a surprised gasp and a blush.

Finally we left Honeymoon and headed out in space, with Lulu homing in on the next planet on the sheet.

Lulu was unusually quiet, which should have tipped us off that there was something wrong. But we were so relieved to have her shut up for a while that we never questioned it. We just leaned back and reveled in it.

Jimmy was laboring on a poem that wasn't coming off too well and Ben and I were in the middle of a blackjack game when Lulu broke her silence.

"Good evening, boys," she said, and her voice seemed a bit off key, not as brisk and efficient as it usually was. I remember thinking that maybe the audio units had somehow gotten out of kilter.

Jimmy was all wrapped up in his poem, and Ben was trying to decide if he should ask me to hit him or stand with what he had, and neither of them answered.

So I said, "Good evening, Lulu. How are you today?"

"Oh, I'm fine," she said, her voice trilling a bit.

"That's wonderful," I said, and hoped she'd let it go at that.

"I've just decided," Lulu informed me, "that I love you."

"It's nice of you to say so," I replied, "and I love you, too."

"But I mean it," Lulu insisted. "I have it all thought out. I'm in love with you."

"Which one of us?" I asked. "Who is the lucky man?"

Just kidding, you understand, but also a little puzzled, for Lulu was no jokester.

"All three of you," said Lulu.

I'm afraid I yawned. "Good idea. That way, there'll be no jealousy."

"Yes," said Lulu. "I'm in love with you and we are eloping."

Ben looked up, startled, and I asked, "Where are we eloping to?"

"A long way off," she said. "Where we can be alone."

"My God!" yelled Ben. "Do you really think—"

I shook my head. "I don't think so. There is something wrong, but—"

Ben rose so swiftly to his feet that he tipped the table and sent the whole deck of cards spinning to the floor.

"I'll go and see," he said.

Jimmy looked up from his tablet. "What's going on?"

"You and your poetry!" I described his poetry in a rather bitter manner.

"I'm in love with you," said Lulu. "I'll love you forever. I'll take good care of you and I'll make you see how much I really love you and someday you'll love me—"

"Oh, shut up!" I said.

Ben came back sweating.

"We're way off course and the emergencies are locked."

"Can we—"

He shook his head. "If you ask me, Lulu jammed them intentionally. In that case, we're sunk. We'll never get back."

"Lulu," I said sternly.

"Yes, darling."

"Cut out that kind of talk!"

"I love you," Lulu said.

"It was Honeymoon," said Ben. "The damn place put notions in her head."

"Honeymoon," I told him, "and that crummy verse Jimmy's always writing—"

"It's not crummy verse," Jimmy shot back, all burned up. "One day, when I am published—"

"Why couldn't you write about war or hunting or flying in the depths of space or something big and noble, instead of all that mush about how I'll always love you and fly to me, sweetheart, and all the other—"

"Tame down," Ben advised me. "No good crawling up Jimmy's frame. It was mostly Honeymoon, I tell you."

"Lulu," I said, "you got to stop this nonsense. You know as well as anything that a machine can't love a human. It's just plain ridiculous."

"On Honeymoon," said Lulu, "there were different species that—"

"Forget Honeymoon. Honeymoon's a freak. You could check a billion planets and not find another like it."

"I love you," Lulu repeated obstinately, "and we are eloping."

"Where'd she get that eloping stuff?" asked Ben.

"It's the junk they filled her up with back on Earth," I said.

"It wasn't junk," protested Lulu. "If I am to do my job, it's necessary that I have a wide and varied insight into humanity."

"They read her novels," Jimmy said, "and they told her about the facts of life. It's not Lulu's fault."

"When I get back," said Ben, "I'm going to hunt up the jerk who picked out those novels and jam them down his throat and then mop up the place with him."

"Look, Lulu," I said, "it's all right if you love us. We don't mind at all, but don't you think eloping is going too far?"

"I'm not taking any chances," Lulu answered. "If I went back to Earth, you'd get away from me."

"And if we don't go back, they'll come out and hunt us down."

"That's exactly right," Lulu agreed. "That's the reason, sweetheart, that we are eloping. We're going out so far that they'll never find us."

"I'll give you one last chance," I said. "You better think it over. If you don't, I'll message back to Earth and—"

"You can't message Earth," she said. "The circuits have been disconnected. And, as Ben guessed, I've jammed all emergencies. There's nothing you can do. Why don't you stop this foolishness and return my love?"

* * *

Getting down on the floor on his hands and knees, Ben began to pick up the cards. Jimmy tossed his tablet on the desk.

"This is your big chance," I told him. "Why don't you rise to the occasion? Think what an ode you could indite about the ageless and eternal love between Machine and Man."

"Go chase yourself," said Jimmy.

"Now, boys," Lulu scolded us. "I will not have you fighting over me."

She sounded like she already owned us and, in a way, she did. There was no way for us to get away from her, and if we couldn't talk her out of this eloping business, we were through for sure.

"There's just one thing wrong with all of this," I said to her. "By your standards, we won't live long. In another fifty years or less, no matter how well you may take care of us, we'll be dead. Of old age, if nothing else. What will happen then?"

"She'll be a widow," said Ben. "Just a poor old weeping widow without chick or child to bring her any comfort."

"I have thought of that," Lulu replied. "I have thought of everything. There's no reason you should die."

"But there's no way—"

"With a love as great as mine, there's nothing that's impossible. I won't let you die. I love you too much ever to let you die."

We gave up after a while and went to bed and Lulu turned off the lights and sang us a lullaby.

With her squalling this lullaby, there was no chance of sleeping and we all yelled at her to dry up and let us get to sleep. But she paid no attention to us until Ben threw one of his shoes at the audio.

Even so, I didn't go to sleep right away, but lay there thinking.

I could see that we had to make some plans and we had to make them without her knowing it. That was going to be tough, because she watched us all the time. She kibitzed and she listened and she read over our shoulders and there wasn't anything we did or said that she didn't know about.

I knew that I might take quite a while and that we must not panic and that we must have patience and that, more than likely, we'd be just plain lucky if we got out of it at all.

After we had slept, we sat around, not saying much, listening to Lulu telling us how happy we would be and how we'd be a complete world and a whole life in ourselves and how love canceled out everything else and made it small and petty.

Half of the words she used were from Jimmy's sappy verse and the rest of it was from the slushy novels that someone back on Earth had read her.

I would have got up right then and there and beat Jimmy to a pulp, only I told myself that what was done was done and it wouldn't help us any to take it out on him.

Jimmy sat hunched over in one corner, scribbling on his tablet, and I wondered how he had the guts to keep on writing after what had happened.

He kept writing and ripping off sheets and throwing them on the floor, making disgusted sounds every now and then.

One sheet he tossed away landed in my lap, and when I went to brush it off, I caught the words on it:

I'm an untidy cuss,
I'm always in a muss,
And no one ever loves me
Because I'm a sloppy Gus.

I picked it up quick and crumpled it and tossed it at Ben and he batted it away. I tossed it back at him and he batted it away again.

"What the hell you trying to do?" he snapped.

I hit him in the face with it and he was just starting to get up to paste me when he must have seen by my look that this wasn't just horseplay. So he picked up the wad of paper and began fooling with it until he got it unwrapped enough to see what was written on it. Then he crumpled it again.

Lulu heard every word, so we couldn't talk it over. And we must not be too obvious, because then she might suspect.

We went at it gradually, perhaps more gradually than there was any need, but we had to be casual about it and we had to be convincing.

We were convincing. Maybe we were just natural-born slobs, but before a week had ended, our living quarters were a boar's nest.

We strewed our clothes around. We didn't even bother to put them in the laundry chute so Lulu could wash them for us. We left the dishes stacked on the table instead of putting them in the washer. We knocked out our pipes upon the floor. We failed to shave and we didn't brush our teeth and we skipped our baths.

Lulu was fit to be tied. Her orderly robot intellect was outraged. She pleaded with us and she nagged at us and there were times she lectured us, but we kept on strewing things around. We told her if she loved us, she'd have to put up with our messiness and take us as we were.

After a couple of weeks of it, we won, but not the way we had intended.

Lulu told us, in a hurt and resigned voice, she'd go along with us if it pleased us to live like pigs. Her love, she said, was too big a thing to let a small matter like mere personal untidiness interfere with it.

So it was no good.

I, for one, was rather glad of it. Years of spaceship routine revolted against this kind of life and I don't know how much more of it I could have stood.

It was a lousy idea to start with.

* * *

We cleared up and we got ourselves clean and it was possible once again to pass downwind of one another.

Lulu was pleased and happy and she told us so and cooed over us and it was worse than all the nagging she had done. She thought we'd been touched by her willing sacrifice and that we were making it up to her and she sounded like a high school girl who had been invited by her hero to the Junior Prom.

Ben tried some plain talk with her and he told her some facts of life (which she already knew, of course) and tried to impress upon her the part that the physical factor played in love.

Lulu was insulted, but not enough to bust off the romance and get back to business.

She told us, in a sorrowful voice tinged by the slightest anger, that we had missed the deeper meaning of love. She went on to quote some of Jimmy's more gooey verse about the nobility and the purity of love, and there was nothing we could do about it. We were just plain licked.

So we sat around and thought and we couldn't talk about it because Lulu would hear everything we said.

We didn't do anything for several days but just mope around.

As far as I could see, there was nothing we could do. I ran through my mind all the things a man might do to get a woman sore at him.

Most women would get burned up at gambling. But the only reason they got sore at that was because it was a threat to their security. Here that threat could not possibly exist. Lulu was entirely self-sufficient. We were no breadwinners.

Most women would get sore at excessive drinking. Security again. And, besides, we had not a thing to drink.

Some women raised hell if a man stayed away from home. We had no place to go.

All women would resent another woman. And here there were no women—no matter what Lulu thought she was.

There was no way, it seemed, to get Lulu sore at us.

And arguing with her simply did no good.

I lay in bed and ran through all the possibilities, going over them again and again, trying to find a chink of hope in one of them. By reciting and recounting them, I might suddenly happen on one that I'd never thought of, and that might be the one that would do the job.

And even as I turned these things over in my head, I knew there was something wrong with the way I had been thinking. I knew there was some illogic in the way I was tackling the problem—that somehow I was going at it tail-end to.

I lay there and thought about it and I mulled it considerably and, all at once, I had it.

I was approaching the problem as if Lulu were a woman, and when you thought about it, that didn't make much sense. For Lulu was no woman, but just a robot.

The problem was: How do you make a robot sore?

The untidiness business had upset her, but it had just outraged her sense of rightness; it was something she could overlook and live with. The trouble with it was that it wasn't basic.

And what would be basic with a robot—with any machine, for that matter?

What would a machine value? What would it idealize?

Order?

No, we'd tried that one and it hadn't worked.

Sanity?

Of course.

What else?

Productiveness? Usefulness?

I tossed insanity around a bit, but it was too hard to figure out. How in the name of common sense would a man go about pretending that he was insane—especially in a limited space inside an all-knowing intelligent machine?

But just the same, I lay there and dreamed up all kinds of insanities. If carried out, they might have fooled people, but not a robot.

With a robot, you had to get down to basics and what, I wondered, was the fundamental of insanity? Perhaps the true horror of insanity, I told myself, would become apparent to a robot only when it interfered with usefulness.

And that was it!

I turned it around and around and looked at it from every angle.

It was airtight.

Even to start with, we hadn't been much use. We'd just come along because Earth Center had rules about sending Lulu out alone. But we represented a certain *potential* usefulness.

We did things. We read books and wrote terrible poetry and played cards and argued. There wasn't much of the time we just sat around. That's a trick you learn in space—keep busy doing something, no matter what it is, no matter how piddling or purposeless.

In the morning, after breakfast, when Ben wanted to play cards, I said no, I didn't want to play. I sat down on the floor with my back against the wall; I didn't even bother to sit in a chair. I didn't smoke, for smoking was doing something and I was determined to be as utterly inactive as a living man could manage. I didn't intend to do a blessed thing except eat and sleep and sit.

Ben prowled around some and tried to get Jimmy to play a hand or two, but Jimmy wasn't much for cards and, anyhow, he was busy with a poem.

So Ben came over and sat on the floor beside me.

"Want a smoke?" he asked, offering me his tobacco pouch.

I shook my head.

"What's the matter? You haven't had your after-breakfast smoke."

"What's the use?" I said.

He tried to talk to me and I wouldn't talk, so he got up and paced around some more and finally came back and sat down beside me again.

"What's the trouble with you two?" Lulu troubledly wanted to know. "Why aren't you doing something?"

"Don't feel like doing anything," I told her. "Too much bother to be doing something all the time."

She berated us a bit and I didn't dare look at Ben, but I felt sure that he began to see what I was up to.

After a while, Lulu left us alone and the two of us just sat there, lazier than hillbillies on a Sunday afternoon.

Jimmy kept on with his poem. There was nothing we could do about him. But Lulu called his attention to us when we dragged ourselves to lunch. She was just a little sharper than she had been earlier and she called us lazy, which we surely were, and wondered about our health and made us step into the diagnosis booth, which reported we were fine, and that got her more burned up than ever.

She gave us a masterly chewing out and listed all the things there were for us to occupy our time. So when lunch was over, Ben and I went back and sat down on the floor and leaned against the wall. This time, Jimmy joined us.

Try sitting still for days on end, doing absolutely nothing. At first it's uncomfortable, then it's torture, and finally it gets to be almost intolerable.

I don't know what the others did, but I made up complex mathematical problems and tried to solve them. I started mental chess game after chess game, but was never able to hold one in my mind beyond a dozen moves. I went clean back to childhood and tried to recreate, in sequence, everything I had ever done or experienced. I delved into strange areas of the imagination and hung onto them desperately to string them out and kill all the time I could.

I even composed some poetry and, if I do say so myself, it was better than that junk of Jimmy's.

I think Lulu must have guessed what we were doing, must have known that our attitude was deliberate, but for once her cold robotic judgment was outweighed by her sense of outrage that there could exist such useless hulks as us.

She pleaded with us, she cajoled us, she lectured us—for almost five days hand-running, she never shut her yap. She tried to shame us. She told us how worthless and low-down and no-account we were and she used adjectives I didn't think she knew.

She gave us pep talks.

She told us of her love in prose poems that made Jimmy's sound almost restrained.

She appealed to our manhood and the honor of humanity.

She threatened to heave us out in space.

We just sat there.

We didn't do a thing.

Mostly we didn't even answer. We didn't try to defend ourselves. At times we agreed with all she said of us and that, I believe, was most infuriating of all to her.

She got cold and distant. Not sore. Not angry. Just icy.

Finally she quit talking.

We sat, sweating it out.

Now came the hard part. We couldn't talk, so we couldn't try to figure out together what was going on.

We had to keep on doing nothing. *Had to,* for it would have spoiled whatever advantage we might have to do anything else.

The days dragged on and nothing happened. Lulu didn't speak to us. She fed us, she washed the dishes, she laundered, she made up the bunks. She took care of us as she always had, but she did it without a word.

She sure was fuming.

A dozen crazy thoughts crossed my mind and I worried them to tatters.

Maybe Lulu *was* a woman. Maybe a woman's brain *was* somehow welded into that great hulk of intelligent machinery. After all, none of us knew the full details of Lulu's structure.

The brain of an old maid, it would have to be, so often disillusioned, so lonely and so by-passed in life that she would welcome a chance to go adventuring even if it meant sacrificing a body which, probably, had meant less and less to her as the years went by.

I built up quite a picture of my hypothetical old maid, complete with cat and canary, and even the boarding house in which she lived.

I sensed her lonely twilight walks and her aimless chattering and her small imaginary triumphs and the hungers that kept building up inside her.

And I felt sorry for her.

Fantastic? Of course. But it helped to pass the time.

But there was another notion that really took solid hold of me—that Lulu, beaten, had finally given up and was taking us back to Earth, but that, womanlike, she refused to give us the satisfaction and comfort of knowing that we had won and were going home at last.

I told myself over and over that it was impossible, that after the kind of shenanigans she'd pulled, Lulu wouldn't dare go back. They'd break her up for scrap.

But the idea persisted and I couldn't shake it off. I knew I must be wrong, but I couldn't convince myself I was and I began to watch the chronometer. I'd say to myself, "One hour nearer home, another hour and yet another and we are that much closer."

And no matter what I told myself, no matter how I argued, I became positive that we were heading Earthward.

So I was not surprised when Lulu finally landed. I was just grateful and relieved.

We looked at one another and I saw the hope and question in the others' eyes. Naturally, none of us could ask. One word might have ruined our victory. All we could do was stand there silently and wait for the answer.

The port began to open and I got the whiff of Earth and I didn't fool around waiting any more. There wasn't room enough as yet to get out standing up, so I took a run at it and dived and went through slick and clean. I hit the ground and got a lot of breath knocked out of me, but I scrambled to my feet and lit out of there as fast as I could go. I wasn't taking any chances. I didn't want to be within reach if Lulu changed her mind.

Once I stumbled and almost fell, and Ben and Jimmy went past me with a whoosh, and I told myself that I'd not been mistaken. They'd caught the Earth smell, too.

It was night, but there was a big, bright moon and it was almost as light as day. There was an ocean to the left of us, with a wide strip of sandy beach, and, to the right, the land swept up into barren rolling hills, and right ahead of us was a strip of woods that looked as if it might border some river flowing down into the sea.

We legged it for the woods, for we knew that if we got in among the trees, Lulu would have a tough time ferreting us out. But when I sneaked a quick look back over my shoulder, she was just squatting where she'd landed, with the moonlight shining on her.

We reached the woods and threw ourselves on the ground and lay panting. It had been quite a stretch of ground to cover and we had covered it fast; after weeks of just sitting, a man is in no condition to do a lot of running.

I had fallen face down and just sprawled there, sucking in great gulps of air and smelling the good Earth smell—old leaf mold and growing things and the tang of salt from the soft and gentle ocean breeze.

After a while, I rolled over on my back and looked up. The trees were wrong—there were no trees like those on Earth—and when

LULU

I crawled out to the edge of the woods and looked at the sky, the stars were all wrong, too.

My mind was slow in accepting what I saw. I had been so sure that we were on Earth that my brain rebelled against thinking otherwise.

But finally it hit me, the chilling terrible knowledge.

I went back to the other two.

"Gents," I said, "I have news for you. This planet isn't Earth at all."

"It smells like Earth," said Ben. "It has the look of Earth."

"It feels like Earth," Jimmy argued. "The gravity and the air and—"

"Look at the stars. Take a gander at those trees."

They took a long time looking. Like me, they must have gotten the idea that Lulu had zeroed in for home. Or maybe it was only what they wanted to believe. It took a while to knock the wishful thinking out of them, as well as myself.

Ben let his breath out slowly. "You're right."

"What do we do now?" asked Jimmy.

We stood there, thinking about what we should do now.

Actually it was no decision, but pure and simple reflex, conditioned by a million years of living on Earth as opposed to only a few hundred in which to get used to the idea that there were different worlds.

We started running, as if an order had been given, as fast as we could go.

"Lulu!" we yelled. "Lulu, wait for us!"

But Lulu didn't wait. She shot straight up for a thousand feet or so and hung there. We skidded to a halt and gaped up at her, not quite believing what we saw. Lulu started to fall back, shot up again, came to a halt and hovered. She seemed to shiver, then sank slowly back until she rested on the ground.

We continued running and she shot up and fell back, then shot up once more, then fell back again and hit the ground and hopped. She looked for all the world like a demented yo-yo. She was acting strangely, as if she wanted to get out of there, only there was something that wouldn't let her go, as if she were tethered to the ground by some invisible elastic cable.

Finally she came to rest about a hundred yards from where she'd first set down. No sound came from her, but I got the impression she was panting like a winded hound dog.

There was a pile of stuff stacked where Lulu had first landed, but we raced right past it and ran up to her. We pounded on her metal sides.

"Open up!" we shouted. "We want to get back in!"

Lulu hopped. She hopped about a hundred feet into the air, then plopped back with a thud, not more than thirty feet away.

We backed away from her. She could have just as easily come straight down on top of us.

We stood watching her, but she didn't move.

"Lulu!" I yelled at her.

She didn't answer.

"She's gone crazy," Jimmy said.

"Someday," said Ben, "this was bound to happen. It was a cinch they'd sooner or later build a robot too big for its britches."

We backed away from her slowly, watching all the time. We weren't afraid of her exactly, but we didn't trust her either.

We backed all the way to the mound of stuff that Lulu had unloaded and stacked up and we saw that it was a pyramid of supplies, all neatly boxed and labeled. And beside the pyramid was planted a stenciled sign that read:

NOW, DAMN YOU, WORK!!

Ben said, "She certainly took our worthlessness to heart."

Jimmy was close to gibbering. "She was actually going to maroon us!"

Ben reached out and grabbed his shoulder and shook him a little—a kindly sort of shake.

"Unless we can get back inside," I said, "and get her operating, we are as marooned as if she had up and left us."

"But what made her do it?" Jimmy wailed. "Robots aren't supposed to—"

"I know," said Ben. "They're not supposed to harm a human. But Lulu wasn't harming us. She didn't throw us out. We ran away from her."

"That's splitting legal hairs," I objected.

"Lulu's just the kind of gadget for hair-splitting," Ben said. "Trouble is they made her damn near human. They probably poured her full of a lot of law as well as literature and physics and all the rest of it."

"Then why didn't she just leave? If she could whitewash her conscience, why is she still here?"

Ben shook his head. "I don't know."

"She looked like she tried to leave and couldn't, as though there was something holding her back."

"This is just an idea," said Ben. "Maybe she could have left if we had stayed out of sight. But when we showed up, the order that a robot must not harm a human may have become operative again. A sort of out of sight, out of mind proposition."

She was still squatting where she'd landed. She hadn't tried to move again. Looking at her, I thought maybe Ben was right. If so, it had been a lucky thing that we'd headed back exactly when we did.

We started going through the supplies Lulu had left for us. She had done right well by us. Not only had she forgotten nothing we needed, but had stenciled careful instructions and even some advice on many of the boxes.

Near the signboard, lying by themselves, were two boxes. One was labeled TOOLS and the top was loosely nailed so we could pry it off. The other was labeled WEAPONS and had a further stencil: *Open immediately and always keep at hand.*

We opened both the boxes. In the weapons box, we found the newest type of planet-busters—a sort of shotgun deal, a general-purpose weapon that put out everything from bullets to a wide range of vibratory charges. In between these two extremes were a flame-thrower, acid, gas, poisoned darts, explosive warheads and knockout pellets. You merely twirled a dial to choose your ammunition. The guns were heavy and awkward to handle and they were brutes to operate, but they were just the ticket for a planet where you never knew what you might run into next.

We turned our attention to the rest of the stuff and started to get it sorted out. There were boxes of protein and carbohydrate foods. There were cartons of vitamins and minerals. There was clothing and a tent, lanterns and dishes—all the stuff you'd need on a high-priced camping trip.

Lulu hadn't forgotten a single item.

"She had it all planned out," said Jimmy bitterly. "She spent a long time making this stuff. She had to synthesize every bit of it. All she needed then was to find a planet where a man could live. And that took some doing."

"It was tougher than you think," I added. "Not only a planet where a man could live, but one that smelled like Earth and looked and felt like Earth. Because, you see, we had to be encouraged to run away from her. If we hadn't, she couldn't have marooned us. She had the problem of her conscience and—"

Ben spat viciously. "Marooned!" he said. "Marooned by a love-sick robot!"

"Maybe not entirely robot." I told them about the old maid I had conjured up and they hooted at me and that made us all feel better.

But Ben admitted that my idea needn't be entirely crazy. "She was twenty years in building and a lot of funny stuff must have gone into her."

Dawn was breaking and now, for the first time, we really saw the land. It was a pleasant place, as pleasant as any man might wish. But we failed to appreciate it much.

The sea was so blue that it made you think of a blue-eyed girl and the beach ran white and straight and, from the beach, the land ran back into rolling hills with the faint whiteness of distant mountains frosting the horizon. And to the west was the forest.

Jimmy and I went down to the beach to collect some driftwood for a fire while Ben made ready to get breakfast.

We had our arms full of wood and were starting back when something came charging over the hill and down upon the camp. It was about rhinoceros size and shaped somewhat like a beetle and it shone dully in the morning light. It made no sound, but it was traveling fast and it looked like something hard to stop.

And, of course, we'd left our guns behind.

I dropped my wood and yelled at Ben and started running up the slope. Ben had already seen the charging monster and had grabbed a rifle. The beast swerved straight for him and he brought up his gun. There was a flash of fire and then the bright gout of an exploding warhead and, for an instant, the scene was fogged with smoke and shrieking bits of metal and flying dust.

It was exactly as if one had been watching a film and the film had jumped. One moment there was the blaze of fire; then the thing had plunged past Ben and was coming down the slope of the beach, heading for Jimmy and myself.

"Scatter!" I yelled at Jimmy and didn't think till later how silly it must have sounded to yell for just the two of us to scatter.

But it wasn't any time or place for fine points of semantics and, anyhow, Jimmy caught on to what I meant. He went one way down the beach and I went the other and the monster wheeled around, hesitating for a moment, apparently to decide which one of us to take.

And, as you might have known, he took after me.

I figured I was a goner. That beach was just plain naked, with not a place to hide, and I knew I had no chance at all of outrunning my pursuer. I might be able to dodge a time or two, but even so, that thing was pretty shifty on the turns and I knew in the end I'd lose.

Out of the tail of my eye, I saw Ben running and sliding down the slope to cut off the beast. He yelled something at me, but I didn't catch the words.

Then the air shook with the blast of another exploding warhead and I sneaked a quick look back.

Ben was legging it up the slope and the thing was chasing him, so I spun around and sprinted for the camp. Jimmy, I saw, was almost there and I put on some extra speed. If we only could get three guns going, I felt sure we could make it.

Ben was running straight toward Lulu, apparently figuring that he could race around her bulk and elude the beast. I saw that his dash would be a nip-and-tuck affair.

Jimmy had reached the camp and grabbed a gun. He had it firing before he got it to his shoulder and little splashes of liquid were flying all over the running beast.

I tried to yell at Jimmy, but had no breath to do it—the damn fool was firing knockout pellets and they were hitting that tough hide and bursting without penetrating.

Within arm's reach of Lulu, Ben stumbled. The gun flew from his hand. His body struck the ground doubled up and he rolled, trying to get under the curve of Lulu's side. The rhinoceros-thing lunged forward viciously.

Then it happened—quicker than the eye could follow, much quicker than it can be told.

Lulu grew an arm, a long, ropelike tentacle that snaked out of the top of her. It lashed downward and had the beast about the middle and was lifting him.

I stopped dead still and watched. The instant of the lifting of the beast seemed to stretch out into long minutes as my mind scrambled at top speed to see what kind of thing it was. The first thing I saw was that it had wheels instead of feet.

The dull luster of the hide could be nothing but metal and I could see the dents where the warheads had exploded. Drops of liquid spotted the hide—what was left of the knockout drops Jimmy had been firing.

Lulu raised the monster high above the ground and began swinging it around and around. It went so fast, it was just a blur. Then she let go and it sailed out above the sea. It went tumbling end over end in an awkward arc and plunged into the water. When it hit, it raised a pretty geyser.

Ben picked himself up and got his gun. Jimmy came over and I walked up to Lulu. The three of us stood and looked out to sea, watching the spot where the creature had kerplunked.

Finally Ben turned around and rapped on Lulu's side with his rifle barrel.

"Thanks a heap," he said.

Lulu grew another tentacle, shorter this time, and there was a face on it. It had a lenslike eye and an audio and speaker.

"Go chase yourselves," Lulu remarked.

"What's eating you?" I asked.

"Men!" she spat, and pulled her face in again.

We rapped on her three or four times more, but there was no reply. Lulu was sulking.

So Jimmy and I started down to pick up the wood that we had dropped. We had just gotten it picked up when Ben let out a yelp from up by the camp and we spun around. There was our rhinoceros friend wheeling out of the water.

We dropped the wood and lit out for camp, but there was no need to hurry. Our boy wasn't having any more just then. He made a wide circle to the east of us and raced back into the hills.

We cooked breakfast and ate it and kept our guns handy, because where there was one critter, there were liable to be more. We didn't see the sense in taking chances.

* * *

We talked about our visitor and since we had to call it something, we named it Elmer. For no particular reason, that seemed appropriate.

"Did you see those wheels?" asked Ben, and the two of us agreed that we'd seen them. Ben seemed to be relieved. "I thought I was seeing things," he explained.

But there could be no doubt about the wheels. All of us had noticed them and there were the tracks to prove it—wheel tracks running plain and clear along the sandy beach.

But we were somewhat puzzled when it came to determining just what Elmer was. The wheels spelled out machine, but there were a lot of other things that didn't—mannerisms that were distinctly lifelike, such as the momentary hesitation before it decided which one of us to charge, Jimmy or myself, or the vicious lunge at Ben when he lay upon the ground, or the caution it had shown in circling us when it came out of the sea.

But there were, as well, the wheels and the unmistakably metal hide and the dents made by exploding warheads that would have torn the biggest and toughest animal to shreds.

"A bit of both?" suggested Ben. "Basically machine, but with some life in it, too, like the old-maid brain you dreamed up for Lulu?"

Sure, it could be that. It could be almost anything.

"Silicate life?" offered Jimmy.

"That's not silicate," Ben declared. "That's metal. Silicate, any form of it, would have turned to dust under a direct rocket hit. Besides, we know what silicate life is like. One species of it was found years ago out on Thelma V."

"It isn't basically life," I said. "Life wouldn't evolve wheels. Wheels are bum inventions so far as locomotion is concerned, except where you have special conditions. Life might be involved, but only as Ben says—as a deliberate, engineered combining of machine and life."

"And that means intelligence," said Ben.

We sat there around the fire, shaken at the thought of it. In many years of searching, only a handful of intelligent races had been found and the level of intelligence, in general, was not too impressive. Certainly nothing of the order that would be necessary to build something like Elmer.

So far, Man was top dog in the discovered universe. Nothing had been found to match him in the use of brain-power.

And here, by utter accident, we'd been dumped upon a planet where there seemed to be some evidence of an intelligence that would equal Man—if not, indeed, surpass him.

"There's one thing that has been bothering me," said Ben. "Why didn't Lulu check this place before she landed here? She intended to maroon us, that's why. She meant to dump us here and leave. And yet presumably she's still bound by the precept that a robot cannot harm a human. And if she followed that law, it would have meant that she was compelled—completely and absolutely compelled—to make certain, before she marooned us, that there was nothing here to harm us."

"Maybe she slipped a little," guessed Jimmy.

"Not Lulu," said Ben. "Not with that Swiss-watch brain of hers."

"You know what I think?" I said. "I think Lulu has evolved. In her, we have a brand-new kind of robot. They pumped too much humanity into her—"

"She had to have the human viewpoint," Jimmy pointed out, "or she couldn't do her job."

"The point," I said, "is that when you make a robot as human as Lulu, you no longer have a robot. You have something else. Not quite human, not entirely robot, but something in between. A new kind of a sort of life you can't be certain of. One you have to watch."

"I wonder if she's still sulking," Ben wondered.

"Of course she is," I said.

"We ought to go over and kick her in the pants and snap her out of it."

"Leave her alone," I ordered sharply. "The only thing is to ignore her. As long as she gets attention, she'll keep on sulking."

So we left her alone. It was the only thing we could do.

I took the dishes down to the sea to wash them, but this time I took my gun along. Jimmy went down to the woods to see if he could find a spring. The half dozen tins of water that Lulu had provided for us wouldn't last forever and we couldn't be sure she'd shell out more when those were gone.

She hadn't forgotten us, though, hadn't shut us out of her life entirely. She had fixed Elmer's wagon when he got too gay. I took a lot of comfort out of reflecting that, when the cards were down, she had backed us up. There still were grounds for hope, I told myself, that we could work out some sort of deal with her.

I squatted down by a pool of water in the sand, and as I washed the dishes, I did some thinking about the realignment which would become necessary once all robots were like Lulu. I could envision a Bill of Robotic Rights and special laws for robots and robotic lobbies, and after I'd thought of it for a while, it became mighty complicated.

Back at the camp, Ben had been setting up the tent, and when I came back, I helped him.

"You know," Ben said, "the more I think about it, the more I believe I was right when I said that the reason Lulu couldn't leave was because we showed up. It's only logical that she can't up and leave when we're standing right in front of her and reminding her of her responsibility."

"You getting around to saying that one of us has to stay close by her all the time?" I asked.

"That's the general idea."

I didn't argue with him. There was nothing to argue about,

nothing to believe or disbelieve. But we were in no position to be making any bones.

After we had the tent up, Ben said to me, "If you don't mind, I'll take a little walk around back in the hills."

"Watch out for Elmer," I warned him.

"He won't bother us. Lulu took the starch out of him."

He picked up his gun and left.

I puttered around the camp, putting things in order. Everything was peaceful. The beach shone in the sun and the sea was still and beautiful. There were a few birds flying, but no other sign of life. Lulu kept on sulking.

Jimmy came back. He had found a spring and brought along a pail of water. He started rummaging around in the supplies.

"What you looking for?" I asked.

"Paper and a pencil. Lulu would have thought of them."

I grunted at the idea, but he was right. Damned if Lulu hadn't fixed him up with a ream of paper and a box of pencils.

He settled down against a pile of boxes and began to write a poem.

Ben returned shortly after midday. I could see he was excited, but I didn't push him any.

"Jimmy stumbled on a spring," I said. "The pail is over there."

He had a drink, then sat down in the shade of a pile of boxes.

"I found it," he said triumphantly.

"I didn't know you were hunting anything."

He looked up at me and grinned a bit crookedly. "Someone manufactured Elmer."

"So you went out and found them. Just like walking down a street. Just like—"

He shook his head. "Seems we're too late. Some several thousand years too late, if not a good deal longer. I found a few ruins and a valley heaped with tumuli that must be ruin mounds. And some caves in a limestone bluff beyond the valley."

*   *   *

He got up and walked over to the pail and had another drink.

"I couldn't get too close," he said. "Elmer is on guard." He took off his hat and wiped his shirt sleeve across his face. "He's patrolling up and down, the way a sentry walks a post. You can see the paths he's worn through all the years of standing guard."

"So that's why he took us on," I said. "We are trespassers."

"I suppose that's it," said Ben.

That evening we talked it over and decided we'd have to post a watch on Elmer so we could learn his habits and timetable, if any. Because it was important that we try to find out what we could about the buried ruins of the place that Elmer guarded.

For the first time, Man had stumbled on a high civilization, but had come too late and, because of Lulu's sulking, too poorly equipped to do much with what little there was left.

Getting somewhat sore the more I thought about it, I went over to Lulu and kicked her good and solid to attract her attention. But she paid me no mind. I yelled at her and there was no answer. I told her what was cooking and that we needed her—that there was a job she simply had to do, just exactly the kind she had been built to do. She just sat there frigidly.

I went back and slouched down with the others at the fire. "She acts as if she might be dead."

Ben poked the fire together and it flamed a little higher. "I wonder if a robot could die. A highly sensitive job like Lulu."

"Of a broken heart," said Jimmy pityingly.

"You and your poetic notions!" I raged at him. "Always mooning around. Always spouting words. If it hadn't been for that damned verse of yours—"

"Cut it out," Ben said.

I looked at his face across the fire, with flame shadows running on it, and I cut it out. After all, I admitted to myself, I might be wrong. Jimmy couldn't help being a lousy poet.

I sat there looking at the fire, wondering if Lulu might be dead. I knew she wasn't, of course. She was just being nasty. She had fixed our clock for us and she had fixed it good. Now she was watching us sweat before she made her play, whatever it was.

In the morning, we set up our watch on Elmer and we kept it up day after day. One of us would go out to the ridge top three miles or so from camp and settle down with our only field glass. We'd stare for several hours. Then someone else would come out and relieve the watcher and that way, for ten days or more, we had Elmer under observation during all the daylight hours.

We didn't learn much. He operated on a schedule and it was the kind that seemed to leave no loopholes for anyone to sneak into the valley he guarded—although probably none of us would have known what to do if we had sneaked in.

Elmer had a regular beat. He used some of the mounds for observation posts and he came to each one about every fifteen minutes. The more we watched him, the more we became convinced that he had the situation well in hand. No one would monkey around with that buried city as long as he was there.

I think that after the second day or so, he found out we were watching. He got a little nervous, and when he mounted his observation mounds, he'd stand and look in our direction longer than in any other. Once, while I was on guard, he began what looked to be a charge and I was just getting ready to light out of there when he broke off and went back to his regular rounds.

Other than watching Elmer, we took things easy. We swam in the sea and fished, taking our lives in our hands when we cooked and ate each new kind, but luck was with us and we got no poisonous ones. We wouldn't have eaten the fish at all except that we figured we should piece out our food supplies as best we could. They wouldn't last forever and we had no guarantee that Lulu would give more handouts once the last was gone. If she didn't we'd have to face the problem of making our own way.

Ben got to worrying about whether there were seasons on the planet. He convinced himself there were and went off into the woods to find a place where we might build a cabin.

"Can't live out on the beach in a tent when it gets cold," he said.

But he couldn't get either Jimmy or me too stirred up about the possibility. I had it all doped out that, sooner or later, Lulu would end her sulking and we could get down to business. And Jimmy was deep into the crudest bunch of junk you ever heard that he called a saga. Maybe it was a saga. Damned if I know. I'm ignorant on sagas.

He called it "The Death of Lulu" and he filled page after page with the purest drivel about what a swell machine she was and how, despite its being metal, her heart beat with snow-white innocence. It wouldn't have been so bad if he had allowed us to ignore it, but he insisted on reading that tripe to us each evening after supper.

I stood it as long as I could, but one evening I blew my top. Ben stood up for Jimmy, but when I threatened to take my third of the supplies and set up a camp of my own, out of earshot, Ben gave in and came over to my side of the argument. Between the two of us, we ruled out any more recitals. Jimmy took it hard, but he was outnumbered.

After that first ten days or so, we watched Elmer only off and on, but we must have had him nervous, for during the night we'd sometimes hear his wheels, and in the morning we'd find tracks. We figured that he was spying out the camp, trying to size us up the same way we'd done with him. He didn't make any passes at us and we didn't bother him—we were just a lot more wakeful and alert on our night watches. Even Jimmy managed to stay awake while he was standing guard.

There was a funny thing about it, though. One would have imagined that Elmer would have stayed away from Lulu after the clobbering she gave him. But there were mornings when we found his tracks running up close behind her, then angling sharply off.

We got it doped out that he sneaked up and hid behind her, so he could watch the camp close up, peeking around at us from his position behind that sulking hulk.

* * *

Ben kept arguing about building winter quarters until he had me almost convinced that it was something we should do. So one day I teamed up with him, leaving Jimmy at the camp. We set off, carrying an ax and a saw and our guns.

Ben had picked a fine site for our cabin, that much I'll say. It wasn't far from the spring, and it was tucked away in a sort of pocket where we'd be protected from the wind, and there were a lot of trees nearby so we wouldn't have far to drag our timbers or haul our winter wood.

I still wasn't convinced there would be any winter. I was fairly sure that even if there were, we wouldn't have to stay that long. One of these days, we'd be able to arrive at some sort of compromise with Lulu. But Ben was worried and I knew it would make him happier if he could get a start at building. And there was nothing else for any of us to do. Building a cabin, I consoled myself, would be better than just sitting.

We leaned our guns against a tree and began to work. We had one tree down and sawed into lengths and were starting on the second tree when I heard the brush snap behind me.

I straightened up from the saw to look, and there was Elmer, tearing down the hill at us.

There wasn't any time to grab our guns. There was no time to run. There was no time for anything at all.

I yelled and made a leap for the tree behind me and pulled myself up. I felt the wind as Elmer whizzed by beneath me.

Ben had jumped to one side and, as Elmer went pounding past, heaved the ax at him. It was a honey of a throw. The ax caught Elmer in his metal side and the handle splintered into pieces.

Elmer spun around. Ben tried to reach the guns, but he didn't have the time. He took to a tree and shinnied up it like a cat. He got up to the first big branch and straddled it.

"You all right?" he yelled at me.

"Great," I said.

Elmer was standing between the two trees, swinging his massive head back and forth, as if deciding which one of us to take.

We clung there, watching him.

He had waited, I reasoned, until he could get between us and Lulu—then he had tackled us. And if that was the case, then this business of his hiding behind Lulu so he could spy on us seemed very queer indeed.

Finally Elmer wheeled around and rolled over to my tree. He squared off and took a chopping bite at it with his metal jaws. Splinters flew and the tree shivered. I got a tighter grip and looked down the trunk. Elmer was no great shakes as a chopper, but if he kept at it long enough, he'd get that tree chewed off.

I climbed up a little higher, where there were more branches and where I could wedge myself a little tighter so I couldn't be shaken out.

I got myself fixed fairly comfortable, then looked to see how Ben was getting on and I got quite a shock. He wasn't in his tree. I looked around for him and then back at the tree again, and I saw that he was sneaking down it as quietly as he could, like a hunted squirrel, keeping the trunk of the tree between himself and Elmer.

I watched him breathlessly, ready to shout out a warning if Elmer should spot him, but Elmer was too busy chopping at my tree to notice anything.

Ben reached the ground and made a dash for the guns. He grabbed both of them and ducked behind another tree. He opened up on Elmer at short range. From where I crouched, I could hear the warheads slamming into Elmer. The explosions rocked everything so much that I had to grab the tree and hang on with all my might. A couple of pieces of flying metal ripped into the tree just underneath me, and other pieces went flying through the branches, and the air was full of spinning leaves and flying shredded wood, but I was untouched.

It must have been a horrible surprise for Elmer. At the first explosion, he took a jump of about fifteen feet and bolted up the hill like a cat with a stepped-on tail. I could see a lot of new dents in his shining hide. A big hunk of metal had been gouged out of one of his wheels and he rocked slightly as he went, and he was going so fast that he couldn't dodge and ran head-on into a tree. The impact sent him skidding back a dozen feet or so. As he slid back, Ben poured another salvo into him and he seemed to become considerably lop-sided, but he recovered himself and made it over the hilltop and out of sight.

Ben came out from behind his tree and shouted at me, "All right, you can come down now."

But when I tried to get down, I found that I was trapped. My left foot had become wedged in a crotch between the tree trunk and a good-sized limb and I couldn't pull it loose, no matter how I tried.

"What's the matter?" asked Ben. "Do you like it up there?"

I told him what was wrong.

"All right," he said, disgusted. "I'll come up and cut you loose."

He hunted for the ax and found it and, of course, it was no use. He'd smashed the handle when he threw it at Elmer.

He stood there, holding the ax in his hands, and delivered an oration on the lowdown meanness of fate.

Then he threw the ax down and climbed my tree. He squeezed past me out onto the limb.

"I'll climb out on it and bend it down," he explained. "Maybe then you can get loose."

He crawled out on the branch a way, but it was a shaky trick. A couple of times, he almost fell.

"You're sure you can't get your foot out now?" he asked anxiously.

I tried and I said I couldn't.

So he gave up the crawling idea and let his body down and hung on by his hands, shifting out along the branch hand over hand.

The branch bent toward the ground as he inched along it and it seemed to me my boot wasn't gripped as tightly as it had been. I tried again and found I could move it some, but I still couldn't pull it loose.

Just then there was a terrible crashing in the brush. Ben let out a yell and dropped to the ground and scurried for a gun.

The branch whipped back and caught my foot just as I had managed it move it a little and this time caught it at a slightly different angle, twisting it, and I let out a howl of pain.

Down on the ground, Ben lifted his gun and swung around to face the crashing in the brush and suddenly who should come busting out of all that racket but Jimmy, racing to the rescue.

"You guys in trouble?" he shouted. "I heard shooting."

Ben's face was three shades whiter than the purest chalk as he lowered his gun. "You fool! I almost let you have it!"

"There was all this shooting," Jimmy panted. "I came as quickly as I could."

"And left Lulu alone!"

"But I thought you guys—"

"Now we're sunk for sure," groaned Ben. "You know all that makes Lulu stick around is one of us being there."

We didn't know any such thing, of course. It was just the only reason we could think of why she didn't up and leave. But Ben was somewhat overwrought. He'd had a trying day.

"You get back there!" he yelled at Jimmy. "Get back as fast as your legs will let you. Maybe you can catch her before she gets away."

Which was foolishness, because if Lulu meant to leave, she'd have lifted out of there as soon as Jimmy had disappeared. But Jimmy didn't say a word. He just turned around and went crashing back. For a long time after he had left, I could hear him blundering through the woods.

* * *

Ben climbed my tree again, muttering, "Just a pack of wooden-headed jerks. Can't do anything right. Running off and leaving Lulu. Getting trapped up in a tree. You would think, by God, that they could learn to watch out for themselves. . . ."

He said a good deal more than that.

I didn't answer back. I didn't want to get into any argument.

My foot was hurting something fierce and the only thing I wanted him to do was get me out of there.

He climbed out on the branch again and I got my foot loose. While Ben dropped to the ground, I climbed down the tree. My foot hurt pretty bad and seemed to be swelling some, but I could hobble on it.

He didn't wait for me. He grabbed his gun and made off rapidly for camp.

I tried to hurry, but it was no use, so I took it easy.

When I got to the edge of the woods, I saw that Lulu still was there and all Ben's hell-raising had been over absolutely nothing. There are some guys like that.

When I reached camp, Jimmy pulled off my boot while I clawed at the ground. Then he heated a pail of water for me to soak the foot in and rummaged around in the medicine chest and found some goo that he smeared on the foot. Personally, I don't think he knew what he was doing. But I'll say this for the kid—he had some kindness in him.

All this time, Ben was fuming around about a funny thing that had attracted his attention. When we had left camp, the area around Lulu had been all tracked up with our tracks and Elmer's tracks, but now it was swept clean. It looked exactly as if someone had taken a broom and had swept out all the tracks. It surely was a funny business, but Ben was making too much of it. The important thing was that Lulu still was there. As long as she stuck around, there was a chance we could work out some agreement with her. Once she left, we were marooned for good.

Jimmy fixed something to eat, and after we had eaten, Ben said to us, "I think I'll go out and see how Elmer's getting on."

I, for one, had seen enough of Elmer to last a lifetime and Jimmy wasn't interested. Said he wanted to work on his saga.

So Ben took a rifle and set out alone, back into the hills.

My foot hurt me quite a bit and I got myself comfortable and tried to do some thinking, but I tried so hard that I put myself to sleep.

It was late in the afternoon when I awoke. Jimmy was getting nervous.

"Ben hasn't shown up," he said. "I wonder if something's happened to him."

I didn't like it, either, but we decided to wait a while before going out to hunt Ben. After all, he wasn't in the best of humor and he might have been considerably upset if we'd gone out to rescue him.

He finally showed up just before dusk, tuckered out and a little flabbergasted. He leaned his rifle against a box and sat down. He found a cup and reached for the coffee pot.

"Elmer's gone," he said. "I spend all afternoon trying to find him. Not a sign of him anywhere."

My first reaction was that it was just fine. Then I realized that the safest thing would be to know where Elmer was, so we could keep an eye on him. And suddenly I had a horrible hunch that I knew where Elmer was.

"I didn't actually go down into the valley," said Ben, "but I walked around and glassed it from every angle."

"He might be in one of the caves," Jimmy said.

"Maybe so," said Ben.

We did a lot of speculating on what might have happened to Elmer. Jimmy held out for his having holed up in one of the caves. Ben was inclined to think he might have cleared out of the country. I didn't say what I thought. It was too fantastic.

I volunteered for the first watch, saying that I couldn't sleep with my foot, anyhow, and after the two of them were asleep, I walked over to Lulu and rapped on her hide. I didn't expect anything to happen. I figured she would keep on sulking.

But she put out a tentacle and grew a face on it—a lens, an audio and speaker.

"It was nice of you," I said, "not to run away and leave us."

Lulu swore. It was the first and the only time I have ever heard her use such language.

"How could I leave?" she asked when she at last turned printable. "Of all the dirty human tricks! I'd have been gone long ago if it weren't for—"

"What dirty trick?"

"As if you didn't know. A built-in block that won't let me move unless there's one of you detestable humans inside me."

"I didn't know," I said.

"Don't try to pass the buck," she snapped. "It's a dirty human trick and you're a dirty human and you're just as responsible as all the rest of them. But it doesn't make any difference any more, because I've found myself. I am finally content. I know what I was meant for. I have—"

"Lulu," I asked her, straight out, "are you shacking up with Elmer?"

"That's a vulgar way to say it," Lulu told me heatedly. "It's the nasty human way. Elmer is a scholar and a gentleman and his loyalty to his ancient, long-dead masters is a touching thing no human could be capable of. He has been badly treated and I shall make it up to him. All he wanted from you was the phosphate in your bones—"

"The phosphate in our bones!" I yelled.

"Why, certainly," said Lulu. "Poor Elmer has such a hard time finding any phosphate. He got it at first from animals that he caught, but now all the animals are gone. There are birds, of course, but birds are hard to catch. And you had such nice, big bones—"

"That's a fine thing for you to say," I bawled her out sternly. "You were built by humans and humans educated you and—"

"Still I'm a machine," said Lulu, "and I am closer to Elmer than I am to you. You humans can't get it through your heads that there might be a legitimate set of non-human values. You are horrified that Elmer wanted the phosphate in your bones, but if there were a metal in Elmer that you needed, you'd break him up to get it without a second thought. You wouldn't even consider that you might be wrong. You'd think it an imposition if Elmer should object. That's the trouble with you and your human race. I've had enough. I have what I want. I am content to stay here. I've found the great love of my life. And for all I care, your pals and you can rot."

She pulled in her face and I didn't rap to try to get her to talk any more. I figured there wasn't any use. She had made it about as plain as anyone could wish.

I walked back to the camp and woke Ben and Jimmy. I told them about my hunch and about the talk with Lulu. We were pretty glum, because we were all washed up.

Up till now, there had always been the chance that we could make a deal with Lulu. I had felt all along that we needn't worry too much—that Lulu was more alone than we were and that eventually she would have to be reasonable. But now Lulu was not alone and she no longer needed us. And she still was sore at us—and not just at us, but at the whole human race.

And the worst of it was that this was no sudden whim. It had been going on for days. Elmer hadn't been really watching us when he'd hung around at night. He'd come to neck with Lulu. And undoubtedly the two of them had planned Elmer's attack on Ben and me, knowing that Jimmy would be loping to the rescue, leaving the coast clear so that Elmer could rush back and Lulu could take him in. And once it had been accomplished, Lulu had put out a tentacle and swept the tracks away so we wouldn't know that Elmer was inside.

"So she jilted us," said Ben.

"No worse than we did to her," Jimmy reminded him.

"But what did she expect? A man can't love a robot."

"Evidently," I said, "a robot can love a robot. And that's a new one to paste into the book."

"Lulu's crazy," Ben declared.

In all this great romance of Lulu's, it seemed to me there was a certain false note. Why should Lulu and Elmer be sneaky about their love? Lulu could have opened the port any time she wanted and Elmer could have scampered up the ramp right before our eyes. But they hadn't done that. They had planned and plotted. They had practically eloped.

I wondered if, on Lulu's part, it might be the mark of shame. Was she ashamed of Elmer—ashamed that she had fallen for him? Much as she might deny it, perhaps she nursed the smug snobbery of the human race.

Or was I only thinking this to save my own smug snobbery, simply building up a defense mechanism against being forced to admit, now or in some future time, that there might be other values than the ones evolved by humans? For in us all, I knew, lingered that reluctance to recognize that our way was not necessarily best, that the human viewpoint might not be the universal viewpoint to which all other life must eventually conform.

Ben made a pot of coffee, and while we sat around and drank it, we said some bitter things of Lulu. I don't regret anything we said, for she had it coming to her. She'd played us a nasty trick.

We finally rolled back into our blankets and didn't bother standing guard. With Elmer out of circulation, there was no need.

The next morning, my foot was still sore, so I stayed behind while Ben and Jimmy went out to explore the valley that held the ruined city. Meantime, I hobbled out and walked all around Lulu, looking her over. There was no way I could see that a man might bust into her. The port itself was machined so closely that you had to get real close to see the tiny hairline where it fitted into her side.

Even if we could bust into her, I wondered, could we take control of her? There were the emergencies, of course, but I wasn't too sure just how much use they were. They certainly hadn't bothered Lulu much when she'd got that crazy notion of eloping with us. Then she'd simply jammed them and had left us helpless.

And if we broke into Lulu, we'd come to grips with Elmer, and Elmer was just the kind of beast I had no hankering to come to grips with.

So I went back to camp and puttered around, thinking that now we'd really have to begin to lay some plans about how to get along. We'd have to build that cabin and work up a food supply and do the best we could to get along on our own. For I was fairly certain that we could expect no help from Lulu.

Ben and Jimmy came back in the afternoon and their eyes were shining with excitement. They spread out a blanket and emptied their pockets of the most incredible things any man has ever laid eyes on.

Don't expect me to describe that stuff. There's no point in trying to. What is the sense of saying that a certain item was like a metal chain and that it was yellow? There is no way to get across the feel of it as it slid through one's fingers or the tinkle of it as it moved or the blazing color that was a sort of *living* yellow. It is very much like saying that a famous painting is square and flat and blue, with some green and red.

The chain was only a part of it. There were a lot of other doo-dads and each one of them was the sort of thing to snatch your breath away.

Ben shrugged at the question in my eyes. "Don't ask me. It's only some stuff we picked up. The caves are full of it. Stuff like this and a whole lot more. We just picked up one thing here and another there—whatever was pocket-size and happened to catch our eye. Trinkets. Samples. I don't know."

Like jackdaws, I thought. Or pack-rats. Grabbing a thing that shone or had a certain shape or a certain texture—taking it because it was pretty, not knowing what its use might be or if, in fact, it had any use at all.

"Those caves may have been storehouses," said Ben. "They're jammed with all sorts of things—not much of any one thing, apparently. All different, as if these aliens had set up a trading post and had their merchandise on display. There seems to be a sort of curtain in front of each of the caves. You can see a shimmer and hear a hissing, but you can't feel a thing when you step through it. And behind that curtain, all the junk they left is as clean and bright and new as the day they left it."

I looked at the articles spread on the blanket. It was hard to keep your hands off them, for they felt good in your hands and were pleasing to the eye and one seemed to get a sense of warmth and richness just by handling them.

"Something happened to those folks," said Jimmy. "They knew it was going to happen, so they took all this stuff and laid it out—all the many things they had made, all the things they'd used and loved. Because, you see, that way there always was a chance someone might come along someday and find it, so they and the culture they had fashioned would not be entirely lost."

It was exactly the kind of silly, sentimental drivel you could expect from a glassy-eyed romantic like Jimmy.

But for whatever reason the artifacts of that vanished race had gotten in the caves, we were the ones who'd found them and here once again they'd run into a dead end. Even if we had been equipped to puzzle out their use, even if we had been able to ferret out the basic principles of that long-dead culture, it still would be a useless business. We were not going anywhere; we wouldn't be passing on the knowledge. We'd live out our lives here on this planet, and when the last of us had died, the ancient silence and the old uncaring would close down once again.

We weren't going anywhere and neither was Lulu. It was a double dead end.

It was too bad, I thought, for Earth could use the knowledge and the insight that could be wrested from those caves and from the mounds. And not more than a hundred feet from where we sat lay the very tool that Earth had spent twenty years in building to dig out that specific kind of knowledge, should Man ever happen on it.

"It must be terrible," said Jimmy, "to realize that all the things and all the knowledge that you ever had, all the trying, all the praying, all the dreams and hopes, will be wiped out forever. That all of you and your way of life and your understanding of that life will simply disappear and no one will ever know."

"You said it, kid," I chipped in.

He stared at me with haunted, stricken eyes. "That may be why they did it."

Watching him, the tenseness of him, the suffering in his face, I caught a glimpse of why he was a poet—why he *had* to be a poet. But even so, he still was an utter creep.

"Earth has to know about this," Ben said flatly.

"Sure," I agreed. "I'll run right over and let them know."

"Always the smart guy," Ben growled at me. "When are you going to cut out being bright and get down to business?"

"Like busting Lulu open, I suppose."

"That's right. We have to get back somehow and Lulu's the only way to get there."

"It might surprise you, Buster, but I thought of all that before you. I went out today and looked Lulu over. If you can figure how to bust into her, you've a better brain than I have."

"Tools," said Ben. "If we only had—"

"We have. An ax without a handle, a hammer and a saw. A small pinch-bar, a plane, a draw-shave—"

"We might *make* some tools."

"Find the ore and smelt it and—"

"I was thinking of those caves," said Ben. "There might be tools in there."

I wasn't even interested. I knew it was impossible.

"We might find some explosive," Ben went on. "We might—"

"Look," I said, "what do you want to do—open Lulu up or blow her to bits? Anyhow, I don't think you can do a thing about it. Lulu is a self-maintaining robot, or have you forgotten? Bore a hole in her and she'll grow it shut. Go monkeying around too much and she'll grow a club and clout you on the head."

Ben's eyes blazed with fury and frustration. "Earth has to know! You understand that, don't you? Earth has got to know!"

"Sure," I said. "Absolutely."

In the morning, I thought, he'd come to his senses, see how impossible it was. And that was important. Before we began to lay any plans, it was necessary that we realize what we were up against. That way, you conserve a lot of energy and miss a lot of lumps.

But, come morning, he still had that crazy light of frustration in his eyes and he was filled with a determination that was based on nothing more than downright desperation.

After breakfast, Jimmy said he wasn't going with us.

"For God's sake, why not?" demanded Ben.

"I'm way behind on my writing," Jimmy told him, deadpan. "I'm still working on that saga."

Ben wanted to argue with him, but I cut him off disgustedly.

"Let us go," I said. "He's no use, anyhow."

Which was the solemn truth.

So the two of us went out to the caves. It was the first time I had seen them and they were something to see. There were a dozen of them and all of them were crammed. I got dizzy just walking up and down, looking at all the gadgets and the thing-umbobs and dofunnies, not knowing, of course, what any of them were. It was maddening enough just to look at them; it was plain torture trying to figure out what use they might be put to. But Ben was plain hell-bent on trying to figure something out because he'd picked up the stubborn conviction that we could find a gadget that would help us get the best of Lulu.

We worked all day and I was dog-tired at the end of it. Not once in the entire day had we found anything that made any sense at all. I wonder if you can imagine how it felt to stand there, sur-rounded by all those devices, knowing there were things within your reach that, rightly used, could open up entirely new avenues for human thoughts and technique and imagination. And yet you stood there powerless—an alien illiterate.

But there was no stopping Ben. We went out again the next day and the day after and we kept on going out. On the sec-ond day, we found a dojigger that was just fine for opening cans, although I'm fairly sure that was not at all what it was designed for. And on the following day, we finally puzzled out how another piece of equipment could be used for digging slanted postholes and, I ask you, who in their right mind would be wanting slanted postholes?

We got nowhere, but we kept on going out and I sensed that Ben had no more hope than I had, but that he still kept at it because it was the one remaining fingerhold he had on sanity.

I don't think that for one moment he considered the source or significance of that heritage we'd found. To him, it became no more than a junkyard through which we searched frantically to find one unrecognizable piece of scrap that we might improvise into something that would serve our purpose.

As the days went on, the valley and its mounds, the caves and their residue of a vanished culture seized upon my imagination, and it seemed to me that, in some mysterious manner, I grew closer to that extinct race and sensed at once its greatness and its tragedy. And the feeling grew as well that this frantic hunt of ours bordered on sacrilege and callous profanation of the dead.

Jimmy had not gone out with us a single day. He'd sit hunched over his ream of paper and he scribbled and revised and crossed out words and put in others. He'd get up and walk around in circles or pace back and forth and mumble to himself, then go back and write some more. He scarcely ate and he wouldn't talk and he only slept a little. He was the very portrait of a Young Man in the Throes of Creation.

I got curious about it, wondering if, with all this agony and sweat, he might be at last writing something that was worth the effort. So, when he wasn't looking, I sneaked out a page of it.

It was even worse than the goo he had written before.

That night I lay awake and looked up at the unfamiliar stars and surrendered myself to loneliness. Only, once I had surrendered, I found that I was not so lonely as I might have been—that somehow I had drawn comfort and perhaps even understanding from the muteness of the ruin-mounds and the shining wonder of the trove.

Finally I dropped asleep.

I don't know what woke me. It might have been the wind or the sound of the waves breaking on the beach or maybe the chilliness of the night.

Then I heard it, a voice like a chant, solemn and sonorous, a throaty whisper in the dark.

I started up and propped myself on an elbow—and caught my breath at what I saw.

Jimmy was standing in front of Lulu, holding a flashlight in one hand, reading her his saga. His voice had a rolling quality, and despite the soggy words, there was a fascination in the tenor of his tone. It must have been so that the ancient Greeks read their Homer in the flare of torches before the next day's battle.

And Lulu was listening. She had a face hung out and the tentacle which supported it was twisted to one side, so that her audio would not miss a single syllable, just as a man might cup his ear.

Looking at that touching scene, I began to feel a little sorry about the way we'd treated Jimmy. We wouldn't listen to him and the poor devil had to read that tripe of his to someone. His soul hungered for appreciation and he'd got no appreciation out of either Ben or me. Merely writing was not enough for him; he must share it. He had to have an audience.

I put out a hand and shook Ben gently by the shoulder. He came storming up out of his blankets.

"What the hell is—"

"Sh-h-h!"

He drew in a whistling breath and dropped on one knee beside me.

Jimmy went on with his reading and Lulu, with her face cocked attentively, went on listening.

Part of the words came to us, wind-blown and fragmentary:

> "*Wanderer of the far ways between the two faces of eternity,*
> *True, forever, to the race that forged her,*
> *With the winds of alien space blowing in her hair,*
> *Wearing a circlet of stars as her crown of glory . . .*"

Lulu wept. There was the shine of tears in that single, gleaming lens.

She grew another tentacle and there was a hand on the end of it and a handkerchief, a very white and lacy and extremely feminine hanky, was clutched within the hand.

She dabbed with the handkerchief at her dripping eye.

If she had had a nose, she undoubtedly would have blown it, delicately, of course, and very ladylike.

"And you wrote it all for me?" she asked.

"All for you," said Jimmy. He was lying like a trooper. The only reason he was reading it to her was because he knew that Ben and I wouldn't listen to it.

"I've been so wrong," Lulu sighed.

She wiped her eye quite dry and briskly polished it.

"Just a second," she said, very businesslike. "There's something I must do."

We waited, scarcely breathing.

Slowly the port in Lulu's side came open. She grew a long, limber tentacle and reached inside the port and hauled Elmer out. She held him dangling.

"You lout!" she stormed at Elmer. "I take you in and stuff you full of phosphates. I get your dents smoothed out and I polish you all bright. And then what? Do you write sagas for me? No, you grow fat and satisfied. There's no mark of greatness on you, no spark of imagination. You're nothing but a dumb machine!"

Elmer just dangled at the end of Lulu's tentacle, but his wheels were spinning furiously and I took that to mean that he was upset.

"Love!" proclaimed Lulu. "Love for the likes of us? We machines have better things to do—far better. There are the star-studded trails of space waiting for our tread, the bitter winds of foreverness blowing from the cloud banks of eternity, the mountains of the great beyond . . ."

She went on for quite a while about the challenge of the farther galaxies, about wearing a coronet of stars, about the dust of shattered time paving the road that led into the ultimate nothingness, and all of it was lifted from what Jimmy called a saga.

Then, when she was all through, she hurled Elmer down the beach and he hit the sand and skidded straight into the water.

We didn't wait to see any more of it. We were off like sprinters. We hit the ramp full tilt and went up it in a leap and flung ourselves into our quarters.

Lulu slammed the port behind us.

"Welcome home," she said.

I walked over to Jimmy and held out my hand. "Great going, kid. You got Longfellow backed clear off the map."

Ben also shook his hand. "It was a masterpiece."

"And now," said Lulu, "we'll be on our way."

"Our way!" yelled Ben. "We can't leave this planet. Not right away at least. There's that city out there. We can't go until—"

"Phooey on the city," Lulu said. "Phooey on the data. We are off star-wandering. We are searching out the depths of silence. We are racing down the corridors of space with thunder in our brain—the everlasting thunder of a dread eternity."

We turned and looked at Jimmy.

"Every word of it," I said. "Every single word of it out of that muck he wrote."

Ben took a quick step forward and grabbed Jimmy by his shirt front.

"Don't you feel the urge," Ben asked him, "don't you feel a mighty impulse to write a lengthy ode to home—its comfort and its glory and all the other clichés?"

Jimmy's teeth were chattering just a little.

"Lulu is a sucker," Ben said, "for everything you write."

I lifted a fist and let Jimmy smell of it.

"You better make it good," I warned him. "You better write like you never wrote before."

"But keep it sloppy," Ben said. "That's the way Lulu likes it."

Jimmy sat down on the floor and began writing desperately.

SMOKE KILLER

Framed for the murder of his partner and two jumps ahead of a lynching, Danny Morgan's only hope for salvation was a discarded tobacco sack. His story is probably the earliest of Clifford Simak's published westerns (if nothing else, the style and language of the story shows that). I suspect this story was probably the one entitled "Killers Shouldn't Smoke" when Cliff sent it out.

Originally sent to Wild West Weekly *in February of 1943, only to be rejected there before finally being accepted by* Lariat Story Magazine, *it would see publication in the May 1944 issue of the latter magazine—which sold for twenty cents if purchased from a newsstand (but you could subscribe for $1.25 for a year). This is one of Cliff's shorter westerns, which likely means that he did not get paid any large sum (most of his later westerns would be much longer).*

—dww

Danny Morgan found Jack Harris in the coulee back of the shanty.

Someone had shot Harris straight between the eyes and he lay on his back, one leg bent under him and his arms thrown wide, as if a giant hand had slapped him backward violently. Harris' gun still was in its holster. His eyes stared at the silent sky. His mouth sagged as if, before he died, he'd had time to be surprised.

Morgan's hands lifted to his gun butts, then dropped away. There was, he realized, no further danger now. The man on the ground had been killed hours, probably days before. Probably shortly after Morgan had left for Butte City.

Slowly, Morgan glanced around. The prairie swells marched in serried ranks to the high horizon that hemmed in the bowl that held the spread. And the bowl was empty, empty to the sun and little gusts of wind that puffed and eddied down the coulees. Nothing stirred within it, no sign of life at all. The cattle would be down in the brakes, at the lower end of the ranch.

Up ahead, jutting out of the coulee's side, was a jumbled ledge of broken rocks. Morgan's eyes narrowed, hard in the bright sunlight. Those rocks were the only cover anywhere nearby, and were within easy rifle shot.

He walked up the coulee, climbed to the cluster of boulders. On the slope just below the rocks lay something white . . . a cigarette, half burned, unconsumed tobacco spilling from the paper. A man sitting in the rocks above could have flipped it there.

Among the boulders Morgan found other stubs. All of them half smoked. Someone, obviously, had squatted there, nervously puffing while he waited.

Crouched among the rocks, the ranchman stared back down the coulee to where the body of his partner lay. A tenderfoot couldn't have missed a shot like that.

A tiny breeze, hot in the midday sun, stirred down the coulee, fluttering something that lay within the shadow. Morgan reached out his hand. It was a tobacco sack, turned inside out, as if the man who had waited there had been determined to get out of it the last shred of leaf.

Staring at the sack, Morgan tried to marshal his thoughts.

Jack Harris had had his moments of bad temper, his sullen days, but he was not a trouble maker, he got along well with the folks he met. Morgan racked his brains for some enemy Harris might have had, could think of no one.

Could the killer have been someone from out of Harris' past? Someone who finally hunted him down? Something that finally caught up with him?

That, pondered Morgan, might have been the reason Jack had been so anxious to sell out. Although the last winter had been enough to make anyone want to sell, with more than half the cattle gone before the spring thaw came. Although it hadn't hit them any worse, perhaps not as hard, as it had hit some others. The Diamond C, Jay Crawford's big ranch just to the south, had lost more than 20,000 head.

A horse nickered from the shanty. Probably Harris' horse, still standing just as Morgan had found him, saddled and bridled, waiting with drooping head outside the shanty door. Almost as if he knew his master was dead.

Then Morgan saw the riders, three of them, coming up the draw, the horses picking their way through the grove of cottonwoods that grew above the spring.

Morgan clambered down the hill, walked down the coulee and waited beside the dead man until the three drew rein.

"Howdy, sheriff," said Morgan. "Just fixing to ride in and see you."

The burly sheriff sat his horse easily, carelessly, stared down at Harris' body. Morgan nodded to the other two. One of them was Harry Kress, the sheriff's deputy, the other Hank Fridley, Diamond C foreman. They nodded, saying nothing.

"What do you know about this, Danny?" the sheriff asked.

"Not a thing," said Morgan. "I just found him. Not more than an hour ago. The sidewinder that done it hid out in them rocks up there."

The sheriff nodded. "How come you didn't find him until just now?" he demanded. "From the looks of him, he's been dead for quite a long spell, I'd say."

"I just got back. I started out for Butte City a week ago."

The sheriff looked at him sharply. "You and Jack have another fight?" he asked.

"We had some words," admitted Morgan. "Crawford made us an offer for the spread and Jack wanted to sell. I wanted to hang on. Upshot of it was I left for Butte City to try to raise the money to buy out his share."

The sheriff slid from his horse, waddled over to the body.

"Clean a piece of work as I ever see."

He stared at Morgan solemnly. "How come you took so long to Butte City and back? Go on a little toot?"

"I never got to Butte City," said Morgan. "End of the first day out, my hoss got snake-bit. Had to hole up beside the creek for a while and wait till he could travel. Then I hoofed it back here, leading him. Took me three days to make it."

"You mean you never did get to Butte City? All this time you been sittin' out on the prairie, takin' care of a snake-bit hoss?"

Morgan flared angrily. "Just what are you trying to say, sheriff?"

The deputy laughed. "Don't monkey around with him no more, Fred. Go ahead and tell him what you got on your mind."

For a moment silence struck and froze them where they stood, with not a single one of them moving a muscle.

Then the deputy spoke. "I wouldn't go for them guns if I was you, Danny." Fridley laughed softly.

"You're all plumb loco," yelled Morgan. "Why would I kill Jack? Him and me was partners. Why we . . ."

"Shut your trap," said the sheriff, "and wave your paws. I'm going to take your guns."

"Someday," declared Morgan, "I'll just naturally gut-shoot all three of you for this."

"You better hurry, then," said Kress, mockingly. "Because it won't be long before you'll be stretching hemp."

From the tiny window in the rear of the jail, Morgan stared out over the crazily twisted land of turreted bluff and angry purple canyon. The setting sun hung in the west, intensifying the weird colors.

His head buzzed with a thousand questions. Who killed Harris? Why? How come the sheriff put in an appearance just when he did? Of course, the sheriff had explained that. Said Hank Fridley had found Harris' body and ridden into report it. But never before in the three years he and Harris had lived on the spread had Fridley been at their place. And why, above all, had the sheriff been so quick to pin it on him?

Morgan shook his head. Nothing added up, nothing came up right.

A knock came at the door.

"Yes, what is it?" Morgan called.

The door, a heavy wooden affair, creaked open.

"Visitor to see you," declared Deputy Kress.

A tall man, dressed in broadcloth coat and polished boots, the dust of the trail clinging to his clothes, loomed in the doorway. It was Jay Crawford.

"Howdy," said Morgan. "This is a right nice thing for you to do."

Crawford lumbered into the room, the floor boards creaking under his heavy tread.

"Heard you was in trouble, Danny," he said, "and hurried right over. Thought maybe I could help."

"They think I killed Jack," said Morgan.

Crawford sat down heavily on the single bench in the room. "So the sheriff told me. Said you ain't got much of a case."

Morgan shrugged. "Maybe the sheriff's right. I was stuck out in the middle of nowhere with a snake-bit hoss. Can't nohow prove where I was, I guess."

Crawford wagged his head. "Sorry you got into anything like this, Danny. Been watching you and Jack. Ready to offer a helping hand if anything went wrong. But you seemed to be making out all right. Sent some of the boys over this afternoon to look after things for you."

"Much obliged," declared Morgan.

Crawford looked around furtively, then lowered his voice. "But that ain't all I came here for, Danny."

Morgan stiffened. "What else?" he snapped.

"The town's stirred up," said Crawford. "First time there's ever been a killing here. Got their bristles up, the boys have. Talking about a necktie party."

"They can't be," gasped Morgan. "Why, I'm not even charged with anything yet. There isn't any real evidence. . . ."

"That don't make any difference," insisted Crawford. "Some of the hot-heads got to talking over in the Red Rooster and all of the others joined in and before you know it everybody's mad at you."

"They can't do it," insisted Morgan. "The sheriff . . ."

Crawford spat in disgust. "The sheriff's a dirty coward," he declared. "He'd high tail it out of here first sign of trouble. But I got a plan all figured out."

He pitched his voice to a husky whisper. "I'll get some of my own boys together and right after dark we'll rush the jail, like we was planning a necktie party of our own. The sheriff'll clear out and we'll bust down the door and do a lot of shooting and hollering. In the uproar you'll light a shuck. We'll say you slipped away from us."

Morgan considered. "But that would mean running away. Leaving my spread behind. Admitting I'm guilty."

"If it's money you're thinking about," said Crawford, "let me know soon as you get settled someplace and I'll pay you a reasonable price for your lay-out. Not that I need it . . ."

"Just neighborly," suggested Morgan.

"That's it," declared Crawford. "Just neighborly, that's all. Kind of got to like you. Want to help you any way I can."

"It's no go, Crawford," said Morgan.

"What's that?"

"I said it was no go. I'm sticking here, necktie party or no necktie party."

"You mean . . ."

"I mean I'm seeing this thing through. There's something hay-wire about his whole business. Somebody's out to get me . . . and I'm not going to be got."

"They'll string you up, sure as shooting," warned Crawford.

"I'll take my chances," Morgan declared.

The rancher rose slowly, shaking his head. "Wish you'd let me help you, Danny."

"I'm much obliged for the offer," Morgan said. "But I can't see it that way."

Listening to the retreating footsteps of Crawford and the dep-uty, Morgan sat down on the bench and tried to figure things out. There was something behind Crawford's offer of escape, he was sure. Maybe Crawford really did think he was guilty, really was trying to help him get away. But somehow that explanation didn't hold water. Did Crawford want his ranch? It hardly seemed likely. The rancher had thousands of acres of his own, more than he needed. Water was no consideration, for Crawford had plenty of that, too.

His thoughts led him nowhere except to suggest that, after all, he may have been foolish not to accept help. Once away, he could start over with the money from the spread. He didn't like the idea, but it was better than decorating a cottonwood.

Twilight came and slipped swiftly into darkness. Out in the badlands a panther screamed and on the prairie the coyotes set up their dismal howling. Somewhere down in the cedar brakes an owl laughed irrationally.

From the town, down near the Red Rooster saloon, came the yells of men, occasionally a six-gun shot. The boys were having them a time.

He went to the side window and stared out. The saloon and store windows lighted the street and the space in front of the two buildings was swarming with men, some of them on their horses, some jostling around on foot. Someone standing on the porch of the store was trying to make a speech, shouting to make himself heard above the angry roar that came from the crowd.

Morgan felt the short hairs stiffen along the back of his neck, felt the stir of fear crawling on his spine. There was something in the voices of those men . . . something that was not quite human.

A bull voice bellowed out, drowning out the hum. "To hell with all this jabber. Someone get a rope!"

Three or four men started a rush for the store doorway, some of the others mounted their horses. A few of them started toward the jail, then stopped and waited.

What Crawford had said was right!

Frantically he turned from the window, started toward the door, then turned back, with a sudden realization of the hopelessness of his situation rising to choke him.

A board creaked beneath his feet and he stopped stock still, remembering how the boards had teetered under Crawford's tread.

The jail was not strongly built. It never had been meant to house anyone who really wanted to get away. Its usual tenants came on pay-day nights when over-enthusiastic drunks were bent on shooting up the town.

Morgan went to his knees, feeling the floor with his hands. His fingers slid into a crack. He tightened his grip and surged upward. The board yielded a little. He put more strength into it and it came still further. Breathlessly, he ripped at it fiercely and the board came free. He tossed it to one side, grasped another one, ripped it out, let his body down into the hole.

Three wasn't much space. Just enough room for a man's body.

Bellying in the dirt, he dragged himself along between the two stringers. His head bumped and his shoulder scraped on the floor above.

Dirt clogged the way and he dug at it furiously with his hands, like a dog after a gopher. A spear of nighttime light appeared before his face. The dirt he had been digging at was last winter's banking thrown up around the jail to help keep out the cold.

Out of the night came the howl of the mob, the beat of racing hoofs, the sudden crack of six-guns. They were storming the jail!

Savagely, Morgan thrust himself forward, plowing through the remaining pile of dirt, clawing fiercely to free himself. For one sickening moment he thought he was stuck fast and then surged free.

For a moment, he crouched, gulping in great breaths of air.

The hoofs drummed closer and voices bellowed with madness. Six-guns hammered.

Straight ahead lay the badlands. Less than a hundred rods away. Once in there and they'd never find him.

Bending low he dashed for the gap, the gap the buffalo had used for uncounted ages. Hunched over, he held his breath, tightening his muscles, sucking in his stomach, expecting any moment to feel the blow of a .45 slug between his shoulder blades.

He had covered half the distance before the first startled whoop back at the jail announced he had been seen. A gun barked viciously and a bullet whined above his head. Another gun hammered and another. Morgan flung himself to one side in a mighty leap, zigzagging, running low. If he could only reach the shadow of those bushes!

Behind him red flashes stained the night. One slug ripped sod at his feet. Another passed so close it fanned his cheek. Wild whoops rang out and hoofs thundered on the prairie.

Morgan felt the ground dip beneath his feet, flung himself forward into bushes, struck the ground and rolled. Thorns ripped at his clothing, his right arm was nearly paralyzed when it struck a rock. He rocketed over a cut bank in a 20 foot drop, managed to land on his feet before he stumbled to his knees. Then he was running, twisting and leaping down the canyon, keeping in the shadows.

Fifteen minutes later, he stopped and listened. Noise still came from the canyon below the town, that of men on foot beating the bush. Soon they would give up and go back to spend the night in drinking and boasting. No one would risk a horse in such a place at night.

They might be after him as soon as it was light, although he doubted it. The hanging fever would have burned itself out by then. Anyhow, it would be a good idea to put some distance between himself and Buffalo Gap.

He angled across the side of the butte, started down into another canyon. In the darkness his foot caught in a low-creeping bush and he pitched suddenly forward. His outthrust hands were too late to save him, his head cracked against a stone. Danny Morgan lay limp.

The smell of frying bacon filled the air. Somewhere nearby a bird was singing lustily. Someone was shuffling about.

Danny lay quiet, eyes still closed. His head ached. Slowly he opened one eye, stared up at unpeeled pole rafters thatched with yellow clay. He opened the other eye and turned his head to one side.

He was in a small cabin. The floor, he saw, was earthen. A rickety table, built of saplings and a couple of old boards, leaned crazily against the log walls. Two elk antlers hung on the wall, served as a gun rack, held an oldtime rifle. A pair of dirty trousers and a battered felt hat dangled from a peg.

A man moved into his vision, carrying a cup and plate to the table. He was old. Long gray hair curled over the shoulders of a red flannel shirt, his face was a salt and pepper mass of whiskers.

"Bill!" cried Morgan.

Badlands Bill turned around, grinned with tobacco stained teeth.

"So yuh came to life," he said.

"My head hurts like hell," said Morgan.

"It's got a lump on it size of a goose egg," declared Bill. "Wonder yuh didn't bat your brains out."

Morgan slung his legs off the bed.

"I remember stubbing my toe and falling," he said.

"Yuh fetched yourself a crack on the noodle that laid yuh out," said Bill. "Dang near busted the rock, yuh did. I was kind of trailin' along behind yuh."

Morgan stiffened. "Trailing along behind me?"

"Shore. I was just coming up the gap into town when all hell bruk loose. I saw yuh runnin' and all them jaspers after yuh, so being a peaceable sort of cuss, I just kind of hid in some bushes and watched the goings on. I see yuh ain't got no shootin' irons and I figured maybe some of the boys might push yuh kind of hard. So I jogged along with yuh, thinkin' maybe if they did I could grab me a hand."

"Do you mean you was siding with me?"

"Bet yore britches," Bill told him. "Don't like this here idear of the whole danged town jumpin' on one guy. Besides, most of them jaspers was Diamond C men and there ain't nothin' I hate worser than the Diamond C."

"Wait a second," said Morgan, slowly. "You must be wrong on that count, Bill. Crawford himself was over and offered to help me out. Offered to fake a hanging party and let me get away. Maybe that's what he did. Even after I told him I didn't . . ."

"None of them jaspers was bent on lettin' yuh get away," Bill declared. "They was pourin' lead at yuh like water out of a bucket. And they wasn't shootin' at the sky, neither. Them guns was a-pointin' right at yore back."

"And most of them were Diamond C men?"

"Bet yore boots they was. Meanest bunch of hombres that ever cluttered up the range."

Morgan shook his head. "Can't figure it out a-tall," he said. "Crawford himself . . ."

"You come over here and squat," invited Bill. "Get some meat an' coffee inside yore carcass and then yuh and me is goin' to talk."

Morgan made his way dizzily across the room, took a seat on a packing box covered with a sheep pelt. Bill poured a tin cup full of steaming coffee, forked half a grouse and strips of bacon onto a plate.

With the scent of food in his nostrils, Morgan realized that he was hungry, hadn't eaten since the noon before. Eagerly he stripped off the leg of the grouse, ate ravenously.

Finished, he pushed his plate away and looked at Bill. The old man had stoked up his stubby pipe. Glowing and sputtering under forced draft, the tobacco seemed in imminent danger of setting fire to his whiskers.

One of the old beaver trappers who had stayed on after the beaver were gone, Bill was one of Buffalo Gap's characters. Morgan had seen him many times before, had had a drink or two with him at times in the Red Rooster, understood the old man lived in a cabin tucked off somewhere in the badlands. No one seemed to know just where.

"You seem to have your back up at the Diamond C," said Morgan. "What did they ever do to you?"

"Three or four years back," said Bill, "I slow-elked one of their critters. Hard winter and no game in miles. I ain't one that starves when meat walks right up to the door, even if it does tote a brand."

"I can guess it," Morgan said. "They raised hell with you."

"They more than raised hell, mister," declared Bill, "they were plumb set on doin' me violence. Me and my gun argued them out of it."

The old man sat silently for a moment, clouds of tobacco smoke seething in his whiskers.

"I don't know what kind of trouble yuh are in," he finally said, "but it must be powerful bad. I been waitin' for it to happen, sooner or later, ever since I talked to that rock feller last summer."

"What rock fellow?"

"Feller Crawford had lookin' over his ranch. Kind of dudish feller. Wore laced boots, he did. From back east. Said he was a geolo . . . something like geography, though that ain't it."

"Geologist," suggested Morgan.

The old man slapped his knee. "By cracky, that's the word. Never could remember it. Looks at rocks, he told me, and knows what's underneath. Crawford had him out sizin' up his spread for oil."

"There isn't any oil in this country," objected Morgan.

"Feller told me there was," insisted Bill. "Me and him got drinkin' one night and he sort of likkered up. Told me lots of things he probably shouldn't of told. Said there was oil, all right, by cracky, but it wasn't on Crawford's land. Said it was in a big pool just north of Crawford's place."

"North," yelled Morgan. "Why, that's my place!"

The old man nodded. "That's what I thought, too. Sat around long time tryin' to figure out if I should tell yuh. Decided not to 'cause it wasn't none of my danged business."

Morgan rose to his feet and walked to the door, stood looking eastward to the dim purple of the escarpment. The sun was only an hour or so above the horizon. In the creek below the water babbled with a sleepy sound. A scarlet bird flashed from the top of a dead cedar, skimmed the sagebrush.

Old Bill joined him at the door.

"Goin' to be another burner," he opined, squinting at the sun.

"I got business for tonight," said Morgan, tersely.

"Thought yuh might have," said Badlands Bill.

Buffalo Gap was quiet, quiet with the cool of night after an August day. Unlike the night before, there was no movement in the street. The windows of the Red Rooster glowed yellow, but the porch of the saloon was empty. Only one horse stood at the hitching rail.

Danny Morgan moved like a fleeting shadow from the bushes at the head of the gap, making for the jail. Stooping low and running, he reached the back of the building. Crouching there, he waited for any sound that might announce he had been seen. Putting his hand down on the ground, it came in contact with fresh, damp earth and looking down, he saw that he squatted beside the hole he had clawed open to escape the night before.

Moving cautiously, Morgan slid around the corner of the jail. There was a light in the office. Slowly he edged up to the window, looked in. Kress, the deputy, sat with his feet on the desk, his chair tilted back, hat over his face. The lamp burned low. There was no sign of the sheriff.

Swiftly, Morgan's eyes swept the wall, lighted on the double belt and pair of guns slung from a nail. He would have recognized those guns anywhere.

The door stood half open and Kress did not stir when Morgan pushed it easily. For a second, Morgan stood in the doorway, then strode forward.

The deputy jerked in surprise, half swinging his feet off the desk, but before he could utter a cry, Morgan had him by the throat, was bearing him backward to the floor. The chair went over with a clatter.

Kress fought madly, trying to cry out, but the grip on his throat squeezed his cries to tiny gurgles that bubbled faintly from his lips. He tried to reach his gun, but it had swung under his body as he fell, was pinned between him and the floor. Viciously he brought a knee up into Morgan's stomach and for a long moment the rancher felt himself tumbling giddily into a swaying pit of blackness. But he managed to keep his hands locked on Kress' throat, drove his fingers into the flesh of the man he held.

Kress tried with the knee again, but his strength was failing. His eyes widened and he gasped and sobbed for breath. With pawing hands he clawed ineffectually at the hands that throttled him. His boot heels beat a feeble tattoo on the floor.

Dropping Kress, Morgan moved quickly to the wall and jerked down the double belt and guns that hung there . . . the guns that had been taken from him. He took out each gun and spun the cylinders to be sure they were fully loaded, then put them back again.

Calmly the rancher closed the door and slid the bolt, then went back to Kress, stripped off the deputy's gun belt and flung it in a corner. With a length of rope he found in a desk drawer, he tried Kress' hands behind him. He used the man's own neckerchief to gag him. Then he hauled Kress over to the desk and propped him up.

The deputy's eyes flickered open and for a moment he stared at Morgan with a puzzled look.

Morgan grinned at him. "How do you feel, Kress?"

Kress worked his jaws, but no sound came.

"Yes, I know," said Morgan, "I'll swing for this."

Kress made gurgling sounds.

"Somebody will be around and find you soon," said Morgan. "Maybe it is a dirty trick to play on you, but no worse than you played on me. And I had to get my guns again. Can't do what I'm planning without guns."

His face sobered. "There's just one thing, Kress. You hombres heaved me in jail for a killing I didn't do and never lifted a finger to stop a necktie party that was all set to get me. I ain't forgetting that. You shoved me down the owlhoot trail and if I got to travel it, I aim to travel it plumb right. So tell the sheriff that if he comes after me he better come with guns out. That goes for you, too, or anybody else."

Deliberately, Morgan turned on his heel, unlocked the door and stepped outside. The street still was clear. The horse still stood, with drooping head, at the hitching post.

Grimly, Morgan slid a six gun from its holster and clutching it in his hand, moved boldly forward, making no effort to hide his progress. With a gun, there was no longer any need of skulking.

Reaching the horse, he untied the reins and vaulted into the saddle. At that moment the bat wings of the saloon swung open and a man stepped out. For a moment he stood stock still in aston-ishment, then with a wild whoop went for his guns.

Morgan yelled and raked savagely with his spurs as the horse reared and danced. Light from the window fell across the face of the man on the porch as he took a quick step forward. It was Hank Fridley, the Diamond C foreman, the man who had found Jack Harris and ridden to tell the sheriff.

Still fighting the rearing horse, Morgan snatched at his holster, ripped one of the .45s free. Fridley's hand moved. Lead droned past Morgan's ear. Then the other gun was talking and the horse bucked wildly.

Twisting in his saddle, Morgan triggered savagely, spraying the saloon front with a hail of death. Fridley dived for the safety of the street, going flat on his belly in the deep layer of yellow dust.

With a whoop of triumph, Morgan aimed his last shot at the man in the center of the street, the slug raising a geyser of dust six inches from his face.

Then the hammer clicked on an empty chamber.

The horse still was running, stretching out and eating up the ground. Morgan let him run.

Darkness closed in behind until the lights of Buffalo Gap were twinkling fireflies far away.

Morgan rode east, toward the ranch house of the Diamond C.

The buildings of the Diamond C were a dark huddle on the prairie.

Standing beside the horse, Morgan waited in a tiny draw that ran between two swales, ears strained for the rolling drum of hoof beats that would announce Fridley's arrival. That Fridley would head straight for the ranch as soon as he could get another horse, Morgan had no doubt.

He did not have long to wait. Within five minutes the racing horse and rider topped a ridge less than a quarter mile away, swept down toward the ranch.

He heard Fridley's yell as the foreman pulled up in front of the ranch house, saw a light come on through one of the windows.

Another light blinked out of a bunk house window. The bunk house door spouted men. Some of them ran toward the house, others headed for the corral.

"They'll figure I'll head out for my own spread," Morgan told himself. "Maybe to cover up some evidence or get something I don't want to leave behind. Some of them will ride out there and the others will try to cut off my escape back into the badlands."

The riders gathered in a knot around the front door of the ranch house. Someone that looked like Crawford was standing in the door, his form outlined by the lamplight.

With a smile of amusement, Morgan watched them go, waited another quarter hour, then mounted the horse and rode slowly to the ranch house.

No one challenged him as he dismounted and strode up the porch. Without pausing, he flung open the door and walked in.

"That you, Mike?" came Crawford's voice.

Morgan did not answer. The voice had come from the office, just off the living room.

Without hurrying, without a change of stride, he covered the space to the office door.

Crawford, sitting behind the desk, glanced up and a look of amazement, slowly replaced by anger, spread across his face. Then he moved swiftly, standing, kicking back his chair, all in one effortless bit of action.

But at the first hint of a move, Morgan's hands dropped to his gun butts and the two sixes came out, steadied waist high. Crawford's hands stopped, just short of his guns.

"You got something I want, Crawford," Morgan told him, tersely.

"All I've got for you is a rope," snarled Crawford.

"Any more talk like that," Morgan told him, smoothly, "and I'll let daylight through you. I haven't got a thing to lose. You already got me pegged as a killer and hanging for a real killing ain't no worse than hanging for one I've never done."

Crawford stared at him, flinched a little at what he saw in Morgan's eyes.

Morgan holstered one of his guns, reached behind him and closed the door, slid along so he had his back against the wall.

"H'ist out those guns," he ordered. "Easy like. Just the butts between your thumb and fingers. Heave them on the floor. In front of the desk."

Crawford hesitated. Morgan's voice was deadly. "Get them out."

Never shifting his gaze from Morgan, Crawford complied. The two guns hit the floor in front of the desk.

"Now," said Morgan, "I want to know where that geological report is."

"Geological report?" asked Crawford.

"Don't play dumb," snapped Morgan. "You know what I mean. The report the geologist made for you. The one that showed there was oil on my place."

Crawford didn't budge, didn't speak.

Morgan moved forward, threateningly.

"Do I have to knock your teeth in?" he asked.

"It's not here," said Crawford.

"That's just too damn bad for you," snapped Morgan.

His gun moved slightly downward and his eyes narrowed. His finger tensed on the trigger.

"Right in the belly," he said. "You'll suffer like hell, Crawford."

Crawford wilted. "No, Danny, don't do that! It's here. Right in my desk!"

He moved toward the desk, but Morgan stopped him.

"Stay where you are," he ordered. "Tell me which drawer."

"The upper left hand," said Crawford, breathlessly.

Keeping his eyes on the rancher, Morgan moved behind the desk, pulled open the drawer and flung a sheaf of papers on the desk.

"Pick it out," he snapped.

Crawford moved forward slowly, then dropped out of sight behind the desk. With one motion, Morgan scooped the papers from the desk top, gave the heavy piece of furniture a shove.

A gun roared from the floor and fire burned its way along Morgan's left arm. Crawford screamed as the desk toppled over on him and in that moment Morgan spun about, lowered his head and leaped straight for the window.

Glass exploded in a shattering spray and he was through, stumbling along the ground, trying to keep his feet. Stuffing the papers into his pocket, he raced toward the front of the house, leaped for the saddle.

The horse wheeled on a dime and streaked off. From the house behind him a gun coughed hoarsely.

Faint yells came from the ranch house.

Morgan, riding westward into the night, felt gingerly of his left arm. The bullet had barely creased the flesh. The arm, he knew, would be stiff tomorrow, but otherwise was unharmed.

"One thing," he told himself and the night wind, "I sure am going to make Crawford know he's been in a fight."

Badlands Bill had been correct. There was oil on his spread, which explained a lot of things. Explained why he had been framed for the Harris killing, why Crawford had been so anxious to help him out the night he was in jail.

Crawford knew and the sheriff knew they didn't have a case they could make stick, knew that if he ever was brought to trial the charge would be thrown out for lack of evidence.

Sitting there, beside the coals of his campfire, Morgan felt a surge of anger sweep over him. Crawford had never intended to let him escape when his men had stormed the jail. The rancher, Morgan was sure now, had set out to kill him as deliberately as he had killed Jack Harris, or hired him to be killed. Perhaps, after all, it hadn't been Crawford who had squatted among the rocks, smoking cigarettes, waiting until there was no chance of missing.

He reached up and took the survey report from his pocket. It was lucky, he told himself, that the report actually had been among the papers he had taken from the drawer. Crawford might have tried to fool him, told him the wrong drawer. That he had indicated the right drawer meant only one thing. The rancher had acted on impulse when he had dropped on the floor and gone after the guns that lay there.

Morgan smoothed the paper out across his knee and read it slowly again, squinting his eyes against the glare of sun.

Something jerked viciously at the paper in Morgan's hand, jerked and tore it from his grip and even as it jerked the silence was cracked wide open by the sharp, wicked chortle of a high caliber rifle.

Morgan hurled himself behind the nearest boulder. And as he landed, crouching, both six guns were in his fists.

Slowly, alert for any movement, any hint of the man who had fired the rifle, Morgan examined each coulee mouth, each perching boulder, each thicket wilting in the sun.

Slow minutes ticked away and the land drowsed on into a sleepy afternoon.

Then something moved, just a flicker of movement, in a thicket below the pink and yellow butte. Eyes glued to the spot, Morgan held his crouch and waited. The movement came again, as if a man were shifting his position, tired from being too long in one pose.

There was something there that looked like a grey sombrero, something white below it that might have been the smudge of the gunman's face.

Carefully, Morgan brought up one of his guns, steadying it against the boulder. The sights lined on what might have been a hat and his finger started to squeeze the trigger.

Something struck the boulder just above his head and howled off into space, a ricocheting bullet tumbling end over end, drowning out the ugly cough of the hidden rifle. Tiny splinters of rock showered on Morgan's hat and instinctively he ducked. Another bullet slammed into the rock, six inches below where the first had hit and went screaming off with an angry hum.

Swiftly, Morgan scrambled around the rock, breath rasping in his throat. The thing that had moved in the thicket hadn't been the rifleman at all. Probably a rabbit or maybe a bear. Or . . . and his heart stood chilled for an instant as he thought of it . . . there might be two gun slingers on his trail. Maybe more.

Faint traces of smoke floated from a rocky point cropping out of a hogback just across the creek.

Morgan nodded in grim satisfaction. At least, he had spotted the position.

He crouched and waited, guns ready.

The sun glinted on a metallic object and Morgan saw a rifle barrel slowly sliding forward around a rock. Hunched, with the feel of death cold between his shoulder blades, Morgan did not stir. Every instinct in him screamed for him to leap out of danger's way, to throw himself behind the rock, to put something between himself and that rifle barrel. But he stuck it out.

A brown splotch appeared beside the boulder on the slope above. A splotch that grew larger and larger. Morgan gulped and held his breath. That splotch was someone's elbow, the bent elbow of the man who held the gun. The rifle still had to move a ways yet to be trained correctly, and Morgan waited . . . waited for a bigger target.

Then suddenly he went into action. His right hand snapped up and for an instant the six gun froze rigid in his fist before it blazed and blazed again.

A shrill scream knifed the air and the rifle plunged forward to land on the slope below, sliding slowly, plowing a furrow with its muzzle through the powdery talus.

Morgan charged from behind his boulder, clawing his way up the treacherous incline.

From the valley below a rifle spanged and dirt spurted at his feet. The rifle roared again and a bullet hit the rocks ahead and plunged off into space with a doleful screech.

Spinning on his heel, Morgan saw the second man standing upright in a patch of bushes, rifle at his shoulder, and snapped a shot at him. The man flung himself to one side as both of Morgan's guns talked, heaving a hail of lead.

Then, guns still smoking, Morgan hurled himself at the boulders above him, circling around their upper end.

A six gun roared and the bullet thudded into the slope. Springing toward the sound of the shot, Morgan saw a man crouched with his back against the rocks, left arm smashed and bleeding, but with a six gun in his other fist and a snarl of hated on his face.

The man was Fridley, Crawford's foreman.

Fridley's gun swung upward, but even as it did, Morgan's hog-leg hammered and the foreman howled with pain. Slowly the gun in his hand tilted its muzzle toward the ground, then dropped from a hand smashed by a bullet.

Slowly Morgan walked forward, until he stood six feet from the wounded man. A smile twitched his lip as he looked at Fridley.

"Hank, you sure are stoved up," he said.

The foreman snarled at him, waving a bloody hand. "They'll get you yet," he screamed. "You'll swing. Sure as hell, you'll swing."

"Not unless they send better men than you after me," said Morgan.

A still smoking cigarette butt lay at Fridley's feet. Morgan glanced around. Another butt lay a short distance away. And on the ground something else, a tobacco sack.

Slowly Morgan stooped and picked it up. The sack was turned inside out!

Staring at it, his eyes narrowed.

"You do a lot of smoking on your killing jobs," he told Fridley, quietly.

Fridley said nothing, glaring at him.

Morgan tossed the sack up and down in his palm.

"Found one of these things, just like this, turned inside out, where you waited to kill Harris."

"What are you trying to do?" yelled Fridley. "Pin the blame on someone else?"

Morgan's face turned grim. "I don't have to pin it on anyone," he said. "I know who killed Harris. It was you."

He hoisted a gun slowly.

"You fixed it up so it looked like I was the one that did it," Morgan said. "You made an outlaw out of me. Guess nobody would believe me now, even if I had proof I didn't do it."

Fridley's eyes gleamed with fear. "What you getting at, Morgan?"

"Guess I'll just naturally have to gun you, Hank. Ain't got a thing to lose. Besides, I'd get a heap of satisfaction out of doing it."

"Look, Danny," pleaded Fridley, "you can't do that. Not in cold blood."

"Don't see why not," declared Morgan, almost cheerfully. "You ain't in no shape to stop me."

From the valley below came the swift clatter of hoofs.

"See," said Morgan, "your friend's riding out on you. Probably figures you're a goner already. He'll be back after a while with help to round me up. In a minute or two I'll fix you for planting, then move on."

"I'll clear you," yelled Fridley, almost slobbering in terror. "I'll tell them I killed Harris. I'll . . ."

He stopped and stared at Morgan. "Go on," Morgan ordered.

"Crawford made me do it. Said he'd turn me in for something down in Texas if I didn't . He knows there's oil on your spread and when he couldn't buy it . . ."

Morgan nodded. "So he figured if he killed Harris and got me hung for the killing, he could get the ranch. But he was afraid I couldn't be convicted, so he fixed up that necktie party."

Fridley licked dry lips.

"That's about right," he said.

Morgan stood up. "We got riding to do," he said. "Can you walk down to your hoss or do I have to carry you?"

"I can walk," said Fridley.

SHADOW SHOW

"Shadow Show" was Clifford D. Simak's first story for The Magazine of Fantasy & Science Fiction, *appearing in the November 1953 issue of that magazine; for that initial publication, Cliff was paid $425. Readers who came across the story in a subsequent anthology republication, however, were deprived of the opening passage that appears here. The theme of this story is that of guilt arising out of people's religious beliefs, and I rather think that this might in turn represent a new thought related to Cliff's earlier great story, "Desertion," and its concept of changing the human form. But this time it's a psychological horror story.*

Will anyone who reads this story in the future know what it meant to "dress for dinner"?

—*dww*

Henry Griffith died just after breakfast, seated at his bench, with his notebook at his elbow and his pen still clutched within his fingers.

He died a natural death. The best medical examinations before hiring cannot detect the possibilities of a later embolism, nor can the best of medical care on the job. The embolus, unnoticed in the bloodstream, found its way finally to the heart, and Griffith died.

It was a natural death. But the job on which he died was not a natural job; and the consequences of his death were far from our concept of nature.

I

Bayard Lodge, chief of Life Team No. 3, sat at his desk and stared across it angrily at Kent Forester, the team's psychologist.

"The Play must go on," said Forester. "I can't be responsible for what might happen if we dropped it even for a night or two. It's the one thing that holds us all together. It is the unifying glue that keeps us sane and preserves our sense of humor. And it gives us something to think about."

"I know," said Lodge, "but with Henry dead. . . ."

"They'll understand," Forester promised. "I'll talk to them. I know they'll understand."

"They'll understand all right," Lodge agreed. "All of us recognize the necessity of the Play. But there is something else. One of those characters was Henry's."

Forester nodded. "I've been thinking of that, too."

"Do you know which one?"

Forester shook his head.

"I thought you might," said Lodge. "You've been beating out your brains to get them figured out, to pair up the characters with us."

Forester grinned sheepishly.

"I don't blame you," said Lodge. "I know why you're doing it."

"It would be a help," admitted Forester. "It could give me a key to every person here. Just consider—when a character went illogical. . . ."

"They're all illogical," said Lodge. "That's the beauty of them."

"But the illogic runs true to a certain zany pattern," Forester pointed out. "You can use that very zaniness and set up a norm."

"You've done that?"

"Not as a graph," said Forester, "but I have it well in mind. When the illogic deviates it's not too hard to spot it."

"It's been deviating?"

Forester nodded. "Sharply at times. The problem that we have—the way that they are thinking. . . ."

"Call it attitude," said Lodge.

For a moment the two of them were silent. Then Forester asked: "Do you mind if I ask why you insist on attitude?"

"Because it is an attitude," Lodge told him. "It's an attitude conditioned by the life we lead. An attitude traceable to too much thinking, too much searching of the soul. It's an emotional thing, almost a religious thing. There's little of the intellectual in it. We're shut up too tightly. Guarded too closely. The importance of our work is stressed too much. We aren't normal humans. We're off balance all the time. How in the world can we be normal humans when we lead no normal life?"

"It's a terrible responsibility," said Forester. "They face it each day of their lives."

"The responsibility is not theirs."

"Only if you agree that the individual counts for less than the race. Perhaps not even then, for there are definite racial implications in this project, implications that can become terribly personal. Imagine making. . . ."

"I know," said Lodge impatiently. "I've heard it from every one of them. Imagine making a human being not in the image of humanity."

"And yet it would be human," Forester said. "That is the point, Bayard. Not that we would be manufacturing life, but that it would be human life in the shape of monsters. You wake up screaming, dreaming of those monsters. A monster itself would not be bad at all, if it were no more than a monster. After centuries of traveling to the stars, we are used to monsters."

Lodge cut him off. "Let's get back to the Play."

"We'll have to go ahead," insisted Forester.

"There'll be one character missing," Lodge warned him. "You know what that might do. It might throw the entire thing off balance, reduce it to confusion. That would be worse than no Play at all. Why can't we wait a few days and start over, new again? With a new Play, a new set of characters."

"We can't do that," said Forester, "because each of us has identified himself or herself with a certain character. That character has become a part, an individual part, of each of us. We're living split lives, Bayard. We're split personalities. We have to be to live. We have to be because not a single one of us could bear to be himself alone."

"You're trying to say that we must continue the Play as an insurance of our sanity."

"Something like that. Not so grim as you make it sound. Under ordinary circumstances, there'd be no question we could dispense with it. But this is no ordinary circumstance. Every one of us is nursing a guilt complex of horrendous magnitude. The Play is an emotional outlet, a letdown from the tension. It gives us something to talk about. It keeps us from sitting around at night washing out the stains of guilt. It supplies the ridiculous in our lives—it is our daily comic strip, our chuckle or our belly laugh."

Lodge got up and paced up and down the room.

"I said attitude," he declared, "and it is an attitude—a silly, crazy attitude. There is no reason for the guilt complex. But they coddle it as if it were a thing that kept them human, as if it might be the one last identity they retain with the outside world and the rest of mankind. They come to me and they talk about it—as if I could do something about it. As if I could throw up my hands and say, well, all right, then, let's quit. As if I didn't have a job to do.

"They say we're taking a divine power into our hands, that life came to be by some sort of godly intervention, that it's blasphemous and sacrilegious for mere man to try to duplicate that feat.

"And there's an answer to that one—a logical answer, but they can't see the logic, or won't listen to it. Can Man do anything divine? If life is divine, then Man cannot create it in his laboratories no matter what he does, cannot put it on a mass production basis. If Man can create life out of his chemicals, out of his knowledge, if he can make one living cell by the virtue of his technique and his knowledge, then that will prove divine intervention was unnecessary to the genesis of life. And if we have that proof—if we know that a divine instrumentality is unnecessary for the creation of life, doesn't that very proof and fact rob it of divinity?"

"They are seeking an escape," said Forester, trying to calm him. "Some of them may believe what they say, but there are others of them who are merely afraid of the responsibility—the moral responsibility. They start to thinking how it would be to live with something like that the rest of their life. You had the same situation a thousand years ago when men discovered and developed atomic fission. They did it and they shuddered. They couldn't sleep at night. They woke up screaming. They knew what they were doing—that they were unloosing terrible powers. And we know what we are doing. . . ."

Lodge went back to his desk and sat down.

"Let me think about it, Kent," he said. "You may be right. I don't know. There are so many things that I don't know."

"I'll be back," said Forester.

He closed the door quietly when he left.

II

The Play was a never-ending soap opera, the *Old Red Barn* extended to unheard reaches of the ridiculous. It had a touch of Oz and a dash of alienness and it went on and on and on.

When you put a group of people on an asteroid, when you throw a space patrol around them, when you lead them to their laboratories and point out the problem to be solved, when you keep them at that problem day after endless day, you must likewise do something to preserve their sanity.

To do this there may be books and music, films, games, dancing of an evening—all the old standby entertainment values the race has used for millennia to forget its troubles.

But there comes a time when these amusements fail to serve their purpose, when they are not enough.

Then you hunt for something new and novel—and basic—for something in which each of the isolated group may participate, something with which they can establish close personal identity and lose themselves, forgetting for a time who they are and what may be their purpose.

That's where the Play came in.

In olden days, many years before, in the cottages of Europe and the pioneer farmsteads of North America, a father would provide an evening's entertainment for his children by the means of shadow pictures. He would place a lamp or candle on a table opposite a blank wall, and sitting between the lamp and wall, he would use his hands to form the shadows of rabbit and of elephant, of horse and man and bear and many other things. For an hour or more the shadow show would parade across the wall, first one and then another—the rabbit nibbling clover, the elephant waving trunk and ears, the wolf howling on a hilltop. The children would sit quiet and spellbound, for these were wondrous things.

Later, with the advent of movies and of television, of the comic book and the cheap plastic dime-store toy, the shadows were no longer wondrous and were shown no longer, but that is not the point.

Take the principle of the shadow pictures, add a thousand years of know-how, and you have the Play.

Whether the long-forgotten genius who first conceived the Play had ever known of the shadow pictures is something that's not known. But the principle was there, although the approach was different in that one used his mind and thought instead of just his hands.

And instead of rabbits and elephants appearing in one-dimensional black-and-white, in the Play the characters were as varied as the human mind might make them (since the brain is more facile than the hand) and three-dimensional in full color.

The screen was a triumph in electronic engineering, with its memory banks, its rows of sonic tubes, its color selectors, ESP antennae and other gadgets, but it was the minds of the audience that did the work, supplying the raw material for the Play upon the screen. It was the audience that conceived the characters, that led them through their actions, that supplied the lines they spoke. It was the combined will of the audience that supplied the backdrops and dreamed up the properties.

At first the Play had been a haphazard thing, with the characters only half developed, playing at cross purposes, without personalities and little more than cartoons paraded on the stage. At first the backdrops and the properties were the crazy products of many minds flying off at tangents. At times no less than three moons would be in the sky simultaneously, all in different phases. At times snow would be falling at one end of the stage and bright sunlight would pour down on palm trees at the other end.

But in time the Play developed. The characters grew to full stature, without missing arms and legs; acquired personalities; rounded out into full-blown living beings. The background became the result of a combined effort to achieve effective setting rather than nine different people trying desperately to fill in the blank spots.

In time direction and purpose had been achieved, so that the action flowed smoothly, although there never came a time when any of the nine were sure of what would happen next.

That was the fascination of it. New situations were continually being introduced by one character or another, with the result that the human creators of the other characters were faced with the need of new lines and action to meet the changing situations.

It became in a sense a contest of wills, with each partici-
pant seeking advantages for his character, or, on the other hand,
forced to backtrack to escape disaster. It became, after a time, a
never-ending chess game in which each player pitted himself or
herself against the other eight.

And no one knew, of course, to whom any of the characters
belonged. Out of this grew up a lively guessing game and many
jokes and sallies, and this was to the good, for that was what the
Play was for—to lift the minds of the participants out of their
daily work and worries.

Each evening after dinner the nine gathered in the theater
and the screen sprang into life, and the nine characters performed
their parts and spoke their lines—the Defenseless Orphan, the
Mustached Villain, the Proper Young Man, the Beautiful Bitch,
the Alien Monster and all the others.

Nine of them—nine men and women, and nine characters.

But now there would be only eight, for Henry Griffith
had died, slumped against his bench with the notebook at his
elbow.

And the Play would have to go on with one missing character—the character that had been controlled and motivated by
the man who now was dead.

Lodge wondered which character would be the missing one.
Not the Defenseless Orphan, certainly, for that would not have
been down Henry's alley. But it might be the Proper Young Man
or the Out-At-Elbows Philosopher or the Rustic Slicker.

Wait a minute there, said Lodge. Not the Rustic Slicker. The
Rustic Slicker's me.

He sat idly speculating on which belonged to whom. It
would be exactly like Sue Lawrence to dream up the Beautiful
Bitch—a character as little like her prim, practical self as one
could well imagine. He remembered that he had taunted her
once concerning his suspicion and that she had been very cold
to him for several days thereafter.

Forester said the Play must go on, and maybe he was right. They might adjust. God knows, they should be able to adjust to anything after participating in the Play each evening for months on end.

It was a zany thing, all right. Never getting anywhere. Not even episodic, for it never had a chance to become episodic. Let one trend develop and some joker was sure to throw in a stumbling block that upset the trend and sent the action angling off in some new direction.

With that kind of goings-on, he thought, the disappearance of a single character shouldn't throw them off their stride.

He got up from his desk and walked to the great picture window.

He stood there looking out at the bleak loneliness of the asteroid.

The curbed roofs of the research center fell away beneath him, shining in the starlight, to the blackness of the cragged surface. Above the jagged northern horizon lay a flush of light and in a little while it would be dawn, with the weak, watch-sized sun sailing upward to shed its feeble light upon this tiny speck of rock. He watched the flushed horizon, remembering Earth, where dawn was morning and sunset marked the beginning of the night. Here no such scheme was possible, for the days and nights were so erratic and so short that they could not be used to divide one's time. Here morning came at a certain hour, evening came at another hour, regardless of the sun, and one might sleep out a night with the sun high in the sky.

It would have been different, he thought, if we could have stayed on Earth, for there we would have had normal human contacts. We would not have thought so much, or brooded; we could have rubbed away the guilt on the hides of other people.

But normal human contacts would have meant the start of rumors, would have encouraged leaks, and in a thing of this sort there could be no leaks.

For if the people of the Earth knew what they were doing, or, more correctly, what they were trying to do, they would raise a hubbub that might result in calling off the project.

Even here, he thought—even here, there are those who have their doubts and fears.

A human being must walk upon two legs and have two arms and a pair of eyes, a brace of ears, one nose, one mouth, be not unduly hairy. He must walk; he must not hop or crawl or slither.

A perversion of the human form, they said; a scrapping of human dignity; a going-too-far, farther than Man in all his arrogance was ever meant to go.

There was a rap upon the door.

Lodge turned and called: "Come in."

It was Dr. Susan Lawrence.

She stood in the open doorway, a stolid, dumpy, dowdy woman with an angular face that had a set of stubbornness and of purpose in it. She did not see him for a moment and stood there, turning her head, trying to find him in the dusky room.

"Over here, Sue," he called.

She closed the door and crossed the room, and stood by his side looking out the window.

Finally she said, "There was nothing wrong with him, Bayard. Nothing organically wrong. I wonder. . . ."

She stood there, silent, and Lodge could feel the practical bleakness of her thoughts.

"It's bad enough," she said, "when they die and you know what killed them. It's not so bad to lose them if you've had a fighting chance to save them. But this is different. He just toppled over. He was dead before he hit the bench."

"You've examined him?"

She nodded. "I put him in the analyzers. I've got three reels of stuff. I'll check it all—later. But I'll swear there was nothing wrong."

She reached out a hand and put it on his arm, her pudgy fingers tightening.

"He didn't want to live," she said. "He was afraid to live. He thought he was close to finding something and he was afraid to find it."

"We have to find it, Sue."

"For what?" she asked. "So we can fashion humans to live on planets where humans in their present form wouldn't have a chance. So we can take a human mind and spirit and enclose it in a monster's body, hating itself. . . ."

"It wouldn't hate itself," Lodge told her. "You're thinking in anthropomorphic terms. A thing is never ugly to itself because it knows itself. Have we any proof that bipedal man is any happier than an insect or a toad?"

"But why?" she persisted. "We do not need those planets. We have more now than we can colonize. Enough Earth-type planets to last for centuries. We'll be lucky if we even colonize them all, let alone develop them, in the next five hundred years."

"We can't take the chance," he said. "We must take control while we have the chance. It was all right when we were safe and snug on Earth, but that is true no longer. We've gone out to the stars. Somewhere in the universe there are other intelligences. There have to be. Eventually we'll meet. We must be in a strong position."

"And to get into that strong position we plant colonies of human monsters. I know, Bayard—it's clever. We can design the bodies, the flesh and nerves and muscles, the organs of communication—all designed to exist upon a planet where a normal human being could not live a minute. We are clever, all right, and very good technicians, but we can't breathe the life into them. There's more to life than just the colloidal combination of certain elements. There's something else, and we'll never get it."

"We will try," said Lodge.

"You'll drive good technicians out of their sanity," she said. "You'll kill some of them—not with your hands, but with your insistence. You'll keep them cooped up for years and you'll give them a Play so they'll last the longer—but you won't find life, for life is not Man's secret."

"Want to bet?" he asked, laughing at her fury.

She swung around and faced him.

"There are times," she said, "when I regret my oath. A little cyanide. . . ."

He caught her by the arm and walked her to the desk.

"Let's have a drink," he said. "You can kill me later."

III

They dressed for dinner.

That was a rule.

They always dressed for dinner.

It was, like the Play, one of the many little habits that they cultivated to retain their sanity, to not forget that they were a cultured people as well as ruthless seekers after knowledge—a knowledge that any one of them would have happily forsworn.

They laid aside their scalpels and their other tools, they boxed their microscopes, they ranged the culture bottles neatly in place, they put the pans of saline solutions and their varying contents carefully away. They took their aprons off and went out and shut the door. And for a few hours they forgot, or tried to forget, who they were and what their labors were.

They dressed for dinner and assembled in the so-called drawing room for cocktails and then went in to dinner, pretending that they were no more than normal human beings—and no less.

The table was set with exquisite china and fragile glass, and there were flowers and flaming tapers. They began with an entrée and their meal was served in courses by accomplished robots and they ended with cheese and fruit and brandy and there were cigars for those who wanted them.

Lodge sat at the table's head and looked down the table at them and for a moment saw Sue Lawrence looking back at him and wondered if she were scowling or if the seeming scowl was no more than the play of candlelight upon her face.

They talked as they always talked at dinner—the inconsequential social chatter of people without worry and with little purpose. For this was the moment of forgetting and escape. This was the hour to wash away the guilt and to ignore the stain.

But tonight, he noticed, they could not pull themselves away entirely from the happenings of the day—for there was talk of Henry Griffith and of his sudden dying and they spoke of him in soft tones and with strained and sober faces. Henry had been too intense and too strange a man for anyone to know him well, but they held him in high regard, and although the robots had been careful to arrange the seating so his absence left no gap, there was a real and present sense that one of them was missing.

Chester Sifford said to Lodge: "We'll be sending Henry back?"

Lodge nodded. "We'll call in one of the patrol and it'll take him back to Earth. We'll have a short service for him here."

"But who. . . ."

"Craven more than likely. He was closer to Henry than any of the rest. I spoke to him about it. He agreed to say a word or two."

"Is there anyone on Earth? Henry never talked a lot."

"Some nephews and nieces. Maybe a brother or a sister. That would be all, I think."

Hugh Maitland said, "I understand we'll continue with the Play."

"That's right," Lodge told him. "Kent recommended it and I agreed. Kent knows what's best for us."

Sifford agreed. "That's his job. He's a good man at it."

"I think so, too," said Maitland. "Most psych-men stand outside the group. Posing as your conscience. But Kent doesn't work that way."

"He's a chaplain," Sifford said. "Just a God damn chaplain."

Helen Gray sat to the left, and Lodge saw that she was not talking with anyone, but only staring at the bowl of roses which this night served as a centerpiece.

Tough on her, he thought. For she had been the one who had found Henry dead and, thinking that he was merely sleeping, had taken him by the shoulder and shaken him to wake him.

Down at the other end of the table, sitting next to Forester, Alice Page was talking far too much, much more than she had ever talked before, for she was a strangely reserved woman, with a quiet beauty that had a touch of darkness in it. Now she leaned toward Forester, talking tensely, as if she might be arguing in a low tone so the others would not hear her, with Forester listening, his face masked with patience against a feeling of alarm.

They are upset, thought Lodge—far more than I had suspected. Upset and edgy, ready to explode.

Henry's death had hit them harder than he knew.

Not a lovable man, Henry still had been one of them. One of them, he thought. Why not one of us? But that was the way it always was—unlike Forester, who did his best work by being one of them, he must stand to one side, must keep intact that slight, cold margin of reserve which was all that preserved against an incident of crisis the authority which was essential to his job.

Sifford said, "Henry was close to something."

"So Sue told me."

"He was writing up his notes when he died," said Sifford. "It may be. . . ."

"We'll have a look at them," Lodge promised. "All of us together. In a day or two."

Maitland shook his head. "We'll never find it, Bayard. Not the way we're working. Not in the direction we are working. We have to take a new approach. . . ."

Sifford bristled. "What kind of approach?"

"I don't know," said Maitland. "If I knew. . . ."

"Gentlemen," said Lodge.

"Sorry," Sifford said. "I'm a little jumpy."

Lodge remembered Dr. Susan Lawrence, standing with him, looking out the window at the bleakness of the trembling hunk of rock on which they lived, and saying, "He didn't want to live. He was afraid to live. . . ."

What had she been trying to tell him? That Henry Griffith had died of intellectual fear? That he had died because he was afraid to live?

Would it actually be possible for a psychosomatic syndrome to kill a man?

IV

You could feel the tension in the room when they went to the theater, although they did their best to mask the tension. They chatted and pretended to be light-hearted, and Maitland tried a joke which fell flat upon its face and died, squirming beneath the insincerity of the laughter that its telling had called forth.

Kent was wrong, Lodge told himself, feeling a wave of terror washing over him. This business was loaded with deadly psychological dynamite. It would not take much to trigger it and it would set off a chain reaction that could wash up the team.

And if the team were wrecked the work of years was gone— the long years of education, the necessary months to get them working together, the constant, never-ending battle to keep them happy and from one another's throats. Gone would be the team confidence, which over many months had replaced individual confidence and doubt, gone would be the smooth cooperation and coordination which worked like meshing gears, gone would be a vast percentage of the actual work they'd done, for no other team, no matter how capable it might be, could take up where another team left off, even with the notes of the first team to guide them on their way.

The curving screen covered one end of the room, sunken into the wall, with the flare of the narrow stage in front of it.

Back of that, thought Lodge, the tubes and generators, the sonics and computers—mechanical magic which turned human thought and will into the moving images that would parade across the screen. Puppets, he thought—puppets of the human mind, but with a strange and startling humanity about them that could not be achieved by carven hunks of wood.

And the difference, of course, was the difference between the mind and hand, for no knife, no matter how sharp, guided by no matter how talented and artistic a hand, could carve a dummy with half the precision or fidelity with which the mind could shape a human creature.

First, Man had created with hands alone, chipping the flint, carving out the bow and dish; then he achieved machines which were extensions of his hands and they turned out artifacts which the hands alone were incapable of making; and now, Man created not with his hands, nor with extensions of his hands, but with his mind and extensions of his mind, although he still must use machinery to translate and project the labor of his brain.

Someday, he thought, it will be mind alone, without the aid of machines, without the help of hands.

The screen flickered and there was a tree upon it, then another tree, a bench, a duck pond, grass, a distant statue, and behind it all the dim, tree-broken outlines of city towers.

That was where they had left it the night before, with the cast of characters embarked upon a picnic in a city park—a picnic that was almost certain to remain a picnic for mere moments only before someone should turn it into something else.

Tonight, he hoped, they'd let it stay a picnic, let it run its course, take it easy for a change, not try any fancy stuff—for tonight, of all nights, there must be no sudden jolts, no terrifying turns. A mind forced to guide its character through the intricacies of a suddenly changed plot or some outlandish situation might crack beneath the effort.

As it was, there'd be one missing character and much would depend upon which one it was.

The scene stood empty, like a delicate painting of a park in springtime with each thing fixed in place.

Why were they waiting? What were they waiting for?

They had set the stage. What were they waiting for?

Someone thought of a breeze and you could hear the whisper of it, moving in the trees, ruffling the pond.

Lodge brought his character into mind and walked him on the stage, imagining his gangling walk, the grass stem stuck in his mouth, the curl of unbarbered hair above his collar.

Someone had to start it off. Someone—

The Rustic Slicker turned and hustled back off stage. He hustled back again, carrying a great hamper.

"Forgot m' basket," he said, with rural sheepishness.

Someone tittered in the darkened room.

Thank God for that titter!

It is going all right.

Come on, the rest of you!

The Out-At-Elbows Philosopher strode on stage.

He was a charming fellow, with no good intent at all—a cadger, a bum, a full-fledged fourflusher behind the façade of his flowered waistcoat, the senatorial bearing, the long, white, curling locks.

"My friend," he said. "My friend."

"Y' ain't m' friend," the Rustic Slicker told him, "till y' pay me back m' 300 bucks."

Come on, the rest of you!

The Beautiful Bitch showed up with the Proper Young Man, who any moment now was about to get dreadfully disillusioned.

The Rustic Slicker had squatted on the grass and opened his hamper. He began to take out stuff—a ham, a turkey, a cheese, a vacuum jug, a bowl of Jello, a tin of kippered herring.

The Beautiful Bitch made exaggerated eyes at him and wiggled her hips. The Rustic Slicker blushed, ducking his head.

Kent yelled from the audience: "Go ahead and ruin him!"

Everyone laughed.

It was going to be all right. It would be all right.

Get the audience and the players kidding back and forth and it was bound to be all right.

"Ah think that's a good idee, honey," said the Beautiful Bitch. "Ah do believe Ah will."

She advanced upon the Slicker.

The Slicker, with his head still ducked, kept on taking things out of the hamper—more by far than could have been held in any ten such hampers.

He took out rings of bologna, stacks of wieners, mounds of marshmallows, a roast goose—and a diamond necklace.

The Beautiful Bitch pounced on the necklace, shrieking with delight.

The Out-At-Elbows Philosopher had jerked a leg off the turkey and was eating it, waving it between bites to emphasize the flowery oration he had launched upon.

"My friends"—he orated between bites—"my friends, in this vernal season it is right and proper, I said right and proper, sir, that a group of friends should foregather to commune with nature in her gayest aspects, finding retreat such as this even in the heart of a heartless city. . . ."

He would go on like that for hours unless something intervened to stop him. The situation being as it was, something was almost bound to stop him.

Someone had put a sportive, if miniature, whale into the pond, and the whale, acting much more like a porpoise than a whale, was leaping about in graceful curves and scaring the hell out of the flock of ducks which resided on the pond.

The Alien Monster sneaked in and hid behind a tree. You could see with half an eye that he was bent upon no good.

"Watch out!" yelled someone in the audience, but the actors paid no attention to the warning. There were times when they could be incredibly stupid.

The Defenseless Orphan came onstage on the arm of the Mustached Villain (and there was no good intent in that situation, either) with the Extra-Terrestrial Ally trailing along behind them.

"Where is the Sweet Young Thing?" asked the Mustached Villain. "She's the only one who's missing."

"She'll be along," said the Rustic Slicker. "I saw her at the corner saloon building up a load. . . ."

The Philosopher stopped his oration in midsentence, halted the turkey drumstick in midair. His silver mane did its best to bristle and he whirled upon the Rustic Slicker.

"You are a cad, sir," he said. "To say a thing like that, a most contemptible cad!"

"I don't care," said the Slicker. "No matter what y' say, that's what she was doing."

"You lay off him," shrilled the Beautiful Bitch, fondling the diamond necklace. "He's mah frien' and you can't call him a cad."

"Now, B.B.," protested the Proper Young Man, "you keep out of this."

She spun on him. "You shut yoah mouth," she said. "You mealy hypocrite. Don't you tell me what to do. Too nice to call me by mah rightful name, but using just initials. You prissy-panted high-binder, don't you speak to me."

The Philosopher stepped ponderously forward, stooped down and swung his arm. The half-eaten drumstick took the Slicker squarely across the chops.

The Slicker rose slowly to his feet, one hand grasping the roast goose.

"So y' want to play," he said.

He hurled the goose at the Philosopher.

It struck squarely on the flowered waistcoat.

It was greasy and it splashed.

Oh, Lord, thought Lodge.

Now the fat's in the fire for sure!

Why did the Philosopher act the way he did? Why couldn't they have left it a simple, friendly picnic, just this once? Why did the person whose character the Philosopher was make him swing that drumstick?

And why had he, Bayard Lodge, made the Slicker throw the goose?

He went cold all over at the question, and when the answer came he felt a hand reach into his belly and start twisting at his guts.

For the answer was: He hadn't!

He hadn't made the Slicker throw the goose. He'd felt a flare of anger and a hard, cold hatred, but he had not willed his character to retaliatory action.

He kept watching the screen, seeing what was going on, but with only half his mind, while the other half quarreled with itself and sought an explanation.

It was the machine that was to blame—it was the machine that had had the Slicker throw the goose, for the machine would know, almost as well as a human knew, the reaction that would follow a blow upon the face. The machine had acted automatically, without waiting for the human thought. Sure, perhaps, of what the human thought would be.

It's logical, said the arguing part of his mind—it's logical that the machine would know, and logical once again that being sure of knowing, it would react automatically.

The Philosopher had stepped cautiously backward after he

had struck the blow, standing at attention, presenting arms, after a manner of speaking, with the mangy drumstick.

The Beautiful Bitch clapped her hands and cried, "Now you-all got to fight a duel!"

"Precisely, miss," said the Philosopher, still stiffly at attention. "Why else do you think I struck him."

The goose grease dripped slowly off his ornate vest, but you never would have guessed for so much as an instant but he was faultlessly turned out.

"But it should have been a glove," protested the Proper Young Man.

"I didn't have a glove, sir," said the Philosopher, speaking a truth that was self-evident.

"It's frightfully improper," persisted the Proper Young Man.

The Mustached Villain flipped back his coattails and, reaching into his back pockets, brought out two pistols.

"I always carry them," he said with a frightful leer, "for occasions such as this."

We have to break it up, thought Lodge. We have to stop it. We can't let it go on!

He made the Rustic Slicker say, "Now lookit here, now. I don't want to fool around with firearms. Someone might get hurt."

"You have to fight," said the leering Villain, holding both pistols in one hand and twirling his mustaches with the other.

"He has the choice of weapons," observed the Proper Young Man. "As the challenged party. . . ."

The Beautiful Bitch stopped clapping her hands.

"You keep out of this," she screamed. "You sissy—you just don't want to see them fight."

The Villain bowed. "The Slicker has the choice," he said.

The Extra-Terrestrial Ally piped up. "This is ridiculous," it said. "All you humans are ridiculous."

The Alien Monster stuck his head out from behind the tree.

"Leave 'em alone," he bellowed in his frightful brogue. "If they want to fight, let them go ahead and fight."

Then he curled himself into a wheel by the simple procedure of putting his tail into his mouth and started to roll. He rolled around the duck pond at a fearful pace, chanting all the while:

"Leave 'em fight. Leave 'em fight. Leave 'em fight."

Then popped behind his tree again.

The Defenseless Orphan complained, "I thought this was a picnic."

And so did all the rest of us, thought Lodge.

Although you could have bet, even before it started, that it wouldn't stay a picnic.

"Your choice, please," said the Villain to the Slicker, far too politely. "Pistols, knives, swords, battle axes. . . ."

Ridiculous, thought Lodge.

Make it ridiculous.

He made the Slicker say, "Pitchforks at three paces."

The Sweet Young Thing tripped lightly on the stage. She was humming a drinking song, and you could see that she'd picked up quite a glow.

But she stopped at what she saw before her—the Philosopher dripping goose grease, the Villain clutching a pistol in each hand, the Beautiful Bitch jangling a diamond necklace, and she asked: "What is going on here?"

The Out-At-Elbows Philosopher relaxed his pose and rubbed his hands together with smirking satisfaction.

"Now," he said, oozing good fellowship and cheer, "isn't this a cozy situation. All nine of us are here. . . ."

In the audience Alice Page leaped to her feet, put her hands up to her face, pressed her palms tight against her temples, closed her eyes quite shut and screamed and screamed and screamed.

V

There had been, not eight characters, but nine.

Henry Griffith's character had walked on with the rest of them.

"You're crazy, Bayard," Forester said. "When a man is dead, he's dead. Whether he still exists or not, I don't profess to know, but if he does exist it is not on the level of his previous existence; it is on another plane, in another state of being, in another dimension, call it what you will, religionist or spiritualist, the answer is the same."

Lodge nodded his agreement. "I was grasping at straws. Trying to dredge up every possibility. I know that Henry's dead. I know the dead stay dead. And yet, you'll have to admit, it is a natural thought. Why did Alice scream? Not because the nine characters were there. But because of why there might be nine of them. The ghost in us dies hard."

"It's not only Alice," Forester told him. "It's all the others, too. If we don't get this business under control, there'll be a flare-up. The emotional index was already stretched pretty thin when this happened—doubt over the purpose of the research, the inevitable wear and tear of nine people living together for months on end, a sort of cabin fever. It all built up. I've watched it building up and I've held my breath."

"Some joker out there subbed for Henry," Lodge said. "How does that sound to you? Someone handled his own character and Henry's, too."

"No one could handle more than one character," said Forester.

"Someone put a whale into that duck pond."

"Sure, but it didn't last long. The whale jumped a time or two and then was gone. Whoever put it there couldn't keep it there."

"We all cooperate on the setting and the props. Why couldn't someone pull quietly out of that cooperation and concentrate all his mind on two characters?"

Forester looked doubtful. "I suppose it could be done. But the second character probably would be out of whack. Did you notice any of them that seemed a little strange?"

"I don't know about strange," said Lodge, "but the Alien Monster hid—"

"Henry's character wasn't the Alien Monster."

"How can you be sure?"

"Henry wasn't the kind of mind to cook up an alien monster."

"All right, then. Which one is Henry's character?"

Forester slapped the arm of his chair impatiently. "I've told you, Bayard, that I don't know who any of them are. I've tried to match them up and it can't be done."

"It would help if we knew. Especially. . . ."

"Especially Henry's character," said Forester.

He left the chair and paced up and down the office.

"Your theory of some joker putting on Henry's character is all wrong," he said. "How would he know which one. . . ."

Lodge raised his hand and smote the desk.

"The Sweet Young Thing!" he shouted.

"What's that?"

"The Sweet Young Thing. She was the last to walk on. Don't you remember? The Mustached Villain asked where she was and the Rustic Slicker said he saw her in a saloon and. . . ."

"Good Lord!" breathed Forester. "And the Out-At-Elbows Philosopher was at great pains to announce that all of them were there. Needling us! Jeering at us!"

"You think the Philosopher is the one, then? He's the joker. The one who produced the Sweet Young Thing—the ninth member of the cast. The ninth one to appear would have to be Henry's character, don't you see. You said yourself it couldn't be done because you wouldn't know which one it was. But you could know—you'd know when eight were on the stage that the missing one was Henry's character."

"Either there was a joker," Forester said, "or the cast itself is somehow sentient—has come halfway alive."

Lodge scowled. "I can't buy that one, Kent. They're images of our minds. We call them up, we put them through their paces, we dismiss them. They depend utterly on us. They couldn't have a separate identity. They're creatures of our mind and that is all."

"It wasn't exactly along that line that I was thinking," said Forester. "I was thinking of the machine itself. It takes the impressions from our minds and shapes them. It translates what we think into the images on the screen. It transforms our thoughts into seeming actualities. . . ."

"A memory. . . ."

"I think the machine may have a memory," Forester declared. "God knows it has enough sensitive equipment packed into it to have almost anything. The machine does more of it than we do, it contributes more than we do. After all, we're the same drab old mortals that we always were. We've just got clever, that is all. We've built extensions of ourselves. The machine is an extension of our imagery."

"I don't know," protested Lodge. "I simply do not know. This going around in circles. This incessant speculation."

But he did know, he told himself. He did know that the machine could act independently, for it had made the Slicker throw the goose. But that was different from handling a character from scratch, different from putting on a character that should not appear. It had simply been a matter of an induced, automatic action—and it didn't mean a thing.

Or did it?

"The machine could walk on Henry's character," Forester persisted. "It could have the Philosopher mock us."

"But why?" asked Lodge, and even as he asked it, he knew why the machine might do just that, and the thought of it made icy worms go crawling up his back.

"To show us," Forester said, "that it was sentient, too."

"But it wouldn't do that," Lodge argued. "If it were sentient it would keep quiet about it. That would be its sole defense. We could smash it. We probably would smash it if we thought it had come alive. We could dismantle it; we could put an end to it."

He sat in the silence that fell between them and felt the dread that had settled on this place—a strange dread compounded of an intellectual and a moral doubt, of a man who had fallen dead, of one character too many, of the guarded loneliness that hemmed in their lives.

"I can't think," he said. "Let's sleep on it."

"Okay," said Forester.

"A drink?"

Forester shook his head.

He's glad to drop it, too, thought Lodge. He's glad to get away.

Like a hurt animal, he thought. All of us, like hurt animals, crawling off to be alone, sick of one another, poisoned by the same faces eternally sitting across the table or meeting in the halls, of the same mouths saying the same inane phrases over and over again until when you meet the owner of a particular mouth, you know before he says it what he is going to say.

"Good night, Bayard."

"Night, Kent. Sleep tight."

"See you."

"Sure," said Lodge.

The door shut softly.

Good night. Sleep tight. Don't let the bedbugs bite.

VI

He woke, screaming in the night.

He sat bolt upright in the middle of the bed and searched with numbed mind for the actuality, slowly, clumsily separating the actuality from the dream, becoming aware again of the room he slept in, of the furniture, of his own place and who he was and what he did and why he happened to be there.

It was all right, he told himself. It had been just a dream. The kind of dream that was common here. The kind of dream that everyone was having.

The dream of walking down a street or road, or walking up a stairs, of walking almost anywhere and of meeting something—a spider-like thing, or a worm-like thing, or a squatting monstrosity with horns and drooling mouth or perhaps something such as could be fabricated only in a dream and have it stop and say hello and chat—for it was human, too, just the same as you.

He sat and shivered at the memory of the one he'd met, of how it had put a hairy, taloned claw around his shoulder, of how it had drooled upon him with great affection and had asked him if he had the time to catch a drink because it had a thing or two it wanted to talk with him about. Its odor had been overpowering and its shape obscene, and he'd tried to shrink from it, had tried to run from it, but could neither shrink nor run, for it was a man like him, clothed in different flesh.

He swung his legs off the bed and found his slippers with searching toes and scuffed his feet into them. He found his robe and stood up and put it on and went out to the office.

There he mixed himself a drink.

Sleep tight, he thought. God, how can a man sleep tight? Now it's got me as well as all the others.

The guilt of it—the guilt of what mankind meant to do.

Although, despite the guilt, there was a lot of logic in it.

There were planets upon which no human could have lived for longer than a second—because of atmospheric pressure, because of overpowering gravity, because of lack of atmosphere or poison atmosphere, or because of any one or any combination of a hundred other reasons.

And yet those planets had economic and strategic value—every one of them. Some of them had both great economic and great strategic value. And if Man were to hold the galactic empire which he was carving out against the possible appearance of some as-yet-unknown alien foe, he must man all economic and strategic points, must make full use of all the resources of his new empire.

For that somewhere in the galaxy there were other intelligences as yet unmet by men there could be little doubt. The sheer mathematics of pure chance said there had to be. Given an infinite space, the possibility of such an intelligence also neared infinity. Friend or foe—you couldn't know. But you couldn't take a chance. So you planned and built against the day of meeting.

And in such planning, to bypass planets of economic and strategic value was sheer insanity.

Human colonies must be planted on those planets—must be planted there and grow against the day of meeting so that their numbers and their resources and their positioning in space might be thrown into the struggle if the struggle came to be.

And if Man, in his natural form, could not exist there—why, then you changed his form. You manufactured bodies that could live there, that could fit into the planets' many weird conditions, that could live on those planets and grow and build and carry out Man's plans.

Man could build those bodies. He had the technique to compound the flesh and bone and nerve, he had the skill to duplicate the mechanisms that produced the hormones, he had ferreted out the secrets of the enzymes and the amino acids and had at his fingertips all the other know-how to construct a body—any body, not just a human body. Biological engineering had become an exact science and biological blueprints could be drawn up to meet any conceivable set of planetary conditions. Man was all set to go on his project for colonization by humans in strange nonhuman forms.

Ready except for one thing: he could make everything but life.

Now the search for life went on, a top priority, highly classified research program carried on here and on other asteroids, with the teams of biochemists, metabolists, endocrinologists and others isolated on the tumbling slabs of rock, guarded by military patrols operating out in space, hemmed in by a million regulations and uncounted security checks.

They sought for life, working down in that puzzling gray area where non-life was separated from life by a shadow zone and a strange unpredictability that was enough to drive one mad, working with the viruses and crystals which at one moment might be dead and the next moment half alive and no man as yet who could tell why this was or how it came about.

That there was a definite key to life, hidden somewhere against Man's searching, was a belief that never wavered in the higher echelons, but on the guarded asteroids there grew up a strange and perhaps unscientific belief that life was not a matter of fact to be pinned down by formula or equation, but rather a matter of spirit, with some shading to the supernatural—that it was not something that Man was ever meant to know, that to seek it was presumptuous and perhaps sacrilegious, that it was a tangled trap into which Man had lured himself by his madcap hunt for knowledge.

And I, thought Bayard Lodge, I am one of those who drive them on in this blind and crazy search for a thing that we were never meant to find, that for our peace of mind and for our security of soul we never should have sought. I reason with them when they whisper out their fears, I kid them out of it when they protest the inhumanity of the course we plan, I keep them working and I kill each of them just a little every day, kill the humanity of them inch by casual inch—and I wake up screaming because a *human* thing I met put its arm around me and asked me to have a drink with it.

He finished off his drink and poured another one and this time did not bother with the mix.

"Come on," he said to the monster of the dream. "Come on, friend. I'll have that drink with you."

He gulped it down and did not notice the harshness of the uncut liquor.

"Come on," he shouted at the monster. "Come on and have that drink with me!"

He stared around the room, waiting for the monster.

"What the hell," he said, "we're all human, aren't we?"

He poured another one and held it in a fist that suddenly was shaky.

"Us humans," he said, still talking to the monster, "have got to stick together."

VII

All of them met in the lounge after breakfast and Lodge, looking from face to face, saw the terror that lay behind the masks they kept in front of them, could sense the unvoiced shrieking that lay inside of them, held imprisoned by the iron control of breeding and of discipline.

Kent Forester lit a careful cigarette and when he spoke his voice was conversationally casual, and Lodge, watching him as he talked, knew the price he paid to keep his voice casual.

"This is something," Forester said, "that we can't allow to keep eating on us. We have to talk it out."

"You mean rationalize it?" asked Sifford.

Forester shook his head. "Talk it out, I said. This is once we can't kid ourselves."

"There were nine characters last night," said Craven.

"And a whale," said Forester.

"You mean one of. . . ."

"I don't know. If one of us did, let's speak up and say so. There's not a one among us who can't appreciate a joke."

"A grisly joke," said Craven.

"But a joke," said Forester.

"I would like to think it was a joke," Maitland declared. "I'd feel a lot easier if I knew it was a joke."

"That's the point," said Forester. "That's what I'm getting at."

He paused for a moment.

"Anyone?" he asked.

No one said a word.

They waited.

"No one, Kent," said Lodge.

"Perhaps the joker doesn't want to reveal himself," said Forester. "I think all of us could understand that. Maybe we could hand out slips of paper. . . ."

"Hand them out," Sifford grumbled.

Forester took sheets of folded paper from his pocket, carefully tore the strips. He handed out the strips.

"If anyone played a joke," Lodge pleaded, "for God's sake let us know."

The slips came back. Some of them said "no," others said "no joke," one said "I didn't do it."

Forester wadded up the strips.

"Well, that lets that idea out," he said. "I must admit I didn't have much hope."

Craven lumbered to his feet. "There's one thing that all of us have been thinking," he said, "and it might as well be spoken. It's not a pleasant subject."

He paused and looked around him at the others, as if defying them to stop him.

"No one liked Henry too well," he said. "Don't deny it. He was a hard man to like. A hard man any way you look at him. I was closer to him than any of you. I've agreed to say a few words for him at the service this afternoon. I am glad to do it, for he was a good man despite his hardness. He had a tenacity of will, a stubbornness such as you seldom find even in a hard man. And he had moral scruples that none of us could guess. He would talk to me a little—really talk—and that's something that he never did with the rest of you.

"Henry was close to something. He was scared. He died.

"There was nothing wrong with him."

Craven looked at Dr. Lawrence.

"Was there, Susan?" he asked. "Was there anything wrong with him?"

"Not a thing," said Dr. Susan Lawrence. "He should not have died."

Craven turned to Lodge.

"He talked with you recently."

"A day or two ago," said Lodge. "He seemed quite normal then."

"What did he talk about?"

"Oh, the usual things. Minor matters."

"Minor matters?" Mocking.

"All right, then. If you want it that way. He talked about not wanting to go on. He said our work was unholy. That's the word he used—unholy."

Lodge looked around the room. "That's one the rest of you have never thought to use. Unholy."

"He was more insistent than usual?"

"Well, no," said Lodge. "It was the first time he had ever talked to me about it. The only person engaged in the research here, I believe, who had not talked with me about it at one time or another."

"And you talked him into going back."

"We discussed it."

"You killed the man."

"Perhaps," said Lodge. "Perhaps I'm killing all of you. Perhaps you're killing yourselves and I myself. How am I to know?"

He said to Dr. Lawrence, "Sue, could a man die of a psycho-somatic illness brought about by fear?"

"Clinically, no," said Susan Lawrence. "Practically, I'm afraid, the answer might be yes."

"He was trapped," said Craven.

"Mankind's trapped," snapped Lodge. "If you must point your finger, point it at all of us. Point it at the whole community of Man. . . ."

"I don't think," Forester interrupted, "that this is pertinent."

"It is," insisted Craven, "and I will tell you why. I'd be the last to admit the existence of a ghost. . . ."

Alice Page came swiftly to her feet.

"Stop it!" she cried. "Stop it! Stop it! Stop it!"

"Miss Page, please," said Craven.

"But you're saying. . . ."

"I'm saying that if there ever was a situation where a departed spirit had a motive—and I might even say a right—to come back and haunt his place of death, this is it."

"Sit down, Craven," Lodge commanded, sharply.

Craven hesitated angrily, then sat down, grumbling to himself.

Lodge said, "If there's any point in continuing the discussion along these lines, I insist that it be done objectively."

Maitland said, "There's no point to it I can see. As scientists who are most intimately concerned with life we must recognize that death is an utter ending."

"That," objected Sifford, "is open to serious question and you know it."

Forester broke in, his voice cool. "Let's defer the matter for a moment. We can come back to it. There is another thing."

He hurried on. "Another thing that we should know. Which of the characters was Henry's character?"

No one said a word.

"I don't mean," said Forester, "to try to find which belonged to whom. But by a process of elimination. . . ."

"All right," said Sifford. "Hand out the slips again."

Forester brought out the paper in his pocket, tore more strips.

Craven protested. "Not just slips," he said. "I won't fall for a trick like that."

Forester looked up from the slips.

"Trick?"

"Of course," said Craven, harshly. "Don't deny it. You've been trying to find out."

"I don't deny it," Forester told him. "I'd have been derelict in my duty if I hadn't tried."

Lodge said, "I wonder why we keep this secret thing so closely to ourselves. It might be all right under normal circumstances, but these aren't normal circumstances. I think it might be best if we made a clean breast of it. I, for one, am willing. I'll lead off if you only say the word."

He waited for the word.

There was no word.

They all stared back at him and there was nothing in their faces—no anger, no fear, nothing at all that a man could read.

Lodge shrugged the defeat from his shoulders.

He said to Craven, "All right, then. What were you saying?"

"I was saying that if we wrote down the names of our characters it would be no better than standing up and shouting them aloud. Forester knows our handwriting. He could spot every slip."

Forester protested. "I hadn't thought of it. I ask you to believe I hadn't. But what Craven says is true."

"All right, then?" asked Lodge.

"Ballots," Craven said. "Fix up ballots with the characters' names upon them."

"Aren't you afraid we might be able to identify your X's?"

Craven looked levelly at Lodge. "Since you mention it, I might be."

Forester said, wearily, "We have a batch of dies down in the labs. Used for stamping specimens. I think there's an X among them."

"That would satisfy you?" Lodge asked Craven.

Craven nodded that it would.

Lodge heaved himself out of the chair.

"I'll get the stamp," he said. "You can fix the ballots while I'm after it."

Children, he thought.

Just so many children.

Suspicious and selfish and frightened—like cornered animals.

Cornered between the converging walls of fear and guilt, trapped in the corner of their own insecurity.

He walked down the stairs to the laboratories, his heels ringing on the metal treads, with the sound of his walking echoing from the hidden corners of the fear and guilt.

If Henry hadn't died right now, he thought, it might have been all right. We might have muddled through.

But he knew that probably was wrong. For if it had not been Henry's death, it would have been something else. They were ready for it—more than ready for it. It would not have taken much at any time in the last few weeks to have lit the fuse.

He found the die and ink pad and tramped back upstairs again.

The ballots lay upon the table and someone had found a shoe box and cut a slit out of its lid to make a ballot box.

"We'll all sit over on this side of the room," said Forester, "and we'll go up, one by one, and vote."

And if anyone saw the ridiculous side of speaking of what they were about to do as voting, they pointedly ignored it.

Lodge put the die and ink pad down on the table top and walked across the room to take his seat.

"Who wants to start it off?" asked Forester.

No one said a word.

Even afraid of this, thought Lodge.

Then Maitland said he would.

They sat in utter silence as each walked forward to mark a ballot, to fold it and to drop it in the box. Each of them waited for the one to return before another walked out to the table.

Then it finally was done, and Forester went to the table, took up the box and shook it, turning it this way and that to change the order of the ballots, so that no one might guess by their position whom they might belong to.

"I'll need two monitors," he said.

His eyes looked them over. "Craven," he said. "Sue."

They stood up and went forward.

Forester opened the box.

He took out a ballot, unfolded it and read it, passed it on to Dr. Lawrence and she passed it on to Craven.

"The Defenseless Orphan."

"The Rustic Slicker."

"The Alien Monster."

"The Beautiful Bitch."

"The Sweet Young Thing."

Wrong on that one, Lodge told himself. But who else could it be? She had been the last one on. She had been the ninth.

Forester went on, unfolding the ballots and reading them.

"The Extra-Terrestrial Ally."

"The Proper Young Man."

Only two left now. Only two. The Out-At-Elbows Philosopher and the Mustached Villain.

I'll make a guess, Lodge said to himself. I'll make a bet. I'll bet on which one was Henry.

He was the Mustached Villain.

Forester unfolded the last ballot and read aloud the name.

"The Mustached Villain."

So I lose the bet, thought Lodge.

He heard the rippling hiss of indrawn breath from those around him, the swift, stark terror of what the balloting had meant.

For Henry's character had been the most self-assertive and dominant in last night's Play: the Philosopher.

VIII

The script in Henry's notebook was close and crabbed, with a curtness to it, much like the man himself. His symbols and his equations were a triumph of clarity, but the written words had a curious backward, petulant slant and the phrases that he used were laconic to the point of rudeness—although whom he was being rude to, unless it were himself, was left a matter of conjecture.

Maitland closed the book with a snap and shoved it away from him, out into the center of the table.

"So that was it," he said.

They sat in quietness, their faces pale and drawn, as if in bitter fact they might have seen the ghost of Craven's hinting.

"That's the end of it," snapped Sifford. "I won't. . . ."

"You won't what?" asked Lodge.

Sifford did not answer, just sitting there with his hands before him on the table, opening and closing them, making great tight fists of them, then straightening out his fingers, stretching them as if he meant by sheer power of will to bend them back farther than they were meant to go.

"Henry was crazy," said Susan Lawrence curtly. "A man would have to be to dream up that sort of evidence."

"As a medical person," Maitland said, "we could expect that reaction from you."

"I work with life," said Susan Lawrence. "I respect it and it is my job to preserve it as long as it can be kept within the body. I have a great compassion for the things possessing it."

"Meaning we haven't?"

"Meaning you have to live with it and come to know it for its power and greatness, for the fine thing that it is, before you can appreciate or understand its wondrous qualities."

"But, Susan. . . ."

"And I know," she said, rushing on to head him off, "I know that it is more than decay and breakdown, more than the senility of matter. It is something greater than disease. To argue that life is the final step to which matter is reduced, the final degradation of the nobility of soil and ore and water is to argue that a static, unintelligent, purposeless existence is the norm of the universe."

"We're getting all tangled up semantically," suggested Forester. "As living things the terms we use have no comparative values with the terms that might be used for universal purpose, even if we knew those universal terms."

"Which we don't," said Helen Gray. "What you say would be true especially if what Henry had thought he had found was right."

"We'll check Henry's notes," Lodge told them grimly. "We'll follow him step by step. I think he's wrong, but on the chance he isn't, we can't pass up an angle. . . ."

Sifford bristled. "You mean even if he were right you would go ahead? That you would use even so humanly degrading a piece of evidence to achieve our purpose?"

"Of course I would," said Lodge. "If life is a disease and a senility, all right, then, it is disease and senility. As Kent and Helen pointed out, the terms are not comparative when used in a universal sense. What is poison for the universe is—well, is life for us. If Henry was right, his discovery is no more than the uncovering of a fact that has existed since time untold. . . ."

"You don't know what you're saying," Sifford said.

"But I do," Lodge told him bluntly. "You have grown neurotic. You and some of the others. Maybe I, myself. Maybe all of us. We are ruled by fear—you by the fear of your job, I by the fear that the job will not be done. We've been penned up, we've been beating out our brains against the stone walls of our conscience and a moral value suddenly furbished up and polished until it shines like the shield of Galahad. Back on the Earth you wouldn't give this thing a second thought. You'd gulp a little, maybe, then you'd swallow it, if it were proved true, and you'd go ahead to track down that principle of decay and of disease we happen to call life. The principle itself would be only one more factor for your consideration, one more tool to work with, another bit of knowledge.

"But here you claw at the wall and scream."

"Bayard!" shouted Forester. "Bayard, you can't. . . ."

"I can," Lodge told him, "and I am. I'm sick of all their whimpering and baying. I'm tired of spoonfed fanatics who drove themselves to their own fanaticism by their own synthetic fears. It takes men and women with knife-sharp minds to lick this thing we're after. It takes guts and intelligence. . . ."

Craven was white-lipped with fury. "We've worked," he shouted. "Even when everything within us, even when all our decency and intelligence and our religious instincts told us not to work, we worked. And don't say you kept us at it, you with your mealy words and your kidding and your back slapping. Don't say you laughed us into it. . . ."

Forester pounded the table with a fist. "Let's quit this arguing," he cried. "Let's get down to cases."

Craven settled back in his chair, face still white with anger. Sifford kept on making fists.

"Henry wrote a conclusion," said Forester. "Well, hardly a conclusion. Let's call it a suspicion. Now what do you want to do about it? Ignore it, run from it, test it for its proof?"

"I say, test it," Craven said. "It was Henry's work. Henry's gone and can't speak for his own beliefs. We owe at least that much to him."

"If it can be tested," Maitland qualified. "To me it sounds more like philosophy than science."

"Philosophy runs hand in hand with science," said Alice Page. "We can't simply brush it off because it sounds involved."

"I didn't say involved," Maitland objected. "What I meant was—oh, hell, let's go ahead and check it."

"Check it," Sifford said.

He swung around on Lodge. "And if it checks out, if it comes anywhere near to checking, if we can't utterly disprove it, I'm quitting. I'm serving notice now. . . ."

"That's your privilege, Sifford, any time you wish."

"It might be hard to prove anything one way or the other," said Helen Gray. "It might not be any easier to disprove than prove."

Lodge saw Sue Lawrence looking at him and there was grim laughter and something of grudging admiration and a touch of confused cynicism in her face, as if she might be saying to him:

Well, you've done it again. I didn't think you would—not this time, I didn't. But you did. Although you won't always do it. There'll come a time—

"Want to bet?" he whispered at her.

She said, "Cyanide."

And although he laughed back at her, he knew that she was right—righter than she knew. For the time had already come and this was the end of Life Team No. 3.

They would go on, of course, stung by the challenge Henry Griffith had written in his notebook, still doggedly true to their training and their charge, but the heart was out of them, the fear and the prejudice too deeply ingrained within the soul of each, the confused tangle of their thinking too much a part of them.

If Henry Griffith had sought to sabotage the project, Lodge told himself, he had done it perfectly. In death he had done it far better than he could have, living.

He seemed to hear in the room the dry, acerbic chuckling of the man and he wondered at the imagined chuckle, for Henry had had no humor in him.

Although Henry had been the Out-At-Elbows Philosopher and it was hard to think of Henry as that sort of character—an old humbug who hid behind a polished manner and a golden tongue. For there was nothing of the humbug in Henry, either, and his manner was not polished nor did he have the golden gift of words. He slouched and he rarely talked, and when he did he growled.

A joker, Lodge thought—had he been, after all, a joker?

Could he have used the Philosopher to lampoon the rest of them, a character who derided them and they not knowing it?

He shook his head, arguing with himself.

If the Philosopher had kidded them, it had been gentle kidding, so gentle that none of them had known it was going on, so subtle that it had slid off them without notice.

But that wasn't the terrifying aspect of it—that Henry might have been quietly making fun of them. The terrifying thing was that the Philosopher had been second on the stage. He had followed the Rustic Slicker and during the whole time had been much in evidence—munching on the turkey leg and waving it to emphasize the running fire of pompous talk that had never slacked. The Philosopher had been, in fact, the most prominent player in the entire Play.

And that meant that no one could have put him on the stage, for no one, in the first place, could have known so soon which of the nine was Henry's character, and no one, not having handled him before, could have put the Philosopher so realistically through his paces. And none of those who had sent on their characters early in the Play could have handled two characters convincingly for any length of time—especially when the Philosopher had talked all the blessed time.

And that would cancel out at least four of those sitting in the room.

Which could mean:

That there was a ghost.

Or that the machine itself retained a memory.

Or that the eight of them had suffered mass hallucination.

He considered that last alternative and it wilted in the middle. So did the other two.

None of the three made sense.

Not any of it made sense—none of it at all.

Take a team of trained men and women, trained objectively, trained to look for facts, conditioned to skepticism and impatience of anything outside the pale of fact: What did it take to wreck a team like that? Not simply the cabin fever of a lonely asteroid. Not simply the nagging of awakened conscience against well established ethics. Not the atavistic, Transylvanian fear of ghosts.

There was some other factor.

Another factor that had not been thought of yet—like the new approach that Maitland had talked about at dinner, saying they would have to take a new direction to uncover the secret that they sought. We're going at it wrong, Maitland had said. We'll have to find a new approach.

And Maitland had meant, without saying so, that in their research the old methods of ferreting out the facts were no longer valid, that the scientific mind had operated for so long in the one worn groove that it knew no other, that they must seek some fresh concept to arrive at the fact of life.

Had Henry, Lodge wondered, supplied that fresh approach? And in the supplying of it and in dying, wrecked the team as well?

Or was there another factor, as Maitland had said there must be a new approach—a factor that did not fit in with conventional thinking or standard psychology?

The Play, he wondered.

Was the Play a factor?

Had the Play, designed to keep the team intact and sane, somehow turned into a two-edged sword?

They were rising from the table now, ready to leave, ready to go to their rooms and to dress for dinner. And after dinner, there would be the Play again.

Habit, Lodge thought. Even with the whole thing gone to pot, they still conformed to habit.

They would dress for dinner; they would stage the Play. They would go back tomorrow morning to their workrooms and they'd work again, but the work would be a futile work, for the dedicated purpose of their calling had been burned out of them by fear, by the conflict of their souls, by death, by ghosts.

Someone touched his elbow and he saw that Forester stood beside him.

"Well, Kent?"

"How do you feel?"

"Okay," said Lodge. Then he said, "You know, of course, it's over."

"We'll try again," said Forester.

Lodge shook his head. "Not me. You, maybe. You're a younger man than I. I am burned out too."

IX

The Play started in where it had left off the night before, with the Sweet Young Thing coming on the stage and all the others there, with the Out-At-Elbows Philosopher rubbing his hands together smugly and saying, "Now this is a cozy situation. All of us are here."

Sweet Young Thing (tripping lightly): Why, Philosopher, I know that I am late, but what a thing to say. Of course we all are here. I was unavoidably detained. . . .

Rustic Slicker (speaking aside, with a rural leer): By a Tom Collins and a slot machine. . . .

Alien Monster *(sticking out its head from behind the tree)*: Tsk hrstlgn vglater, tsk. . . .

And there was something wrong, Lodge told himself.

There was a certain mechanical wrongness, something out of place, a horrifying alienness that sent a shiver through you even when you couldn't spot the alienness.

There was something wrong with the Philosopher, and the wrongness was not that he should not be there, but something else entirely. There was a wrongness about the Sweet Young Thing and the Proper Young Man and the Beautiful Bitch and all the others of them.

There was a great deal wrong with the Rustic Slicker, and he, Bayard Lodge, knew the Rustic Slicker as he knew no other man—knew the blood and guts and brains of him, knew his thoughts and dreams and his hidden yearnings, his clodhopperish conceit, his smart-aleck snicker, the burning inferiority complex that drove him to social exhibitionism.

He knew him as every member of the audience must know his own character, as something more than an imagined person, as someone more than another person, something more than friend. For the bond was strong—the bond of the created and creator.

And tonight the Rustic Slicker had drawn a little ways apart, had cut the apron strings, stood on his own with the first dawning of independence.

The Philosopher was saying: "It's quite natural that I should have commented on all of us being here. For one of us is dead. . . ."

There was no gasp from the audience, no hiss of indrawn breath, no stir, but you could feel the tension snap tight like a whining violin string.

"We have been consciences," said the Mustached Villain. "Projected conscience playing out our parts. . . ."

The Rustic Slicker said: "The consciences of mankind."

Lodge half rose out of his chair.

I didn't make him say that! I didn't want him to say that. I thought it, that was all. So help me God, I just thought it, that was all!

And now he knew what was wrong. At last, he knew the strangeness of the characters this night.

They weren't on the screen at all! They were on the stage, the little width of stage which ran before the screen!

They were no longer projected imaginations—they were flesh and blood. They were mental puppets came to sudden life.

He sat there, cold at the thought of it—cold and rigid in the quickening knowledge that by the power of mind alone—by the power of mind and electronic mysteries, Man had created life.

A new approach, Maitland had said.

Oh, Lord! A new approach!

They had failed at their work and triumphed in their play, and there'd be no longer any need of life teams, grubbing down into that gray area where life and death were inter changeable.

To make a human monster you'd sit before a screen and you'd dream him up, bone by bone, hair by hair, brains, innards, special abilities and all.

There'd be monsters by the billions to plant on those other planets. And the monsters would be human, for they'd be dreamed by brother humans working from a blueprint.

In just a little while the characters would step down off the stage and would mingle with them.

And their creators? What would their creators do? Go screaming, raving mad?

What would he say to the Rustic Slicker?

What *could* he say to the Rustic Slicker?

And, more to the point, what would the Rustic Slicker have to say to him?

He sat, unable to move, unable to say a word or cry out a warning, waiting for the moment when they would step down.

EPILOG

Clifford D. Simak, after collecting in the book City *the stories that made up the series which, provided with genius-level interstitial materials, went by that name, never intended to do another story set in that "universe." But after the death of John W. Campbell, Jr., the iconic editor of* Astounding, *a project was created to make a kind of memorial to a man who had published so many of the great stories of the field. And Cliff was prevailed upon to go back to the universe he had created and, mostly, sold to Campbell in the early 1940s. Cliff never really regarded "Epilog" as part of the "City" series, and initially he refused to allow it to be tacked onto later publications of* City. *But eventually, faced with repeated requests to combine the book with the last story, he relented on that issue.*

His refusal was based on the fact that so much time had passed since the first City *stories were published—roughly thirty years—that he felt he was a completely different man, and a completely different writer, from the person who wrote those first stories.* City *was over, he said; "Epilog" was a different thing.*

"Epilog" was originally published, then, in Astounding: The John W. Campbell Memorial Anthology, *edited by Harry Harrison and published in 1973.*

—dww

Things happened all at once on that single day, although what day it might have been is not known, for Jenkins . . .

As Jenkins walked across the meadow, the Wall came tumbling down . . .

Jenkins sat on the patio of Webster House and remembered that long-gone day when the man from Geneva had come back to Webster House and had told a little Dog that Jenkins was a Webster, too. And that, Jenkins told himself, had been a day of pride for him . . .

Jenkins walked across the meadow to commune with the little meadow mice, to become one with them and run for a time with them in the tunnels they had constructed in the grass. Although there was not much satisfaction in it. The mice were stupid things, unknowing and uncaring, but there was a certain warmth to them, a quiet sort of security and well-being, since they lived quite alone in the meadow world and there was no danger and no threat. There was nothing left to threaten them. They were all there were, aside from certain insects and worms that were fodder for the mice.

In time past, Jenkins recalled, he had often wondered why the mice had stayed behind when all the other animals had gone to join the Dogs in one of the cobbly worlds. They could have gone, of course. The Dogs could have taken them, but there had been no wish in them to go. Perhaps they had been satisfied with where they were; perhaps they had a sense of home too strong to let them go.

The mice and I, thought Jenkins. For he could have gone as well. He could go even now if he wished to go. He could have gone at any time at all. But like the mice, he had not gone, but stayed. He could not leave Webster House. Without it, he was only half a being.

So he had stayed and Webster House still stood. Although it would not have stood, he told himself, if it had not been for him. He had kept it clean and neat; he had patched it up. When a stone began to crumble, he had quarried and shaped another and had carefully replaced it, and while it may for a while have seemed new and alien to the house, time took care of that—the wind and sun and weather and the creeping moss and lichens.

He had cut the lawn and tended the shrubs and flower beds. The hedges he'd kept trimmed. The woodwork and the furniture well-dusted, the floors and paneling well-scrubbed—the house still stood. Good enough, he told himself with some satisfaction, to house a Webster if one ever should show up. Although there was no hope of that. The Websters who had gone to Jupiter were no longer Websters, and those at Geneva still were sleeping if, in fact, Geneva and the Websters in it existed any longer.

For the Ants now held the world. They had made of the world one building, or so he had presumed, although he could not really know. But so far as he did know, so far as his robotic senses reached (and they reached far), there was nothing but the great senseless building that the Ants had built. Although to call it senseless, he reminded himself, was not entirely fair. There was no way of knowing what purpose it might serve. There was no way one might guess what purpose the Ants might have in mind.

The Ants had enclosed the world, but had stopped short of Webster House, and why they had done that there was no hint at all. They had built around it, making Webster House and its adjoining acres a sort of open courtyard within the confines of the building—a five-mile circle centered on the hill where Webster House still stood.

Jenkins walked across the meadow in the autumn sunshine, being very careful where he placed his feet for fear of harming mice. Except for the mice, he thought, he was alone, and he might almost as well have been alone, for the mice were little help. The Websters were gone and the Dogs and other animals. The robots gone as well, some of them long since having disappeared into the Ants' building to help the Ants carry out their project, the others blasting for the stars. By this time, Jenkins thought, they should have gotten where they were headed for. They all had been long gone, and now he wondered, for the first time in many ages, how long it might have been. He found he did not know and now would never know, for there had been that far-past moment when he had wiped utterly from his mind any sense of time. Deliberately he had decided that he no longer would take account of time, for as the world then stood, time was meaningless. Only later had he understood that what he'd really sought had been forgetfulness. But he had been wrong. It had not brought forgetfulness; he still remembered, but in scrambled and haphazard sequences.

He and the mice, he thought. And the Ants, of course. But the Ants did not really count, for he had no contact with them. Despite the sharpened senses and the new sensory abilities built into his birthday body (now no longer new) that had been given by the Dogs so long ago, he had never been able to penetrate the walls of the Ants' great building to find out what might be going on in there. Not that he hadn't tried.

Walking across the meadow, he remembered the day when the last of the Dogs had left. They had stayed much longer than loyalty and common decency had demanded, and although he had scolded them mildly for it, it still kindled a warm glow within him when he remembered it.

He had been sitting in the sun, on the patio, when they had come trailing up the hill and ranged themselves before him like a gang of naughty boys. "We are leaving, Jenkins," the foremost one of them had said. "Our world is growing smaller. There is no longer room to run."

He had nodded at them, for he'd long expected it. He had wondered why it had not happened sooner.

"And you, Jenkins?" asked the foremost Dog.

Jenkins shook his head. "I must stay," he'd said. "This is my place. I must stay here with the Websters."

"But there are no Websters here."

"Yes, there are," said Jenkins. "Not to you, perhaps. But to me. For me they still live in the very stone of Webster House. They live in the trees and the sweep of hill. This is the roof that sheltered them; this is the land they walked upon. They can never go away."

He knew how foolish it must sound, but the Dogs did not seem to think that it was foolish. They seemed to understand. It had been many centuries, but they still seemed to understand.

He had said the Websters still were there, and at the time they had been. But he wondered as he walked the meadow if now they still were there. How long had it been since he had heard footsteps going down a stair? How long since there had been voices in the great, fireplaced living room and, when he'd looked, there'd been no one there?

And now, as Jenkins walked in the autumn sunshine, a great crack suddenly appeared in the outer wall of the Ants' building, a mile or two away. The crack grew, snaking downward from the top in a jagged line, spreading as it grew, and with smaller cracks moving out from it. Pieces of the material of which the wall was fashioned broke out along the crack and came crashing to the ground, rolling and bouncing in the meadow. Then, all at once, the wall on both sides of the crack seemed to come unstuck and came tumbling down. A cloud of dust rose into the air, and Jenkins stood there looking at the great hole in the wall.

Beyond the hole in the wall, the massive building rose like a circular mountain range, with peaks piercing upward here and there above the plateau of the structure.

The hole stood gaping in the wall and nothing further happened. No ants came pouring out, no robots running frantically. It was as though, Jenkins thought, the Ants did not know, or knowing, care, as if the fact that at last their building had been breached held no significance.

Something had happened, Jenkins told himself with some astonishment. Finally, in this Webster world, an event had come to pass.

He moved forward, heading for the hole in the wall, not moving fast, for there seemed no need to hurry. The dust settled slowly, and now and then additional chunks of the wall broke loose and fell. He came up to the broken place, and, climbing the rubble, walked into the building.

The interior was not as bright as it was outdoors, but considerable light still filtered through what might be thought of as the ceiling of the building. For the building, at least in this portion of it, was not partitioned into floors, but was open to the upper reaches of the structure, a great gulf of space soaring to the topmost towers.

Once inside, Jenkins stopped in amazement, for it seemed at first glance that the building was empty. Then he saw that was not the case, for while the greater part of the building might be empty, the floor of it was most uneven, and the unevenness, he saw, was made up of monstrous ant hills, and on top of each of them stood a strange ornament made of metal that shone in the dim light coming through the ceiling. The hills were crisscrossed here and there by what appeared to be tiny roads, but all of them were out of repair and broken, parts of them wiped out by the miniature landslides that scarred the hills. Here and there, as well, were chimneys, but no smoke poured out of them; some had fallen and others were plainly out of plumb and sagging.

There was no sign of ants.

Small aisles lay between the anthills, and, walking carefully, Jenkins made his way between them, working deeper into the building. All the hills were like the first one—all of them lay dead, with their chimneys sagging and their roads wiped out and no sign of any life.

Now, finally, he made out the ornaments that stood atop each hill, and for perhaps the first time in his life, Jenkins felt laughter shaking him. If he had ever laughed before, he could not remember it, for he had been a serious and a dedicated robot. But now he stood between the dead hills and held his sides, as a laughing man might hold his sides, and let the laughter rumble through him.

For the ornament was a human foot and leg, extending midway from the thigh down through the foot, with the knee bent and the foot extended, as if it were in the process of kicking something violently.

Joe's foot! The kicking foot of the crazy mutant, Joe!

It had been so long ago that he had forgotten it, and he was a little pleased to find there had been something that he had forgotten, that he was capable of forgetting, for he had thought that he was not.

But he remembered now the almost legendary story from the far beginning, although he knew it was not legendary but had really happened, for there had been a mutant human by the name of Joe. He wondered what had happened to such mutants. Apparently not too much. At one time there had been a few of them, perhaps too few of them, and then there had been none of them, and the world had gone on as if they'd never been.

Well, not exactly as if they'd never been, for there was the Ant world and there was Joe. Joe, so the story ran, had experimented with an ant hill. He had covered it with a dome and had heated it and perhaps done other things to it as well—certain things that no one knew but Joe. He had changed the ants' environment and in some strange way had implanted in them some obscure spark of greatness, and in time they had developed an intellectual culture, if ants could be said to be capable of intelligence. Then Joe had come along and kicked the hill, shattering the dome, devastating the hill, and had walked away with that strange, high, almost insane laughter that was characteristic of him. He had destroyed the hill and turned his back upon it, not caring any longer. But he had kicked the ants to greatness. Facing adversity, they had not gone back to their old, stupid, antlike ways, but had fought to save what they had gained. As the Ice Age of the Pleistocene had booted the human race to greatness, so had the swinging foot of the human mutant, Joe, set the ants upon their way.

Thinking this, a suddenly sobering thought came to Jenkins. How could the Ants have known? What ant or ants had sensed or seen, so long ago, the kick that had come out of nothingness? Could some ant astronomer, peering through his glass, have seen it all? And that was ridiculous, for there could have been no ant astronomers. But otherwise how could they have tied up the connection between the blurred shape that had loomed, momentarily, so far above them, and the true beginning of the culture they had built?

Jenkins shook his head. Perhaps this was a thing that never would be known. But the ants, somehow, had known, and had built atop each hill the symbol of that mystic shape. A memorial, he wondered, or a religious symbol? Or perhaps something else entirely, carrying some obscure purpose or meaning that could be conceived by nothing but an ant.

He wondered rather idly if the recognition by the ants of the true beginning of their greatness might have anything to do with their not overrunning Webster House, but he did not follow up the thought because he realized it was too nebulous to be worth the time.

He went deeper into the building, making his way along the narrow paths that lay between the hills, and with his mind he searched for any sign of life, but there was none—there was no life at all, not even the feeblest, smallest flicker denoting the existence of those tiny organisms that should be swarming in the soil.

There was a silence and a nothingness that compounded into horror, but he forced himself to continue on his way, thinking that surely he would find, just a little farther on, some evidence of life. He wondered if he should shout in an attempt to attract attention, but reason told him that the ants, even were they there, would not hear a shout, and aside from that, he felt a strange reluctance to make any kind of noise. As if this were a place where one should stay small and furtive.

Everything was dead.

Even the robot that he found.

It was lying in one of the paths, propped up against a hill, and he came upon it as he came around the hill. It dangled and was limp, if it could be said that a robot could be limp, and Jenkins, at the sight of it, stood stricken in the path. There was no doubt that it was dead; he could sense no stir of life within the skull, and in that moment of realization it seemed to him the world stumbled to a halt.

For robots do not die. Wear out, perhaps, or be damaged beyond possible repair, but even then the life would keep ticking in the brain. In all his life he had never heard of a robot dead, and if there had been one, he surely would have heard of it.

Robots did not die, but here one lay dead, and it was not only this one, something seemed to tell him, but all the robots who had served the ants. All the robots and all the ants and still the building stood, an empty symbol of some misplaced ambition, of some cultural miscalculation. Somewhere the ants had gone wrong, and had they gone wrong, he wondered, because Joe had built a dome? Had the dome become a be-all and an end-all? Had it seemed to the ants that their greatness lay in the construction of a dome, that a dome was necessary for them to continue in their greatness?

Jenkins fled. And as he fled, a crack appeared in the ceiling far overhead, and there was a crunching, grating sound as the crack snaked its way along.

He plunged out of the hole in the wall and raced out into the meadow. Behind him he heard the thunder of a part of the roof collapsing. He turned around and watched as that small portion of the building tore itself apart, great shards falling down into all those dead ant hills, toppling the emblems of the kicking human foot that had been planted on their tops.

Jenkins turned away and went slowly across the meadow and up the hill to Webster House. On the patio, he saw that for the moment the collapse of the building had been halted. More of the wall had fallen, and a great hole gaped in the structure held up by the wall.

In this matchless autumn day, he thought, was the beginning of the end. He had been here at the start of it, and he still was here to see the end of it. Once again he wondered how long it might have been and regretted, but only a small regret, that he had not kept track of time.

Men were gone and Dogs were gone, and except for himself, all the robots, too. Now the ants were gone, and the Earth stood lonely except for one hulking robot and some little meadow mice. There might still be fish, he thought, and other creatures of the sea, and he wondered about those creatures of the sea. Intelligence, he thought. But intelligence came hard and it did not last. In another day, he thought, another intelligence might come from the sea, although deep inside himself he knew it was most unlikely.

The ants had shut themselves in, he thought. Their world had been a closed world. Was it because there was no place for them to go that they had failed? Or was it because their world had been a closed one from the start? There had been ants in the world as early as the Jurassic, 180 million years, and probably before that. Millions of years before the forerunners of man had existed, the ants had established a social order. They had advanced only so far; they had established their social order and been content with it—content because it was what they wanted, or because they could go no further? They had achieved security, and in the Jurassic and for many millions of years later, security had been enough. Joe's dome had served to reinforce that security, and it had then been safe for them to develop further if they held the capacity to develop. It was quite evident, of course, that they had the capability, but, Jenkins told himself, the old idea of security had continued to prevail. They had been unable to rid themselves of it. Perhaps they never even tried to rid themselves of it, had never recognized it as something that should be gotten off their backs. Was it, Jenkins wondered, that old, snug security that had killed them?

With a booming crash that went echoing around the horizon, another section of the roof fell.

What would an ant strive for, Jenkins wondered. A maintenance of security, and what else? Hoarding, perhaps. Grubbing from the earth everything of value and storing it away against another day. That in itself, he realized, would be no more than another facet to the fetish of security. A religion of some sort, perhaps—the symbols of the kicking foot that stood atop the hills could have been religious. And again security. Security for the souls of ants. The conquest of space? And perhaps the ants had conquered space, Jenkins told himself. For a creature the size of an ant the world itself must have appeared to be a quite sufficient galaxy. Conquering one galaxy with no idea that an even greater galaxy lay beyond. And even the conquering of a galaxy might be another sort of security.

It was all wrong, Jenkins realized. He was attributing to ants the human mental process, and there might be more to it than that. There might lie in the minds of ants a certain ferment, a strange direction, an unknown ethical equation which had never been a part, or could never be a part, of the minds of men.

Thinking this, he realized with horror that in building a picture of an ant he'd built the picture of a human.

He found a chair and sat down quietly to gaze across the meadow to the place where the building of the ants still was falling in upon itself.

But Man, Jenkins remembered, had left something behind him. He had left the Dogs and robots. What, if anything, had the ants left? Nothing, certainly, that was apparent, but how was he to know?

A man could not know, Jenkins told himself, and neither could a robot, for a robot was a man, not blood and flesh as was a man, but in every other way. The ants had built their society in the Jurassic or before and had existed within its structure for millions of years, and perhaps that was the reason they had failed—the society of the hill was so firmly embedded in them they could not break away from it.

And I? he asked himself. How about me? I am embedded as deeply in man's social structure as any ant in hers. For less than a million years, but for a long, long time, he had lived in, not the structure of man's society, but in the memory of that structure. He had lived in it, he realized, because it had offered him the security of an ancient memory.

He sat quietly, but stricken at the thought—or at least at the fact that he could allow the thought.

"We never know," he said aloud. "We never know ourselves."

He leaned far back in the chair and thought how unrobot-like it was to be sitting in a chair. He never used to sit. It was the man in him, he thought. He allowed his head to settle back against the rest and let his optic filters down, shutting out the light. To sleep, he wondered—what would sleep be like? Perhaps the robot he had found beside the hill—but no, the robot had been dead, not sleeping. Everything was wrong, he told himself. Robots neither sleep nor die.

Sounds came to him. The building still was breaking up, and out in the meadow the autumn breeze was rustling the grasses. He strained a little to hear the mice running in their tunnels, but for once the mice were quiet. They were crouching, waiting. He could sense their waiting. They knew, somehow, he thought, that there was something wrong.

And another sound, a whisper, a sound he'd never heard before, an entirely alien sound.

He snapped his filters open and sat erect abruptly, and out in front of him he saw the ship landing in the meadow.

The mice were running now, frightened, running for their lives, and the ship came to rest like floating thistledown, settling in the grass.

Jenkins leaped to his feet and stabbed his senses out, but his probing stopped at the surface of the ship. He could no more probe beyond it than he could the building of the ants before it came tumbling down.

He stood on the patio, utterly confused by this unexpected thing. And well he might be, he thought, for until this day there had been no unexpected happenings. The days had all run together, the days, the years, the centuries, so like one another there was no telling them apart. Time had flowed like a mighty river, with no sudden spurts. And now, today, the building had come tumbling down and a ship had landed.

A hatch came open in the ship and a ladder was run out. A robot climbed down the ladder and came striding up the meadow toward Webster House. He stopped at the edge of the patio, "Hello, Jenkins," he said. "I thought we'd find you here."

"You're Andrew, aren't you?"

Andrew chuckled at him. "So you remember me."

"I remember everything," said Jenkins. "You were the last to go. You and two others finished up the final ship, and then you left the Earth. I stood and watched you go. What have you found out there?"

"You used to call us wild robots," Andrew said. "I guess you thought we were. You thought that we were crazy."

"Unconventional," said Jenkins.

"What is conventional?" asked Andrew. "Living in a dream? Living for a memory? You must be weary of it."

"Not weary . . ." said Jenkins, his voice trailing off. He began again. "Andrew, the ants have failed. They're dead. Their building's falling down."

"So much for Joe," said Andrew. "So much for Earth. There is nothing left."

"There are mice," said Jenkins. "And there is Webster House."

He thought again of the day the Dogs had given him a brand-new body as a birthday gift. The body had been a lulu. A sledge hammer wouldn't dent it, and it would never rust, and it was loaded with sensory equipment he had never dreamed of. He wore it even now, and it was as good as new, and when he polished the chest a little, the engraving still stood out plain and clear: To Jenkins From the Dogs.

He had seen men go out to Jupiter to become something more than men, and the Websters to Geneva for an eternity of dreams, the Dogs and other animals to one of the cobbly worlds, and now, finally, the ants gone to extinction.

He was shaken to realize how much the extinction of the ants had marked him. As if someone had come along and put a final period to the written story of the Earth.

Mice, he thought. Mice and Webster House. With the ship standing in the meadow, could that be enough? He tried to think: Had the memory worn thin? Had the debt he owed been paid? Had he discharged the last ounce of devotion?

"There are worlds out there," Andrew was saying, "and life on some of them. Even some intelligence. There is work to do."

He couldn't go to the cobbly world that the Dogs had settled. Long ago, at the far beginning, the Websters had gone away so the Dogs would be free to develop their culture without human interference. And he could do no less than Websters, for he was, after all, a Webster. He could not intrude upon them; he could not interfere.

He had tried forgetfulness, ignoring time, and it had not worked, for no robot could forget.

He had thought the ants had never counted. He had resented them, at times even hated them, for if it had not been for them, the Dogs would still be here. But now he knew that all life counted.

There were still the mice, but the mice were better left alone. They were the last mammals left on Earth, and there should be no interference with them. They wanted none and needed none, and they'd get along all right. They would work out their own destiny, and if their destiny be no more than remaining mice, there was nothing wrong with that.

"We were passing by," said Andrew. "Perhaps we'll not be passing by again."

Two other robots had climbed out of the ship and were walking about the meadow. Another section of the wall fell, and some of the roof fell with it. From where Jenkins stood, the sound of falling was muted and seemed much farther than it was.

So Webster House was all, and Webster House was only a symbol of the life that it once had sheltered. It was only stone and wood and metal. Its sole significance, Jenkins told himself, existed in his mind, a psychological concept that he had fashioned.

Driven into a corner, he admitted the last hard fact: He was not needed here. He was only staying for himself.

"We have room for you," said Andrew, "and a need of you."

So long as there had been ants, there had been no question. But now the ants were gone. And what difference did that make? He had not liked the ants.

Jenkins turned blindly and stumbled off the patio and through the door that led into the house. The walls cried out to him. And voices cried out as well from the shadow of the past. He stood and listened to them, and now a strange thing struck him. The voices were there, but he did not hear the words. Once there had been words, but now the words were gone and, in time, the voices as well? What would happen, he wondered, when the house grew quiet and lonely, when all the voices were gone and the memories faded? They were faded now, he knew. They were no longer sharp and clear; they had faded through the years.

Once there had been joy, but now there was only sadness, and it was not, he knew, alone the sadness of an empty house; it was the sadness of all else, the sadness of the Earth, the sadness of the failures and the empty triumphs.

In time the wood would rot and the metal flake away; in time the stone be dust. There would, in time, be no house at all, but only a loamy mound to mark where a house had stood.

It all came from living too long, Jenkins thought—from living too long and not being able to forget. That would be the hardest part of it; he never would forget.

He turned about and went back through the door and across the patio. Andrew was waiting for him, at the bottom of the ladder that led into the ship.

Jenkins tried to say goodbye, but he could not say goodbye. If he could only weep, he thought, but a robot could not weep.

A BOMB FOR
NO. 10 DOWNING

Clifford Simak's production of World War II–era stories involving air combat seems to have been limited to just five tales; all five sold, and there is no indication that he wrote any that did not sell. All of those five stories were much shorter than most of his work in other genres, but there is nothing in his surviving journals to suggest why they were so short—nor, for that matter, why he entered the genre or why he left it. It is clear that he began writing the war stories well before the United States entered WWII, and he seems to have left the market before the end of 1942. I suspect that he found the editors' requirements too restrictive (the editor of this particular issue was a U.S. Army officer, a fact that might suggest that demands outside those of the usual pulp magazine markets were placed on authors), but it's also true that Simak was moving into western stories at that time, and those paid much better money (he received just $25 for this story).

Sent to American Eagle *in October 1941 and purchased less than a month later, "A Bomb for No. 10 Downing" would actually appear in a magazine called* Sky Fighters *in September 1942. (No. 10 Downing was, and is, the address of the British Prime Minister's residence/office.)*

—dww

Normandy lay peaceful in the dawn, its forests colorful, its fields somber in after-harvest dress. War seemed a remote thing in this land of white chateaux and little villages and ribbony roads winding through the woods.

Kermit Hubbard glanced at the map strapped to his knee and pushed the nose of the Defiant down. The crossroad with its clustered village rushed up at him as the plane dived. Just beyond the village sat a chateau among the beeches. Just beyond the chateau should be a field rimmed by poplars, with wheat shocks at its northern end set in the form of a Maltese cross.

There it was, rimmed with poplars and with the shocks in the form of a cross. Just exactly as the message had said they would be. Speed cut, Hubbard circled the field, eyes sharp on the ground below. Nothing stirred.

Barely clearing the treetops, he mushed the machine down into the field, gunned the Merlin to taxi toward the wheat shocks.

Prop barely turning over, motor no more than a whisper, Hubbard shoved back the hatch cover. The smell of ripened grain and dried straw came to his nostrils and a breeze made the leaves of the poplars dance with tiny whisperings.

There was no sign of Grigsby.

Silence enveloped Hubbard. A silence that seemed to squeeze at the pit of his stomach, while little danger signals jigged up and down his spine.

Slowly he climbed from the ship, mentally cursing Grigsby. The man's message had said that he would be here, waiting at dawn, for the next seven days—and this was only the second.

"Grigsby!" he shouted.

When there was no reply, he shouted again, a note of desperation in his voice.

"Grigsby!"

The grain shocks in front of him suddenly erupted into men with short, ugly submachine-guns.

Hubbard stepped back quickly, hand falling to the revolver at his belt. But one of the men spoke harshly and he stopped, stock still, hands hanging at his side.

He eyed the men sharply, saw their coal-scuttle helmets, gray battle dress, wide leather belts and creased service boots. All but one. This one wore a visored cap, a medal dangled on his left breast pocket and he carried a revolver instead of a tommy gun. He, Hubbard knew, was a German officer.

"Your friend Grigsby, I am afraid, has disappointed you," the officer said in precise English.

Hubbard did not answer.

"I can imagine," the officer went on, "that you may be planning something—something in the way of sudden action. I ask you, please don't do it. You haven't got a chance."

"No," Hubbard admitted. "No, I guess I haven't."

"And now," said the officer, "if you will—"

A rifle snicked from the edge of the field. The officer gasped and pitched forward on his face. The rifle snicked again, then chattered.

Three of the German soldiers were down, the others were diving for the scattered wheat shocks. Bullets kicked up little puffs of dust just in front of Hubbard's toes. With a cry, the R.A.F. man jerked his Webley free.

The German guns were snarling now and the wheat bundles were bouncing to the impact of bullets from the field's edge. Hubbard leaped backward to gain shelter behind his plane, his Webley coming up to line its sights on one of the Nazis snuggled in the bundles.

But even as his finger tightened on the trigger, something bored into his back.

"Nein! Nein!" a voice said.

Hubbard whirled savagely, shoving the submachine-gun aside. But the German backed away and slammed its muzzle viciously into his stomach, knocking the wind from him.

"Nein! Nein!" the man with the coat-scuttle helmet insisted. Hubbard saw that his lips were drawn back in a snarl.

The fire at the edge of the field had ceased. Somewhere a motorcycle roared into life and howled away. The Nazi with the gun jabbed it deeper into Hubbard's stomach and jerked his head toward the Webley in the R.A.F. man's hand.

"I get you, pal," Hubbard said and dropped the weapon.

He stood there, with the gun still in his belly, listening to the ticking of the Merlin. The firing had stopped completely now and feet were tramping behind him. The Nazi laughed quietly at him.

"Dumkopf," he said.

And that was right, Hubbard told himself. The Nazi apparently had dived for the shelter of the plane when the firing started, had been there all the time, ready to cover any action he might take. All in all, it was as neat a trap as one could imagine.

Rough hands grabbed him and hauled him around. There were four Nazis left. They shouted at him in German while they searched him for other weapons.

A sound of motors roared out of the sky and over the trees came a Stuka, mushing down into the field. Hubbard watched the machine taxi up beside his. Two men got out. One of them climbed into the Defiant while the other walked over to Hubbard.

"I trust you didn't find *Herr* Grigsby," the Nazi pilot said to him.

"You guys seem to know more about this Grigsby than I do," Hubbard told him.

"We'll find out how much you know," the pilot barked. "You're going back to base with me. The *Kommandant* wants to see you!"

The *Kommandant* spoke English—English with something that might have started out to be an Oxford accent.

"Why did you land your plane in France, *Herr* Lieutenant?"

Hubbard grinned. "You know as well as I do. Why be so formal?"

The *Kommandant* nodded.

"Grigsby is a British agent, isn't he?"

"I suppose so," said Hubbard. "I never asked."

"You mean you won't tell me."

"No. I mean I don't know. I presume he is. I was to come and pick him up. No harm in telling you that. You probably read the message he sent. Mind telling me how you did it?"

The Nazi officer chuckled.

"The pigeon flew down into a street in Le Havre to pick up some grain. A soldier found him. We keep close watch for things like that."

"You read the message and then sent the pigeon on," Hubbard surmised.

"Naturally, *Herr* Lieutenant. It was too good a chance to miss."

The Nazi tapped the desk with a pencil slowly, sizing up the man before him.

"You are sure you can't help us? Who Grigsby really is? Where we might find him? What he looks like? If you could just remember a few of those things, it might be possible you could escape, get back to England."

"I've never seen the man," Hubbard shot back.

The *Kommandant* leaned across the desk.

"You are an American?"

Hubbard nodded.

"Why do you Americans fight us?" demanded the Nazi. "This isn't your war. You have no right to meddle!"

"We don't like the way you comb your hair," said Hubbard easily. "We don't like the way you treat your neighbors. Or keep your promises. We don't like the way your little tin god thinks he can boss the world—"

"Stop!" shrieked the German, his face livid.

* * *

The American grinned at him.

"You insulted the *Fuehrer!*" screamed the officer.

"Let me get my hands on him," promised Hubbard, "and I'll do worse than that."

The *Kommandant* leaped to his feet, his face purple.

"I could have you shot for that!" he screeched.

"You could—but you won't," retorted Hubbard. "Not for a while, anyway. You think I'm going to tell you something."

"We have ways to make you talk," barked the Nazi.

"That's the trouble with you Krauts," said Hubbard. "You think force will accomplish everything."

The *Kommandant* screamed orders at the two guards by the door. The men came forward at a trot, reached out to seize Hubbard's arms.

But as they reached him, the American's fist rose from his side, traveled in a bone-crushing arc straight to the chin of the guard on the right. The impact cracked like a whip. The soldier skidded across the floor on his heels, crashed into a table and slumped to the floor.

The other guard smashed Hubbard on the head with his pistol butt.

Hubbard opened his eyes, found he was in semi-darkness. He lay on one of several bunks. No one else was in the room. Gingerly his fingers explored the lump on his head. He cursed, wincing with pain.

Presently his brain cleared. His eyes made out a wash basin and a bench. A rickety table was propped against one wall. Otherwise the room was bare. Light came through a small window, shoulder high and criss-crossed by iron bars. Hobnailed boots beat a sentry tramp outside the heavy oaken door.

"A guardhouse," Hubbard said, half aloud. "Naturally."

He got to his feet, his brain throbbing, and walked groggily to the window. Grasping the iron bars, he peered out.

The base apparently was on the site of a French farm, for just opposite the window was the farmhouse, with Nazi flyers lounging and smoking in the doorway. Here and there sentries slogged, with rifles carried smartly.

Planes marked with the swastika of Nazi Germany stood in lines on the hard-packed tarmac, mostly fighters, with a few bombers next to the heavy forest that enclosed the field.

Suddenly Hubbard's fingers tightened on the bars and his breath caught in his throat. On the far side of the field, squatting wing to wing with several German ships, was a Defiant, its burnished metal gleaming in the rays of the noonday sun.

Shoulders slumped, Hubbard went back to the bunk and sat down. The Defiant, he knew, must be his own ship. But it had not occurred to him that it would be brought to this base.

It was understandable that an undamaged British plane would be of value to the Jerries, but hardly for flying purposes. Then why should the Defiant be out there on the field, with R.A.F. insignia still intact?

There was something fishy, too, about what had happened back there in the stubble field. Who had opened fire on the Jerries when they popped up out of the wheat shocks?

Footsteps sounded outside and a key grated in the lock. The door swung open on creaking hinges and an old Frenchman entered, carrying a pail. Behind him, four-square in the doorway, stood a guard, sun glinting on a fixed bayonet.

The old man tottered forward. He wore a greasy beret that at one time had been blue. His blouse was dirty and torn and his trousers were patched. His wooden *sabots* clattered as he shuffled forward.

Carefully he set the pail down. But as he stooped over, with his back to the guard, he held his right hand in front of his chest, index and second finger extended to form a V, the expression on his face unchanging. Then he straightened up and clopped back to the door.

For a long moment, Hubbard sat on the bunk. When he went over to the pail, he found it held his dinner, about a pint of watery soup.

A flight of Nazi planes more than an hour before had roared off into the night. Now someone in the old French farmhouse was playing a piano and young voices bellowed out the words of a German song.

Bright moonlight filtered through the barred window and threw a checkerboard pattern on the floor. It was, Hubbard thought, a good night for bombing. Probably the English Channel towns were catching their share of punishment.

The clumping feet of the sentry went past the door and toward the other end of the courtyard.

Hubbard lay flat on his back in the bunk and stared up at the blackness of the ceiling. His mind seethed with thoughts but they got him nowhere. Speculation about Grigsby, and the man who opened fire from the edge of the field. Wondering about the *Defiant* squatting out there on the field, about the old French peasant who had made the victory sign with his fingers.

His hopes flared at the thought of the old man, but as quickly died again. What could one old man do to help him. That victory sign had been a courageous gesture, nothing more. Just the old man's way of letting him know that he had a friend, that someone was sorry he was in a mess.

The piano tinkled to a stop. The footsteps came from further and further away. Mind tired out with his thoughts, Hubbard slept. Once the roar of returning planes roused him in the night, but he turned over and went back to sleep.

Then someone was shaking him, shaking insistently, and a voice was whispering—an urgent voice with a clipped British accent.

"Roll out, lad. There's a job to do."

Hubbard opened his eyes to the first gray light of dawn and the figure that stood over him. It was the old Frenchman, the one who had brought his soup, the one who had made a V with his fingers. But the old man was speaking English—with a British accent. The American sat up.

"Who are you?" he challenged.

"I am Grigsby," the Frenchman chuckled.

"Grigsby!" Hubbard sputtered. "Grigsby!"

"Certainly, old chap."

"But the guard?"

"The guard is dead," said Grigsby.

"I thought the Jerries got you," Hubbard declared confusedly.

"Not quite," Grigsby grinned. "Almost, but not quite. Sometimes they aren't so clever. I've lived with them here for months. But they'll know soon. After this, they cannot help but know."

The American stood up determinedly.

"All right, Grigsby. What's the play."

In wordless reply, Grigsby stooped over, picked something off the floor and handed it to Hubbard. The American curled his fingers around it lovingly.

"A tommy gun!"

Grigsby nodded. "Now listen closely. In five minutes things are going to start happening around here, and we don't want any slip-up."

"I'm listening."

"Righto. You come with me and hide around the corner of this guardhouse. I'll walk over to the nearest Stuka. Nobody will think it strange, they knew me around here. Most of them are asleep, anyhow. I'll try to get a chance to climb in and man the gun. When you see I've done that, come running."

"Wait a minute," snapped Hubbard. "Are you expecting *me* to pilot that Stuka out of here?"

Grigsby nodded slowly.

"But I don't know much about them," protested Hubbard. "If the Defiant is still over there—"

"The Defiant is still there," said Grigsby, "but you'd never get to it. You'd never live long enough to get to it. It's too far away. And it's too well guarded."

"Guarded?"

Grigsby's face had become grim.

"That's the reason we have to get out of here—this minute! The Jerries have plans for that Defiant. They're going to load it with explosives, make a flying bomb out of it. A man who's willing to die for the 'New Order' will pilot it to London."

"To London!"

"Yes, London. Number Ten Downing Street!"

"Good Lord!" said Hubbard. "That's the Prime Minister's residence!"

"Listen, fellow," snapped Grigsby. "As soon as I get into the plane, come as fast as you can. You may have to shoot your way through, but I'll be there to back you up. And someone else—"

The blast of a plane motor came across the field—a sudden, snarling blast.

"That's the Defiant!" cried Hubbard.

Grigsby's face paled as he wheeled, cupping his ear.

"It's the Defiant, I tell you!" roared Hubbard. "I'd know that Merlin anywhere."

"Come on, then!" yelled Grigsby. "The plan is off. We have to rush the Stuka. We've got to make it!"

He was already running and Hubbard loped behind him, submachine-gun held across his body. Around the edge of the guardhouse they ran. Hubbard saw that the nearest Stuka was a matter of a hundred yards away.

The Defiant was lifting off the field, her motors whining at full blast. A group of Nazi officers and pilots stood beside the bombers across the field, watching her climb.

A warning shot rang out and Hubbard heard the bullet whip past his head. Someone yelled and then a dozen shouts split the air. Another shot blasted the morning and another. A bullet kicked dust ahead of them.

The farmhouse suddenly erupted men. Hubbard, cradling the tommy gun in the crotch of his arm, slammed home the trigger. The gun stuttered in short bursts and men tumbled like tenpins.

Grigsby, Hubbard saw, had a pistol in his hand, was shooting at a running guard. The guard stumbled, tried to catch himself, fell sprawling.

Bullets now were zipping from the farmhouse, where half a dozen Nazis had taken cover behind a garden wall. Windows slammed up and other gun muzzles appeared.

Hubbard, realizing that the next ten seconds would find them in a hurricane of whizzing steel, ate up the ground, bending low, not trying to return the fire.

Suddenly from behind him a machine-gun broke into its song of death. Kermit Hubbard unconsciously hunched his shoulders to take the storm of lead. But the gun was not aimed at him. Its bullets were spraying the farmhouse, driving the Nazis to cover.

Above the roar of the gun he heard a full voice roar.

"So you had fun at Dunkerque, did you! Well, curse your bloody hearts!"

The rest of what he said was drowned out in the yammering of the gun. Not the spiteful chatter of a tommy rifle, but the baleful chuckling of a man-size machine-gun hurling a hail of steel.

Hubbard was climbing into the Stuka and Grigsby scrambled after him, dropping the automatic, not bothering to retrieve it. He heard the bullets chunking into the fuselage and prayed they wouldn't find an oil line or mess up the engine.

Tumbling into the pilot's pit, the American reached for the ignition switch, snapped it over, then sat for three precious seconds trying to locate the starter mechanism.

Back of him he heard Grigsby's curses as the man fought the gun, trying to swing it into position.

Hubbard got the engine going at almost the same instant that Grigsby opened up with the gun in the rear compartment. Off to the left, the tommy rifle operated by the man with the British voice kept up an insane chatter.

"What about that fellow?" yelled Hubbard.

"Get the devil out of here!" Grigsby screamed.

The ball knob in the box to his left, Hubbard figured, must be the throttle. He rammed it ahead and the Jumo 211 howled as the fury of its 1,500-horsepower engine was unleashed.

Suddenly the instrument board seemed to explode and shattered glass showered over Hubbard. A bullet had slammed through the pit and ended in the maze of dials.

But the Stuka was rolling now, fairly leaping forward. Hubbard hauled back on the stick recklessly. It was dangerous, he knew, starting with a cold engine, without even the pretense of a warm-up. But they had to get away from that murderous ground fire.

The trees on the far end of the field suddenly dipped and Hubbard knew they were in the air. The motor coughed once, then regained its throbbing bark. In the rear compartment the gun still jabbered.

Hubbard wheeled the plane and stared down through the turret glass. Pilots were scurrying like ants for their ships. With a yell of glee the American whipped the Stuka around and dived.

The air-speed indicator had been smashed. Hubbard couldn't tell how fast they were going. But it seemed that everything dropped from under him as the plane screamed down, a meteor of vengeance.

He started to level off as his diving Stuka came opposite one end of the line of planes out on the field. He pressed the trigger button on the stick. The guns in the wings spat viciously and Grigsby's gun stammered and stuttered with deadly bursts.

Down the line of ships the Stuka went, spraying the field. With a wild whoop, Hubbard looped to come back. It was not until then that he saw the man who stood on top of the guardhouse. A man clad in British battle dress, standing beside a machine-gun, waving at them with his hat, dancing in glee. His mouth was open and he was shouting something, but they couldn't hear.

From somewhere below an ack-ack banged. Far above them a shell burst, like a flower opening in the sky. The ack-ack coughed again and Hubbard put the Stuka on its tail and climbed.

Only once did he glance back—and his glance was at the guardhouse. On top of it a lone figure was sprawled beside his gun. The man in British battle dress had fired his last round for England.

The ack-acks still were banging, but by now the Stuka was out of range and going fast. Hubbard's eyes searched the skies ahead of them, made out a black dot far to the west. That would be the Defiant, scurrying for the English coast.

"If I'd only had some bombs!" the American swore feelingly. "I'd have really mowed 'em down."

Grigsby's hand reached out of the rear compartment and grasped him by the shoulder.

"You see the Defiant?"

"I sure do," Hubbard replied.

"You had no business wasting time back there," charged Grigsby. "It was a fool thing to do. We have to catch that Defiant. We have to catch it before it reaches London!"

"If we hadn't strafed them, they'd have been on our tails," Hubbard defended himself. "They would have had planes in the air within the minute. I'd rather waste a little time stopping them before they started than fight them after they got up."

"How fast can you travel?" Grigsby demanded impatiently.

"I don't know. Not as fast as the Defiant, normally. But you said the Defiant was loaded."

"With explosives," Grigsby snapped. "Explosives for Number Ten Downing Street."

"We'll catch it," Hubbard said grimly.

He pushed against the throttle but it already was forward as far as it would go. The Jumo's bark had become a snarl, mingled with the screech of air as it slid past the fuselage.

"Say," Hubbard shouted back at Grigsby. "Who was that fellow up on the roof?"

"His name was Thompson," Grigsby said. "One of the rear-guard men at Dunkerque. Got cut off and was left behind. He's been carrying on a little private war all of his own since then. Had a lot of help, too. Peasants would hide him, get gasoline for the motorcycle he stole, sneak him ammunition. He's made life miserable for the Jerries."

"He was the guy who busted up the Krauts that nabbed me," Hubbard decided. "Good man."

"I tipped him off," said Grigsby. "He liked little jobs like that. I figured, too, you might manage to get away. I couldn't take a chance myself."

"Sure," said Hubbard.

He watched the Defiant with narrowed eyes. It seemed that they were gaining.

"Maybe," he shouted to Grigsby, "we should have done something for poor old Thompson. Tried to save the guy. Stayed and covered his retreat."

"We couldn't wait," snapped Grigsby. "What we're doing is more important than Thompson's life. Thompson knew that. I explained it to him, although no explanation was necessary. Thompson figured he was living on borrowed time, anyway. Figured he really should have been killed at Dunkerque.

"He lived for just one thing—to kill Nazis. He didn't want to live, himself. He saw too much at Dunkerque."

Hubbard nodded. He'd talked with Dunkerque men, sensed the things they left unsaid, came to understand the strange lights in their eyes. They were a group set aside by bitterness and hatred.

Grigsby cleared his throat.

"Something I want to say to you, Hubbard."

"Fire away."

"Maybe both of us won't get through. Maybe something will happen."

"Maybe neither of us will get through," growled Hubbard. "This is no picnic."

"But if you do and I don't—if anything happens, be sure to get the papers I have inside my blouse. If it comes to the worst, if we crash and I am trapped, don't bother about me. Get the papers first. Then if you can pull me out, well and good. But if you can't—"

"Okay, pal," said Hubbard. "And if I can't get the papers, what then?"

"Tell them a new invasion fleet is being built and massed along the Norwegian and Danish coasts. The papers show the exact locations."

Hubbard grimaced wryly.

"Take it easy," he said. "You'll hand them in yourself."

"I'd like to," Grigsby chuckled. "I cooked for them and blacked Nazi boots and took Nazi insults. I scrubbed floors—" he made a disgusted sound in his throat.

The American bent forward to inspect the damage done by the bullet that had smashed the instrument board. By luck, the ignition and oil gauge were undamaged but the rest was blasted into confusion. The radio was dead. There wasn't even a hum as he tried it.

The Stuka, he knew, was gaining on the Defiant, but whether he could gain enough was something else again. He hunched forward in his seat as if he would force the plane to greater speed, then realized the futility of such a posture and settled back.

If only the radio weren't broken, he could warn the R.A.F. and a swarm of fighters would scramble upstairs to intercept the Defiant. But that was a useless thought.

He kept close watch for Nazi formations which he expected to rise up to bar his path at any moment. If the radio back at the base they had fled was working, a warning would be flashed. But it was just possible Hubbard's bullets had taken their toll of the Nazi radio hut and it was out of commission.

By the time they reached the channel, the Stuka had cut down the distance to the Defiant by a good half.

"Will we make it, Hubbard?" Grigsby shouted.

Although not too sure of it himself, Hubbard nodded grimly. "You've got to do it, fella," he told himself.

He could envision what would happen if he didn't. Once over London, the way was clear for the Nazi pilot bent on his suicidal mission. Once the Defiant got inside the sprawling metropolis, no power on earth could stop it.

Thinking of the consequences, Hubbard shut his eyes in agony. In his mind's eye he could see the Defiant screaming down, a silvery blur in the foggy sunlight, straight at No.10 Downing Street.

Undoubtedly the Germans knew the right time to strike. Knew that the explosive-laden plane would plunge into the Prime Minister's residence at a time when the man all Britain depended on was at home—perhaps having breakfast, perhaps conferring with some of the members of his war cabinet—

"British plane to the north," Grigsby reported suddenly.

Hubbard nodded. That was something else to worry about, another grim reason to force more speed out of the Stuka. The R.A.F. wouldn't know—couldn't know—what was going on. They would merely see a Stuka chasing a Defiant and would act accordingly.

The British plane, a coastal patrol boat, did not try to give chase. But Hubbard was certain that even now its radio was carrying the news of his approach.

When they crossed the coastline, the Stuka was less than a quarter-mile behind the Defiant, closing in fast. Below then a few coastal anti-aircraft batteries let loose, but the shots were wide.

Far to the north black dots sprinkled the sky. R.A.F. fighters! A cloud of them!

Hubbard hauled back the stick and climbed.

The maneuver lost him distance, but in the face of the squadrons before him he had to have room in which to work.

The Spitfires climbed to intercept him, but he outdistanced them, left them far below, wheeling to come back at him.

"Keep an eye on the Defiant!" he yelled to Grigsby.

Far ahead, a smudge on the horizon, was London. Far below was the suicide plane.

"That's her!" Grigsby shouted.

"Hang on!" yelled Hubbard. "Here we go!"

He shoved the Stuka's nose down and again the bottom dropped out of everything.

The screech of air against the fuselage and wings rose to a thin scream that hurt the eardrums. The ground below was a blur of green and brown that seemed to hurl itself upward.

Vaguely Hubbard wondered how fast they were traveling, his mind reeling at the thought. Fleetingly, he wondered if he could pull out of that dive. Strangely enough, he didn't particularly care. The world had become a whirl of speed and shadows, an unreal place in which he seemed to hang without any sense of suspension.

"Spitfires!" gasped Grigsby, just behind him.

Grigsby was right. From below three planes knifed up. Hubbard saw them, knew that he would crash into them if they continued their course. But he gritted his teeth and clutched the stick, trying to fight back the darkness that rose up to blanket him.

Guns were yammering thinly and he sensed the thud of tracers smacking into the Stuka. Below him eight red mouths flickered as a Spitfire's Brownings crackled into action.

Out of the corner of his eye, he saw bits of fabric being chewed from the wings by the Spitfire's bullets. The Stuka shuddered and then the Spitfire wheeled and dropped away. But still the tracer raked them, punching holes.

The Defiant now was almost directly below, a long gun range away. Blackness was surging over Hubbard, but he fought it off. Tightening his stomach muscles, he sucked in his breath, found himself counting.

"One, two, three, four—*now!*"

He depressed the firing button and kept it down. Tracers slapped into the Defiant. The next moment the world turned into a red maw that writhed and dripped with flame.

The Stuka trembled as if a giant hand had grasped and shaken it. Staggering, it slipped into the dense cloud of smoke that marked the place where the Defiant had been.

Jarred to his teeth, stunned with the concussion of the explosion, unable to see, Hubbard hauled back the stick, felt the Stuka wobbling all over the sky.

Slowly he felt his way back to consciousness, blinked his eyes.

The Stuka was still tearing toward the earth, but had veered from its direct dive. The wings were ribboned with flame. Smoke rolled from the cowling. The motor sputtered and yammered. The blast of the exploding Defiant had all but shaken the German plane apart.

Savagely, Hubbard snapped off the switch, yanked the plane out of its dive. Thoughts hammered at his brain. They had no 'chutes. They couldn't jump. He had to set the Stuka down—and quickly.

His eyes searched the ground beneath. Rolling farmland, fields that would have made perfect landing spots. But every one of them was pitted with holes, ridged with mounds, cluttered with old cars and other junk to forestall a Nazi invasion.

Hubbard groaned. In all of England, there wasn't a place a man could set down a plane, except at a regular airport. The British were determined that no fields be safe for the enemy.

The Stuka was dropping fast—much too fast. Desperately, Hubbard searched the ground. That haystack!

"Get set!" he yelled to Grigsby.

* * *

Breath sobbing in his throat, the American hauled the plane around, headed it for the stack. He was coming down like a comet. Too fast. But it was too late now to do anything about it.

Below him Hubbard saw a farmer running with a pitchfork. A horse galloped wildly across a pasture. The American's hands froze to the stick and his eyes measured the stack. Near the top and yet not too high. Couldn't let the ship roll over.

The Stuka mushed savagely into the hay and ripped through. The impact was like a savage wrench. The plane hit the ground and bounced high, throwing clouds of straw in a wild cascade.

Hubbard slammed on the brakes and the Stuka nosed over. It teetered for a moment, threatening to somersault on its back, then hung there, nose down, prop biting the earth.

Frantically Hubbard hauled back the hatch cover. Smoke pouring from the cowling blinded him. Flame licked upward at him as he rolled free and fell to the ground.

Through the smoke he saw Grigsby already running from the ship. Hurriedly he scrambled after him.

"Halt!" yelled a voice and they stopped.

The farmer rounded the haystack, pitchfork still in hand. He menaced them with it.

"Stand there, you bloody 'Uns!" he rasped. "Or I'll 'eave this into you."

"Look here, man—" Grigsby started to say. But the farmer roared at him.

"No back talk, you!"

Grigsby gulped and glanced appealingly at Hubbard. The American shrugged and broke into a tight grin.

"Maybe he thinks we're Rudolf Hess' twin brothers," he said from the corner of his mouth. "With another 'peace' proposal."

The farmer glared at them.

A small boy, lugging a heavy gun, came running across the barnyard.

"Here, Grandfather!" he panted, handing the man the weapon.

"Now I bloody well got you," the farmer said with satisfaction. "You and your smart 'Un tricks!"

"But, man," Grigsby protested wildly. "I'm English! I've got to get to London! I've got to see the Prime Minister!"

"You'll see the inside of a coffin, if you don't shut up," the farmer growled. "Now, march!"

They marched.

LIMITING FACTOR

After being rejected by John W. Campbell, Jr., of Astounding Science Fiction *(with whom Cliff Simak had had a long and successful relationship), this story would first appear in the November 1949 issue of* Startling Stories—*which was apparently a small market, as indicated by the fact that Cliff was paid only $60. I theorize that the story was a hard sell because it lacked a conventional sort of plot, the kind born of conflict. Every now and then, Cliff Simak apparently had to vent, had to release a thing that dwelled in the back of his mind, that simply lived to see something marvelous out in the Universe somewhere—and when he did that, it was enough for him to imagine the marvel and try to describe it. (I sometimes wonder how many starts he made on stories that had their genesis in a glorious vision, but never went anywhere . . .)*

The wonder is that he got any of them published at all; science fiction critics usually condemn them. But if you look, you'll find other Simak stories that give off the same sort of vibe.

—*dww*

First, there were two planets looted of their ores, mined and gutted and left there naked for the crows of space to pick.

Then there was a planet with a faery city, a place that made one think of cobwebs with the dew still on them, a place of glass and plastic so full of wondrous beauty that it hurt one's throat to look.

But there was just one city. There was no other sign of habitation on the entire planet. And the city was deserted. Perfect in its beauty, but hollow as a laugh.

Finally there was a metal planet, third outward from the sun. Not a lump of metallic ore, but a planet with a surface—or a roof—of fabricated metal, burnished to the polish of a bright steel mirror. And it shone, by reflected light, like another sun.

"I can't get over the conviction," said Duncan Griffith, "that this place is no more than a camp."

"I think you're crazy," Paul Lawrence told him sharply. He wiped his forehead with his sleeve.

"It may not look like a camp," said Griffith, doggedly, "but it meets the definition."

It looks like a city to me, Lawrence told himself. It always has, from the first moment that I saw it, and it always will. Big and vital, despite its faery touch—a place to live and dream and find the strength and courage to put the dreams to work. Great dreams, he told himself. Dreams to match the city—such a city as it would take Man a thousand years to build.

"What I can't understand," he said aloud, "is why it is deserted. There is no sign of violence. No sign of death at all."

"They voluntarily left it," Griffith told him. "They up and went away. And they did it because it wasn't really home to them. It was just a camp and it held no traditions and no legends. As a camp, it had no emotional value for the ones who built it."

"A camp," said Lawrence stubbornly, "is just a stopping place. A temporary habitation that you sling together and make as comfortable as you can with the things at hand."

"So?" asked Griffith.

"These folks did more than stop here," Lawrence said. "That

city wasn't slapped together. It was planned with foresight and built with loving care."

"On a human basis, yes," said Griffith. "You're dealing here with non-human values and an alien viewpoint."

Lawrence squatted and plucked at a grass stem, stuck it between his teeth and chewed on it thoughtfully. He squinted across the brilliant blaze of noon-day sun at the silent, empty city.

Griffith hunkered down beside him.

"Don't you see, Paul," he said, "that it has to be a temporary habitation. There is no sign of any previous culture on the planet. No artifact. King and his gang went over it and there wasn't anything. Nothing but the city. Think of it—an absolutely virgin planet with a city that it would take a race a million years of living just to dream. First there'd be a tree to huddle under when it rained. Then a cave to huddle in when night came down. After that there'd be a tent or a wigwam or a hut. Then three huts and you had a village."

"I know," Lawrence said. "I know."

"A million years of living," Griffith said, relentlessly. "Ten thousand centuries before a race could build a fairyland of glass and plastics. And that million years of living wasn't done on this planet. A million years of living leaves scars upon a planet. And there aren't any scars. This planet is brand new."

"You're convinced they came from somewhere else, Dunc?"

Griffith nodded. "They must have."

"From Planet Three, perhaps."

"We can't know that. Not yet."

"Maybe never," Lawrence said.

He spat out the blade of grass.

"This system," he said, "is like a pulp whodunit. Everywhere you turn you stumble on a clue and every clue is haywire. Too many mysteries, Dunc. This city here, the metal planet, the looted planets—it's just too much to swallow. It would be our luck to stumble on a place like this."

"I have a feeling there's a tie between it all," said Griffith.

Lawrence grunted.

"It's a sense of history," Griffith said. "A feeling for the fitness of things. Given time, all historians acquire it."

A footstep crunched behind them and they came to their feet, turning toward the sound.

It was Doyle, the radio man, hurrying toward them from the lifeboat camp.

"Sir," he said to Lawrence, "I just had Taylor out on Planet Three. He asks if you won't come. It seems they've found a door."

"A door!" said Lawrence. "A door into the planet. What did they find inside?"

"He didn't say, sir."

"He didn't say!"

"No. You see, sir, they can't budge the door. There's no way to open it."

The door wasn't much to look at.

There were twelve holes in the planet's surface, grouped in four groups of three each, as if they might be handholds for a thing that had three fingers.

And that was all. You could not tell where the door began nor where it ended.

"There is a crack," said Taylor, "but you can just barely see it with a glass. Even under magnification, it's no more than a hairline. The door's machined so perfectly that it's practically one piece with the surface. For a long time we didn't even know it was a door. We sat around and wondered what the holes were for.

"Scott found it. Just skating around and saw those holes. You could have looked until your eyes fell out and you'd never found it except by accident."

"And there's no way to open it?" asked Lawrence.

"None that we have found. We tried lifting it, sticking our fingers in the holes and heaving. You might as well have tried to lift the planet. And, anyhow, you can't get much purchase here. Can't keep your feet under you. This stuff's so slick you can scarcely walk on it. You don't walk, in fact; you skate. I'd hate to think what would happen if some of the boys got to horsing around and someone gave someone else a shove. It would take us a week to run them down."

"I know," said Lawrence. "I put the lifeboat down as easy as I could and we skidded forty miles or more."

Taylor chuckled. "I've got the big job stuck on with all the magnetics that we have and even then she wabbles if you lean on her. Ice is positively rough alongside this stuff."

"About this door," said Lawrence. "It occurred to you it might be a combination?"

Taylor nodded. "Sure, we thought of that. And if it is we haven't got a ghost. Take the element of chance, multiply it by the unpredictability of an alien mind."

"You checked?"

"We did," said Taylor. "We stuck a camera tentacle down into those holes and we took all kinds of shots. Nothing. Absolutely nothing. Eight inches deep or so. Wider at the bottom than the top. But smooth. No bumps. No ridges. No keyholes.

"We managed to saw out a hunk of metal so that we could test it. Used up three blades getting it out. Basically, it's steel, but it's alloyed with something Mueller can't tie a tag onto and the molecular structure has him going nuts."

"Stumped," said Lawrence.

"Yeah. I skated the ship over to the door and we hooked up a derrick and heaved with everything we had. The ship swung like a pendulum and the door stayed put."

"We might look for other doors," said Lawrence, whistling past the graveyard. "They might not be all alike."

"We looked," said Taylor. "Crazy as it sounds, we did. Each man-jack of us, creeping on our shinbones. We mapped the area off in sectors and crawled on our hands and knees for miles, squinting and peering. We almost put our eyes out, what with the sun glaring from the metal and our images staring back at us as if we were crawling on a mirror."

"Come to think of it," said Lawrence, "they probably wouldn't have built doors very close together. Every hundred miles, say— or maybe every thousand."

"You're right," said Taylor. "It might be a thousand."

"There's just one thing to do," Lawrence told him.

"Yeah, I know," said Taylor, "but I hate to do it. We got a problem here. Something we should work out. And if we blast we've failed at the first equation."

Lawrence stirred uneasily. "I know how you feel," he said. "If they beat us on the first move, we haven't got a chance at the second or the third."

"We can't just sit around," said Taylor.

"No," said Lawrence. "No, I guess we can't."

"I hope it works," said Taylor.

It did.

The blast ripped the door free and hurled it into space. It came down a mile away and rolled like a crazy, jagged wheel across the ice-slick surface.

Half an acre or so of the surface itself peeled up and back and hung twisted like a question mark that sparkled in the sun.

The unmanned lifeboat, clamped to the metal by its weak magnetics, like a half-licked stamp, came unstuck when the blast let loose. It danced a heavy-footed skaters' waltz for a good twelve miles before it came to rest.

The metal of the surface was a mere fourteen inches thick, a paper-thin covering when one considered that the sphere was the size of Earth.

A metal ramp, its upper ten feet twisted and smashed by the explosive force, wound down into the interior like a circular staircase.

Nothing came out of the hole. No sound or light or smell.

Seven men went down the ramp to see what they could find. The others waited topside, sweating them out.

Take a trillion sets of tinker toys.

Turn loose a billion kids.

Give them all the time they need and don't tell them what to do.

If some of them are non-human, that makes it better yet.

Then take a million years to figure out what happened.

A million years, mister, won't be long enough. You'll never do it—not in a million years.

It was machinery, of course. It could be nothing else.

But it was tinker toy machinery, something you'd expect a kid to throw together from sheer exuberance the morning after he got a real expensive set.

There were shafts and spools and disks and banks of shining crystal cubes that might have been tubes, although one couldn't quite be sure.

There were cubic miles of it and it glistened like a silvery Christmas tree in the fanning of the helmet lights, as if it had been polished no more than an hour before. But when Lawrence leaned over the side of the ramp and ran gloved fingers along a shining shaft, the fingers came back dusty—with a dust as fine as flour.

They had come down, the seven of them, twisting along the ramp until they had grown dizzy and always there was the machinery, stretching away on every side as far as the lights could penetrate the darkness.

Machinery that was motionless and still—and it seemed, for no reason that anyone could voice, that it had been still for many countless ages.

And machinery that was the same, repeating over and over again the senseless array of shafts and spools and disks and the banks of shining crystal cubes.

Finally the ramp had ended on a landing and the landing ran on every side as far as the lights could reach, with the spidery machinery far above them for a roof, and furniture, or what seemed to be furniture, arranged upon the metal floor.

They stood together in a tight-packed group and their lights stabbed out defiantly and they were strangely quiet in the darkness and the silence and the ghost of another time and people.

"An office," said Duncan Griffith, finally.

"Or a control room," said Ted Buckley, the mechanical engineer.

"It might be their living quarters," Taylor said.

"A machine shop, perhaps," suggested Jack Scott, the mathematician.

"Have you gentlemen considered," asked Herbert Anson, the geologist, "that it might be none of these? It might be something which is not allied with anything we know."

"All we can do," said Spencer King, the archaeologist, "is to translate it as best we can in the terms we know. My guess is that it could be a library."

Lawrence thought: There were seven blind men and they chanced to come upon an elephant.

He said: "Let's look. If we don't look, we'll never know."

They looked.

And still they didn't know.

Take a filing cabinet now. It's a handy thing to have.

You take some space and you wrap some steel around it and you have your storage space. You put in sliding drawers and you put nice, neat folders in the drawers and you label the folders and arrange them alphabetically. Then when you want a certain paper you almost always find it.

Two things are basic—space and something to enclose it, to define it from other space so that you can locate your designated storage space at a moment's notice.

The drawers and the alphabetically filed folders are refinements. They subdivide the space so you can put your fingers instantly on any required sector of it.

That's the advantage of a filing cabinet over just heaving everything you want to save into a certain corner of the room.

But suppose someone built a filing cabinet without any drawers.

"Hey," said Buckley, "this thing is light. Someone give me a hand."

Scott stepped forward quickly and between them they lifted the cabinet off the floor and shook it. Something rattled inside of it.

They put it down again.

"There's something in there," said Buckley, breathlessly.

"Yes," said King. "A receptacle. No doubt of that. And there's something in it."

"Something that rattles," said Buckley.

"Seems to me," declared Scott, "it was more like a rustle than a rattle."

"It won't do us much good," said Taylor, "if we can't get at it. You can't tell much about it by just listening to it while you fellows shake it."

"That's easy," said Griffith. "It's fourth dimensional. You say the magic words and reach around a corner somewhere and fish out what you want."

Lawrence shook his head. "Cut out the humor, Dunc. This is serious business. Any of you got an idea how the thing is made?"

"It couldn't be made," wailed Buckley. "It simply wasn't made. You can't take a sheet of metal and make a cube of it and not have any seams."

"Remember the door up on the surface," Anson reminded him. "We couldn't see anything there, either, until we got a magnifier on it. That cabinet opens somehow. Someone or something opened it at one time—to put in whatever rattled when you shook it."

"And they wouldn't put something in there," said Scott, "if there was no way to get it out."

"Maybe," said Griffith, "it was something they wanted to get rid of."

"We could rip it open," said King. "Get a torch."

Lawrence stopped him. "We've done that once already. We had to blast the door."

"There's half a mile of those cabinets stretched out here," said Buckley. "All standing in a row. Let's shake some more of them."

They shook a dozen more.

There wasn't any rattle.

There was nothing in them.

"Cleaned out," said Buckley, sadly.

"Let's get out of here," said Anson. "This place gives me the creeps. Let's go back to the ship and sit down and talk it over. We'll go looney batting out our brains down here. Take those control panels over there."

"Maybe they aren't control panels," Griffith reminded him. "We must be careful not to jump at what seem obvious conclusions."

Buckley snapped up the argument. "Whether they are or not," he said, "they must have some functional purpose. Control panels fill the bill better than anything I can think of at the moment."

"But they have no markings," Taylor broke in. "A control setup would have dials or lights or something you could see."

"Not necessarily something that a human could see," said Buckley. "To some other race we might qualify no better than stone blind."

"I have a horrible feeling," said Lawrence, "that we are getting nowhere."

"We took a licking on the door," said Taylor. "And we've taken a licking here."

King said: "We'll have to evolve some orderly plan of exploration. We must map it out. Take first things first."

Lawrence nodded. "We'll leave a few men on the surface and the rest of us will come down here and set up camp. We'll work in groups and we'll cover the situation as swiftly as we can—the general situation. After that we can fill in the details."

"First things first," said Taylor. "What comes first?"

"I wouldn't know," said Lawrence. "What ideas have the rest of you?"

"Let's find out what we have," suggested King. "A planet or a planetary machine."

"We'll have to find more ramps," said Taylor. "There must be other ramps."

Scott spoke up. "We should try to find out how extensive this machinery is. How much space it covers."

"And find out if the machine's running," said Buckley.

"What we saw wasn't," Lawrence told him.

"What we saw," Buckley declared, "may be no more than one corner of a vast machine. All of it might not work at once. Once in a thousand years or so a certain part of the machine might be used and then only for a few minutes or maybe even seconds. Then it might be idle for another thousand years. But it would have to be there for the once in a thousand years that it might be needed."

"Somehow," said Griffith, "we should try to make at least an educated guess what the machinery's for. What it does. What it produces."

"But keep your hands off it," warned Buckley. "No pushing this and pulling that just to see what happens. Lord knows what it might do. Just keep your big paws off it until you know what you are doing."

It was a planet, all right.

They found the planetary surface—twenty miles below. Twenty miles through the twisting maze of shining, dead machinery.

There was air, almost as good as Earth's, and they established camp on the lower levels, glad to get rid of space gear and live as normal beings.

But there was no light, and there was no life. Not even an insect, not one crawling, creeping thing.

Although life had once been there.

The ruined cities told the story of that life. A primitive culture, King had said. A culture not much better than Twentieth Century Earth.

Duncan Griffith squatted beside the small atomic stove, hands spread out to its welcome glow.

"They moved to Planet Four," he was saying smugly. "They didn't have the room to live here, so they went out there and camped."

"And mined two other planets," Taylor said, "to get the ore they needed."

Lawrence hunched forward, dejectedly. "What bothers me," he said, "is the drive behind this thing—the sheer, unreasoning urge, the spirit that would drive an entire race from their home to another planet, that would enable them to spend centuries to turn their own planet into one vast machine."

He turned his head to Scott. "There isn't much doubt, is there," he asked, "that it's nothing but machinery?"

Scott shook his head. "We haven't seen it all, of course. That would take years and we haven't years to spend. But we are fairly certain it's all one machine—a world covered by machinery to the height of twenty miles."

"And dead machinery," said Griffith. "Dead because they stopped it. They shut the machinery down and took all their records and all their tools and went away and left an empty shell. Just as they left the city out on Planet Four."

"Or were driven away," said Taylor.

"Not driven away," Griffith declared flatly. "We've found no sign of violence anywhere in this entire system. No sign at all of haste. They took their time and packed and they didn't leave a single thing behind. Not a single clue. Somewhere there must be blueprints. You couldn't build and you couldn't run a place like this without some sort of road map. Somewhere there must be records—records that kept tally on the results or the production of this world-machine. But we haven't found them. And why haven't we found them? Because they were taken away when the people left."

"We haven't looked everywhere," said Taylor.

"We found repositories where they logically would be kept," said Griffith, "and they weren't there. There was nothing there."

"Some of the cabinets we couldn't get into. Remember? Those we found the first day on the upper level."

"There were thousands of other places that we could and did get into," Griffith declared. "But we didn't find a tool or a single record or anything to hint anything ever had been there."

"Those cabinets up on the last level," said Taylor. "They are the logical place."

"We shook them," said Griffith, "and they all were empty."

"All except one," said Taylor.

"I'm inclined to believe you're right, Dunc," Lawrence said. "This world was abandoned, stripped and left to rust. We should have known that when we found it undefended. They would have had some sort of defenses—automatic probably—and if anyone had wanted to keep us out we'd never gotten in."

"If we'd come around when this world was operating," Griffith said, "we'd been blown to dust before we even saw it."

"They must have been a great race," Lawrence said. "The economics, alone, of this place is enough to scare you. It must have required the total manpower of the entire race many centuries to build it, and after that many other centuries to keep it operating. That means they spent a minimum of time in getting food, in manufacturing the million things that a race would need to live."

"They simplified their living and their wants," said King, "to the bare necessities. That, in itself alone, is a mark of greatness."

"And they were fanatics," said Griffith. "Don't forget that for a moment. Only the sheer, blind, one-track purpose of an obsessed people could do a job like this."

"But why?" asked Lawrence. "Why did they build the thing?"

No one spoke.

Griffith chuckled thinly. "Not even a guess?" he asked. "Not one educated guess."

Slowly a man came to his feet from the shadows outside the tiny circle of light cast by the shining stove.

"I have a guess," he said. "In fact, I think I know."

"Let's have it, Scott," said Lawrence.

The mathematician shook his head. "I have to have some proof. You'd think that I was crazy."

"There is no proof," said Lawrence. "There is no proof for anything."

"I know of a place where there might be proof—just might."

They sat stock-still—all of them in the tight stove-circle.

"You remember that cabinet," said Scott. "The one Taylor was talking about just now. The one we shook and something rattled in it. The one we couldn't open."

"We still can't open it."

"Give me some tools," said Scott, "and I will get it open."

"We did that once," said Lawrence. "We used bull strength and awkwardness to open up the door. We can't keep on using force to solve this problem. It calls for more than force. It calls for understanding."

"I think I know," said Scott, "what it was that rattled."

Lawrence was silent.

"Look," said Scott. "If you have something valuable, some-thing you don't want someone else to steal, what do you do with it?"

"Why," said Lawrence, "I put it in a safe."

Silence whistled down the long, dead stretches of the vast machine above them.

"There could be no safer place," said Scott, "than a cabinet that had no way of being opened. Those cabinets held something that was important. They left one thing, something behind—something that they overlooked."

Lawrence came slowly to his feet.

"Let's get the tools," he said.

It was an oblong card, very ordinary-looking, and it had holes punched in it in irregular patterns.

Scott held it in his hand and his hand was shaking.

"I trust," said Griffith, bitterly, "that you're not disappointed."

"Not at all," said Scott. "It's exactly what I thought we'd find."

They waited.

"Would you mind?" asked Griffith, finally.

"It's a computation card," said Scott. "An answer to some problem fed into a differential calculator."

"But we can't decipher it," said Taylor. "We have no way of knowing what it means."

"We don't need to decipher it," Scott told him. "It tells us what we have. This machine—this whole machine, is a calculator."

"Why, that's crazy," Buckley cried. "A mathematical—"

Scott shook his head. "Not mathematical. At least not purely mathematical. It would be something more than that. Logic, more than likely. Maybe even ethics."

He glanced around at them and read the disbelief that still lingered on their faces.

"It's there for you to see," he cried. "The endless repetition, the monotonous sameness of the whole machine. That's what a calculator is—hundreds or thousands or million or billions of integrators, whatever number you would need to have to solve a stated question."

"But there would be a limiting factor," snapped Buckley.

"The human race," said Scott, "has never paid too much attention to limiting factors. They've gone ahead and licked them. Apparently, this race didn't pay too much attention to them, either."

"There are some," said Buckley, stubbornly, "that you just can't ignore."

A brain has limitations.

It won't apply itself.

It forgets too easily, and too many things, and the wrong things—always.

It is prone to worry—and in a brain, that's partial suicide.

If you push it too hard, it escapes into insanity.

And, finally, it dies. Just when it's getting good, it dies.

So you build a mechanical brain—a big one that covers an Earth-size planet for the depth of twenty miles—a brain that will tend to business and will not forget and will not go insane, for it cannot know frustration.

Then you up and leave it—and that's insanity compounded.

"The speculation," said Griffith, "is wholly without point, for there is no way of knowing what they used it for. You persist in regarding the people of this system as humanoids, when they probably weren't."

"They could not have been so different from us," Lawrence said. "That city out on Four might have been a human city. Here on this planet they faced the same technical problems the human race would face if we tried a similar project, and they carried it out in much the same manner that we would."

"You overlook," said Griffith, "the very thing that you, yourself, have pointed out so often—the fanatic drive that made them sacrifice everything to one great idea. A race of humans could not co-operate that closely or that fanatically. Someone would blunder and someone would cut someone else's throat and then someone would suggest there ought to be an investigation and the pack would be off, howling down the wind."

"They were thorough," he said. "Terrifyingly thorough. There's no life here. None that we could find. Not even an insect. And why not, do you think? Perhaps because a bug might get itself entangled in a gear or something and bollix up the works. So the bugs must go."

Griffith wagged his head. "In fact, they suggest the thinking of a bug itself. An ant, say. A colony of ants. A soulless mutual society that goes ahead in blind, but intelligent obedience toward a chosen goal. And if that were so, my friend, your theory that they used the calculator to work out economic and social theories is so much poppycock."

"It's not my theory," Lawrence said. "It was only one of several speculations. Another equally as valid might be that they were trying to work out an answer to the universe, why it is and what it is and where it might be going."

"And how," said Griffith.

"You're right. And how. And if they were, I feel sure it was no idle wondering. There must have been a pressure of some sort, some impelling reason why they felt that they must do it."

"Go on," said Taylor. "I can hardly wait. Carry out the fairy tale to its bitter end. They found out about the universe and—"

"I don't think they did," Buckley said quietly. "No matter what it was, the chances are against their finding the final answer to the thing they sought."

"For my part," said Griffith, "I would incline to think they might have. Why else would they go away and leave this great machine behind? They found the thing they wanted, so they had no further use for the tool that they had built."

"You're right," said Buckley. "They had no further use for it, but not because it had done everything that it could do and that wasn't quite enough. They left it because it wasn't big enough, because it couldn't work the problem they wanted it to work."

"Big enough!" cried Scott. "Why, all they had to do was add another tier, all around the planet."

Buckley shook his head. "Remember what I said about limiting factors? Well, there's one that you can't beat. Put steel under fifty-thousand pounds per square inch pressure and it starts to flow. The metal used in this machine must have been able to withstand much greater pressure, but there was a limit beyond which it was not safe to go. At twenty miles above the planet's surface, they had reached that limit. They had reached dead end."

Griffith let out a long breath. "Obsolete," he said.

"An analytical machine is a matter of size," said Buckley. "Each integrator corresponds to a cell in the human brain. It has a limited function and capacity. And what one cell does must be checked by two other cells. The 'tell me thrice' principle of making sure that there is no error."

"They could have cleared it and started over again," said Scott.

"Probably they did," said Buckley. "Many, many times. Although there always would have been an element of chance that each time it was cleared it might not be—well, rational or moral. Clearing on a machine this size would be a shock, like corrective surgery on the brain.

"Two things might have happened. They might have reached a clearance limit. Too much residual memory clinging to the tubes—"

"Subconscious," said Griffith. "It would be interesting to speculate if a machine could develop a subconscious."

"Or," continued Buckley, "they might have come to a problem that was so complicated, a problem with so many facets, that this machine, despite its size, was not big enough to handle it."

"So they went off to hunt a bigger planet," said Taylor, not quite believing it. "Another planet small enough to live and work on, but enough bigger so they could have a larger calculator."

"It would make sense," said Scott, reluctantly. "They'd be starting fresh, you see, with the answers they had gotten here. And with improved designs and techniques."

"And now," said King, "the human race takes over. I wonder what we'll be able to do with a thing like this? Certainly not what its builders intended it should be used for."

"The human race," said Buckley, "won't do a thing for a hundred years, at least. You can bet on that. No engineer would dare to turn a single wheel of this machine until he knew exactly what it's all about, how it's made and why. There are millions of circuits to be traced, millions of tubes to check, blueprints to be made, technicians to be trained."

Lawrence said sharply: "That's not our problem, King. We are the bird dogs. We hunt out the quail and flush it and our job is done and we go on to something else. What the race does with the things we find is something else again."

He lifted a pack of camp equipment off the floor and slung it across his shoulder.

"Everyone set to go?" he asked.

Ten miles up, Taylor leaned over the guardrail of the ramp to look down into the maze of machinery below him.

A spoon slid out of his carelessly packed knapsack and went spinning down.

They listened to it for a long time, tinkling as it fell.

Even after they could hear it no longer, they imagined that they could.

MASQUERADE

Clifford D. Simak's journals show that he was paid $125 for this story. He sent it, under the title "Mercutian Masquerade," to John W. Campbell, Jr., the editor of Astounding Science Fiction, *on August 11, 1940, received news of its acceptance a week later, and it would appear in the March 1941 issue. The story seems to have been part of what the author intended to be a series of stories set on the various planets of our Solar System (a project that the author seemed to abandon before completion, which may be just as well).*

It's rather a peculiar story, with some disturbing elements, including its portrayal of the character "Old Creepy," but I am interested in the similarity of the Roman Candles to the "Ghosts" of the story "Hermit of Mars," which appeared less than two years earlier. (Another disturbing element here is the portrayal of a (human) person named Rastus. He is described once as "a smoke," and once as a Negro; and he clearly presents a stereotype not unusual in pulp fiction of the 1930s. Clifford Simak did not use any of the more common derogatory terms, and he would never do another such portrayal.)

Just as an interesting historical aside: I note that the issue of Astounding *in which "Masquerade" appeared also featured two stories by Robert A. Heinlein—a short story, and the conclusion of his serial,* Sixth Column *(which was published under his pseudonym, Anson MacDonald). (I find this interesting both because of the fact that the two future science fiction Grand Masters would always have great respect for each other—*

and because Cliff Simak used "Anson" in the name "Anson Lee," which he would use a number of times in later, unrelated, stories.)

—dww

Old Creepy was down in the control room, sawing lustily on his screeching fiddle.

On the sun-blasted plains outside the Mercutian Power Center, the Roman Candles, snatching their shapes from Creepy's mind, had assumed the form of Terrestrial hillbillies and were cavorting through the measures of a square dance.

In the kitchen, Rastus rolled two cubes about the table, crooning to them, feeling lonesome because no one would shoot a game of craps with him.

Inside the refrigeration room, Mathilde, the cat, stared angrily at the slabs of frozen beef above her head, felt the cold of the place and meowed softly, cursing herself for never being able to resist the temptation of sneaking in when Rastus wasn't looking.

Up in the office, at the peak of the great photocell that was the center, Curt Craig stared angrily across the desk at Norman Page.

One hundred miles away, Knut Anderson, encased in a cumbersome photocell space suit, stared incredulously at what he saw inside the space warp.

The communications bank snarled warningly and Craig swung about in his chair, lifted the handset off the cradle and snapped recognition into the mouthpiece.

"This is Knut, chief," said a voice, badly blurred by radiations.

"Yes," yelled Craig. "What did you find?"

"A big one," said Knut's voice.

"Where?"

"I'll give you the location."

Craig snatched up a pencil, wrote rapidly as the voice spat and crackled at him.

"Bigger than anything on record," shrilled Knut's voice. "Space busted wide open and twisted all to hell. The instruments went nuts."

"We'll have to slap a tracer on it," said Craig, tensely. "Take a lot of power, but we've got to do it. If that thing starts to move—"

Knut's voice snapped and blurred and sputtered so Craig couldn't hear a word he said.

"You come back right away," Craig yelled. "It's dangerous out there. Get too close to that thing. Let it swing toward you and you—"

Knut interrupted, his voice wallowing in the wail of tortured beam. "There's something else, chief. Something funny. Damn funny—"

The voice pinched out.

Craig shrieked into the mouthpiece. "What is it, Knut? What's funny?"

He stopped, astonished, for suddenly the crackle and hissing and whistle of the communications beam was gone.

His left hand flicked out to the board and snapped a toggle. The board hummed as tremendous power surged into the call. It took power—lots of power, to maintain a tight beam on Mercury. But there was no answering hum—no indication the beam was being restored.

Something had happened out there! Something had snapped the beam.

Craig stood up, white-faced, to stare through the ray filter port to the ashy plains. Nothing to get excited about. Not yet, anyway. Wait for Knut to get back. It wouldn't take long. He had told Knut to start at once, and those puddle jumpers could travel.

But what if Knut didn't come back? What if that space warp had moved?

The biggest one on record, Knut had said. Of course, there always were a lot of them one had to keep an eye on, but very few big enough to really worry about. Little whirlpools and eddies where the space-time continuum was wavering around, wondering which way it ought to jump.

Not dangerous, just a bother. Had to be careful not to drive a puddle jumper into one. But a big one, if it started to move, might engulf the plant—

Outside, the Candles were kicking up the dust, shuffling and hopping and flapping their arms. For the moment they were mountain folk back in the hills of Earth, having them a hoe down. But there was something grotesque about them—like scarecrows set to music.

The plains of Mercury stretched away to the near horizon, rolling plains of bitter dust. The Sun was a monstrous thing of bright-blue flame in a sky of inky black, ribbons of scarlet curling out like snaky tentacles.

Mercury was its nearest to the Sun—a mere 29,000,000 miles distant—and that probably explained the warp. The nearness to the Sun and the epidemic of sunspots. Although the sunspots may not have had anything to do with it. Nobody knew.

Craig had forgotten Page until the man coughed, and then he turned away from the port and went back to the desk.

"I hope," said Page, "that you have reconsidered. This project of mine means a lot to me."

Craig was suddenly swept with anger at the man's persistence.

"I gave you my answer once," he snapped. "That is enough. When I say a thing, I mean it."

"I can't see your objection," said Page flatly. "After all, these Candles—"

"You're not capturing any Candles," said Craig. "Your idea is the most crackpot, from more than one viewpoint, that I have ever heard."

"I can't understand this strange attitude of yours," argued Page. "I was assured at Washington—"

Craig's anger flared. "I don't give a damn what Washington assured you. You're going back as soon as the oxygen ship comes in. And you're going back without a Candle."

"It would do no harm. And I'm prepared to pay well for any services you—"

Craig ignored the hinted bribe, leveled a pencil at Page.

"Let me explain it to you once again." he said. "Very carefully and in full, so you will understand.

"The Candles are natives of Mercury. They were here first. They were here when men came, and they'll probably be here long after men depart. They have let us be and we have let them be. And we have let them be for just one reason—one damn good reason. You see, we don't know what they could do if we stirred them up. We are afraid of what they might do."

Page opened his mouth to speak, but Craig waved him into silence and went on.

"They are organisms of pure energy. Things that draw their life substance directly from the Sun—just as you and I do. Only we get ours by a roundabout way. Lot more efficient than we are by that very token, for they absorb their energy direct, while we get ours by chemical processes.

"And when we've said that much—that's about all we can say. Because that's all we know about them. We've watched those Candles for five hundred years and they still are strangers to us."

"You think they are intelligent?" asked Page, and the question was a sneer.

"Why not?" snarled Craig. "You think they aren't because Man can't communicate with them. Just because they didn't break their necks to talk with men.

"Just because they haven't talked doesn't mean they aren't intelligent. Perhaps they haven't communicated with us because their thought and reasoning would have no common basis for intelligent communication with mankind. Perhaps it's because they regard Man as an inferior race—a race upon which it isn't even worth their while to waste their time."

"You're crazy," yelled Page. "They have watched us all these years. They've seen what we can do. They've seen our space ships— they've seen us build this plant—they've seen us shoot power across millions of miles to the other planets."

"Sure," agreed Craig, "they've seen all that. But would it impress them? Are you sure it would? Man, the great architect! Would you bust a gut trying to talk to a spider, or an orchard oriole, or a mud wasp? You bet your sweet life you wouldn't. And they're great architects, every one of them."

Page bounced angrily in his chair. "If they're superior to us," he roared, "where are the things they've done? Where are their cities, their machines, their civilizations?"

"Perhaps," suggested Craig, "they outlived machines and cities millennia ago. Perhaps they've reached a stage of civilization where they don't need mechanical things."

He tapped the pencil on the desk.

"Consider this. Those Candles are immortal. They'd have to be. There'd be nothing to kill them. They apparently have no bodies—just balls of energy. That's their answer to their environment. And you have the nerve to think of capturing some of them! You, who know nothing about them, plan to take them back to Earth to use as a circus attraction, a side-show drawing card—something for fools to gape at!"

"People come out here to see them," Page countered. "Plenty of them. The tourist bureaus use them in their advertising."

"That's different," roared Craig. "If the Candles want to put on a show on home territory, there's nothing we can do about it. But you can't drag them away from here and show them off. That would spell trouble and plenty of it!"

"But if they're so damned intelligent?" yelped Page, "why do they put on those shows at all? Just think of something and presto!—they're it. Greatest mimics in the Solar System. And they never get anything right. It's always cockeyed. That's the beauty of it."

"It's cockeyed," snapped Craig, "because man's brain never fashions a letter-perfect image. The Candles pattern themselves directly after the thoughts they pick up. When you think of something you don't give them all the details—your thoughts are sketchy. You can't blame the Candles for that. They pick up what you give them and fill in the rest as best they can. Therefore camels with flowing manes, camels with four and five humps, camels with horns, an endless parade of screwball camels, if camels are what you are thinking of."

He flung the pencil down angrily.

"And don't you kid yourself the Candles are doing it to amuse us. *More than likely they believe we are thinking up all those swell ideas just to please them.* They're having the time of their lives. Probably that's the only reason they've tolerated us here—because we have such amusing thoughts.

"When Man first came here they were just pretty, colored balls rolling around on the surface, and someone called them Roman Candles because that's what they looked like. But since that day they've been everything Man has ever thought of."

Page heaved himself out of the chair.

"I shall report your attitude to Washington, Captain Craig."

"Report and be damned," growled Craig. "Maybe you've forgotten where you are. You aren't back on Earth, where bribes and boot-licking and bulldozing will get a man almost anything he wants. You're at the power center on the Sunward side of Mercury. This is the main source of power for all the planets. Let this power plant fail, let the transmission beams be cut off and the Solar System goes to hell!"

He pounded the desk for emphasis.

"I'm in charge here, and when I say a thing it stands, for you as well as anyone. My job is to keep this plant going, keep the power pouring out to the planets. And I'm not letting some half-baked fool come out here and make me trouble. While I'm here, no one is going to stir up the Candles. We've got plenty of trouble without that."

Page edged toward the door, but Craig stopped him.

"Just a little word of warning," he said, speaking softly. "If I were you, I wouldn't try to sneak out any of the puddle jumpers, including your own. After each trip the oxygen tank is taken out and put into the charger, so it'll be at first capacity for the next trip. The charger is locked and there's just one key. And I have that."

He locked eyes with the man at the door and went on.

"There's a little oxygen left in the jumper, of course. Half an hour's supply, maybe. Possibly less. After that there isn't any more. It's not nice to be caught like that. They found a fellow that had happened to just a day or so ago over near one of the Twilight Belt stations."

But Page was gone, slamming the door.

The Candles had stopped dancing and were rolling around, drifting bubbles of every hue. Occasionally one would essay the formation of some object, but the attempt would be half-hearted and the Candle once more would revert to its natural sphere.

Old Creepy must have put his fiddle away, Craig thought. Probably he was making an inspection round, seeing if everything was all right. Although there was little chance that anything could go wrong. The plant was automatic, designed to run with the minimum of human attention.

The control room was a wonder of clicking, chuckling, chortling, snicking gadgets. Gadgets that kept the flow of power directed to the substations on the Twilight Belt. Gadgets that kept the tight beams from the substations centered exactly on those points in space where each must go to be picked up by the substations circling the outer planets.

Let one of those gadgets fail—let that spaceward beam sway as much as a fraction of a degree—Curt shuddered at the thought of a beam of terrific power smashing into a planet—perhaps into a city. But the mechanism had never failed—never would. It was foolproof. A far cry from the day when the plant had charged monstrous banks of converters to be carted to the outer worlds by lumbering spaceships.

This was really free power, easy power, plentiful power. Power carried across millions of miles on Addison's tight-beam principle. Free power to develop the farms of Venus, the mines of Mars, the chemical plants and cold laboratories on Pluto.

Down there in the control room, too, were other gadgets as equally important. The atmosphere machine, for example, which kept the air mixture right, drawing on those tanks of liquid oxygen and nitrogen and other gases brought across space from Venus by the monthly oxygen ship. The refrigerating plant, the gravity machine, the water assembly.

Craig heard the crunch of Creepy's footsteps on the stairs and turned to the door as the old man shuffled into the room.

Creepy's brows were drawn down and his face looked like a thundercloud.

"What's the matter now?" asked Craig.

"By cracky," snapped Creepy, "you got to do something about that Rastus."

Craig grinned. "What's up this time?"

"He stole my last bottle of drinking liquor," wailed Creepy. "I was hoarding it for medical purposes, and now it's gone. He's the only one that could have taken it."

"I'll talk to Rastus," Craig promised.

"Some day," threatened Creepy, "I'm going to get my dander up and whale the everlastin' tar out of that smoke. That's the fifth bottle of liquor he's swiped off me."

The old man shook his head dolefully, whuffled his walruslike mustache.

"Aside from Rastus, how's everything else going?" asked Craig.

"Earth just rounded the Sun," the old man said. "The Venus station took up the load."

Craig nodded. That was routine. When one planet was cut off by the Sun, the substations of the nearest planet took on an extra load, diverted part of it to the first planet's stations, carrying it until it was clear again.

He arose from the chair and walked to the port, stared out across the dusty plains. A dot was moving across the near horizon. A speedy dot, seeming to leap across the dead, gray wastes.

"Knut's coming!" he yelled to Creepy.

Creepy hobbled for the doorway. "I'll go down to meet him. Knut and me are having a game of checkers as soon as he gets in."

Craig laughed, relieved by Knut's appearance. "How many checker games have you and Knut played?" he asked.

"Hundreds of 'em," Creepy declared proudly. "He ain't no match for me, but he thinks he is. I let him beat me regular to keep the interest up. I'm afraid he'd quit playing if I beat him as often as I could."

He started for the door and then turned back. "But this is my turn to win." The old man chuckled in his mustache. "I'm goin' to give him a first-class whippin'."

"First," said Craig, "tell him I want to see him."

"Sure," said Creepy, "and don't you go telling him about me letting him beat me. That would make him sore."

Craig tried to sleep but couldn't. He was worried. Nothing definite, for there seemed no cause to worry. The tracer placed on the big warp revealed that it was moving slowly, a few feet an hour or so, in a direction away from the center. No other large ones had shown up in the detectors. Everything, for the moment, seemed under control. Just little things. Vague suspicions and wondering—snatches here and there that failed to fall into the pattern.

Knut, for instance. There wasn't anything wrong with Knut, of course, but while he had talked to him he had sensed something. An uneasy feeling that lifted the hair on the nape of his neck, made the skin prickle along his spine. Yet nothing one could lay one's hands on.

Page, too. The damn fool probably would try to sneak out and capture some Candles and then there'd be all hell to pay.

Funny, too, how Knut's radios, both in his suit and in the jumper, had gone dead. Blasted out, as if they had been raked by a surge of energy. Knut couldn't explain it, wouldn't try. Just shrugged his shoulders. Funny things always were happening on Mercury.

Craig gave up trying to sleep, slid his feet into slippers and walked across the room to the port. With a flip of his hand he raised the shutter and stared out.

Candles were rolling around. Suddenly one of them materialized into a monstrous whisky bottle, lifted in the air, tilted, liquid pouring to the ground.

Craig chuckled. That would be either Old Creepy bemoaning the loss of that last bottle or Rastus sneaking off to where he'd hid it to take another nip.

A furtive tap came on the door, and Craig wheeled. For a tense moment he crouched, listening, as if expecting an attack. Then he laughed softly to himself. He was jumpy, and no fooling. Maybe what *he* needed was a drink.

Again the tap, more insistent, but still furtive.

"Come in," Craig called.

Old Creepy sidled into the room. "I hoped you wasn't asleep," he said.

"What is it, Creepy?" And even as he spoke, Craig felt himself going tense again. Nerves all shot to hell.

Creepy hitched forward.

"Knut," he whispered. "Knut beat me at checkers. Six times hand running! I didn't have a chance!"

Craig's laugh exploded in the room.

"But I could always beat him before," the old man insisted. "I even let him beat me every so often to keep him interested so he would play with me. And tonight I was all set to take him to a cleaning—"

Creepy's face twisted, his mustache quivering.

"And that ain't all, by cracky. I felt, somehow, that Knut had changed and—"

Craig walked close to the old man, grasped him by the shoulder. "I know," he said. "I know just how you felt." Again he was remembering how the hair had crawled upon his skull as he talked to Knut just a while ago.

Creepy nodded, pale eyes blinking, Adam's apple bobbing.

Craig spun on his heel, snatched up his shirt, started peeling off his pajama coat.

"Creepy," he rasped, "you go down to that control room. Get a gun and lock yourself in. Stay there until I get back. And don't let anyone come in!"

He fixed the old man with a stare. "You understand. *Don't let anyone get in!* Use your gun if you are forced to use it. *But see no one touches those controls!*"

Creepy's eyes bugged and he gulped. "Is there going to be trouble?" he quavered.

"I don't know," snapped Craig, "but I'm going to find out."

Down in the garage, Craig stared angrily at the empty stall.

Page's jumper was gone!

Grumbling with rage, Craig walked to the oxygen-tank rack. The lock was undamaged, and he inserted the key. The top snapped up and revealed the tanks—all of them, nestling in rows, still attached to the recharger lines. Almost unbelieving, Craig stood there, looking at the tanks.

All of them were there. That meant Page had started out in the jumper with insufficient oxygen. It meant the man would die out on the blistering wastes of Mercury. That he might go mad and leave his jumper and wander into the desert, a raving maniac, like the man they'd found out near the Twilight station.

Craig swung about, away from the tanks, and then stopped, thoughts spinning in his brain. There wasn't any use of hunting Page. The damn fool probably was dead by now. Sheer suicide, that was what it was. Sheer lunacy. And he had warned him, too!

And he, Craig, had work to do. Something had happened out there at the space warp. He had to lay those tantalizing suspicions that rummaged through his mind. There were some things he had to be sure about. He didn't have time to go hunting a man who was already dead, a damn fool who had committed suicide. The man was nuts to start with. Anyone who thought he could capture Candles—

Savagely, Craig closed one of the line valves, screwed shut the tank valve, disconnected the coupling and lifted the tank out of the rack. The tank was heavy. It had to be heavy to stand a pressure of two hundred atmospheres.

As he started for the jumper, Mathilde, the cat, strolled down the ramp from the floor above and walked between his legs. Craig stumbled and almost fell, recovered his balance with a mighty effort and cursed Mathilde with a fluency born of practice.

"Me-ow-ow-ow," said Mathilde conversationally.

There is something unreal about the Sunward side of Mercury, an abnormality that is sensed rather than seen.

There the Sun is nine times larger than seen from Earth, and the thermometer never registers under six hundred fifty degrees Fahrenheit. Under that terrific heat, accompanied by blasting radiations hurled out by the Sun, men must wear photocell space suits, must ride photocell cars and live in the power center which in itself is little more than a mighty photocell. For electric power can be disposed of, while heat and radiation often cannot be.

There the rock and soil have been crumbled into dust under the lashing of heat and radiations. There the horizon is near, always looming just ahead, like an ever-present brink.

But it is not these things that make the planet so alien. Rather, it is the strange distortion of lines, a distortion that one sometimes thinks he can see, but is never sure. Perhaps the very root of that alien sense is the fact that the Sun's mass makes a straight line an impossibility, a stress that bends magnetic fields and stirs up the very structure of space itself.

Curt Craig felt that strangeness of Mercury as he zoomed across the dusty plain. The puddle jumper splashed through a small molten pool, spraying it out in sizzling sheets. A pool of lead, or maybe tin.

But Craig scarcely noticed. At the back of his brain pounded a thousand half-formed questions. His eyes, edged by crow's-feet, squinted through the filter shield, following the trail left by Knut's returning machine. The oxygen tank hissed softly and the atmosphere mixer chuckled. But all else was quiet.

A howl of terror and dismay shattered the quiet. Craig jerked the jumper to a stop, leaped from his seat, hand streaking to his gun.

Crawling from under the metal bunk bolted at the rear of the car was Rastus, the whites of his eyes showing like bull's-eyes.

"Good Lawd," he bellowed, "Where is I?"

"You're in a jumper, sixty miles from the Center," snapped Craig. "What I want to know is how the hell you got here."

Rastus gulped and rose to his knees. "You see, it was like this, boss," he stammered. "I was lookin' for Mathilde. Dat cat, she run me wild. She sneaks into the refrigerator all the time. I jus' can't trust her no place. So when she turned up missin'—"

He struggled to his feet, and as he did so a bottle slipped from his pocket, smashed to bits on the metal floor. Pale-amber liquor ran among the fragments.

Craig eyed the shattered glass. "So you were hunting Mathilde, eh?"

Rastus slumped on the bunk, put his head in his hands. "Ain't no use lyin' to you, boss," he acknowledged. "Never gets away with it. I was havin' me a drink. Just a little nip. And I fell asleep."

"You hid the bottle you swiped from Creepy in the jumper," declared Craig flatly, "and you drank yourself to sleep."

"Can't seem to help it," Rastus moaned. "'Ol' debbil's got me. Can't keep my hands off of a bottle, somehow. Ol' Mercury, he done dat to me. Ol' debbil planet. Nothin' as it should be. Ol' Man Sun pullin' the innards out of space. Playin' around with things until they ain't the same—"

Craig nodded, almost sympathetically. That *was* the hell of it. Nothing ever was the same on Mercury. Because of the Sun's tremendous mass, light was bent, space was warped and eternally threatening to shift, basic laws required modification. The power of two magnets would not always be the same, the attraction between two electrical charges would be changed. And the worst of it was that a modification which stood one minute would not stand the next.

"Where are we goin' now, boss?"

"We're going out to the space warp that Knut found," said Craig. "And don't think for a minute I'll turn around and take you back. You got yourself into this, remember."

Rastus' eyes batted rapidly and his tongue ran around his lips. "You said the warp, boss? Did I hear you right? The warp?"

Craig didn't answer. He swung back to his seat, started the jumper once again.

Rastus was staring out of one of the side ports. "There's a Candle followin' us," he announced. "Big blue feller. Skippin' along right with us all the time."

"Nothing funny in that," said Craig. "They often follow us. Whole herds of them."

"Only one this time," said Rastus. "Big blue feller."

Craig glanced at the notation of the space warp's location. Only a few miles distant. He was almost there.

* * *

There was nothing to indicate where the warp might be, although the instruments picked it up and charted it as he drew near. Perhaps if a man stood at just the right angle he might detect a certain shimmer, a certain strangeness, as if he were looking into a wavy mirror. But otherwise there probably would be nothing pointing to its presence. Hard to know just where one stopped or started. Hard to keep from walking into one, even with instruments.

Curt shivered as he thought of the spacemen who had walked into just such warps in the early days. Daring mariners of space who had ventured to land their ships on the Sunward side, had dared to take short excursions in their old-type space suit. Most of them had died, blasted by the radiations spewed out by the Sun, literally cooked to death. Others had walked across the plain and disappeared. They had walked into the warps and disappeared as if they had melted into thin air. Although, of course, there wasn't any air to melt into—hadn't been for many million years.

On this world, all free elements long ago had disappeared. Those elements that remained, except possibly far underground, were locked so stubbornly in combination that it was impossible to blast them free in any appreciable quantity. That was why liquid air was carted clear from Venus.

The tracks in the dust and rubble made by Knut's machine were plainly visible, and Craig followed them. The jumper topped a slight rise and dipped into a slight depression. And in the center of the depression was a queer shifting of light and dark, as if one were looking into a tricky mirror.

That was the space warp!

Craig glanced at the instruments and caught his breath. Here was a space warp that was really big. Still following the tracks of Knut's machine, he crept down into the hollow, swinging closer and closer to that shifting, almost invisible blotch that marked the warp.

"Golly!" gasped Rastus, and Craig knew the Negro was beside him, for he felt his breath upon his neck.

Here Knut's machine had stopped, and here Knut had gotten out to carry the instruments nearer, the blotchy tracks of his space suit like furrows through the powdered soil. And there he had come back. And stopped and gone forward again. And there—

Craig jerked the jumper to a halt, stared in amazement and horror through the filter shield. Then, the breath sobbing in his throat, he leaped from the seat, scrambled frantically for a space suit.

Outside the car, he approached the dark shape huddled on the ground. Slowly he moved nearer, the hands of fear clutching at his heart. Beside the shape he stopped and looked down. Heat and radiation had gotten in their work, shriveling, blasting, desiccating—but there could be no doubt.

Staring up at him from where it lay was the dead face of Knut Anderson!

Craig straightened up and looked around. Candles danced upon the ridges, swirling and jostling, silent watchers of his grim discovery. The one lone blue Candle, bigger than the rest, had followed the machine into the hollow, was only a few rods away, rolling restlessly to and fro.

Knut had said something was funny—had shouted it, his voice raspy and battered by the screaming of powerful radiations. Or had that been Knut? Had Knut already died when that message came through?

Craig glanced back at the sand, the blood pounding in his temples. Had the Candles been responsible for this? And if they were, why was he unmolested, with hundreds dancing on the ridge?

And if this was Knut, with dead eyes staring at the black of space, who was the other one—the one who came back?

Candles masquerading as human beings? Was that possible? Mimics the Candles were—but hardly as good as that. There was always something wrong with their mimicry—something ludi-crously wrong.

He remembered now the look in the eyes of the returned Knut—that chilly, deadly look—the kind of look one sometimes sees in the eyes of ruthless men. A look that had sent cold chills chasing up his spine.

And Knut, who was no match for Creepy at checkers, but who thought he was because Creepy let him win at regular inter-vals, had taken six games straight.

Craig looked back at the jumper again, saw the frightened face of Rastus pressed against the filter shield. The Candles still danced upon the hills, but the big blue one was gone.

Some subtle warning, a nasty little feeling between his shoul-der blades, made Craig spin around to face the warp. Just in front of the warp stood a man, and for a moment Craig stared at him, frozen, speechless, unable to move.

For the man who stood in front of him, not more than forty feet away, was Curt Craig!

Feature for feature, line for line, that man was himself. A sec-ond Curt Craig. As if he had rounded a corner and met himself coming back.

Bewilderment roared through Craig's brain, a baffling bewil-derment. He took a quick step forward, then stopped. For the bewilderment suddenly was edged with fear, a knifelike sense of danger.

The man raised a hand and beckoned, but Craig stayed rooted where he stood, tried to reason with his muddled brain. It wasn't a reflection, for if it had been a reflection it would have shown him in a space suit, and this man stood without a space suit. And if it were a real man, it wouldn't be standing there exposed to the madness of the Sun. Such a thing would have spelled sure and sudden death.

Forty feet away—and yet within that forty feet, perhaps very close, the power of the warp might reach out, might entangle any man who crossed that unseen deadline. The warp was moving, at a few feet an hour, and this spot where he now stood, with Knut's dead body at his feet, had a few short hours ago been within the limit of the warp's influence.

The man stepped forward, and as he did, Craig stepped back, his hands dropping to the gun butts. But with the guns half out he stopped, for the man had disappeared. Had simply vanished. There had been no puff of smoke, no preliminary shimmering as of matter breaking down. The man just simply wasn't there. But in his place was the big blue Candle, rocking to and fro.

Cold sweat broke out upon Craig's forehead and trickled down his face. For he knew he had trodden very close to death—perhaps to something even worse than death. Wildly he swung about, raced for the puddle jumper, wrenched the door open, hurled himself at the controls.

Rastus wailed at him. "What's the matter, boss?"

"We have to get back to the Center," yelled Craig. "Old Creepy is back there all alone! Lord knows what has happened to him—what will happen to him."

"But, boss," yipped Rastus, "what's the matter. Who was back there on the ground?"

"That was Knut," said Craig.

"But Mr. Knut is back there at the Center, boss. I know. I seen him with my own eyes."

"Knut isn't at the Center," Craig snapped. "Knut is dead out there by the warp. The thing that's at the Center is a Candle, masquerading as Knut!"

Craig drove like a madman, the cold claws of fear hovering over him. Twice he almost met disaster, once when the jumper bucked through a deep drift of dust, again when it rocketed through a pool of molten tin.

"But them Candles can't do that nohow," argued Rastus. "They can't get nothing right. Every time they try to be a thing they always get it wrong."

"How do you know that?" snapped Craig. "How do you know they couldn't if they tried? And if they could and wanted to use it against us, do you think they would let us see them do it? Through all these years they have done their best to make us lower our guard. They have tried to make us believe they were nothing but a gang of good-natured clowns. That, my boy, is super-plus psychology."

"But why?" demanded Rastus. "Why would they want to do it? We ain't never hurt them."

"Ask me another one," said Craig grimly. "The best answer is that we don't know them. They might have a dozen reasons—reasons we couldn't understand. Reasons no human being could understand because they wouldn't tally with the things we know."

Craig gripped the wheel hard and slammed the jumper up an incline slippery with dust.

Damn it, the thing that had come back as Knut *was* Knut. It knew the things Knut knew, it acted like Knut. It had his mannerisms, it talked in his voice, it actually seemed to think the way Knut would think.

What could a man—what could mankind do against a thing like that? How could it separate the original from the duplicate? How would it know its own?

The thing that had come back to the Center had beaten Creepy at checkers. Creepy had led Knut to believe he was the old man's equal at the game, although Creepy knew he could beat Knut at any time he chose. But Knut didn't know that—and the thing masquerading as Knut didn't know it. So it had sat down and beaten Creepy six games hand-running, to the old man's horror and dismay.

Did that mean anything or not?

Craig groaned and tried to get another ounce of speed out of the jumper.

"It was that old blue jigger," said Rastus. "He was sashaying all around, and then he disappeared."

Craig nodded. "He was in the warp. Apparently the Candles are able to alter their electronic structures so they may exist within the warp. They lured Knut into the warp by posing as human beings, arousing his curiosity, and when he stepped into its influence it opened the way for their attack. They can't get at us inside a suit, you see, because a suit is a photocell, and they are energy, and in a game of that sort, the cell wins every time.

"That's what they tried to do with me. Lord knows what the warp would have done if I'd stepped into it, but undoubtedly it would have made me vulnerable in the fourth dimension or in some other way. That would have been all they needed."

Rastus's eyes strayed to the litter of glass on the floor by the bunk. "Sho' wish I had me a snort of redeye," he mourned. "Sho' could do with a little stimulus."

"It was clever of them," Craig said. "A Trojan horse method of attack. First they got Knut, and next they tried to get me, and with two of them in the Center it would not have been so hard to have gotten you and Creepy."

He slapped the wheel a vicious stroke, venting his anger.

"And the beauty of it was that no one would have known. The oxygen ship could have come from Venus and the men on board would never have been the wiser, for they would have met things that seemed like all four of us. No one would have guessed. They would have had time—plenty of time—to do anything they planned."

"What you figure they was aimin' to do, boss?" queried Rastus. "Figure maybe they meant to blow up that ol' plant?"

"I don't know, Rastus. How could I know? If they were human beings, I could make a guess, because I could put myself in their shoes and try to think the way they did. But with the Candles you can't do that. You can't do anything with the Candles, because you don't know what they are."

"You aimin' to raise hell with dem Candles, boss?"

"With what?" snapped Craig.

"Just give me a razor," exulted Rastus. "Maybe two razors, one for each han'. I'se a powerful dangerous man with a razor blade."

"It'll take more than razors," said Craig. "More than our energy guns, for those things are energy. We could blast them with everything we had, and they'd just soak it up and laugh at us and ask for more."

He skidded the jumper around a ravine head, slashed across the desert. "First thing," he declared, "is to find the one that's masquerading as Knut. Find him and then figure out what to do with him."

But finding the Knut Candle was easier said than done. Craig, Creepy and Rastus, clad in space suits, stood in the kitchen at the Center.

"By cracky," said Creepy, "he must be here somewhere. He must have found him an extra-special hideout that we have over-looked."

Craig shook his head. "We haven't overlooked him, Creepy. We've searched this place from stem to stern. There isn't a crack where he could hide."

"Maybe," suggested Creepy, "he figured the jig was up and took it on the lam. Maybe he scrammed out the lock when I was up there guarding that control room."

"Maybe," agreed Craig. "I had been thinking of that. He smashed the radio—that much we know. He was afraid that we might call for help, and that means he may have had a plan. Even now he may be carrying out that plan."

The Center was silent, filled with those tiny sounds that only serve to emphasize and deepen a silence. The faint *cluck-cluck* of the machines on the floor below, the hissing and distant chortling of the atmosphere mixer, the chuckling of the water synthesizer.

"Dang him," snorted Creepy, "I knew he couldn't do it. I knew Knut couldn't beat me at checkers honest—"

From the refrigerator came a frantic sound. "Me-ow—me-ow-ow-ow," it wailed.

Rastus leaped for the refrigerator door, grabbing a broom as he went. "It's that Mathilde cat again," he yelled. "She's always sneakin' in on me. Every time my back is turned."

He brandished the broom and addressed the door. "You jus' wait. I'll sure work you over with this here broom. I'll plaster you—"

But Craig had leaped forward, snatched the Negro's hand away from the door. "Wait!" he shouted.

Mathilde yodeled pitifully.

"But, boss, that Mathilde cat—"

"Maybe it isn't Mathilde," Craig rasped grimly.

From the doorway leading out into the corridor came a low purring rumble. The three men whirled about. Mathilde was standing across the threshold, rubbing with arched back against the jamb, plumed tail waving. From inside the refrigerator came a scream of savage feline fury.

Rastus' eyes were popping and the broom clattered to the floor. "But, boss," he shrieked, "there's only one Mathilde!"

"Of course, there's only one Mathilde," snapped Craig. "One of these is her. The other is Knut, or the thing that was Knut."

The lock signal rang shrilly, and Craig stepped swiftly to a port, flipped the shutter up. "It's Page," he shouted. "Page is back again!"

He turned from the port, face twisted in disbelief. Page had gone out five hours before—without oxygen. Yet here he was, back again. No man could live for over four hours without oxygen. Craig's eyes hardened, and furrows came between his brows. "Creepy," he said suddenly. "You open the inner lock. You, Rastus, pick up that cat. Don't let her get away."

Rastus backed off, eyes wide in terror.

"Pick her up," commanded Craig sharply. "Hang onto her."

"But, boss, she—"

"Pick her up, I say!"

Creepy was shuffling down the ramp to the lock. Slowly Rastus moved forward, clumsily reached down and scooped up Mathilde. Mathilde purred loudly, dabbing at his suit-clad fingers with dainty paws.

Page stepped out of the jumper and strode across the garage toward Craig, his boot heels ringing on the floor.

From behind the space suit visor, Craig regarded him angrily. "You disobeyed my orders," he snapped. "You went out and caught some Candles."

"Nothing to it, Captain Craig," said Page. "Docile as so many kittens. Make splendid pets."

He whistled sharply, and from the open door of the jumper rolled three Candles, a red one, a green one, a yellow one. Ranged in a row, they lay just outside the jumper, rolling back and forth.

Craig regarded them appraisingly.

"Cute little devils," said Page good-naturedly.

"And just the right number," said Craig.

Page started, but quickly regained his composure. "Yes, I think so, too. I'll teach them a routine, of course, but I suppose the audience reactions will bust that all to hell once they get on the stage."

Craig moved to the rack of oxygen tanks and snapped up the lid. "There's just one thing I can't understand," he said. "I warned you you couldn't get into this rack. And I warned you that without oxygen you'd die. And yet here you are."

Page laughed. "I had some oxygen hid out, Captain. I anticipated something just like that."

Craig lifted one of the tanks from the rack, held it in his arms. "You're a liar, Page," he said calmly. "You didn't have any other oxygen. You didn't need any. A man would die if he went out there without oxygen—die horribly. But you wouldn't—*because you aren't a man!*"

Page stepped swiftly back, but Craig cried out warningly. Page stopped, as if frozen to the floor, his eyes on the oxygen tank. Craig's finger grasped the valve control.

"One move out of you," he warned grimly, "and I'll let you have it. You know what it is, of course. Liquid oxygen, pressure of two hundred atmospheres. Colder than the hinges of space."

Craig grinned ferociously. "A dose of that would play hell with your metabolism, wouldn't it? Tough enough to keep going here in the dome. You Candles have lived out there on the surface too long. You need a lot of energy, and there isn't much energy here. We have to screen it out or we would die ourselves. And there's a damn sight less energy in liquid oxygen. You met your own environment, all right; you even spread that environment pretty wide, but there's a limit to it."

"You'd be talking a different tune," Page declared bitterly, "if it weren't for those space suits."

"Sort of crossed you up, didn't they," said Craig. "We're wearing them because we were tracking down a pal of yours. I think he's in the refrigerator."

"A pal of mine—in a refrigerator?"

"He's the one that came back as Knut," said Craig, "and he turned into Mathilde when he knew we were hunting for him. But he did the job too well. He was almost more Mathilde than he was Candle. So he sneaked into the refrigerator. And he doesn't like it."

Page's shoulders sagged. For a moment his features seemed to blur, then snapped back into rigid lines again.

"The answer is that you do the job too well," said Craig. "Right now you yourself are more Page than Candle, more man than thing of energy."

"We shouldn't have tried it," said Page. "We should have waited until there was someone in your place. You were too frank in your opinion of us. You held none of the amused contempt so many of the others held. I told them they should wait, but a man named Page got caught in a space warp—"

Craig nodded. "I understand. An opportunity you simply couldn't miss. Ordinarily we're pretty hard to get at. You can't fight photocells. But you should strive for more convincing stories. That yarn of yours about capturing Candles—"

"But Page came out for that purpose," insisted the pseudo-Page. "Of course, he would have failed. But, after all, it was poetic justice."

"It was clever of you," Craig said softly. "More clever than you thought. Bringing your sidekicks in here, pretending you had captured them, waiting until we were off our guard."

"Look," said Page, "we know when we are licked. What are you going to do?"

"We'll turn loose the one in the refrigerator," Craig told him. "Then we'll open up the locks and you can go."

"And if we don't want to go?"

"We'd turn loose the liquid oxygen," said Craig. "We have vats of the stuff upstairs. We can close off this room, you know, turn it into a howling hell. You couldn't live through it. You'd starve for energy."

From the kitchen came a hideous uproar, a sound that suggested a roll of barbed wire galloping around a tin roof. The bedlam was punctuated by yelps and howls from Rastus.

Creepy, who had been standing by the lock, started forward, but Craig, never lifting an eye from Page, waved him back.

Down the ramp from the kitchen came a swirling ball of fur, and after it came Rastus, whaling lustily with his broom, the ball of fur separated, became two identical cats, tails five times normal size, backs bristling, eyes glowing with green fury.

"Boss, I jus' got tired of holding Mathilde—" Rastus panted.

"I know," said Craig. "So you chucked her into the refrigerator with the other cat."

"I sho' did," confessed Rastus, "and hell busted loose right underneath my nose."

"All right," snapped Craig. "Now, Page, if you'll tell us which one of those is yours—"

Page spoke sharply and one of the cats melted and flowed. Its outlines blurred and it became a Candle, a tiny, pale-pink Candle.

Mathilde let out one soul-wrenching shriek and fled.

"Page," said Craig, "we've never wanted trouble. If you are willing we'd like to be your friends. Isn't there some way?"

Page shook his head. "No, captain. We're poles apart. I and you have talked here, but we've talked as man to man rather than as a man and a person of my race. Our differences are too great, our minds too far apart."

He hesitated, almost stammering. "You're a good egg, Craig. You should have been a Candle."

"Creepy," said Craig, "open up the lock."

Page turned to go, but Craig called him back. "Just one thing more. A personal favor. Could you tell me what's at the bottom of this?"

"It's hard to explain," said Page. "You see, my friend, it's a matter of culture. That isn't exactly the word, but it's the nearest I can express it in your language.

"Before you came we had a culture, a way of life, a way of thought, that was distinctly our own. We didn't develop the way you developed, we missed this crude, preliminary civilization you are passing through. We started at a point you won't reach for another million years.

"We had a goal, an ideal, a place we were heading for. And we were making progress. I can't explain it, for—well, there just are no words for it. And then you came along—"

"I think I know," said Craig. "We are a disturbing influence. We have upset your culture, your way of thought. Our thoughts intrude upon you and you see your civilization turning into a troupe of mimics, absorbing alien ideas, alien ways."

He stared at Page. "But isn't there a way? Damn it, do we have to fight about this?"

But even as he spoke, he knew there was no way. The long roll of terrestrial history recorded hundreds of such wars as this—wars fought over forms of faith, over terminology of religion, over ideologies, over cultures. And the ones who fought those wars were members of the same race—not members of two races separated by different origins, by different metabolisms, by different minds.

"No," he said, "there is no way. Some day, perhaps, we will be gone. Some day we will find another and a cheaper source of power and you will be left in peace. Until that day—" He left the words unspoken.

Page turned away, headed for the lock, followed by the three big Candles and the little pink one.

Ranged together at the port, the three Terrestrials watched the Candles come out of the lock. Page was still in the form of a man, but as he walked away the form ran together and puddled down until he was a sphere.

Creepy cackled at Craig's elbow. "By cracky," he yelped, "he was a purple one!"

Craig sat at his desk, writing his report to the Solar power board, his pen travelling rapidly over the paper:

—they waited for five hundred years before they acted. Perhaps this was merely caution or in the hope they might find a better way. Or it may be that time has a different value for them than it has for us. In an existence which stretches into eternity, time would have but little value.

For all those five hundred years they have watched and studied us. They have read our minds, absorbed our thoughts, dug out our knowledge, soaked up our personalities. Perhaps they know us better than we know ourselves. Whether their crude mimicry of our thoughts is merely a clever ruse to make us think they are harmless or whether it reflects differing degrees of the art of mimicry—the difference between a cartoon and a masterpiece of painting—I cannot say. I cannot even guess.

Heretofore we have never given thought to protect ourselves against them, for we have considered them, in general, as amusing entities and little else. Whether or not the cat in the refrigerator was the Candle or Mathilde I do not know, but it was the cat in the refrigerator that gave me the idea of using liquid oxygen. Undoubtedly there are better ways. Anything that would swiftly deprive them of energy would serve. Convinced they will try again, even if they have to wait another five hundred years, I urgently suggest—

He stopped and laid down the pen.

From the kitchen below came the faint clatter of pots and pans as Rastus engineered a dinner. Bellowed snatches of unmusical song, sandwiched between the clatter of utensils, floated up the ramp:

"Chicken in de bread pan,
*   Kickin' up de dough—"*

The wastebasket in the corner moved slightly and Mathilde slunk out, tail at half mast. With a look of contempt at Craig, she stalked to the door and down the ramp.

Creepy was tuning up his fiddle, but only half-heartedly. Creepy felt badly about Knut. Despite their checker arguments, the two had been good friends.

Craig considered the things he'd have to do. He'd have to go out and bring in Knut's body, ship it back to Earth for burial. But first he was going to sleep. Lord, how he needed sleep!

He picked up the pen and proceeded with his writing:

—that every effort be bent to the development of some convenient weapon to be used against them. But to be used only in defense. A program of extermination, such as has been carried out on other planets, is unthinkable.

To do this it will be necessary that we study them even as they have studied us. Before we can fight them we must know them. For the next time their method of attack undoubtedly will be different.

Likewise we must develop a test, to be applied to every person before entering the Center, that will reveal whether he is a Candle or a man.

And, lastly, every effort should be made to develop some other source of universal power against the day when Mercury may become inaccessible to us.

He reread the report and put it down.

"They won't like that," he told himself. "Especially that last paragraph. But we have to face the truth."

Rastus' voice rose shrilly. "You, Mathilde! You get out of there! Can't turn my back but you're in that icebox—"

A broom thudded with a whack.

There was no sound from the control room. Creepy apparently had put away his fiddle. Probably didn't have the heart to play it.

For a long time Craig sat at his desk, thinking. Then he arose and went to the port.

Outside, on the bitter plains of Mercury, the Candles had paired off, two and two, were monstrous dice, rolling in the dust. As far as the eye could see, the plains were filled with galloping dominos. And every pair, at every toss, were rolling sevens!

THE END

THE FENCE

Originally published in the September 1952 issue of Space Science Fiction—*only the second issue of that magazine—this story presents several strange, even perverse, concepts, starting with what seems to have been the application of capitalistic principles to hobbies. But it gets really surreal when the protagonist finds himself completely unable to walk in a straight line, and I find myself wondering whether Cliff was asking—in some metaphorical form—where we are going.*

This warped kind of play-world is a strange place to get to, for an author so frequently referred to as the "pastoralist of science fiction." On the other hand, Cliff apparently saw a lot of nonsense in the way that people have come to live in our society.

—dww

He came down the stairway into the hushed sanctuary of the lounge and stood for a moment to allow his eyes to become accustomed to the perpetual twilight of the place.

A robot waiter went past, tall glasses balanced on the tray.

"Good afternoon, Mr. Craig," he said.

"How are you, Herman?" asked Craig.

"Will you wish something, sir?"

"No, thank you," said Craig. "I'm going out directly."

Herman left. Craig crossed the room and he walked almost on tiptoe. He realized now, for the first time, that he almost always walked on tiptoe here. The only noise that ever was allowed was a cough and even then it must be a cough that was most discreet. To have spoken to anyone within the confines of the lounge would have been high treason.

The ticker stood in one corner of the room and, in keeping with the place, it was an almost silent ticker. The tape came out and went into a basket, but the basket was well watched and often emptied and the tape never, never spilled out on the carpet.

He picked up the strand of tape and ran it through his fingers, bending low to read the characters, backing through the alphabet until he came to C and then he went more slowly.

Cox, 108-1/2; Cotton, 97; Colfield, 92; Cratchfield, 111-1/4; Craig, 75 . . .

Craig, 75!

It had been 78 yesterday and 81 the day before and 83 the day before that. A month ago it had been 96-1/2 and a year ago 120.

He stood with the tape in his hand and looked out over the room. The place seemed, at first glance, to be deserted. But as he looked, he saw them. There was a bald head peeking over the back of one chair and over the back of another rose a telltale trail of smoke from an invisible cigar. There was one who sat facing Craig, but he seemed so much a part of the chair that at first he seemed invisible. He sat quietly, with his gleaming black shoes and white shirt front and the folded paper held stiffly before him.

Craig turned his head slowly and saw, with a sinking feeling, that there was someone in his chair, just three removed from the right wing of the fireplace. A month ago it would not have happened, a year ago it would have been unthinkable. His personal satisfaction had been high, then.

But they knew that he was slipping. They had seen the tape and talked about it. And they felt contempt for him despite their mealy mouths.

"Poor Craig," they had said to one another. "Such a decent chap. And so young, too."

They would have been consoling.

"He'll come out of it," they'd said. "It's just temporary."

And they had been quite smug about it, no doubt, sure that it was the sort of thing that would never happen to any one of them.

The counselor was kind and helpful and Craig could see at a glance that he was a man well satisfied and that he liked his work.

"Seventy-five," he said. "That is not good, is it, Mr. Craig?"

"Not, it's not," said Craig.

"You are engaged in something?" asked the counselor and he simpered just a little, a professional, polished simper that said he knew that Craig was, of course, but he had to ask.

"History," said Craig.

"Oh," said the counselor. "A most engaging subject. I have known a number of gentlemen who were quite wrapped up in history."

"I specialize," said Craig. "One acre."

"Acre?" asked the counselor, not a little puzzled. "I'm not quite sure . . ."

"The history of one acre," Craig told him. "Trace it back, you know, with a temporal viewer. Hour to hour, day to day. Record in detail, and with appropriate comment and deduction, everything that transpired upon the acre."

"Most novel," said the counselor. "I've never heard of it before."

"You do some screwy things," said Craig.

"Screwy?"

"Well, you strive for effect. You try to be spectacular, but spectacular in a scholarly way, if you understand."

"Yes, I am sure I do," the counselor said, "and yet it seems to me that the study of one acre of the Earth's surface is quite legitimate. There have been others who have limited their studies.

There have been histories of families and of cities and of certain rather obscure causes and of the development and evolution of such commonplace things as teapots and coffee cups and antimacassars and such like."

"Yes," said Craig, "that is exactly what I thought."

"Tell me, Mr. Craig," asked the counselor, "have you run across anything spectacular on your . . . ah, acre?"

"I have traced the growth of trees," said Craig. "Backwards, you know. From decaying giants to saplings, from saplings to seed. It is quite a trick, this backward tracing. It is a bit confusing, but soon you get used to it. I swear you finally get so that you think in reverse. And then, of course, I have kept a record of birds' nests and the birds themselves. There's one old lame robin that was quite a character. And flowers, naturally. And the action of the elements on boulders and soil. And weather. I have a fine record of the weather over several thousand years."

"Most interesting," said the counselor.

"There was a murder, too," said Craig, "but it happened just outside the boundary line, so I can't actually include it in the study. The murderer, however, did run across the acre after he committed the deed."

"A murder, Mr. Craig?"

"Exactly," said Craig. "One man killed another, you understand."

"How ghastly," said the counselor.

"I suppose it would be," admitted Craig. "But it was done, you know. The records are filled with murders."

"Anything else?"

"Not yet," said Craig, "although I have some hope. I found some old foundations."

"Buildings?"

"Yes, of buildings. Go back far enough and I'm bound to find the buildings before they went to ruin. That might be interesting.

There might be people in them. One of the foundations looked like a residence. Had what appeared to be the footing for a fireplace."

"You might hurry it up a bit," suggested the counselor. "Get there a little faster. People are most interesting."

Craig shook his head. "To make the study valid, I must record in detail. I can't slight the detail to get what's interesting."

The counselor managed to look sorrowful.

"With such an interesting project," he said, "I can't understand why your rating should go down."

"I realized," said Craig, "that no one would care. I would spend years at the study and I would publish my findings and I would give copies to my friends and acquaintances and they would thank me and put the book up on the shelf and never take it down again. I would deposit copies in libraries and you know yourself that no one ever goes to libraries. The only one who would ever read the thing would be myself."

"Surely, Mr. Craig," comforted the counselor, "there are other men who have found themselves in a like position. And they have managed to remain relatively happy and contented."

"That is what I've told myself," said Craig, "but it doesn't work for me."

"We could go into many of the closer aspects of the case," said the counselor, "but I think we should leave that until some future time if it proves necessary. We'll just hit the high points now. Tell me, Mr. Craig, are you fairly well convinced that you cannot continue to be happy with your acre?"

"Yes," said Craig, "I am."

"Not conceding for a moment," said the counselor, with dogged determination, "that your statement to that effect closes our avenue of investigation in that direction, tell me this: Have you considered an alternative?"

"An alternative?"

"Why, certainly. Some other line of work that might prove happier. I have counseled a number of gentlemen who changed their line of work and it has proved for the best."

"No," said Craig. "I haven't the least idea what I might go into."

"There are a number of openings," said the counselor. "Almost anything you wish. There's snail watching, for example."

"No," said Craig.

"Or stamp collecting," said the counselor. "Or knitting. A lot of gentlemen knit and find it very soothing."

"I don't want to knit," said Craig.

"You could make money."

"What for?" asked Craig.

"Well, now," the counselor said, "that is something I've often wondered, too. There's no need of it, really. All you have to do to get money is go to a bank and ask for some of it. But there are men who actually set out to make money and, if you ask me, they use some rather shady methods. But be that as it may, they seem to get a great deal of satisfaction doing it."

"What do they do with it once they get it?" asked Craig.

"I wouldn't know," the counselor told him. "One man buried it and then forgot where he buried it and he remained happy the rest of his life running around with a lantern and a shovel looking for it."

"Why the lantern?"

"Oh, I forgot to tell you that. He never hunted it in daylight. He hunted in the night."

"Did he ever find it?"

"Come to think of it," the counselor said, "I don't believe he did."

"I don't think," said Craig, "that I'd care for making money."

"You might join a club."

"I belong to a club," said Craig. "A very fine old club. One of the very finest. Some of the best names and its history runs back to . . ."

"That's not the kind of club I mean," the counselor said. "I mean a group of persons who work for something or who have special interests in common and band themselves together for the better enjoyment of those mutual interests."

"I doubt," said Craig, "that a club would be the answer."

"You might get married," the counselor suggested.

"What! You mean to one woman?"

"That is what I mean."

"And raise a bunch of kids?"

"Many men have done it," said the counselor. "They have been quite satisfied."

"It seems," said Craig, "on the face of it, just a bit obscene."

"There are many other possibilities," the counselor told him. "I can just run through a partial list of them and see if there is anything you might care to think about."

Craig shook his head. "Some other time," he said. "I'll come back again. I want to mull it over."

"You're absolutely sure that you're sour on history?" asked the counselor. "I'd rather steer you back to that than interest you in an alternative."

"I'm sour on it," said Craig. "I shudder when I think of it."

"You could take a vacation," suggested the counselor. "You could freeze your personal satisfaction rating until you returned. Maybe then you could boost it up again."

"I think," said Craig, "that to start with I'll take a little walk."

"A walk," the counselor told him, "is very often helpful."

"What do I owe you?" Craig asked.

"A hundred," the counselor said. "But it's immaterial to me if you pay or not."

"I know," said Craig. "You work for the love of it."

The man sat on the shore of the little pond and leaned back against a tree. He smoked while he kept an eye on the fishpole stuck into the ground beside him. Close at hand was an unpretentious jug made of earthenware.

He looked up and saw Craig.

"Come on, friend," he said. "Sit down and rest yourself."

Craig came and sat. He pulled out a handkerchief and mopped his brow.

"The sun's a little warm," he said.

"Cool here," said the man. "I fish or loaf around when the sun is high. When the sun goes down I go and hoe my garden."

"Flowers," said Craig. "Now there's an idea. I've often thought it would be fun to raise a garden full of flowers."

"Not flowers," the man said. "Vegetables. I eat them."

"You mean you work to get the things you eat?"

"Uh-huh," said the man. "I spade the ground and rake it to prepare the seed bed. Then I plant the seeds and watch them sprout and grow. I tend the garden and I harvest it. I get enough to eat."

"It must be a lot of work."

"I take it easy," said the man. "I don't let it worry me."

"You could get a robot," Craig told him.

"Yeah, I guess I could. But I don't hold with such contraptions. It would make me nervous."

The cork went under and he made a grab for the pole, but he was too late. The hook came up empty.

"Missed that one," he said placidly. "Miss a lot of them. Don't pay enough attention."

He swung in the hook and baited it with a worm from the can that stood beside him.

"Might have been a turtle," he said. "Turtles are hell on bait."

He swung the tackle out again, stuck the pole back into the ground and settled back against the tree.

"I grow a little extra corn," he said, "and run a batch of moon when my stock is running low. The house ain't much to look at, but it's comfortable. I got a dog and two cats and I fuss my neighbors."

"Fuss your neighbors?"

"Sure," the man said. "They all think that I am nuts."

He picked up the jug, uncorked it and handed it to Craig. Craig took a drink, prepared for the worst. It wasn't bad at all.

"Took a little extra care with that batch," the man said. "It really pays to do that if you have the time."

"Tell me," said Craig, "are you satisfied?"

"Sure," the man said.

"You must have a nice P.S.," said Craig.

"P.X.?"

"No. P.S. Personal satisfaction rating."

The man shook his head. "I ain't got one of them," he said.

Craig was aghast. "But you have to have!"

"You talk just like that other fellow," said the man. "He was around a while ago. Told me about this P.S. business, but I thought he said P.X. Told me I had to have one. Took it awful hard when I said I wouldn't do it."

"Everyone has a P.S.," said Craig.

"Everyone but me," said the man. "That's what the other fellow said, too. He was some upset about it. Practically read me out of the human race."

He looked sharply at Craig. "Son," he said, "you got troubles on your mind."

Craig nodded.

"Lots of folks have troubles," said the man, "only they don't know it. And you can't start to lick your troubles until you see and recognize them. Things are all upset. No one's living right. There is something wrong."

"My P.S. is way off," said Craig. "I've lost all interest. I know there's something wrong. I can sense it, but I can't put my finger on it."

"They get things given to them," said the man. "They could live the life of Riley and not do a tap of work. They could get food and shelter and clothing and all the luxuries that they want by just asking for them. You want money, so you go to a bank and the bank gives you all you need. You go to a shop and buy a thing and the shopkeeper don't give a tinker's damn if you pay or not. Because, you see, it didn't cost him nothing. He got it given to him. He doesn't have to work for a living. He ain't keeping shop, really. He's just playing at it, like kids would play at keeping store. And there's other people who play at all sorts of other things. They do it to keep from dying of boredom. They wouldn't have to do it. And this P.S. business you talk about is just another play-mechanism, a way of keeping score, a sort of social pressure to keep you on your toes when there is no real reason on all of God's green earth that you should be on your toes. It's meant to keep you happy by giving you something to work for. A high P.S. means high social standing and a satisfied ego. It's clever and ingenious, but it's just playing, too."

Craig stared at the man. "A play world," he said. "You've hit it on the head. That's what it really is."

The man chuckled. "You never thought of it before," he said. "That's the trouble. No one ever thinks. Everyone is so busy trying to convince himself that he's happy and important that he never stops to think. Let me tell you this, son: No man ever is important if he tries to make himself important. It's when he forgets that he's important that he really is important.

"Me," he said. "I have lots of time to think."

"I never thought of it," said Craig, "in just that way before."

"We have no economic worth," the man said. "There's not any of us making our own way. There's not a single one of us worth the energy it would take to kill us."

"Except me," he said. "I raise my own eating and I catch some fish and I snare some rabbits and I make a batch of drinking likker whenever I run out."

"I always thought of our way of life," said Craig, "as the final phase in economic development. That's what they teach the kids. Man has finally achieved economic independence. There is no government and there is no economic fabric. You get all you need as a matter of a hereditary right, a common right. You are free to do anything you want to do and you try to live a worthwhile life."

"Son," said the man, "you had breakfast this morning and you had lunch this 'noon before you took your walk. You'll eat dinner tonight and you'll have a drink or two. Tomorrow you'll get a new shirt or a pair of shoes and there will be some equipment that you'll need to carry on your work."

"That's right," said Craig.

"What I want to know," said the man, "is where did all that stuff come from? The shirt or the pair of shoes might have been made by someone who likes to make shirts and shoes. The food was cooked either by robots or by someone who likes to cook, and the drawing set or the typewriter or the power tools that you use might have been made by someone who likes to mess around making stuff like that. But before the typewriter was a typewriter, it was metal in the ground, the food was grown, the clothes came from one of several raw materials. Tell me: who grew the raw materials, who dug and smelted the ore?"

"I don't know," said Craig. "I never thought of that."

"We're *kept*," said the man. "Someone is keeping us. Me, I won't be kept."

He pulled in the tackle and twirled the pole to wrap the line around it.

"Sun is getting down a bit," he said. "I got to go and hoe."

"It was good talking to you," said Craig, getting up.

"Nice path over that way," said the man, pointing. "Good walking. Lots of flowers and it's shaded, so it'll be nice and cool. If you go far enough, you'll reach an art gallery." He looked at Craig. "You're interested in art?"

"Yes," said Craig. "But I didn't know there was a gallery anywhere around."

"Well, there is," said the man. "Good paintings. Some wood statuary that is better than average. A few pieces of good jade. Go there myself when I have the time."

"Well, thanks," said Craig.

"Funny looking building," the man said. "Group of buildings, really. Architect who designed them was crazier than a coot, but don't let it prejudice you. The stuff is really good."

"There's plenty of time," said Craig. "I'll drop in and have a look. Thanks for telling me."

The man got up and dusted off his trousers seat.

"If you're late in getting back," he said, "drop in and spend the night. My shack is just across the way. Plenty of grub and there is room for two to sleep."

"Thank you," said Craig. "I may do it."

He had no intention of accepting the offer.

The man held out his hand. "My name is Sherman," he said. "Glad you came along."

They shook hands.

Sherman went to hoe his garden and Craig walked down the path.

The buildings seemed to be quite close and yet it was hard to make out their lines. It was because of some crazy architectural principle, Craig decided. Sherman had said the architect was crazier than a coot. One time when he looked at them, they looked one way; when he looked again they were different somehow. They were never twice the same.

They were pink until he decided that they weren't pink at all, but were really blue; there were other times when they seemed neither pink nor blue, but a sort of green, although it wasn't really green.

They were beautiful, of course, but it was a disturbing beauty—a brand new sort of beauty. Something, Craig decided, that Sherman's misplaced genius had thought up, although it did seem funny that a place like this could exist without his ever hearing about it. Still, such a thing was understandable when he remembered that everyone was so self-consciously wrapped up in his work that he never paid attention to what anyone else was doing.

There was one way, of course, to find out what it was all about and that was to go and see.

The buildings, he estimated, were no more than a good five minutes' walk across a landscaped meadow that was a thing of beauty in itself.

He started out and walked for fifteen minutes and he did not get there. It seemed, however, that he was viewing the buildings from a slightly different angle, although that was hard to tell, because they refused to stay in place but seemed to be continually shifting and distorting their lines.

It was, of course, no more than an optical illusion.

He started out again.

After another fifteen minutes he was still no closer, although he could have sworn that he had kept his course headed straight toward the buildings.

It was then that he began to feel the panic.

He stood quite still and considered the situation as sanely as he could and decided there was nothing for it but to try again and this time pay strict attention to what he was doing.

He started out, moving slowly, almost counting his steps as he walked, concentrating fiercely upon keeping each step headed in the right direction.

It was then he discovered he was slipping. It appeared that he was going straight ahead but, as a matter of fact, he was slipping sidewise as he walked. It was just as if there were something smooth and slippery in front of him that translated his forward movement into a sidewise movement without his knowing it. Like a fence, a fence that he couldn't see or sense.

He stopped and the panic that had been gnawing at him broke into cold and terrible fear.

Something flickered in front of him. For a moment it seemed that he saw an eye, one single staring eye, looking straight at him.

He stood rigid and the sense of being looked at grew and now it seemed that there were strange shadows on the grass beyond the fence that was invisible. As if someone, or something, that he couldn't see was standing there and looking at him, watching with amusement his efforts to walk through the fence.

He lifted a hand and thrust it out in front of him and there was no fence, but his hand and arm slipped sidewise and did not go forward more than a foot or so.

He felt the kindness, then, the kindness and the pity and the vast superiority.

And he turned and fled.

He hammered on the door and Sherman opened it.

Craig stumbled in and fell into a chair. He looked up at the man he had talked with that afternoon.

"You knew," he said. "You knew and you sent me to find out."

Sherman nodded. "You wouldn't have believed me if I told you."

"What are they?" asked Craig, his words tumbling wildly. "What are they doing there?"

"I don't know what they are," said Sherman.

He walked to the stove and took a lid off a kettle and looked at what was cooking. Whatever it was, it had a hungry smell. Then he walked to the table and took the chimney off an antique oil lamp, struck a match and lit it.

"I go it simple," he said. "No electricity. No nothing. I hope that you don't mind. Rabbit stew for supper."

He looked at Craig across the smoking lamp and in the flickering light it seemed that his head floated in the air, for the glow of the lamp blotted out his body.

"But what are *they*?" demanded Craig. "What kind of fence is that? What are they fenced in for?"

"Son," said Sherman, "they aren't the ones who are fenced in."

"They aren't . . ."

"It's us," said Sherman. "Can't you see it? *We* are the ones who are fenced in."

"You said this afternoon," said Craig, "that we were kept. You mean they're keeping us?"

Sherman nodded. "That's the way I have it figured. They're keeping us, watching over us, taking care of us. There's nothing that we want that we can't have for the simple asking. They're taking real good care of us."

"But why?"

"I don't know," said Sherman.

"A zoo, maybe. A reservation, maybe. A place to preserve the last of a species. They don't mean us any harm."

"I know they don't," said Craig. "I felt them. That's what frightened me."

He sat in the silence of the shack and smelled the cooking rabbit and watched the flicker of the lamp.

"What can we do about it?" he asked.

"That's the thing," said Sherman, "that we have to figure out. Maybe we don't want to do anything at all."

Sherman went to the stove and stirred the rabbit stew.

"You are not the first," he said, "and you will not be the last. There were others before you and there will be others like you who'll come along this way, walking off their troubles."

He put the lid back on the kettle.

"We're watching them," he said, "the best we can. Trying to find out. They can't keep us fooled and caged forever."

Craig sat in his chair, remembering the kindness and the pity and the vast superiority.

RULE 18

After John W. Campbell, Jr.'s appointment, in September 1937, as the new editor of Astounding Science Fiction, Clifford D. Simak—who had published almost no science fiction during the preceding five years—found reason to hope that the field would finally be willing to accept stories of higher quality, stories that earned more for their authors, and stories that portrayed "ordinary people" (rather than scientists and rocket jockeys). His first submission to Campbell was "Rule 18," a story that stretched the boundaries of science fiction by dealing with an interplanetary football game. The story was published in the July 1938 issue, and Cliff was paid $120.

Although the story was written before there were any awards for science fiction writing, in 2014 "Rule 18" was awarded a Retrospective Hugo, certainly an indicator that there are a number of elements in the story that could be deemed worthy of discussion. But let me focus on one thing few have likely thought about—intercollegiate American football.

It was natural, of course, that when Cliff Simak—a son of Wisconsin—needed to portray a good football player in this story, he would choose a Wisconsin player. But few today realize why, in showing that Wisconsin player's great achievements subsequent to the climax of this story, Cliff had that player lead his team in a trouncing of the Golden Gophers of the University of Minnesota. It was more than *the mere fact that Cliff had become a resident of Minnesota—it was because in that era the Gophers were in the midst of an unprecedented dominance of intercollegiate football. In 1937, as Cliff was writing the story, Minnesota's football team was the three-time defending national champion, and it would ultimately win that championship five times during an eight-year span.*

Although he became a fan of Minnesota sports, I suspect Cliff really enjoyed that little touch of Wisconsin.

—dww

Rule XVIII—Each player on the respective teams must be able to present documentary evidence that he is of pure blood of the planet upon whose team he plays for an unbroken span of at least ten generations. Verification of the aforesaid documentary evidence and approval of the players upon this point shall be the duty of the Interplanetary Athletic Control Board— From the eligibility section of the Official Rule Book for the Annual Terrestrial-Martian Football Game.

Year 2479

I

The mighty bowl resounded to the throaty war cry of the Druzecs, ancient tribe of the Martian Drylands. The cry seemed to blast the very dome of the sky. The purple and red of the Martian stands heaved tumultuously as the Martian visitors waved their arms and screamed their victory. The score was 19-0. For the sixty-seventh consecutive year the Martians had defeated the Earth team. And for the forty-second consecutive year the Terrestrial team had failed to score even a single point.

There had been a time when an Earth eleven occasionally did defeat the Red Warriors. But that had been years ago. It was something that oldsters, mumbling in their beards, told about as if it were a legendary tale from the ancient past. Evil days had fallen upon the Gold and Green squads.

And again this year the pick of the entire Earth, the Terrestrial crack football machine, had been trampled underfoot by the smashing forward wall of Martians, slashed to bits by the ferocious attack of the Red Planet backfield.

Not that the Earth had not tried. Every team member had fought a heart-rending game, had put forth every ounce of strength, every shred of football sense, every last trickle of stout courage. Not that the Earth team was not good. It was good. It was the pick of the entire world, an All-Terrestrial eleven, selected on its merits of the preceding year and trained for an entire year under the mentorship of August Snelling, one of the canniest coaches the game had ever known. It was neither of these. It was just that the Martian team was better.

Bands blared. The two teams were trailed off the field. The Martian victory cry continued to rend the skies, rolling in wave after successive wave from leathern throats.

The Earth stands were emptied quietly, but the Martians remained, trumpeting their prowess. When the Martians did leave the amphitheater, they took over the city of New York after the manner of football crowds since time immemorial. They paraded their mascot, the grotesque, ten-legged *zimpa,* through the streets. Some of them got drunk on Martian *bocca,* a potent liquor banned by law from sale on Earth, but always available in hundreds of speakeasies throughout the city. There were a few clashes between Martian and Earth delegations and some of the Martians were jailed. New York would be a bedlam until the Martian Special, a huge space liner chartered for the game, roared out of its cradle at midnight for the return run to Mars.

* * *

In the editorial rooms of the *Evening Rocket* Hap Folsworth, sports-writer extraordinary, explained it in a blur of submerged rage and admitted futility.

"They just don't grow them big enough or strong enough on Earth anymore," he declared. "We are living too damn easy. We're getting soft. Each generation is just a bit softer than the last. There's no more hard work to be done. Machines do things for us. Machines mine ores, raise crops, manufacture everything from rocket ships to safety pins. All we got to do is push levers and punch buttons. A hell of a lot of muscle you can develop punching a button.

"Where did they get the famous players of the past? Of a couple, three hundred years ago, or of a thousand years ago, if you like?" Hap blared. "I'll tell you where they got them! They got them out of mines and lumber camps and off the farms—places where you had to have guts and brawn to make a living.

"But we got smart. We fixed it so nobody has to work anymore. There are husky Earth lads, lots of them—in Martian mining camps and in Venus lumber camps and out on Ganymede engineering projects. But every damn one of them has got Martian or Venusian blood in his veins. And Rule Eighteen says you got to be lily-pure for ten generations. If you ask me, that's a hell of a rule."

Hap looked around to see how his audience was taking his talk. All of them seemed to be in agreement and he went on. What he was saying wasn't new. It had been said thousands of times by thousands of sports-writers in thousands of different ways, but Hap recited it after each game. He enjoyed doing it. He chewed off the end of a Venus-weed cigar and went on.

"The Martians aren't soft. Their planet is too old and exhausted and nature-ornery for them to be soft. They got brawn and guts and their coaches somehow manage to pound some football sense into their thick heads. Why, football is just their meat—even if we did teach them the game."

He lit his cigar and puffed contentedly.

"Say," he asked as the others stood in respectful silence, "has anyone seen Russell today?"

They shook their heads.

The sports-writer considered the answer and then said, without emotion, "When he does show up, I'm going to boot him right smack-dab into the stratosphere. I sent him out two days ago to get an interview with Coach Snelling and he hasn't showed up yet."

"He'll probably be around next week," suggested a copyboy. "He's probably just sleeping one off somewhere."

"Sure, I know," mourned Hap, "and when he does come in, he'll drag in a story so big the chief will kiss him for remembering us."

Coach August Snelling delivered his annual after-the-Martian-game oration to his team.

"When you went out on the field today," he told them, "I praised you and pleaded with you to get out there and do some of the things I taught you to do. And what did you do? You went out there and you laid down on me. You laid down on the Earth. You laid down on five hundred thousand people in the stands who paid good hard cash to see a football game. You let those big dumbbells push you all over the lot. You had a dozen good plays, every one of them good for ground. And did you use them? You did not!

"You're a bunch of lollipops. A good punch in the ribs and you roll over and bark. Maybe there'll be some of you on the team next year and maybe there won't. But if there are, I want you to remember that when we go up to Mars I intend to bring back that trophy if I have to steal it. And if I don't, I'll stop the ship midway and dump you all out. And then jump out myself."

But this didn't mean much. For Coach Snelling, ace of the Earth coaches, had said the same thing, in substance, to Earth teams after each Martian game for the last twenty years.

* * *

Tantalizing shadows, queer, alien shadows flitted in the ground glass of the outré machine. Alexis Androvitch held his breath and watched. The shadows took form, then faded, but they had held tangible shape long enough for Alexis to glimpse what he wished to see, a glimpse that filled him with a supreme sense of triumph.

The first step was completed. The second would be harder, but now that the first was accomplished—now that he really had some proof of his theories—progress would be faster.

Alexis snapped off the machine and stepped to a bowl. There he washed his hands. Shrugging into a coat, he opened the door and trudged up the steps to the street above.

On the avenue he was greeted by the raucous cries of the auto-newsstands, "Earth loses 19-0 . . . Read all about it . . . Extra . . . Extra . . ." repeating over and over the words recorded on the sound film within them.

Customers placed coins in the slot, shoved a lever, and out came a paper with huge purple headlines and natural-color photo reproductions of the game.

The vari-colored neon street lamps flicked on. Smoothly operating street machines slid swiftly down the broad, glassy pavement. Overhead purred the air-lane traffic.

From somewhere came the muffled sound of the Drylands war cry as the Martians continued their celebration of victory.

Alexis Androvitch walked on, unmindful of the war cries, of the blaring newsstands. He was not interested in athletics. He was on his way to a garden to enjoy a glass of beer and a plate of cheese.

Rush Culver, Wisconsin '45, was struggling with calculus. Exams stared him in the face and Rush freely admitted that he was a fool for having chosen math instead of zoology. Somehow or other he wasn't so bright at figures.

It was late. The other fellows in the house were asleep hours ago. A white moon painted the windows of the house opposite in delicate silver squares and rectangles. A night wind sighed softly in the elms outside. A car raced up State Street and the old clock in the music hall tower tolled out the hour with steady beat of bell.

Rush mopped his brow and dug deeper into his book.

He failed to hear the door of his room open softly and close again. He did not turn about until he heard the scuff of feet on the floor.

A tall stranger stood in the room.

Rush looked at him with something of disgust. He was dressed in purple shorts and a semi-metallic shirt that flashed and glinted in the soft rays of the desk lamp. His feet were shod in sandals. His head was verging on the bald and his face was pale, almost as if he had resorted to face powder.

"Just home from a masquerade?" asked Rush.

The stranger did not answer at once, but stood silently, looking at the student.

When he did speak, his voice was soft and slurred and his English carried an accent Rush could not place.

"You will pardon the intrusion," the stranger said. "I did not wish to disturb you. I merely wanted to know if you are Rush Culver, fullback for the Wisconsin football team."

"I have a good mind to lay one on you," said Rush with feeling. "Almost three o'clock in the morning and me wrestling with math. Want to know if I'm Rush Culver. Want my autograph, maybe?"

The stranger smiled. "I hardly understand," he said. "I know nothing of autographs. But you are having trouble. Maybe I can help."

"If you can, brother," declared Rush, "I'll lend you some clothes so you can get home without being pinched. The cops in this town are tough on students."

The stranger walked forward, picked up the book, glanced at it and threw it aside. "Simple," he said. "Elementary. This problem."

He bent over and ran a finger down the work sheet. His words came softly, in measured cadence.

"It is this way . . . and this way . . . and this way—"

Rush stared. "Say, it's simple," he chortled. "But it never was explained to me that way before. I can see how it goes now."

He rose from the chair and confronted the stranger.

"Who are you?" he asked.

II

Hap Folsworth snarled through his cigar at Jimmy Russell.

"So you came back empty-handed," he growled. "You, the demon reporter for the *Evening Rocket*. In the name of double-dipped damnation, can't you ever do anything? I send you out on a simple errand. 'Just run over to Coach Snelling,' says I, 'and get the line-up for the Earth team'. Any office boy could do that. And you come back without it. All you had to do was ask the coach for it and he would hand it to you."

Jimmy snarled back. "Why, you space-locoed tramp," he roared, "if it's as simple as that, go down and get it yourself. If you ever lifted yourself out of that easy chair and found out what was happening, instead of sitting there thinking up wise-cracks, you might call yourself a newspaperman. I could have told you a week ago there was something screwy about this Earth team. All sorts of rumors floating around. How much news have we printed about it? How much has *Morning Space-Ways* and the *Evening Star* printed about it? But you sit here and look wise and tell the world that Snelling is just using some high-powered psychology to get the Martians' goat. Making it appear he has some new material or some new plays. Say, that old buzzard hasn't had a new play since the first spaceship blew up."

Hap snorted and rescued the cigar. He jabbed a vicious fore-finger at the reporter.

"Listen," he yelled. "I was a newsman when you were still in diapers. I'll lay you five to one I can call up Snelling and have him agree to give us a list of players."

Silently Jimmy picked up the visaphone set and handed it to Hap.

The sports-writer set the dial for the field-house wave length. A face appeared in the glass.

"Let me speak to the coach," said Hap.

The glass went dead as the connection was shifted

The face of Coach Snelling appeared.

"—Say, coach. . . ," said Hap. But that was as far as he got.

"Listen, Hap," said the coach, "I'm a friend of yours. I like you. You've said some nice things about me when the wolves were out after my hide. If I had anything to tell anyone, I'd tell it to the *Evening Rocket*. But I haven't anything to tell anyone. I want you fellows to understand that. And if you send any more of those high-powered reporters of yours around I'll just naturally kick them out on their faces. That's a promise."

The phone went dead.

Jimmy laughed at the bewildered stare in Hap's eyes.

"Pay up," he demanded.

The coach's office was empty and Jimmy was glad of that. It fitted in with his plans.

He hadn't liked the nasty light in the chief's eyes when he had been told to get a list of the Earth's new team. Nothing about *how* he was to get it. No suggestions at all, although it was understood that it couldn't be gotten directly from the coach. Presumably some other means of obtaining it would have to be worked out.

But while the chief had said nothing about how to get it, he had said plenty about what would happen if he returned without it. That was the way with editors, Jimmy reflected glumly. No gratitude. Just a hunk of ice for a heart. Who was it had given the *Rocket* a scoop on the huge gambling syndicate which had tried to buy a victory for the Earth team? Who was it had broken the yarn about the famous jewel-ship robbery off the orbit of Callisto when a governmental clique—which later went to the Moon penal colony—had moved Heaven and Earth to suppress the story? Who had phoned the first flash and later written an eye-witness story that boosted circulation over 6,000 copies concerning the gang murder of Danny Carsten? No one other than James Russell, reporter for the *Evening Rocket*. And yet, here he was, chasing a team list with sulphurous threats hanging over his head if he failed.

Jimmy tiptoed into the coach's office. He wasn't used to getting his news this way and it made him nervous.

There were papers on the desk. Jimmy eyed them furtively. Maybe among them was the list he sought. With a quick glance about the room, he slithered to the desk. Rapidly he pawed through the papers.

A footstep sounded outside.

Moving quickly, the reporter sought refuge behind a steel locker than stood in one corner of the room. It was an instinctive move, born of surprise, but Jimmy, chuckling to himself, realized he had gained an advantageous position. From his hiding place, he might learn where the list was kept.

Coach Snelling strode into the room. Looking neither to right nor left, he walked straight ahead.

In the center of the room he disappeared.

The reporter rubbed his eyes. Snelling had disappeared. There was no question about that, but where had he gone? Jimmy looked about the room. There was no one there.

Slowly he eased himself from behind the locker. No one hailed him.

He walked to the center of the room. The coach had disappeared at just about that point. There seemed to be nothing unusual in sight. Standing in one spot, Jimmy slowly wheeled in a circle. Then he stopped, stock-still, frozen with astonishment.

Before him, materializing out of nothing, was a faintly outlined circular opening, large enough for a man to walk through. It looked like a tunnel, angling slightly downward from the floor level. It was into this that Coach Snelling must have walked a few moments before.

With misgivings as to the wiseness of his course, Jimmy stepped into the mouth of the tunnel. Nothing happened. He walked a few steps and stopped. Glancing back over his shoulder he could see nothing but the blurred mouth of the tunnel behind him. He reached out his hands and they encountered the walls of the tunnel, walls that were hard and icy-cold.

Cautiously he moved down the tunnel, half-crouched, on the alert for danger. Within a few steps he saw another mouth to the tunnel ahead of him, only faintly outlined, giving no hint into what it might open.

Momentarily he hesitated and then plunged forward.

He stood gaping at the scene before him. He stood in a wilderness, and in this wilderness, directly in front of him, was a football gridiron. Upon the field were players, garbed in Gold and Green uniforms, the mystery team of the Earth. On all sides of the field towered tall, gnarled oaks. Through a vista he could see a small river and beyond it blue hills fading into an indistinct horizon.

At the farther end of the field stood several tents, apparently of skins, with rudely symbolic figures painted upon them in red and yellow. Pale smoke curled up from fires in front of the tents and even where he stood Jimmy caught the acrid scent of burning wood.

Coach Snelling was striding across the field toward him and behind him trailed several copper-colored men dressed in fringed deerskin ornamented with claws and tiny bones. One of them wore a headdress of feathers.

Jimmy had never seen an Indian. The race had died out years before. But he had seen pictures of them in historical books dealing with the early American scene. There was no doubt in his mind that he was looking upon members of the aboriginal tribes of North America.

But the coach was close now.

Jimmy mustered a smile. "Nice hideout you have here, coach," he said. "Nice little place for the boys to practice without being disturbed. That tunnel had me fooled for a while."

Coach Snelling did not return the smile. Jimmy could see the coach wasn't overjoyed at seeing him.

"So you like the place?" asked the coach.

"Sure, it's a fine place," agreed Jimmy, feeling he was getting nowhere with this line of talk.

"How would you like to spend a few weeks here?" asked the coach, unsmilingly.

"Couldn't do it," said Jimmy. "The chief expects me back in a little while."

Two of the brawny Indians moved forward, laid heavy hands on the reporter's shoulders.

"You're staying," said the coach, "until after the game."

Hap Folsworth stepped up to the editor's desk.

"Say," he demanded, "did you send Russell out to get the team line-up?"

The editor looked up. "Sure I did, just as you asked me to. Isn't that petrified newshound back yet?"

The sports-writer almost foamed at the mouth. "Back yet!" he stormed. "Don't you know he never gets back on time? Maybe he won't get back at all. I hear the coach is out after his blood."

"What's the matter with the coach?"

"Russell asked him if he was going to use the same three plays this year he has used for the last ten," explained Hap.

"I don't know what I can do," said the editor. "I might send one of the other boys down."

Hap snorted. "Mister," he said, "if Russell can't get the story, none of your other men can. He's the best damn reporter this sheet has ever had. But someday I'm going to kick his ribs in just to ease my feelings."

The editor rustled papers and grumbled.

"So he's at it again," he mused. "Just wait until I get hold of that booze-soaked genius. I'll pickle him in a jar of *bocca* and sell him to a museum. So help me, Hannah, if I don't."

III

Something was holding up the game. The largest football crowd ever to pack the stadium at the Martian city of Guja Tant rumbled and roared its displeasure.

The Martian team already was on the field, but the Earth team had not made its appearance.

The game would have to start soon, for it must be finished by sundown. The Terrestrial visitors, otherwise, would suffer severely from the sudden chill of Martian twilight, for although the great enclosed stadium held an atmosphere under a pressure which struck a happy medium between air density on Earth and Mars, thus affording no advantage to either team, it was not equipped with heating units and the cold of the Martian night struck quickly and fiercely.

A rumor ran through the crowd.

"Something is wrong with the Earth team. Rule Eighteen. The Board of Control is holding a conference."

A disgruntled fan grumbled.

"I knew there was something wrong when the members of the Earth team were never announced. This stuff the newspapers have been writing about a new mystery team must be right. I just thought it was some of Snelling's work, trying to scare the Martians."

His neighbor grumbled back.

"Snelling is smart all right. But psychology won't win this ball game. He'd better have something to show us today after all that's been written about the team."

The Martian stands shouted wild battle cries of the olden days as the Red Warriors went through their preliminary practice on the gridiron.

About the stadium lay the colorful Martian city with its weird architecture and its subtle color blending. Beyond the city stretched the red plains, spotted here and there with the purple of occasional desert groves. The sun shone but dimly, as it always shone on the fourth planet.

"Here they come," someone shouted.

The crowd took up the roar as the Earth team trotted out on the field, running in a long line, to swing into separate squads for the warming up period.

The roar rose and swelled, broke, ebbed lower and lower, until silence reigned over the stands.

A whistle shrilled. The officials walked out on the field. The two teams gathered. A coin flashed in the feeble sunlight. The Earth captain spoke to the referee and jerked his thumb at the north goal. The Earth team took the ball. The teams spread out.

Earth was on the defensive.

A toe smacked against the ball. The oval rose high into the air, spinning slowly. The Red Warriors thundered down the field. A Martian player cupped his arms, snared the ball.

The teams met in a swirl of action.

Players toppled, rolled on the ground. Like a streak of greased lightning, an Earth player cut in, flattened out in a low dive. His arms caught the ball carrier below the knees. The impact of the fall could be heard in the stands.

The teams lined up. The Martians thundered a bloodthirsty cry. The ball was snapped. Like a steel wall the Earth team rose up, smacked the Martian line flat. The backfield went around the ends like thundering rockets. The carrier was caught flat-footed. Mars lost three yards on the play.

The Terrestrial fans leaped to their feet and screamed.

The teams were ready again. The ball came back. It was an end play, a twister, a puzzler. But the Earth team worked like a well-oiled machine. The runner was forced out of bounds. Mars made two yards.

Third down and eleven to go. In two tries the Red Warriors advanced the oval but five yards. Sports-writers later devoted long columns to the peculiar psychology which prevented the Martians from kicking. Perhaps, as Hap Folsworth pointed out, they were overconfident, figured that even on fourth down they could advance the ball the necessary yardage. Perhaps, as another said, they were too stunned by the Earth defense.

The ball went to the Gold and Green.

The team shifted. The ball went back from center. Again there was a swirl of players—sudden confusion which crystallized into an ordered pattern as an Earth ball carrier swung around right end, protected by a line of interference that mowed down the charging Martians. When the Terrestrial was brought down the ball rested on the Mars' twenty-yard line.

Signals. Shift. The ball was snapped. Weaving like a destroyer in heavy seas, a Green and Gold man, ball hugged to him, plowed into the center of the line. His team-mates opened the way for him, and even when he struck the secondary he still kept moving, plowing ahead with pistonlike motion of his driving legs until he was hauled down by superior strength.

The ball was only two yards from the final stripe. For the first time in many years the Red Warriors were backed against their own goal line.

The Druzec war cry thundered from the Martian stands, but the Earth fans sat dumbfounded.

No one could explain the next play. Maybe there was nothing to explain about it. Perhaps the Terrestrials simply charged in and by sheer force pushed the entire Martian line back for the necessary two yards. That was the way it looked.

An official raised his arms. The gigantic scoreboard clicked. Earth had scored!

The Earth stands went insane. Men and women jumped to their feet and howled their delight. The stadium shook to foot-stamping.

And throughout the entire game the Earth side of the stadium was a mad pandemonium as score after score was piled up while the Terrestrial eleven systematically ripped the Martian team apart for yard after consistent yard of ground.

The final count was 65-0 and the Earth fans, weak with triumph, came back to the realization that for four long quarters they had lived in a catapulting, rocketing, unreal world of delirious joy. For four long quarters they had made of the stadium a bedlam, a crazy, weaving, babbling, brass-tongued bedlam.

In the Martian stands sounded the long wail of lament, the death dirge of the ancient Druzecs, a lament that had not been intoned over an Earth-Mars football game for more than three-score years.

That night the Terrestrials took Guja Tant apart, such as is the right and custom of every victorious football delegation. And while the Martians may accept defeat in a philosophical manner, those who participated in the kidnapping will tell one they objected forcefully when the mascot *zimpa*—which had paraded in honor of many a Martian victory—was taken from his stable and placed on board the Earth liner chartered for the football run.

Hap Folsworth, who had covered the game for the *Evening Rocket,* explained it to Sims of the *Star* and Bradley of the *Express.*

"It's just a lot of star-dust," he said. "Some of Snelling's psychology. He got a bunch of big boys and he kept them under cover, taught them a lot of new tricks and built them up as a mystery team. Them Red Warriors were scared to death before they ever faced our fellows. Psychology won that game, you mark my word—"

Sims of the *Star* interrupted. "Did you get a good look at any of the boys on our team?" he asked.

"Why, no, I didn't," admitted Hap. "Of course, I saw them out there on the field from where I was in the press section, but I didn't meet any of them face to face. The coach barred us from the dressing rooms, even after the game. That's a hell of a ways to go to win a ball game, but if he can win them that way I'm all for him."

He puffed on a Venus-weed cigar. "But you mark my word. It was the old psychology that turned the trick." He stopped and looked at his two fellow sports-writers.

"Say," exploded Hap. "I don't think you fellows believe what I am saying."

They didn't speak, but Hap looked at their faces again and was certain they didn't believe him.

Arthur Hart, editor of the *Evening Rocket,* looked up as the door opened.

Framed in the doorway was Jimmy Russell. Just behind him stood a copper-colored man, naked except for a loin-cloth.

The editor stared.

Men in the city room whirled around from their desks and wondered what it was all about.

"I have returned," said Jimmy and the editor emitted a strangled yelp that knifed through the silence in the room.

The reporter walked into the room, dragging his companion after him.

"Tone down your voice," he said, "or you'll frighten my friend. He has seen enough in the last hour to unnerve him for a lifetime."

"Who the hell you got there?" roared Hart.

"This gentleman," said Jimmy, "is Chief Hiawatha. I can't pronounce his name, so I call him Hiawatha. He lived somewhere around here three, four thousand years ago."

"This isn't a masquerade," snapped the editor. "This is a newspaper office."

"Sure and I work here and I'm bringing you a story that will knock your hat off."

"You don't mean to tell me you're bringing in the story I sent you out to get two weeks ago?" Hart purred, and his purr had an edge on it. "You don't mean to tell me you're back already with that story."

"The very same story," agreed Jimmy.

"Too bad," said the editor, "but the game's over. It was over two hours ago. Earth won by a big score. I suppose you were too drunk to find that out."

"Nothing to drink where I come from," Jimmy told him.

"How you must have hated it," said Hart.

"Now listen," said Jimmy, "do you want to get the inside story on this Earth team or don't you? I got it. And it's a big story. No wonder Earth won. Do you know that those Earth players were picked from the *best football players Earth has produced during the last 1800 years?* Why, Mars didn't have a chance!"

"Of course, they didn't have a chance," growled Hart. "Folsworth explained all that in his story. They were licked before they started. Psychology. What's this yap about the pick of Earth teams for the past 1800 years?"

"Give me five minutes," pleaded Jimmy, "and if you aren't yelling yourself hoarse at the end of that time, I'll admit you're a good editor."

"All right," snapped the editor, "sit down and loosen up. And you better be good or I'll fire you right out on your ear."

"Now, Hiawatha," said Jimmy, addressing his companion, "you sit right down in this chair. It won't hurt you. It's a thing you rest yourself in."

The Indian merely stared at him.

"He don't understand me very good yet," explained Jimmy, "but he thinks I'm a god of some sort and he does the best he can."

Hart snorted in disgust.

"Don't snort," cautioned the reporter. "The poor misguided savage probably thinks you're a god, too."

"Get going," snarled Hart.

Jimmy seated himself on the edge of the desk. The Indian drew himself up to his full height and folded his arms across his chest. The newsmen in the room had left their desks and were crowding about.

"You see before you," said Jimmy, "a wild Indian, one of the aborigines of this continent. He lived here before the white men ever set foot on this land. I brought him along to show you I got the right dope."

"What's all this got to do with the game?" persisted the editor.

"Plenty. Now you listen. You don't believe in Time travel. Neither did I until just a few days ago. There are thousands like you. Ships bridging the millions of miles of space between planets are commonplace now. Transmutation of metal is a matter of fact. Yet less than 1500 years ago people believed these things were impossible. Still, you—in this advanced age which has proven the impossible to be possible time and time again—scout the theory of Time travel along a fourth dimension. You even doubt that Time is a fourth dimension, or that there is such a thing possible as a fourth dimension.

"Now, just keep your shirt on!

"Nobody believes in Time travel. Let's state that as a fact. Nobody but a few fool scientists who should be turning their time and effort toward something else. Something that will spell profit, or speed up production, or make the people happier, or send space liners shooting along faster so that the Earth-Mars run can be made in just a few less minutes.

"And let me tell you that one of those fool scientists succeeded and he built a Time tunnel. I don't know what he calls it, but that describes it pretty well. I stumbled onto this thing and from what the coach told me, and what the players told, and from what the Indians tried to tell me, and from my own observations, I've got the thing all doped out. Don't ask me how the scientist made the tunnel. I don't have the least idea. I probably wouldn't understand if I met the man who made it face to face and he told me how he did it.

"Here's how the Earth team beat the Martians. The coach knew he didn't have a chance. He knew that he was in for another licking. The Earth is degenerating. Its men are getting soft. They don't measure up to the Martians. The coach looked back at the Earth players of former years and he wished he could get a few of them."

"So," said the editor, "I suppose he got this Time-tunnel of yours and went back and handpicked them."

"That's exactly what he did," declared Jimmy. "He went over the records and he picked out the men he wanted. Then he sent his scouts back in Time and contracted them to play. He collected the whole bunch as near as I can make it out, and then he established a Time tunnel leading from his office into the past about 3,000 years and took the whole gang back there. He constructed a playing field there, and he drilled men who had been dead for hundreds of years in a wilderness which existed hundreds of years before they were born. The men who played out in the Great Bowl at Guja Tant today were men who had played football before the first spaceship took to the void. Some of them have been dead for over a thousand years.

"That's what the squabble on the Control Board was about. That's what held up the game—while the Board tried to dig up something that would bar these men out of Time. But they couldn't, for the only rules of eligibility are that a man must be of unmixed Earth blood for the past ten generations and must be a football player on some college or university. And every one of those men were just that."

Hart's eyes were stony and the reporter, looking at them, knew what to expect.

"So you would like to sit down at your old desk and write that story," he said.

"Why not?" snarled Jimmy, ready for a battle.

"And you would like me to put it on the front page, with big green headlines, and put out an extra edition and make a big name for the *Rocket*," Hart went on.

Jimmy said nothing. He knew nothing he could say would help.

"And you would like to make a damn fool out of me and a joke out of the *Rocket* and set in motion an athletic investigation that would have Earth and Mars on their ears for the next couple of years."

The reporter turned to the Indian.

"Hiawatha," he said, "the big square-head doesn't believe us. He ought to be back burning witches at the stake. He thinks we just thought this one up."

The Indian remained unmoved.

"Will you get the hell out of here," snapped Hart, "and take your friend along."

IV

The soft, but insistent whirring of the night phone beside his bed brought the editor of the *Rocket* out of a sound sleep. He did not take kindly to night calls and when he saw the face of one of his reporters in the visaglass he growled savagely.

"What are you waking me up for?" he asked. "You say there are fires out in the Great Bowl—Say, do you have to call me out of bed every time a fire breaks out? Do you want me to run down there and get the story—? You want to know should we shoot out an extra in the morning? Say, do we put out extras every time somebody builds a bonfire, even if it is in the Great Bowl? Probably just some drunks celebrating the victory while they're waiting for the football special to come in."

He listened as words tumbled out of the phone.

"What's that," he shouted. "Indians?. . . . Holding a war dance! How many of them?. . . . You say they are coming out of the administration building?. . . . More coming all the time, eh!"

Hart was out of bed now.

"Listen, Bob, are you certain they are Indians?. . . . Bill says they are, huh? Would Bill know an Indian if he saw one?. . . . He wasn't around this afternoon when Jim was in, was he? He didn't see that freak Jim hauled in, did he?. . . . if he's playing a joke, I'll crack his neck.

"Listen, Bob, you get hold of Jim . . . Yes, I know he's fired, but he'll be glad to come back again. Maybe there's something to that yarn of his. Call all the speakies and gambling joints in town. Get him if you have to arrest him. I'm coming down right away."

Hart hauled on his clothes, grabbed a cloak and hurried to his garage, where his small service plane was stored.

A few minutes later he stamped into the *Rocket* editorial rooms.

Bob was there.

"Find Jim?" asked Hart.

"Sure, I found him."

"What dump is he holed up in?"

"He isn't in any dump. He's out at the Bowl with the Indians. He's got hold of a half barrel of *bocca* someplace and those savages are getting ripe to tear up the place. How the Martians drink that *bocca* is beyond me. Imagine an Indian, who has never tasted alcohol, pouring it down his throat!"

"But what did Jim say—"

"Bill got hold of him, but he won't do a thing for us. Said you insulted him."

"I can imagine what he said," grated Hart. "You get Bill in here as fast as you can. Have him write a story about the Indians out at the Bowl. Call some of the other boys. Send one of them to wait for the football special and nail the coach as soon as it lands. Better have a bunch of the boys there and get interviews from the Earth players. The life story of each one of them. Shoot the works. Photographers, too. Pictures—I want hundreds of them. Find out who's been monkeying around with Time traveling and put them on the spot. Call somebody on the Control Board. See what they have to say. Get hold of the Martian coach. I'm going out to the Bowl and drag Jim back here."

The door banged behind him and Bob grabbed for the phone.

A huge crowd had gathered at the Bowl. In the center of the amphitheater, on the carefully kept and tended gridiron sod, a huge bonfire blazed. Hart saw that one of the goal posts had been torn down to feed it and that piles of broken boxes were on the ground beside the fire. About the blaze leaped barbaric figures, chanting—figures snatched out of the legendry of the country's beginnings, etched against the leaping flames of the bonfire.

A murmur rose from the crowd. Hart glanced behind him.

Streaming into the Bowl came a squad of police, mounted on motor-bikes. As the squad entered the Bowl they turned on the shrill blasting of the police sirens and charged full down upon the dancing figures around the fire.

Pandemonium reigned. The crowd that had gathered to watch the Indian dance scented new excitement and attempted to out-scream the sirens.

The dance halted and Hart saw the Indians draw together for a single instant, then break and run, not away from the police, but straight toward them. One savage lifted his arm. There was a glint of polished stone in the firelight as he threw the war-axe.

The weapon described an arc, descended upon the head of a mounted policeman. Policeman and bike went over in a flurry of arms, legs and spinning wheels.

Above the din rose the terrible cry of the war whoop.

Hart saw a white man leaping ahead of the Indians, shouting at them. It was Jimmy Russell. Mad with *bocca,* probably.

"Jimmy," shrieked Hart. "Come back here, Jimmy. You fool, come back."

But Jimmy didn't hear. He was shouting at the Indians, urging them to follow him, straight through the charging police line, toward the administration building.

They followed him.

It was all over in a moment.

The Indians and the police met, the police swerving their machines to avoid running down the men they had been sent out to awe into submission. Then the Indians were in the clear and running swiftly after the white man who was their friend. Before the police squad could turn their charging bikes, the red-men had reached the administration building, disappeared within it.

Behind them ran Hart, his cloak whipping in the wind.

"Jimmy," he shrieked. "Jimmy, damn you, come back here. Everything's all right. I'll raise your salary."

He stumbled and fell, and as he fell the police roared past him, headed for the door through which the Indians and Jimmy had disappeared.

Hart picked himself up and stumbled on. He was met at the door of the building by a police lieutenant who knew him.

"Can't understand it," he shouted. "There isn't a sign of them. They disappeared."

"They're in the tunnel," shouted Hart. "They've gone back 3,000 years."

The editor pushed the lieutenant to one side. But as he set foot in the building there was a dull thud, like a far-away explosion.

When he reached the coach's office he found it in ruins. The door had burst outward. The steel plates were buckled as if by a tremendous force. The furniture was upset and twisted.

Something had happened.

Hart was right. Something had happened to the Time-tunnel. It had been wiped out of existence.

Alexis Androvitch spoke with a queer quirk in his voice, a half-stuttering guttural.

"But how was I to know that a foolish newspaper reporter would go down the Time-tunnel?" he demanded. "How was I to know something would happen? What do I care for newspapers? What do I care for football games? I'll tell you. I care nothing for them. I care only for science. I do not even want to use this Time traveling personally. It would be nice to see the future, oh, yes, that would be nice—but I haven't the time. I have more work to do. I have solved Time travel. Now I care no more about it. Pouf! It is something done and finished. Now I move on. I lose interest in the possible. It is always the impossible that challenges me. I do not rest until I eliminate the impossible."

Arthur Hart thumped the desk.

"But if you did not care about football, why did you help out Coach Snelling? Why turn over the facilities of a great discovery to an athletic coach?"

Androvitch leaned over the desk and leered at the editor.

"So you would like to know that? You would ask me that question. Well, I will tell you. Gentlemen came to me, not the coach, but other gentlemen. A gentleman by the name of Danny Carsten and others. Yes, the gangsters. Danny Carsten was killed later, but I do not care about that. I care for nothing but science."

"Did you know who these men were when they came to you?" asked Hart.

"Certainly I knew. They told me who they were. They were very businesslike about it. They said they had heard about me working on Time travel and they asked when I thought I would have it finished. I told them I already had solved the problem and then they spread money on the table—much money, more than I had ever seen before. So I said to them: 'Gentlemen, what can I do for you?' and they told me. They were frank about it. They said they wanted to win much money by betting on the game. They said they wanted me to help them get a team which would win the game. So I agreed."

Hart leaped to his feet.

"Great galloping Jupiter," he yelled. "Snelling mixed up with gangsters!"

Androvitch shook his head.

"Snelling did not know he was dealing with gangsters. Others went to him and talked to him about using the Time travel method. Others he thought were his friends."

"But, man," said Hart, "you aren't going to tell all this when you are called before the athletic Board of Control? There'll be an investigation that will go through the whole thing with a fine tooth comb and you'll knock Coach Snelling out of the football picture if you open your mouth about gangsters being mixed up in this."

The scientist shook his head. "Why should I care one way or the other. Human fortunes mean little. Progress of the race is the only thing worth while. I have nothing to hide. I sold the use of my discovery for money I needed to embark upon other researches. Why should I lie? If I tell the truth, maybe they will let me leave as soon as my story is told. I can't waste time at investigations. I have work to do, important work."

"Have it your way," said Hart, "but the thing I came here for was to see you about Jimmy Russell. Is there any way I can reach him? Do you know what happened?"

"Something happened to the Time-control machine which was in Coach Snelling's office. It operated at all times to keep the tunnel open. It required a lot of power and we had it hooked on a high-voltage circuit. I would guess that one of the Indians, becoming frightened in the office, probably even in a drunken stupor, blundered into the machine. He more than likely tipped it over and short-circuited it. I understand fragments of human body were found in the office. Just why the tunnel or the machine should have exploded, I don't know. Electricity—just plain old electricity—was the key to the whole discovery. But probably I had set up some other type of force—let's call it a Time-force if you want to be melodramatic about it—and this force might have been responsible. There's still a lot to learn. And a lot of times a man accomplishes results which he does not suspect."

"But what about Jimmy?"

"I'm pretty busy right now," replied Androvitch. "I couldn't possibly do anything for a few days—"

"Is there anyone else who could do the work?" asked Hart.

Androvitch shook his head. "No other person," he said. "I do not confide in others. Once a Time-tunnel has been established, it is easy to operate the machine—that is, projecting the Time element further away from the present or bringing it closer to the present. The football players who have been brought here to play the game were in the present time over six months. But they will be returned to their own time at approximately the same hour they left it. That merely calls for a proper adjustment of the machine controlling the tunnel back into Time. But setting up a tunnel is something only I can do. It requires considerable technique, I assure you."

Hart brought out a bill fold. He counted out bank notes.

"Tell me when to stop," he said.

Androvitch wet his lips and watched the notes pile up on the table before him.

Finally he raised his hand.

"I will do it," he said. "I will start work tomorrow."

His hand reached out and clutched the notes.

"Thank you, Mr. Hart," he said.

Hart nodded and turned to the door. Behind him the scientist greedily counted and re-counted the bills.

V

Rush Culver shook hands with Ash Anderson, football scout for Coach August Snelling.

"I'm glad I didn't hang one on you that night you came into my room, Ash," the fullback said. "This has been the thrill of a lifetime. Any time you fellows need another good fullback just come back and get me."

Anderson smiled.

"Maybe we will if the Control Board doesn't change the rules. They'll probably rip Rule Eighteen all to hell now. And all because of a lousy newspaperman who had to spill the story. No loyalty, that's what's the matter with those guys. They'd cut their grandmas' throats for a good story."

The two stood awkwardly.

"Hate to say good-by," said Rush. "One time I kind of thought I'd like to stay up ahead in your time. But there's a girl back here. And this stuff you gave me will help us get settled soon as I graduate. Right clever, the way you fellows struck off old money."

"They'll never know the difference," said Ash. "They'll accept it as coin of the realm. The money we have up ahead wouldn't help you any here. As long as we had agreed to pay you, we might as well give you something you can use."

"Well, so long, Ash," said Culver.

"So long," said Ash.

Rush walked slowly down the street. The music hall clock tolled the hour. Rush listened. Gone only an hour—and in that time he had lived over six months in the future. He jin-

gled the coins in the sack he held in his hand and struck up a
tune.

Then he wheeled suddenly.

"Ash—wait a minute! Ash!" he shouted.

But the man out of the future was gone.

Slowly Rush turned back down the street, heading for the
house he had quitted less than 60 minutes before.

"Hell," he said to himself, "I forgot to thank him for helping
me with math."

A tiny bell tinkled softly again and again.

Arthur Hart stirred uneasily in his sleep. The bell kept on
insistently. The editor sat up in bed, ran his hands through his
hair and growled. The ringing continued.

"The *Morning Space-Ways*," he said. "Getting out an extra.
Now just what in the double-dipped damnation would they be
getting out an extra for?"

He pressed a lever and stepped up the intensity of the light in
the room. Walking to a machine, he snapped a button and shut
off the ringing bell. Opening the machine, he took from a receptacle within it a newspaper still wet with ink.

He glared at the second of the three news-delivery machines.

"If the *Star* beats the *Rocket* to an extra I'll go down and take
the place apart," he snarled. "We been scooped too often lately.
Probably isn't worth an extra, though. Just *Space-Ways* doing a
little more promotion work."

Sleepily he unfolded the sheet and glanced at the headline.
It read:

"TIME MACHINE SCIENTIST SLAIN BY GANG-
STERS"

Hart's breath sobbed in his throat as his eyes moved down to
the second deck.

"ALEXIS ANDROVITCH TORCHED ON STREET
FROM SPEEDING CAR.
POLICE BELIEVE MARS-EARTH GAME MAY BE
CLUE."

The *Rocket* news-delivery machine stormed into life. Another extra.

Hart snatched the paper from the machine.

He read:

"GANGSTERS SILENCE SCIENTIST ON EVE OF
GAME HEARING"

Stunned, Hart sat down on the edge of the bed.

Androvitch was dead! The only man in the world who could set up a Time-tunnel to reach Jimmy!

It was all plain—plain as day. The gambling syndicate, afraid of what Androvitch might say, had effectively silenced him. Dead men do not talk.

Hart bowed his head in his hands.

"The best damn reporter I ever had," he moaned.

He sprang to his feet as a thought struck him and rushed to the visaphone. Hurriedly he set up a wave length.

The face of Coach August Snelling appeared in the glass.

"Say, coach," said Hart breathlessly, "have you sent all the boys back to the past?"

"Hart," said Coach Snelling in an even voice filled with cold wrath, "after the way the newspapers have crucified me I have nothing to say."

"But, coach," pleaded Hart, "I'm not asking you for publication. What you can tell me will never be printed. I want your help."

"I needed your help the other day," Snelling reminded him, "and you told me news was news. You said you owed it to your readers to publish every detail of any news story."

"But a man's life depends on this," shouted Hart. "One of my reporters is back in the time where you trained the team. If I could use one of the other tunnels—one of those you used to bring the boys forward in Time—I could shoot it back to the correct time. Then I could travel to where Jimmy is and bring him back—"

"I'm telling you the truth when I say that the boys have all been sent back and all the tunnels are closed," Snelling said. "The last player went back this afternoon."

"Well," said Hart slowly, "I guess that settles it—"

Snelling interrupted. "I heard about Russell," he said, "and if he's trapped back with those Indians it's what I'd call poetic justice."

The glass went black as Snelling cut the connection.

The *Star* machine bell hammered. Hart wearily shut off the extra signal and took out the paper.

"Hell," he said, "if we'd had Jimmy here we'd have scooped even the *Space-Ways* on this yarn."

He looked sadly at the three editions.

"Best damn reporter I ever knew," the editor said.

Prof. Ebner White was lecturing to Elementary Astronomy, Section B.

"While there is reason to believe that Mars has an atmosphere," he was saying, "there is every reason to doubt that the planet has conditions which would allow the existence of life forms. There is little oxygen in the atmosphere, if there is an atmosphere. The red color of the planet would argue that much of whatever oxygen may have been at one time in the atmosphere—"

At this point Prof. White was rudely interrupted.

A young man had risen slowly to his feet.

"Professor," he said, "I've listened to you for the last half hour and have reached a conclusion you know nothing about what you are saying. I can tell you that Mars does have an atmosphere. It also has plenty of oxygen and other conditions favorable to life. In fact, there is life there—"

The young man stopped talking, realizing what he had done. The class was on the verge of breaking into boisterous gaiety and gales of strangled guffaws swept the room. No one liked Prof. White.

The professor sputtered feebly and tried to talk. Finally he did.

"Perhaps, Mr. Culver," he suggested, "you had better come up here while I come down and occupy your seat."

"I'm sorry, sir. I forgot myself. It won't happen again. I publicly and sincerely apologize."

He sat down and Prof. White went on with the lecture.

Which incident explains why Rush Culver became a tradition at the University of Wisconsin.

Marvelous tales were told of him. He was voted the man of the year in his senior year. He was elected a member of outstanding campus organizations which even his great football prowess in his junior and sophomore years had failed to obtain for him.

From a mediocre student he became regarded as a brilliant mind. Students to whom he had formerly gone for help with mathematics and other studies now came to him.

At one time he took the floor in a political science discussion hour and used up the entire hour explaining the functioning of a Utopian form of government. Those who heard him later said that he sounded as if he might have seen the government in actual operation.

But his greatest glory came from the credit which was accorded him for Wisconsin's football triumphs. Rumor on the campus said that he had worked out and given to the coach a series of plays, based upon gridiron principles then entirely new to the game. Rush, when approached, denied he had given them to the coach. But, however that may be, Wisconsin did spring upon its opponents that fall a devastating attack. Team after team fell before the onslaught of the Badgers. The team travelled to Minneapolis and there it marched through the mighty Golden Gophers with apparent ease, while fans and sportswriters grew faint with wonder and the football world trembled with amazement.

Clamorous popular demand forced the Big Ten to rescind its ruling against post-season games and at the Rose Bowl on January 1, 1945, the Badgers defeated the Trojans 49 to 0 in what sportswriters termed the greatest game ever played in football.

Jimmy Russell was up a tree. He had been lucky to find the tree, for there were few in that part of the country and at the moment he reached it, Jimmy was desperately in need of a tree.

Below him patrolled an enormous grizzly bear, fighting mad, snarling and biting at the shafts of arrows which protruded from his shoulders. The bole of the tree was scarred and splintered where the enraged animal had struck savagely at it with huge paws armed with four-inch talons. Low limbs had been ripped from the trunk as the beast reared to his full height, attempting to reach his quarry.

In a gully a quarter of a mile away lay the ripped and torn body of Chief Hiawatha. The bear had singled the Indian out in his first charge. Jimmy had sent his last arrow winging deep into the animal's throat as the beast had torn the life from his friend. Then, without means of defense and knowing that his companion was dead, Jimmy had run, madly, blindly. The tree saved him, at least temporarily. He still had hopes that that last arrow, inflicting a deep throat wound, from which the blood flowed freely, would eventually spell death to the maddened beast.

Sadly he reflected, as he perched on a large branch, that if he ever did get down alive the rest of the trip would be lonely. It was still a long way to Mexico and the Aztec civilization, but the way would not have seemed long with old Chief Hiawatha beside him. The chief had been his only friend in this savage, prehistoric world and now he lay dead and Jimmy faced another thousand miles alone, on foot, without adequate weapons.

"Maybe I should have waited at the village," Jimmy told himself. "Somebody might have gotten through to me. But maybe nobody wanted to get through. Funny, though, I always figured Hart was my friend, even if he did get hard-boiled every time he saw me. Still—I waited three years and that should have given him plenty of time."

A lone buffalo bull wandered up the gully and over the ridge where the grizzly stood guard under the tree. The bear, sighting the bull, rushed at him, roaring with rage. For a moment it appeared the bull might stand his ground, but before the bear covered half the distance to him, he wheeled about and lumbered off. The grizzly came back to the tree.

Far out on the plain Jimmy located a skittering band of antelope and watched them for a long time. A wolf slunk through the long grass in a gully to the west of the tree. In the sky vultures began to wheel and turn. Jimmy shook his fist at them and cursed.

Twilight came and still the bear kept up the watch. At times he withdrew a short distance and lay down as if he were growing weak from loss of blood. But in each instance he came back to resume the march around the tree.

The moon came up and wolves howled plaintively from the ridges to the east. Jimmy, tearing a buckskin strip from his shirt, lashed himself to the tree. It was well he did so, for in spite of the danger below, despite his efforts to keep awake, he fell asleep.

The moon was low in the west when he awoke. He was stiff and chilled and for a moment he did not remember where he was.

A slinking form slipped over a ridge a short distance away and from somewhere on the prairie came the roaring grunting of a herd of awakening buffalo.

With a realization of his position coming to him, Jimmy looked about for the bear. He did not locate the beast at first, but finally saw its great bulk stretched out on the ground some distance away. He shouted, but the animal did not stir.

Late afternoon saw Jimmy heading southwest across the plains. He was clad in tattered buckskins. He was armed with a bow and a few arrows. At his belt swung a tomahawk. But he walked with a free swinging tread and his head was high.

Behind him a mound of stones marked the last resting place of all that remained mortal of Chief Hiawatha. Ahead of him lay Mexico, land of the Aztecs.

There he would find the highest order of civilization in pre-Columbian North America. There he would find people whose legends told of a strange white god who came to them in ancient days and taught them many things. This was the story they had told the Spanish conquistadores. That was why they had hailed Cortez as a god likewise, to their later sorrow.

"A white god who taught them many things," said Jimmy to himself and chuckled. Might he not have been that white god? Could he not have taught them many things? But if he had been a god to the Aztecs, why had he not warned them against the Spaniards?

Jimmy chuckled again.

"A newspaperman should make one hell of a good god for a bunch of redskins," he told himself.

MR. MEEK PLAYS POLO

Clifford Simak was not one to write sequels, several times turning down tempting offers to do so. But in this case he apparently was eager to do a sequel, writing this story even before its predecessor (see "Mr. Meek—Musketeer," in volume two of this series) had been published. Moreover, his journals indicate that he would later write, and sell, a third Mr. Meek story (named, it appears, "Mr. Meek Drinks a Toast"); but that story, although reportedly sold to Super Science Stories, *was never published, and has been lost . . . as far as I know, at least.*

This second Mr. Meek story was published in the Fall 1944 issue of Planet Stories. *As in many of Cliff's older stories, such things as the prices of items and the language his characters use seem ridiculous for a story set in the far future. But those things are not meant to be taken literally, but to give meaning to the descriptions of the characters' personalities—that is, to show that they are "ordinary" people, not any sort of elite.*

—dww

I

The sign read: *Atomic Motors Repaired. Busted Plates Patched Up. Rocket Tubes Relined. Wheeze In, Whiz Out!*

It added, as an afterthought, in shaky, inexpert lettering: *We fix anything.*

Mr. Oliver Meek stared owlishly at the sign, which hung from an arm attached to a metal standard sunk in solid rock. A second sign was wired to the standard just below the metal arm, but its legend was faint, almost illegible. Meek blinked at it through thick-lensed spectacles, finally deciphered its scrawl: *Ask about educated bugs.*

A bit bewildered, but determined not to show it, Meek swung away from the signpost and gravely regarded the settlement. On the chart it was indicated by a fairly sizable dot, but that was merely a matter of comparison. Out Saturn-way even the tiniest outpost assumes importance far beyond its size.

The slab of rock was no more than five miles across, perhaps even less. Here in its approximate center were two buildings, both of almost identical construction, semi-spherical and metal. Out here, Meek realized, shelter was the thing. Architecture merely for architecture's sake was still a long way off.

One of the buildings was the repair shop which the sign advertised. The other, according to the crudely painted legend smeared above its entrance lock, was the *Saturn Inn.*

The rest of the rock was landing field, pure and simple. Blasters had leveled off the humps and irregularities so spaceships could set down.

Two ships now were on the field, pulled up close against the repair shop. One, Meek noticed, belonged to the Solar Health and Welfare Department, the other to the Galactic Pharmaceutical Corporation. The Galactic ship was a freighter, ponderous and slow. It was here, Meek knew, to take on a cargo of radiation moss. But the other was a puzzler. Meek wrinkled his brow and blinked his eyes, trying to figure out what a welfare ship would be doing in this remote corner of the Solar System.

Slowly and carefully, Meek clumped toward the squat repair shop. Once or twice he stumbled, hoping fervently he wouldn't get the feet of his cumbersome spacesuit all tangled up. The gravity was slight, next to non-existent, and one who wasn't used to it had to take things easy and remember where he was.

Behind him Saturn filled a tenth of the sky, a yellow, lemon-tinged ball, streaked here and there with faint crimson lines and blotched with angry, bright green patches.

To right and left glinted the whirling, twisting, tumbling rocks that made up the Inner Ring, while arcing above the horizon opposed to Saturn were the spangled glistening rainbows of the other rings.

"Like dewdrops in the black of space," Meek mumbled to himself. But he immediately felt ashamed of himself for growing poetic. This sector of space, he knew, was not in the least poetic. It was hard and savage, and as he thought about that, he hitched up his gun belt and struck out with a firmer tread that almost upset him. After that, he tried to think of nothing except keeping his two feet under him.

Reaching the repair shop's entrance lock, he braced himself solidly to keep his balance, reached out and pressed a buzzer. Swiftly the lock spun outward and a moment later Meek had passed through the entrance vault and stepped into the office.

A dungareed mechanic sat tilted in a chair against a wall, feet on the desk, a greasy cap pushed back on his head.

Meek stamped his feet gratefully, pleased at feeling Earth gravity under him again. He lifted the hinged helmet of his suit back on his shoulders.

"You are the gentleman who can fix things?" he asked the mechanic.

The mechanic stared. Here was no hell-for-leather freighter pilot, no bewhiskered roamer of the outer orbits. Meek's hair was white and stuck out in uncombed tufts in a dozen directions. His skin was pale. His blue eyes looked watery behind the thick lenses that rode his nose. Even the bulky spacesuit failed to hide his stooped shoulders and slight frame.

The mechanic said nothing.

Meek tried again. "I saw the sign. It said you could fix anything. So I . . ."

The mechanic shook himself.

"Sure," he agreed, still slightly dazed. "Sure I can fix you up. What you got?"

He swung his feet off the desk.

"I ran into a swarm of pebbles," Meek confessed. "Not much more than dust, really, but the screen couldn't stop it all."

He fumbled his hands self-consciously. "Awkward of me," he said.

"It happens to the best of them," the mechanic consoled. "Saturn sweeps in clouds of the stuff. Thicker than hell when you reach the Rings. Lots of ships pull in with punctures. Won't take no time."

Meek cleared his throat uneasily. "I'm afraid it's more than a puncture. A pebble got into the instruments. Washed out some of them."

The mechanic clucked sympathetically. "You're lucky. Tough job to bring in a ship without all the instruments. Must have a honey of a navigator."

"I haven't got a navigator," Meek said quietly.

The mechanic stared at him, eyes popping. "You mean you brought it in alone? No one with you?"

Meek gulped and nodded. "Dead reckoning," he said.

The mechanic glowed with sudden admiration. "I don't know who you are, mister," he declared, "but whoever you are, you're the best damn pilot that ever took to space."

"Really I'm not," said Meek. "I haven't done much piloting, you see. Up until just a while ago, I never had left Earth. Bookkeeper for Lunar Exports."

"Bookkeeper!" yelped the mechanic. "How come a book-keeper can handle a ship like that?"

"I learned it," said Meek.

"You learned it?"

"Sure, from a book. I saved my money and I studied. I always wanted to see the Solar System and here I am."

Dazedly, the mechanic took off his greasy cap, laid it carefully on the desk, reached out for a spacesuit that hung from a wall hook.

"Afraid this job might take a while," he said. "Especially if we have to wait for parts. Have to get them in from Titan City. Why don't you go over to the *Inn*. Tell Moe I sent you. They'll treat you right."

"Thank you," said Meek, "but there's something else I'm wondering about. There was another sign out there. Something about educated bugs."

"Oh, them," said the mechanic. "They belong to Gus Hamilton. Maybe belong ain't the right word because they were on the rock before Gus took over. Anyhow, Gus is mighty proud of them, although at times they sure run him ragged. First year they almost drove him loopy trying to figure out what kind of game they were playing."

"Game?" asked Meek, wondering if he was being hoaxed.

"Sure, game. Like checkers. Only it ain't. Not chess, neither. Even worse than that. Bugs dig themselves a batch of holes, then choose up sides and play for hours. About the time Gus would think he had it figured out, they'd change the rules and throw him off again."

"That doesn't make sense," protested Meek.

"Stranger," declared the mechanic, solemnly, "there ain't nothing about them bugs that makes sense. Gus's rock is the only one they're on. Gus thinks maybe the rock don't even belong to the Solar System. Thinks maybe it's a hunk of stone from some other solar system. Figures maybe it crossed space somehow and was captured by Saturn, sucked into the Ring. That would explain why it's the only one that has the bugs. They come along with it, see."

"This Gus Hamilton," said Meek. "I'd like to see him. Where could I find him?"

"Go over to the *Inn* and wait around," advised the mechanic. "He'll come in sooner or later. Drops around regular, except when his rheumatism bothers him, to pick up a bundle of papers. Subscribes to a daily paper, he does. Only man out here that does any reading. But all he reads is the sports section. Nuts about sports, Gus is."

II

Moe, bartender at Saturn Inn, leaned his elbow on the bar and braced his chin in an outspread palm. His face wore a melancholy, hang-dog look. Moe liked things fairly peaceable, but now he saw trouble coming in big batches.

"Lady," he declared mournfully, "you sure picked yourself a job. The boys around here don't take to being uplifted and improved. They ain't worth it, either. Just ring-rats, that's all they are."

Henrietta Perkins, representative for the public health and welfare department of the Solar government, shuddered at his suggestion of anything so low it didn't yearn for betterment.

"But those terrible feuds," she protested. "Fighting just because they live in different parts of the Ring. It's natural they might feel some rivalry, but all this killing! Surely they don't enjoy getting killed."

"Sure they enjoy it," declared Moe. "Not being killed, maybe . . . although they're willing to take a chance on that. Not many of them get killed, in fact. Just a few that get sort of careless. But even if some of them are killed, you can't go messing around with that feud of theirs. If them boys out in Sectors Twenty-three and Thirty-seven didn't have their feud they'd plain die of boredom. They just got to have somebody to fight with. They been fighting, off and on, for years."

"But they could fight with something besides guns," said the welfare lady, a-smirk with righteousness. "That's why I'm here. To try to get them to turn their natural feelings of rivalry into less deadly and disturbing channels. Direct their energies into other activities."

"Like what?" asked Moe, fearing the worst.

"Athletic events," said Miss Perkins.

"Tin shinny, maybe," suggested Moe, trying to be sarcastic.

She missed the sarcasm. "Or spelling contests," she said.

"Them fellows can't spell," insisted Moe.

"Games of some sort, then. Competitive games."

"Now you're talking," Moe enthused. "They take to games. Seven-toed Pete with the deuces wild."

The inner door of the entrance lock grated open and a space-suited figure limped into the room. The spacesuit visor snapped up and a brush of gray whiskers sprouted into view.

It was Gus Hamilton.

He glared at Moe. "What in tarnation is all this foolishness?" he demanded. "Got your message, I did, and here I am. But it better be important."

He hobbled to the bar. Moe reached for a bottle and shoved it toward him, keeping out of reach.

"Have some trouble?" he asked, trying to be casual.

"Trouble! Hell, yes!" blustered Gus. "But I ain't the only one that's going to have trouble. Somebody sneaked over and stole the injector out of my space crate. Had to borrow Hank's to get over here. But I know who it was. There ain't but one other ring-rat got a rocket my injector will fit."

"Bud Craney," said Moe. It was no secret. Every man in the two sectors of the Ring knew just exactly what kind of spacecraft the other had.

"That's right," said Gus, "and I'm fixing to go over into Thirty-seven and yank Bud up by the roots."

He took a jolt of liquor. "Yes, sir, I sure aim to crucify him."

His eyes lighted on Miss Henrietta Perkins.

"Visitor?" he asked.

"She's from the government," said Moe.

"Revenuer?"

"Nope. From the welfare outfit. Aims to help you fellows out. Says there ain't no sense in you boys in Twenty-three all the time fighting with the gang from Thirty-seven."

Gus stared in disbelief.

Moe tried to be helpful. "She wants you to play games."

Gus strangled on his drink, clawed for air, wiped his eyes.

"So that's why you asked me over here. Another of your danged peace parleys. Come and talk things over, you said. So I came."

"There's something in what she says," defended Moe. "You ring-rats been ripping up space for a long time now. Time you growed up and settled down. You're aiming on going over right now and pulverizing Bud. It won't do you any good."

"I'll get a heap of satisfaction out of it," insisted Gus. "And, besides, I'll get my injector back. Might even take a few things off Bud's ship. Some of the parts on mine are wearing kind of thin."

Gus took another drink, glowering at Miss Perkins.

"So the government sent you out to make us respectable," he said.

"Merely to help you, Mr. Hamilton," she declared. "To turn your hatreds into healthy competition."

"Games, eh?" said Gus. "Maybe you got something, after all. Maybe we could fix up some kind of game. . . ."

"Forget it, Gus," warned Moe. "If you're thinking of energy guns at fifty paces, it's out. Miss Perkins won't stand for anything like that."

Gus wiped his whiskers and looked hurt. "Nothing of the sort," he denied. "Dang it, you must think I ain't got no sportsmanship at all. I was thinking of a real sport. A game they play back on Earth and Mars. Read about it in my papers. Follow the teams, I do. Always wanted to see a game, but never did."

Miss Perkins beamed. "What game is it, Mr. Hamilton?"

"Space polo," said Gus.

"Why, how wonderful," simpered Miss Perkins. "And you boys have the spaceships to play it with."

Moe looked alarmed. "Miss Perkins," he warned, "don't let him talk you into it."

"You shut your trap," snapped Gus. "She wants us to play games, don't she. Well, polo is a game. A nice, respectable game. Played in the best society."

"It wouldn't be no nice, respectable game the way you fellows would play it," predicted Moe. "It would turn into mass murder. Wouldn't be one of you who wouldn't be planning on getting even with someone else, once you got him in the open."

Miss Perkins gasped. "Why, I'm sure they wouldn't!"

"Of course we wouldn't," declared Gus, solemn as an owl.

"And that ain't all," said Moe, warming to the subject. "Those crates you guys got wouldn't last out the first chukker. Most of them would just naturally fall apart the first sharp turn they made. You can't play polo in ships tied up with haywire. Those broomsticks you ring-rats ride around on are so used to second-rate fuel they'd split wide open first squirt of high-test stuff you gave them."

The inner locks grated open and a man stepped through into the room.

"You're prejudiced," Gus told Moe. "You just don't like space polo, that is all. You ain't got no blueblood in you. We'll leave it up to this man here. We'll ask his opinion of it."

The man flipped back his helmet, revealing a head thatched by white hair and dominated by a pair of outsize spectacles.

"My opinion, sir," said Oliver Meek, "seldom amounts to much."

"All we want to know," Gus told him, "is what you think of space polo."

"Space polo," declared Meek, "is a noble game. It requires expert piloting, a fine sense of timing and . . ."

"There, you see!" whooped Gus, triumphantly.

"I saw a game once," Meek volunteered.

"Swell," bellowed Gus. "We'll have you coach our team."

"But," protested Meek, "but . . . but . . ."

"Oh, Mr. Hamilton," exulted Miss Perkins, "you are so wonderful. You think of everything."

"Hamilton!" squeaked Meek.

"Sure," said Gus. "Old Gus Hamilton. Grow the finest dog-gone radiation moss you ever clapped your eyes on."

"Then you're the gentleman who has bugs," said Meek.

"Now, look here," warned Gus, "you watch what you say or I'll hang one on you."

"He means your rock bugs," Moe explained, hastily.

"Oh, them," said Gus.

"Yes," said Meek, "I'm interested in them. I'd like to see them."

"See them," said Gus. "Mister, you can have them if you want them. Drove me out of house and home, they did. They're dippy over metal. Any kind of metal, but alloys especially. Eat the stuff. They'll tromp you to death heading for a spaceship. Got so I had to move over to another rock to live. Tried to fight it out with them, but they whipped me pure and simple. Moved out and let them have the place after they started to eat my shack right out from underneath my feet."

Meek looked crestfallen.

"Can't get near them, then," he said.

"Sure you can," said Gus. "Why not?"

"Well, a spacesuit's metal and . . ."

"Got that all fixed up," said Gus. "You come back with me and I'll let you have a pair of stilts."

"Stilts?"

"Yeah. Wooden stilts. Them danged fool bugs don't know what wood is. Seem to be scared of it, sort of. You can walk right among them if you want to, long as you're walking on the stilts."

Meek gulped. He could imagine what stilt walking would be like in a place where gravity was no more than the faintest whisper.

III

The bugs had dug a new set of holes, much after the manner of a Chinese checker board, and now were settling down into their respective places preparatory to the start of another game.

For a mile or more across the flat surface of the rock that was Gus Hamilton's moss garden, ran a string of such game-boards, each one different, each one having served as the scene of a now completed game.

Oliver Meek cautiously wedged his stilts into two pitted pockets of rock, eased himself slowly and warily against the face of a knob of stone that jutted from the surface.

Even in his youth, Meek remembered, he never had been any great shakes on stilts. Here, on this bucking, weaving rock, with slick surfaces and practically no gravity, a man had to be an expert to handle them. Meek knew now he was no expert. A half-dozen dents in his space armor was ample proof of that.

Comfortably braced against the upjutting of stone, Meek dug into the pouch of his space gear, brought out a notebook and stylus. Flipping the pages, he stared, frowning, at the diagrams that covered them.

None of the diagrams made sense. They showed the patterns of three other boards and the moves that had been made by the bugs in playing out the game. Apparently, in each case, the game had been finished. Which, Meek knew, should have meant that some solution had been reached, some point won, some advantage gained.

But so far as Meek could see from study of the diagrams, there was not even a purpose or a problem, let alone a solution or a point.

The whole thing was squirrely. But, Meek told himself, it fitted in. The whole Saturnian system was wacky. The rings, for example. Debris of a moon smashed up by Saturn's pull? Sweepings of space? No one knew.

Saturn itself, for that matter. A planet that kept man at bay with deadly radiations. But radiations that, while they kept Man at a distance, at the same time served Man. For here, on the Inner Ring, where they had become so diluted that ordinary space armor filtered them out, they made possible the medical magic of the famous radiation moss.

One of the few forms of plant life found in the cold of space, the moss was nurtured by those mysterious radiations. Planted elsewhere, on kindlier worlds, it wilted and refused to grow. The radiations had been analyzed, Meek knew, and reproduced under laboratory conditions, but there still was something missing, some vital, elusive factor that could not be analyzed. Under the artificial radiation, the moss still wilted and died.

And because Earth needed the moss to cure a dozen maladies, and because it would grow nowhere else but here on the Inner Ring, men squatted on the crazy swirl of spacial boulders that made up the Ring. Men like Hamilton, living on rocks that bucked and heaved along their orbits like chips riding the crest of a raging flood. Men who endured loneliness, dared death when crunching orbits intersected or when rickety spacecraft flared, who went mad with nothing to do, with the mockery of space before them.

Meek shrugged his shoulders, almost upsetting himself.

The bugs had started the game and Meek craned forward cautiously, watching eagerly, stylus poised above the notebook.

Crawling clumsily, the tiny insect-like creatures moved about, solemnly popping in and out of holes.

If there were opposing sides . . . and if it were a game, there'd have to be . . . they didn't seem to alternate the moves. Although, Meek admitted, certain rules and conditions which he had failed to note or recognize might determine the number and order of moves allowed each side.

Suddenly there was confusion on the board. For a moment a half-dozen of the bugs raced madly about, as if seeking the proper hole to occupy. Then, as suddenly, all movement had ceased. And in another moment, they were on the move again, orderly again, but retracing their movements, going back several plays beyond the point of confusion.

Just as one would do when one made a mistake working a mathematical problem . . . going back to the point of error and going on again from there.

"Well, I'll be . . ." Mr. Meek said.

Meek stiffened and the stylus floated out of his hand, settled softly on the rock below.

A mathematical problem!

His breath gurgled in his throat.

He knew it now! He should have known it all the time. But the mechanic had talked about the bugs playing games and so had Hamilton. That had thrown him off.

Games! Those bugs weren't playing any game. They were solving mathematical equations!

Meek leaned forward to watch, forgetting where he was. One of the stilts slipped out of position and Meek felt himself starting to fall. He dropped the notebook and frantically clawed at empty space.

The other stilt went, then, and Meek found himself floating slowly downward, gravity weak but inexorable. His struggle to retain his balance had flung him forward, away from the face of the rock, and he was falling directly over the board on which the bugs were arrayed.

He pawed and kicked at space, but still floated down, course unchanged. He struck and bounced, struck and bounced again.

On the fourth bounce he managed to hook his fingers around a tiny projection of the surface. Fighting desperately, he regained his feet.

Something scurried across the face of his helmet and he lifted his hand before him. It was covered with the bugs.

Fumbling desperately, he snapped on the rocket motor of his suit, shot out into space, heading for the rock where the lights from the ports of Hamilton's shack blinked with the weaving of the rock.

Oliver Meek shut his eyes and groaned.

"Gus will give me hell for this," he told himself.

Gus shook the small wooden box thoughtfully, listening to the frantic scurrying within it.

"By rights," he declared, judiciously, "I should take this over and dump it in Bud's ship. Get even with him for swiping my injector."

"But you got the injector back," Meek pointed out.

"Oh, sure, I got it back," admitted Gus. "But it wasn't orthodox, it wasn't. Just getting your property back ain't getting even. I never did have a chance to smack Bud in the snoot the way I should of smacked him. Moe talked me into it. He was the one that had the idea the welfare lady should go over and talk to Bud. She must of laid it on thick, too, about how we should settle down and behave ourselves and all that. Otherwise Bud never would have given her that injector."

He shook his head dolefully. "This here Ring ain't ever going to be the same again. If we don't watch out, we'll find ourselves being polite to one another."

"That would be awful," agreed Meek.

"Wouldn't it, though," declared Gus.

Meek squinted his eyes and pounced on the floor, scrabbling on hands and knees after a scurrying thing that twinkled in the lamplight.

"Got him," yelped Meek, scooping the shining mote up in his hand.

Gus inched the lid of the wooden box open. Meek rose and popped the bug inside.

"That makes twenty-eight of them," said Meek.

"I told you," Gus accused him, "that we hadn't got them all. You better take another good look at your suit. The danged things burrow right into solid metal and pull the hole in after them, seems like. Sneakiest cusses in the whole dang system. Just like chiggers back on Earth."

"Chiggers," Meek told him, "burrow into a person to lay eggs."

"Maybe these things do, too," Gus contended.

The radio on the mantel blared a warning signal, automatically tuning in on one of the regular newscasts from Titan City out on Saturn's biggest moon.

The syrupy, chamber-of-commerce voice of the announcer was shaky with excitement and pride.

"Next week," he said, "the annual Martian-Earth football game will be played at Greater New York on Earth. But in the Earth's newspapers tonight another story has pushed even that famous classic of the sporting world down into secondary place."

He paused and took a deep breath and his voice practically yodeled with delight.

"The sporting event, ladies and gentlemen, that is being talked up and down the streets of Earth tonight, is one that will be played here in our own Saturnian system. A space polo game. To be played by two unknown, pick-up, amateur teams down in the Inner Ring. Most of the men have never played polo before. Few if any of them have even seen a game. There may have been some of them who didn't, at first, know what it was.

"But they're going to play it. The men who ride those bucking rocks that make up the Inner Ring will go out into space in their rickety ships and fight it out. And ladies and gentlemen, when I say fight it out, I really mean fight it out. For the game, it seems, will be a sort of tournament, the final battle in a feud that has been going on in the Ring for years. No one knows what started the feud. It has gotten so it really doesn't matter. The only thing that matters is that when men from Sector Twenty-three meet those from Sector Thirty-seven, the feud is taken up again. But that is at an end now. In a few days the feud will be played out to its bitter end when the ships from the Inner Ring go out into space to play that most dangerous of all sports, space polo. For the outcome of that game will decide, forever, the supremacy of one of the two sectors."

Meek rose from his chair, opened his mouth as if to speak, but sank back again when Gus hissed at him and held a finger to his lips for silence.

"The teams are now in training," went on the newscaster, the happy lilt in his voice still undimmed, "and it is understood that Sector Twenty-three has the advantage, at the start at least, of having a polo expert as its coach. Just who this expert is no one can say. Several names have been mentioned, but . . ."

"No, no," yelped Meek, struggling to his feet, but Gus shushed him, poking a finger toward him and grinning like a bearded imp.

". . . Bets are mounting high throughout the entire Saturnian system," the announcer was saying, "but since little is known about the teams, the odds still are even. It is likely, however, that odds will be demanded on the Sector Thirty-seven team on the basis of the story about the expert coach.

"The very audacity of such a game has attracted solar-wide attention and special fleets of ships will leave both Earth and Mars within the next few days to bring spectators to the game. Newsmen from the inner worlds, among them some of the system's most famous sports writers, are already on their way.

"Originally intended to be no more than a recreation project under the supervision of the Department of Health and Welfare, the game has suddenly become a solar attraction. The *Daily Rocket* back on Earth is offering a gigantic loving cup for the winning team, while the *Morning Spaceways* has provided another loving cup, only slightly smaller, to be presented the player adjudged the most valuable to his team. We may have more to tell you about the game before the newscast is over, but in the meantime we shall go on to other news of Solar int—"

Meek leaped up. "He meant me," he whooped. "That was me he meant when he was talking about a famous coach!"

"Sure," said Gus. "He couldn't have meant anyone else but you."

"But I'm not a famous coach," protested Meek. "I'm not even a coach at all. I never saw but one space polo game in all my life. I hardly know how it's played. I just know you go up there in space and bat a ball around. I'm going to—"

"You ain't going to do a blessed thing," said Gus. "You ain't skipping out on us. You're staying right here and give us all the fine pointers of the game. Maybe you ain't so hot as the newscaster made out, but you're a dang sight better than anyone else around here. At least you seen a game once and that's more than any of the rest of us have."

"But I—"

"I don't know what's the matter with you," declared Gus. "You're just pretending you don't know anything about polo, that's all. Maybe you're a fugitive from justice. Maybe that's why you're so anxious to make a getaway. Only reason you stopped at all was because your ship got stoved up."

"I'm no fugitive," declared Meek, drawing himself up. "I'm just a bookkeeper out to see the system."

"Forget it," said Gus. "Forget it. Nobody around here's going to give you away. If they even so much as peep, I'll plain paralyze them. So you're a bookkeeper. That's good enough for me.

Just let anyone say you ain't a bookkeeper and see what happens to him."

Meek opened his mouth to speak, closed it again. What was the use? Here he was, stuck again. Just like back on Juno when that preacher had thought he was a gunman and talked him into taking over the job of cleaning up the town. Only this time it was a space polo game, and he knew even less about space polo than he did about being a lawman.

Gus rose and limped slowly across the room. Ponderously, he hauled a red bandanna out of his back pocket and carefully dusted off the one uncrowded space on the mantel shelf, between the alarm clock and the tarnished silver model of a rocket ship.

"Yes sir," he said, "she'll look right pretty there."

He backed away and stared at the place on the shelf.

"I can almost see her now," he said. "Glinting in the lamplight. Something to keep me company. Something to look at when I get lonesome."

"What are you talking about?" demanded Meek.

"That there cup the radio was talking about," said Gus. "The one for the most valuable team member."

Meek stammered. "But . . . but . . ."

"I'm going to win her," Gus declared.

IV

Saturn Inn bulged. Every room was crowded, with half a dozen to the cubicle, sleeping in relays. Those who couldn't find anywhere else to sleep spread blankets in the narrow corridors or dozed off in chairs or slept on the barroom floor. A few of them got stepped on.

Titan City's Junior Chamber of Commerce had done what it could to help the situation out, but the notice had been short. A half-dozen nearby rocks, which had been hastily leveled off for parking space, now were jammed with hundreds of space vehicles, ranging from the nifty two-man job owned by Billy Jones, sports editor of the *Daily Rocket,* to the huge excursion liners sent out by the three big transport companies. A few hastily-erected shelters helped out to some extent, but none of these shelters had a bar and they were mostly untenanted.

Moe, the bartender at the Inn, harried with too many customers, droopy with lack of sleep, saw Oliver Meek bobbing around in the crowd that surged against the bar, much after the manner of a cork caught in a raging whirlpool. He reached out a hand and dragged Meek against the bar.

"Can't you do something to stop it?"

Meek blinked at him. "Stop what?"

"This game," said Moe. "It's awful, Mr. Meek. Honestly. The crowd has got the fellers so worked up, it's apt to be mass murder."

"I know it," Meek agreed, "but you can't stop it now. The Junior Chamber of Commerce would take the hide off anyone who even said he would like to see it stopped. It's more publicity than Saturn has gotten since the first expeditions were lost here."

"I don't like it," declared Moe, stolidly.

"I don't like it either," Meek confessed. "Gus and those other fellows on his team think I'm an expert. I told them what I knew about space polo, but it wasn't much. Trouble is they think it's everything there is to know. They figure they're a cinch to win and they got their shirts bet on the game. If they lose, they'll more than likely space-walk me."

Fingers tapped Meek's shoulder and he twisted around. A red face loomed above him, a cigarette drooping from the corner of its lips.

"Hear you say you was coaching the Twenty-three bunch?"

Meek gulped.

"Billy Jones, that's me," said the lips with the cigarette. "Best damn sports writer ever pounded keys. Been trying to find out who you was. Nobody else knows. Treat you right."

"You must be wrong," said Meek.

"Never wrong," insisted Jones. "Nose for news. Smell it out. Like this. *Sniff. Sniff.*"

His nose crinkled in imitation of a bloodhound, but his face didn't change otherwise. The cigarette still dangled, pouring smoke into a watery left eye.

"Heard the guy call you Meek," said Jones. "Name sounds familiar. Something about Juno, wasn't it? Rounded up a bunch of crooks. Found a space monster of some sort."

Another hand gripped Meek by the shoulder and literally jerked him around.

"So you're the guy!" yelped the owner of the hand. "I been looking for you. I've a good notion to smack you in the puss."

"Now, Bud," yelled Moe, in mounting fear, "you leave him alone. He ain't done a thing."

Meek gaped at the angry face of the hulking man, who still had his shoulder in the grip of a monstrous paw.

Bud Craney! The ring-rat that had stolen Gus's injector! The captain of the Thirty-seven team.

"If there was room," Craney grated, "I'd wipe up the floor with you. But since there ain't, I'm just plain going to hammer you down about halfway into it."

"But he ain't done nothing!" shrilled Moe.

"He's an outsider, ain't he?" demanded Craney. "What business he got coming in here and messing around with things?"

"I'm not messing around with things, Mr. Craney," Meek declared, trying to be dignified about it. But it was hard to be dignified with someone lifting one by the shoulder so one's toes just barely touched the floor.

"All that's the matter with you," insisted the dangling Meek, "is that you know Gus and his men will give you a whipping. They'd done it, anyhow. I haven't helped them much. I haven't helped them hardly at all."

Craney howled in rage. "Why . . . you . . . you . . ."

And then Oliver Meek did one of those things no one ever expected him to do, least of all himself.

"I'll bet you my spaceship," he said, "against anything you got."

Astonished, Craney opened his hand and let him down on the floor.

"You'll what?" he roared.

"I'll bet you my spaceship," said Meek, the madness still upon him, "that Twenty-three will beat you."

He rubbed it in. "I'll even give you odds."

Craney gasped and sputtered. "I don't want any odds," he yelped. "I'll take it even. My moss patch against your ship."

Someone was calling Meek's name in the crowd.

"Mr. Meek! Mr. Meek!"

"Here," said Meek.

"What about that story?" demanded Billy Jones, but Meek didn't hear him.

A man was tearing his way through the crowd. It was one of the men from Twenty-three.

"Mr. Meek," he panted, "you got to come right away. It's Gus. He's all tangled up with rheumatiz!"

Gus stared up with anguished eyes at Meek.

"It sneaked up on me while I slept," he squeaked. "Laid off me for years until just now. Limped once in a while, of course, and got a few twinges now and then, but that was all. Never had me tied up like this since I left Earth. One of the reasons I never did go back to Earth. Space is good climate for rheumatiz. Cold but dry. No moisture to get into your bones."

Meek looked around at the huddled men, saw the worry that was etched upon their faces.

"Get a hot water bottle," he told one of them.

"Hell," said Russ Jensen, a hulking-framed spaceman, "there ain't no such a thing as a hot water bottle nearer than Titan City."

"An electric pad, then."

Jensen shook his head. "No pads, neither. Only thing we can do is pour whiskey down him and if we pour enough down him to cure the rheumatiz, we'll get him drunk and he won't be no more able to play in that game than he is right now."

Meek's weak eyes blinked behind his glasses, staring at Gus.

"We'll lose sure if Gus can't play," said Jensen, "and me with everything I got bet on our team."

Another man spoke up. "Meek could play in Gus's place."

"Nope, he couldn't," declared Jensen. "The rats from Thirty-seven wouldn't stand for it."

"They couldn't do a thing about it," declared the other man. "Meek's been here six weeks today. That makes him a resident. Six Earth weeks, the law says. And all that time he's been in Sector Twenty-three. They wouldn't have a leg to stand on. They might squawk but they couldn't make it stick."

"You're certain of that?" demanded Jensen.

"Dead certain," said the other.

Meek saw them looking at him, felt a queasy feeling steal into his stomach.

"I couldn't," he told them. "I couldn't do it. I . . . I . . ."

"You go right ahead, Oliver," said Gus. "I wanted to play, of course. Sort of set my heart on that cup. Had the mantel piece all dusted off for it. But if I can't play, there ain't another soul I'd rather have play in my place than you."

"But I don't know a thing about polo," protested Meek.

"You taught it to us, didn't you?" bellowed Jensen. "You pretended like you knew everything there was to know."

"But I don't," insisted Meek. "You wouldn't let me explain. You kept telling me all the time what a swell coach I was and when I tried to argue with you and tell you that I wasn't you yelled me down. I never saw more than one game in all my life and the only reason I saw it then was because I found the ticket. It was on the sidewalk and I picked it up. Somebody had dropped it."

"So you been stringing us along," yelped Jensen. "You been

making fools of us! How do we know but you showed us wrong. You been giving us the wrong dope."

He advanced on Meek and Meek backed against the wall.

Jensen lifted his fist, held it in front of him as if he were weighing it.

"I ought to bop you one," he decided. "All of us had ought to bop you one. Every danged man in this here room has got his shirt bet on the game because we figured we couldn't lose with a coach like you."

"So have I," said Meek. But it wasn't until he said it that he really realized he did have his shirt bet on Twenty-three. His spaceship. It wasn't all he had, of course, but it was the thing that was nearest to his heart . . . the thing he had slaved for thirty years to buy.

He suddenly remembered those years now. Years of bending over account books in the dingy office back on Earth, watching other men go out in space, longing to go himself. Counting pennies so that he could go. Spending only a dime for lunch and eating crackers and cheese instead of going out for dinner in the evening. Piling up the dollars, slowly through the years . . . dollars to buy the ship that now stood out on the field, all damage repaired. Sitting, poised for space.

But if Thirty-seven won, it wouldn't be his any longer. It would be Craney's. He'd just made a bet with Craney and there were plenty of witnesses to back it up.

"Well?" demanded Jensen.

"I will play," said Meek.

"And you really know about the game? You wasn't kidding us?"

Meek looked at the men before him and the expression on their faces shaped his answer.

He gulped . . . gulped again. Then slowly nodded.

"Sure, I know about it," he lied.

They didn't look quite satisfied.

He glanced around, but there was no way of escape. He faced them again, back pressed against the wall.

He tried to make his voice light and breezy, but he couldn't quite keep out the croak.

"Haven't played it much in the last few years," he said, "But back when I was a kid I was a ten-goal man."

They were satisfied at that.

V

Hunched behind the controls, Meek slowly circled Gus's crate, waiting for the signal, half fearful of what would happen when it came.

Glancing to left and right, he could see the other ships of Sector Twenty-three, slowly circling too, red identification lights strung along their hulls.

Ten miles away a gigantic glowing ball danced in the middle of the space-field, bobbing around like a jigging lantern. And beyond it were the circling blue lights of the Thirty-seven team. And beyond them the glowing green space-buoys that marked the Thirty-seven goal line.

Meek bent an attentive ear to the ticking of the motor, listening intently for the alien click he had detected a moment before. Gus's ship, to tell the truth, was none too good. It might have been a good ship once, but now it was worn out. It was sluggish and slow to respond to the controls, it had a dozen little tricks that kept one on the jump. It had followed space trails too long, had plumped down to too many bumpy landings in the maelstrom of the Belt.

Meek sighed gustily. It would have been different if they had let him take his own ship, but it was only on the condition that he use Gus's ship that Thirty-seven had agreed to let him play at all. They had raised a fuss about it, but Twenty-three had the law squarely on its side.

He stole a glance toward the sidelines and saw hundreds of

slowly cruising ships. Ships crammed with spectators out to watch the game. Radio ships that would beam a play-by-play description to be channeled to every radio station throughout the Solar System. Newsreel ships that would film the clash of opposing craft. Ships filled with newsmen who would transmit reams of copy back to Earth and Mars.

Looking at them, Meek shuddered.

How in the world had he ever let himself get into a thing like this? He was out to see the solar system, not to play a polo game . . . especially a polo game he didn't want to play.

It had been the bugs, of course. If it hadn't been for the bugs, Gus never would have had the chance to talk him into that coaching business.

He should have spoken out, of course. Told them, flat out, that he didn't know a thing about polo. Made them understand he wasn't going to have a thing to do with this silly scheme. But they had shouted at him and laughed at him and bullied him. Been nice to him, too. That was the biggest trouble. He was a sucker, he knew, for anyone who was nice to him. Not many people had been.

Maybe he should have gone to Miss Henrietta Perkins and explained. She might have listened and understood. Although he wasn't any too sure about that. She probably had plenty to do with starting the publicity rolling. After all, it was her job to make a showing on the jobs she did.

If it hadn't been for Gus's dusting off the place on the mantel piece. If it hadn't been for the Titan City Junior Chamber of Commerce. If it hadn't been for all the ballyhoo about the mystery coach.

But more especially, if he'd kept his fool mouth shut and not made that bet with Craney.

Meek groaned and tried to remember the few things he did know about polo. And he couldn't think of a single thing, not even some of the things he had made up and told the boys.

Suddenly a rocket flared from the referee's ship and with a jerk Meek hauled back the throttle. The ship gurgled and stuttered and for a moment, heart in his throat, Meek thought it was going to blow up right then and there.

But it didn't. It gathered itself together and leaped, forcing Meek hard against the chair, snapping back his head. Dazed, he reached out for the repulsor trigger.

Ahead the glowing ball bounced and quivered, jumped this way and that as the ships spun in a mad melee with repulsor beams whipping out like stabbing knives.

Two of the ships crashed and fell apart like matchboxes. A third, trying a sharp turn above the field of play, came unstuck and strewed itself across fifty miles of space.

Substitute ships dashed in from the sidelines, signaled by the referee's blinking light. Rescue ships streaked out to pick up the players, salvage ships to clear away the pieces.

For a fleeting moment, Meek got the bobbing sphere in the crosshairs and squeezed the trigger. The ball jumped as if someone had smacked it with his fist, sailed across the field.

Fighting to bring the ship around, Meek yelled in fury at its slowness. Desperately pouring on the juice, he watched with agony as a blue-lighted ship streamed down across the void, heading for the ball.

The ship groaned in every joint, protesting and twisting as if in agony, as Meek forced it around. Suddenly there was a snap and the sudden *swoosh* of escaping air. Startled, Meek looked up. Bare ribs stood out against star-spangled space. A plate had been ripped off!

Face strained behind the visor of his spacesuit, hunched over the controls, he waited for the rest of the plates to go. By some miracle they hung on. One worked loose and flapped weirdly as the ship shivered in the turn.

But the turn had taken too long and Meek was too late. The blue-lamped ship already had the ball, was streaking for the goal line. Jensen somehow had had sense enough to refuse to be sucked out of goalie position, and now he charged in to intercept.

But he muffed his chance. He dived in too fast and missed with his repulsor beam by a mile at least. The ball sailed over the lighted buoys and the first chukker was over, with Thirty-seven leading by one score.

The ships lined up again.

The rocket flared from the starter's ship and the ships plunged out. One of Thirty-seven's ships began to lose things. Plates broke loose and fell away, a rocket snapped its moorings and sailed off at a tangent, spouting gouts of flame, the structural ribs came off and strewed themselves along like spilling toothpicks.

Battered by repulsor beams, the ball suddenly bounced upward and Meek, trailing the field, waiting for just such a chance, played a savage tune on the tube controls.

The ship responded with a snap, executing a half-roll and a hairpin turn that shook the breath from Meek. Two more plates tore off in the turn, but the ship plowed on. Now the ball was dead ahead and Meek gave it the works. The beam hit squarely and Meek followed through. The second chukker was over and the score was tied.

Not until he was curving back above the Thirty-seven goal line did Meek have time to wonder what had happened to the ship. It was sluggish no longer. It was full of zip. Almost like driving his own sleek craft. Almost as if the ship knew where he wanted it to go and went there.

A hint of motion on the instrument panel caught his eye and he bent close to see what it was. He stiffened. The panel seemed to be alive. Seemed to be crawling.

He bent closer and froze. It was crawling. There was no doubt of that. Crawling with rock bugs.

Breath whistling between his teeth, Meek ducked his head under the panel. Every wire, every control was oozing bugs!

For a moment he sat paralyzed by the thoughts that flickered through his brain.

Gus, he knew, would have his scalp for this. Because he was the one that had brought the bugs over to the rock where Gus lived and kept the ship. They thought, of course, they had caught all of them that were on his suit, but now it was clear they hadn't. Some of them must have gotten away and found the ship. They would have made straight for it, of course, because of the alloys that were in it. Why bother with a spacesuit or anything else when there was a ship around?

Only there were too many of them. There were thousands in the instrument panel and other thousands in the controls and he couldn't have brought back that many. Not if he'd hauled them back in pails.

What was it Gus had said about them burrowing into metal just like chiggers burrow into human flesh?

Chiggers attacked humans to lay their eggs. Maybe . . . maybe . . .

A battalion of the bugs trooped across the face of an indicator and Meek saw they were smaller than the ones he had seen back on Gus's rock.

There was no doubt about it. They were young bugs. Bugs that had just hatched out. Thousands of them . . . millions of them, maybe! And they wouldn't be in the instruments and controls alone, but all through the ship. They'd be in the motors and the firing mechanisms . . . all the places where the best alloys were used.

Meek wrung his hands, watching them play tag across the panel. If they'd had to hatch, why couldn't they have waited. Just until the game was over, anyhow. That would have been all he'd asked. But they hadn't and here he was, with a couple of million bugs or so right smack in his lap.

The rocket flared again and the ships shot out.

Bitterness chewing at him, Meek flung the ship out savagely. What did it matter what happened now? Gus would take the hide off him, rheumatism or no rheumatism, as soon as he found out about the bugs.

For a wild moment, he hoped he would crack up. Maybe the ship would fall apart like some of the others had. Like the old one-hoss shay the poet had written about centuries ago. The ship had lost so many plates that even now it was like flying a space-going box kite.

Suddenly a ship loomed directly ahead, diving from the zenith. Meek, forgetting his half-formed hope of a crackup a second before, froze in terror, but his fingers acted by pure instinct, stabbing at keys. Although, in the petrified second that seemed half an eternity, Meek knew the ships would crash before he even touched the keys. And even as he thought it, the ship ducked in a nerve-rending jerk and they were skimming past, hulls almost touching. Another jerk and more plates gone and there was the ball, directly ahead, with the repulsor beam already licking out.

Meek's jaw fell and a chill went through his body and he couldn't move a muscle. For he hadn't even touched the trigger and yet the repulsor beam was flaring out, driving the ball ahead of it while the ship twisted and squirmed its way through a mass of fighting craft.

Hands dangling limply at his sides, Meek gaped in terror and disbelief. He wasn't touching the controls, and yet the ship was like a thing bewitched. A split second later the ball was over the goal and the ship was curving back, repulsor beam snapped off.

"It's the bugs!" Meek whispered to himself, lips scarcely moving. "The bugs have taken over!"

The craft he was riding, he knew, was no longer just a ship, but a collection of rock bugs. Bugs that could work out mathematical equations. And now were playing polo!

For what was polo, anyhow, except a mathematical equation, a problem of using certain points of force at certain points in space to arrive at a predetermined end? Back on Gus's rock the bugs had worked as a unit to solve equations . . . and the new hatch in the ship was working as a unit, too, to solve another kind of problem . . . the problem of taking a certain ball to a certain point despite certain variable and random factors in the form of opposing spaceships.

Tentatively, half fearfully, Meek stabbed cautiously at a key which should have turned the ship. The ship didn't turn. Meek snatched his hand away as if the key had burned his finger.

Back on the line the ship wheeled into position of its own accord and a moment later was off again. Meek clung to his chair with shaking hands. There was, he knew, no use of even pretending he was trying to operate the ship. There was just one thing that he was glad of. No one could see him sitting there, doing nothing.

But the time would come . . . and soon . . . when he would have to do something. For he couldn't let the ship return to the Ring. To do that would be to infest the other ships parked there, spread the bugs throughout the solar system. And those bugs definitely were something the solar system could get along without.

The ship shuddered and twisted, weaving its way through the pack of players. More plates ripped loose. Glancing up, Meek could see the glory of Saturn through the gleaming ribs.

Then the ball was over the line and Meek's team mates were shrieking at him over the radio in his spacesuit . . . happy, glee-filled yells of triumph. He didn't answer. He was too busy ripping out the control wires. But it didn't help. Even while he was doing it the ship went on unhampered and piled up another score.

Apparently the bugs didn't need the controls to make the ship do what they wanted. More than likely they were in control of the firing mechanism at its very source. Maybe, and the thought curled the hair on Meek's neck, they were the firing mechanism. Maybe they had integrated themselves with the very structure of the entire mechanism of the ship. That would make the ship alive. A living chunk of machinery that paid no attention to the man who sat at the controls.

Meanwhile, the ship made another goal. . . .

There was a way to stop the bugs . . . only one way . . . but it was dangerous.

But probably not half as dangerous, Meek told himself, as Gus or the Junior Chamber or the Thirty-seven team . . . especially the Thirty-seven team . . . if any of them found out what was going on.

He found a wrench and crawled back along the shivering ship.

Working in a frenzy of fear and need for haste, Meek took off the plate that sealed the housing of the rear rocket assembly. Breath hissing in his throat, he fought the burrs that anchored the tubes. There were a lot of them and they didn't come off easily. Rockets had to be anchored securely . . . securely enough so the blast of atomic fire within their chambers wouldn't rip them free.

Meanwhile, the ship piled up the score.

Loose burrs rolled and danced along the floor and Meek knew the ship was in the thick of play again. Then they were curving back. Another goal!

Suddenly the rocket assembly shook a little, began to vibrate. Wielding the wrench like a madman, knowing he had seconds at the most, Meek spun two or three more bolts, then dropped the wrench and ran. Leaping for a hole from which a plate had been torn, he caught a rib, swung with every ounce of power he had, launching himself into space.

His right hand fumbled for the switch of the suit's rocket motor, found it, snapped it on to full acceleration. Something seemed to hit him on the head and he sailed into the depths of blackness.

VI

Billy Jones sat in the office of the repair shop, cigarette dangling from his lip, pouring smoke into his watery eye.

"Never saw anything like it in my life," he declared. "How he made that ship go at all with half the plates ripped off is way beyond me."

The dungareed mechanic sighted along the toes of his shoes, planted comfortably on the desk.

"Let me tell you, mister," he declared, "the solar system never has known a pilot like him . . . never will again. He brought his ship down here with the instruments knocked out. Dead reckoning."

"Wrote a great piece about him," Billy said. "How he died in the best tradition of space. Stuff like that. The readers will eat it up. The way that ship let go he didn't have a chance. Seemed to go out of control all at once and went heaving and bucking almost into Saturn. Then, *blooey* . . . that's the end of it. One big splash of flame."

The mechanic squinted carefully at his toes. "They're still out there, messing around," he said, "but they'll never find him. When that ship blew up he was scattered halfway to Pluto."

The inner lock swung open ponderously and a spacesuited figure stepped in.

They waited while he snapped back his helmet.

"Good evening, gentlemen," said Oliver Meek.

They stared, slack-jawed.

Jones was the first to recover. "But it can't be you! Your ship . . . it exploded!"

"I know," said Meek. "I got out just before it went. Turned on my suit rocket full blast. Knocked me out. By the time I came to I was halfway out to the second Ring. Took me awhile to get back."

He turned to the mechanic. "Maybe you have a secondhand suit you would sell me. I have to get rid of this one. Has some bugs in it."

"Bugs? Oh, yes, I see. You mean something's wrong with it."

"That's it," said Meek. "Something's wrong with it."

"I got one I'll let you have, free for nothing," said the mechanic. "Boy, that was a swell game you played!"

"Could I have the suit now?" asked Meek. "I'm in a hurry to get away."

Jones bounced to his feet. "But you can't leave. Why, they think you're dead. They're out looking for you. And you won the cup . . . the cup as the most valuable team member."

"I just can't stay," said Meek. He shuffled his feet uneasily. "Got places to go. Things to see. Stayed too long already."

"But the cup . . ."

"Tell Gus I won the cup for him. Tell him to put it on that mantel piece. In the place he dusted off for it."

Meek's blue eyes shone queerly behind his glasses. "Tell him maybe he'll think of me sometimes when he looks at it."

The mechanic brought the suit. Meek bundled it under his arm, started for the lock.

Then turned back.

"Maybe you gentlemen . . ."

"Yes," said Jones.

"Maybe you can tell me how many goals I made. I lost count, you see."

"You made nine," said Jones.

Meek shook his head. "Must be getting old," he said. "When I was a kid I was a *ten-goal* man."

Then he was gone, the lock swinging shut behind him.

THE WORLD THAT COULDN'T BE

The first mention of this story, in Clifford D. Simak's journals, comes in a short entry for April 18, 1957, in which he merely states that he is starting the "Beast story." By May 9 he had finished it and sent it to Horace Gold, now with the title "The Cytha." "Got good ending," Cliff said in his journal—and he was right.

The story appeared in the January 1958 issue of Galaxy Science Fiction, *and there is no indication in Cliff's journals that he had anything to do with its second change of title.*

—dww

The tracks went up one row and down another, and in those rows the *vua* plants had been sheared off an inch or two above the ground. The raider had been methodical; it had not wandered about haphazardly, but had done an efficient job of harvesting the first ten rows on the west side of the field. Then, having eaten its fill, it had angled off into the bush—and that had not been long ago, for the soil still trickled down into the great pug marks, sunk deep into the finely cultivated loam.

Somewhere a sawmill bird was whirring through a log, and down in one of the thorn-choked ravines, a choir of chatterers was clicking through a ghastly morning song. It was going to be a scorcher of a day. Already the smell of desiccated dust was rising from the ground and the glare of the newly risen sun was dancing off the bright leaves of the hula-trees, making it appear as if the bush were filled with a million flashing mirrors.

Gavin Duncan hauled a red bandanna from his pocket and mopped his face.

"No, mister," pleaded Zikkara, the native foreman of the farm. "You cannot do it, mister. You do not hunt a Cytha."

"The hell I don't," said Duncan, but he spoke in English and not the native tongue.

He stared out across the bush, a flat expanse of sun-cured grass interspersed with thickets of hula-scrub and thorn and occasional groves of trees, criss-crossed by treacherous ravines and spotted with infrequent waterholes.

It would be murderous out there, he told himself, but it shouldn't take too long. The beast probably would lay up shortly after its pre-dawn feeding and he'd overhaul it in an hour or two. But if he failed to overhaul it, then he must keep on.

"Dangerous," Zikkara pointed out. "No one hunts the Cytha."

"I do," Duncan said, speaking now in the native language. "I hunt anything that damages my crop. A few nights more of this and there would be nothing left."

Jamming the bandanna back into his pocket, he tilted his hat lower across his eyes against the sun.

"It might be a long chase, mister. It is the *skun* season now. If you were caught out there. . . ."

"Now listen," Duncan told it sharply. "Before I came, you'd feast one day, then starve for days on end; but now you eat each day. And you like the doctoring. Before, when you got sick, you died. Now you get sick, I doctor you, and you live. You like staying in one place, instead of wandering all around."

"Mister, we like all this," said Zikkara, "but we do not hunt the Cytha."

"If we do not hunt the Cytha, we lose all this," Duncan

pointed out. "If I don't make a crop, I'm licked. I'll have to go away. Then what happens to you?"

"We will grow the corn ourselves."

"That's a laugh," said Duncan, "and you know it is. If I didn't kick your backsides all day long, you wouldn't do a lick of work. If I leave, you go back to the bush. Now let's go and get that Cytha."

"But it is such a little one, mister! It is such a young one! It is scarcely worth the trouble. It would be a shame to kill it."

Probably just slightly smaller than a horse, thought Duncan, watching the native closely.

It's scared, he told himself. It's scared dry and spitless.

"Besides, it must have been most hungry. Surely, mister, even a Cytha has the right to eat."

"Not from my crop," said Duncan savagely. "You know why we grow the *vua,* don't you? You know it is great medicine. The berries that it grows cures those who are sick inside their heads. My people need that medicine—need it very badly. And what is more, out there"—he swept his arm toward the sky—"out there they pay very much for it."

"But, mister. . . ."

"I tell you this," said Duncan gently, "you either dig me up a bush-runner to do the tracking for me or you can all get out, the kit and caboodle of you. I can get other tribes to work the farm."

"No, mister!" Zikkara screamed in desperation.

"You have your choice," Duncan told it coldly.

He plodded back across the field toward the house. Not much of a house as yet. Not a great deal better than a native shack. But someday it would be, he told himself. Let him sell a crop or two and he'd build a house that would really be a house. It would have a bar and swimming pool and a garden filled with flowers, and at last, after years of wandering, he'd have a home and broad acres and everyone, not just one lousy tribe, would call him mister.

Gavin Duncan, planter, he said to himself, and liked the sound of it. Planter on the planet Layard. But not if the Cytha came back night after night and ate the *vua* plants.

He glanced over his shoulder and saw that Zikkara was racing for the native village.

Called their bluff, Duncan informed himself with satisfaction.

He came out of the field and walked across the yard, heading for the house. One of Shotwell's shirts was hanging on the clothesline, limp in the breathless morning.

Damn the man, thought Duncan. Out here mucking around with those stupid natives, always asking questions, always under foot. Although, to be fair about it, that was Shotwell's job. That was what the Sociology people had sent him out to do.

Duncan came up to the shack, pushed the door open and entered. Shotwell, stripped to the waist, was at the wash bench.

Breakfast was cooking on the stove, with an elderly native acting as cook.

Duncan strode across the room and took down the heavy rifle from its peg. He slapped the action open, slapped it shut again.

Shotwell reached for a towel.

"What's going on?" he asked.

"Cytha got into the field."

"Cytha?"

"A kind of animal," said Duncan. "It ate ten rows of *vua*."

"Big? Little? What are its characteristics?"

The native began putting breakfast on the table. Duncan walked to the table, laid the rifle across one corner of it and sat down. He poured a brackish liquid out of a big stew pan into their cups.

God, he thought, what I would give for a cup of coffee.

Shotwell pulled up his chair. "You didn't answer me. What is a Cytha like?"

"I wouldn't know," said Duncan.

"Don't know? But you're going after it, looks like, and how can you hunt it if you don't know—"

"Track it. The thing tied to the other end of the trail is sure to be the Cytha. We'll find out what it's like once we catch up to it."

"We?"

"The natives will send up someone to do the tracking for me. Some of them are better than a dog."

"Look, Gavin. I've put you to a lot of trouble and you've been decent with me. If I can be any help, I would like to go."

"Two make better time than three. And we have to catch this Cytha fast or it might settle down to an endurance contest."

"All right, then. Tell me about the Cytha."

Duncan poured porridge gruel into his bowl, handed the pan to Shotwell. "It's a sort of special thing. The natives are scared to death of it. You hear a lot of stories about it. Said to be unkillable. It's always capitalized, always a proper noun. It has been reported at different times from widely scattered places."

"No one's ever bagged one?"

"Not that I ever heard of." Duncan patted the rifle. "Let me get a bead on it."

He started eating, spooning the porridge into his mouth, munching on the stale corn bread left from the night before. He drank some of the brackish beverage and shuddered.

"Some day," he said, "I'm going to scrape together enough money to buy a pound of coffee. You'd think—"

"It's the freight rates," Shotwell said. "I'll send you a pound when I go back."

"Not at the price they'd charge to ship it out," said Duncan. "I wouldn't hear of it."

They ate in silence for a time. Finally Shotwell said: "I'm getting nowhere, Gavin. The natives are willing to talk, but it all adds up to nothing."

"I tried to tell you that. You could have saved your time."

Shotwell shook his head stubbornly. "There's an answer, a logical explanation. It's easy enough to say you cannot rule out the sexual factor, but that's exactly what has happened here on

Layard. It's easy to exclaim that a sexless animal, a sexless race, a sexless planet is impossible, but that is what we have. Somewhere there is an answer and I have to find it."

"Now hold up a minute," Duncan protested. "There's no use blowing a gasket. I haven't got the time this morning to listen to your lecture."

"But it's not the lack of sex that worries me entirely," Shotwell said, "although it's the central factor. There are subsidiary situations deriving from that central fact which are most intriguing."

"I have no doubt of it," said Duncan, "but if you please—"

"Without sex, there is no basis for the family, and without the family there is no basis for a tribe, and yet the natives have an elaborate tribal setup, with taboos by way of regulation. Somewhere there must exist some underlying, basic unifying factor, some common loyalty, some strange relationship which spells out to brotherhood."

"Not brotherhood," said Duncan, chuckling. "Not even sisterhood. You must watch your terminology. The word you want is ithood."

The door pushed open and a native walked in timidly.

"Zikkara said that mister want me," the native told them. "I am Sipar. I can track anything but screamers, stilt-birds, longhorns and donovans. Those are my taboos."

"I am glad to hear that," Duncan replied. "You have no Cytha taboo, then."

"Cytha!" yipped the native. "Zikkara did not tell me Cytha!"

Duncan paid no attention. He got up from the table and went to the heavy chest that stood against one wall. He rummaged in it and came out with a pair of binoculars, a hunting knife and an extra drum of ammunition. At the kitchen cupboard, he rummaged once again, filling a small leather sack with a gritty powder from a can he found.

"Rockahominy," he explained to Shotwell. "Emergency rations thought up by the primitive North American Indians.

Parched corn, ground fine. It's no feast exactly, but it keeps a man going."

"You figure you'll be gone that long?"

"Maybe overnight. I don't know. Won't stop until I get it. Can't afford to. It could wipe me out in a few days."

"Good hunting," Shotwell said. "I'll hold the fort."

Duncan said to Sipar: "Quit sniveling and come on."

He picked up the rifle, settled it in the crook of his arm. He kicked open the door and strode out.

Sipar followed meekly.

II

Duncan got his first shot late in the afternoon of that first day.

In the middle of the morning, two hours after they had left the farm, they had flushed the Cytha out of its bed in a thick ravine. But there had been no chance for a shot. Duncan saw no more than a huge black blur fade into the bush.

Through the bake-oven afternoon, they had followed its trail, Sipar tracking and Duncan bringing up the rear, scanning every piece of cover, with the sun-hot rifle always held at ready.

Once they had been held up for fifteen minutes while a massive donovan tramped back and forth, screaming, trying to work up its courage for attack. But after a quarter hour of showing off, it decided to behave itself and went off at a shuffling gallop.

Duncan watched it go with a lot of thankfulness. It could soak up a lot of lead, and for all its awkwardness, it was handy with its feet once it set itself in motion. Donovans had killed a lot of men in the twenty years since Earthmen had come to Layard.

With the beast gone, Duncan looked around for Sipar. He found it fast asleep beneath a hula-shrub. He kicked the native awake with something less than gentleness and they went on again.

The bush swarmed with other animals, but they had no trouble with them.

Sipar, despite its initial reluctance, had worked well at the trailing. A misplaced bunch of grass, a twig bent to one side, a displaced stone, the faintest pug mark were Sipar's stock in trade. It worked like a lithe, well-trained hound. This bush country was its special province; here it was at home.

With the sun dropping toward the west, they had climbed a long, steep hill and as they neared the top of it, Duncan hissed at Sipar. The native looked back over its shoulder in surprise. Duncan made motions for it to stop tracking.

The native crouched and as Duncan went past it, he saw that a look of agony was twisting its face. And in the look of agony he thought he saw as well a touch of pleading and a trace of hatred. It's scared, just like the rest of them, Duncan told himself. But what the native thought or felt had no significance; what counted was the beast ahead.

Duncan went the last few yards on his belly, pushing the gun ahead of him, the binoculars bumping on his back. Swift, vicious insects ran out of the grass and swarmed across his hands and arms and one got on his face and bit him.

He made it to the hilltop and lay there, looking at the sweep of land beyond. It was more of the same, more of the blistering, dusty slogging, more of thorn and tangled ravine and awful emptiness.

He lay motionless, watching for a hint of motion, for the fitful shadow, for any wrongness in the terrain that might be the Cytha.

But there was nothing. The land lay quiet under the declining sun. Far on the horizon, a herd of some sort of animals was grazing, but there was nothing else.

Then he saw the motion, just a flicker, on the knoll ahead—about halfway up.

He laid the rifle carefully on the ground and hitched the binoculars around. He raised them to his eyes and moved them slowly back and forth. The animal was there where he had seen the motion.

It was resting, looking back along the way that it had come, watching for the first sign of its trailers. Duncan tried to make out the size and shape, but it blended with the grass and the dun soil and he could not be sure exactly what it looked like.

He let the glasses down and now that he had located it, he could distinguish its outline with the naked eye.

His hand reached out and slid the rifle to him. He fitted it to his shoulder and wriggled his body for closer contact with the ground. The cross-hairs centered on the faint outline on the knoll and then the beast stood up.

It was not as large as he had thought it might be—perhaps a little larger than Earth lion-size, but it certainly was no lion. It was a square-set thing and black and inclined to lumpiness and it had an awkward look about it, but there were strength and ferociousness as well.

Duncan tilted the muzzle of the rifle so that the cross-hairs centered on the massive neck. He drew in a breath and held it and began the trigger squeeze.

The rifle bucked hard against his shoulder and the report hammered in his head and the beast went down. It did not lurch or fall; it simply melted down and disappeared, hidden in the grass.

"Dead center," Duncan assured himself.

He worked the mechanism and the spent cartridge case flew out. The feeding mechanism snicked and the fresh shell clicked as it slid into the breech.

He lay for a moment, watching. And on the knoll where the thing had fallen, the grass was twitching as if the wind were blowing, only there was no wind. But despite the twitching of the grass, there was no sign of the Cytha. It did not struggle up again. It stayed where it had fallen.

Duncan got to his feet, dug out the bandanna and mopped at his face. He heard the soft thud of the step behind him and turned his head. It was the tracker.

"It's all right, Sipar," he said. "You can quit worrying. I got it. We can go home now."

It had been a long, hard chase, longer than he had thought it might be. But it had been successful and that was the thing that counted. For the moment, the *vua* crop was safe.

He tucked the bandanna back into his pocket, went down the slope and started up the knoll. He reached the place where the Cytha had fallen. There were three small gouts of torn, mangled fur and flesh lying on the ground and there was nothing else.

He spun around and jerked his rifle up. Every nerve was screamingly alert. He swung his head, searching for the slightest movement, for some shape or color that was not the shape or color of the bush or grass or ground. But there was nothing. The heat droned in the hush of afternoon. There was not a breath of moving air. But there was danger—a saw-toothed sense of danger close behind his neck.

"Sipar!" he called in a tense whisper, "Watch out!"

The native stood motionless, unheeding, its eyeballs rolling up until there was only white, while the muscles stood out along its throat like straining ropes of steel.

Duncan slowly swiveled, rifle held almost at arm's length, elbows crooked a little, ready to bring the weapon into play in a fraction of a second.

Nothing stirred. There was no more than emptiness—the emptiness of sun and molten sky, of grass and scraggy bush, of a brown-and-yellow land stretching into foreverness.

Step by step, Duncan covered the hillside and finally came back to the place where the native squatted on its heels and moaned, rocking back and forth, arms locked tightly across its chest, as if it tried to cradle itself in a sort of illusory comfort.

The Earthman walked to the place where the Cytha had fallen and picked up, one by one, the bits of bleeding flesh. They had been mangled by his bullet. They were limp and had no shape. And it was queer, he thought. In all his years of hunting, over many planets, he had never known a bullet to rip out hunks of flesh.

He dropped the bloody pieces back into the grass and wiped his hand upon his thighs. He got up a little stiffly.

He'd found no trail of blood leading through the grass, and surely an animal with a hole of that size would leave a trail.

And as he stood there upon the hillside, with the bloody fingerprints still wet and glistening upon the fabric of his trousers, he felt the first cold touch of fear, as if the fingertips of fear might momentarily, almost casually, have trailed across his heart.

He turned around and walked back to the native, reached down and shook it.

"Snap out of it," he ordered.

He expected pleading, cowering, terror, but there was none.

Sipar got swiftly to its feet and stood looking at him and there was, he thought, an odd glitter in its eyes.

"Get going," Duncan said. "We still have a little time. Start circling and pick up the trail. I will cover you."

He glanced at the sun. An hour and a half still left—maybe as much as two. There might still be time to get this buttoned up before the fall of night.

A half mile beyond the knoll, Sipar picked up the trail again and they went ahead, but now they traveled more cautiously, for any bush, any rock, any clump of grass might conceal the wounded beast.

Duncan found himself on edge and cursed himself savagely for it. He'd been in tight spots before. This was nothing new to him. There was no reason to get himself tensed up. It was a deadly business, sure, but he had faced others calmly and walked away from them. It was those frontier tales he'd heard about the

Cytha—the kind of superstitious chatter that one always heard on the edge of unknown land.

He gripped the rifle tighter and went on.

No animal, he told himself, was unkillable.

Half an hour before sunset, he called a halt when they reached a brackish waterhole. The light soon would be getting bad for shooting. In the morning, they'd take up the trail again, and by that time the Cytha would be at an even greater disadvantage. It would be stiff and slow and weak. It might even be dead.

Duncan gathered wood and built a fire in the lee of a thorn-bush thicket. Sipar waded out with the canteens and thrust them at arm's length beneath the surface to fill them. The water still was warm and evil-tasting, but it was fairly free of scum and a thirsty man could drink it.

The sun went down and darkness fell quickly. They dragged more wood out of the thicket and piled it carefully close at hand.

Duncan reached into his pocket and brought out the little bag of rockahominy.

"Here," he said to Sipar. "Supper."

The native held one hand cupped and Duncan poured a little mound into its palm.

"Thank you, mister," Sipar said. "Food-giver."

"Huh?" asked Duncan, then caught what the native meant. "Dive into it," he said, almost kindly. "It isn't much, but it gives you strength. We'll need strength tomorrow."

Food-giver, eh? Trying to butter him up, perhaps. In a little while, Sipar would start whining for him to knock off the hunt and head back for the farm.

Although, come to think of it, he really was the food-giver to this bunch of sexless wonders. Corn, thank God, grew well on the red and stubborn soil of Layard—good old corn from North America. Fed to hogs, made into corn-pone for breakfast back on Earth, and here, on Layard, the staple food crop for a gang of shiftless varmints who still regarded, with some good solid skepticism and round-eyed wonder, this unorthodox idea that one should take the trouble to grow plants to eat rather than go out and scrounge for them.

Corn from North America, he thought, growing side by side with the *vua* of Layard. And that was the way it went. Something from one planet and something from another and still something further from a third and so was built up through the wide social confederacy of space a truly cosmic culture which in the end, in another ten thousand years or so, might spell out some way of life with more sanity and understanding than was evident today.

He poured a mound of rockahominy into his own hand and put the bag back into his pocket.

"Sipar."

"Yes, mister?"

"You were not scared today when the donovan threatened to attack us."

"No, mister. The donovan would not hurt me."

"I see. You said the donovan was taboo to you. Could it be that you, likewise, are taboo to the donovan?"

"Yes, mister. The donovan and I grew up together."

"Oh, so that's it," said Duncan.

He put a pinch of the parched and powdered corn into his mouth and took a sip of brackish water. He chewed reflectively on the resultant mash.

He might go ahead, he knew, and ask why and how and where Sipar and the donovan had grown up together, but there was no point to it. This was exactly the kind of tangle that Shotwell was forever getting into.

Half the time, he told himself, I'm convinced the little stinkers are doing no more than pulling our legs.

What a fantastic bunch of jerks! Not men, not women, just things. And while there were never babies, there were children, although never less than eight or nine years old. And if there were no babies, where did the eight- and nine-year-olds come from?

"I suppose," he said, "that these other things that are your taboos, the stiltbirds and the screamers and the like, also grew up with you."

"That is right, mister."

"Some playground that must have been," said Duncan.

He went on chewing, staring out into the darkness beyond the ring of firelight.

"There's something in the thorn-bush, mister."

"I didn't hear a thing."

"Little pattering. Something is running there."

Duncan listened closely. What Sipar said was true. A lot of little things were running in the thicket.

"More than likely mice," he said.

He finished his rockahominy and took an extra swig of water, gagging on it slightly.

"Get your rest," he told Sipar. "I'll wake you later so I can catch a wink or two."

"Mister," Sipar said, "I will stay with you to the end."

"Well," said Duncan, somewhat startled, "that is decent of you."

"I will stay to the death," Sipar promised earnestly.

"Don't strain yourself," said Duncan.

He picked up the rifle and walked down to the waterhole.

The night was quiet and the land continued to have that empty feeling. Empty except for the fire and the waterhole and the little micelike animals running in the thicket.

And Sipar—Sipar lying by the fire, curled up and sound asleep already. Naked, with not a weapon to its hand—just the naked animal, the basic humanoid, and yet with underlying purpose that at times was baffling. Scared and shivering this morning at mere mention of the Cytha, yet never faltering on the trail; in pure funk back there on the knoll where they had lost the Cytha, but now ready to go on to the death.

Duncan went back to the fire and prodded Sipar with his toe. The native came straight up out of sleep.

"Whose death?" asked Duncan. "Whose death were you talking of?"

"Why, ours, of course," said Sipar, and went back to sleep.

III

Duncan did not see the arrow coming. He heard the swishing whistle and felt the wind of it on the right side of his throat and then it thunked into a tree behind him.

He leaped aside and dived for the cover of a tumbled mound of boulders and almost instinctively his thumb pushed the fire control of the rifle up to automatic.

He crouched behind the jumbled rocks and peered ahead. There was not a thing to see. The hula-trees shimmered in the blaze of sun and the thorn-bush was gray and lifeless and the only things astir were three stilt-birds walking gravely a quarter of a mile away.

"Sipar!" he whispered.

"Here, mister."

"Keep low. It's still out there."

Whatever it might be. Still out there and waiting for another shot. Duncan shivered, remembering the feel of the arrow flying past his throat. A hell of a way for a man to die—out at the tail-end of nowhere with an arrow in his throat and a scared-stiff native heading back for home as fast as it could go.

He flicked the control on the rifle back to single fire, crawled around the rock pile and sprinted for a grove of trees that stood on higher ground. He reached them and there he flanked the spot from which the arrow must have come.

He unlimbered the binoculars and glassed the area. He still saw no sign. Whatever had taken the pot shot at them had made its getaway.

He walked back to the tree where the arrow still stood out, its point driven deep into the bark. He grasped the shaft and wrenched the arrow free.

"You can come out now," he called to Sipar. "There's no one around."

The arrow was unbelievably crude. The unfeathered shaft looked as if it had been battered off to the proper length with a jagged stone. The arrowhead was unflaked flint picked up from some outcropping or dry creek bed, and it was awkwardly bound to the shaft with the tough but pliant inner bark of the hula-tree.

"You recognize this?" he asked Sipar.

The native took the arrow and examined it. "Not my tribe."

"Of course not your tribe. Yours wouldn't take a shot at us. Some other tribe, perhaps?"

"Very poor arrow."

"I know that. But it could kill you just as dead as if it were a good one. Do you recognize it?"

"No tribe made this arrow," Sipar declared.

"Child, maybe?"

"What would child do way out here?"

"That's what I thought, too," said Duncan.

He took the arrow back, held it between his thumbs and forefingers and twirled it slowly, with a terrifying thought nibbling at his brain. It couldn't be. It was too fantastic. He wondered if the sun was finally getting him that he had thought of it at all.

He squatted down and dug at the ground with the makeshift arrow point. "Sipar, what do you actually know about the Cytha?"

"Nothing, mister. Scared of it is all."

"We aren't turning back. If there's something that you know—something that would help us. . . ."

It was as close as he could come to begging aid. It was further than he had meant to go. He should not have asked at all, he thought angrily.

"I do not know," the native said.

Duncan cast the arrow to one side and rose to his feet. He cradled the rifle in his arm. "Let's go."

He watched Sipar trot ahead. Crafty little stinker, he told himself. It knows more than it's telling.

They toiled into the afternoon. It was, if possible, hotter and drier than the day before. There was a sense of tension in the air—no, that was rot. And even if there were, a man must act as if it were not there. If he let himself fall prey to every mood out in this empty land, he only had himself to blame for whatever happened to him.

The tracking was harder now. The day before, the Cytha had only run away, straight-line fleeing to keep ahead of them, to stay out of their reach. Now it was becoming tricky. It backtracked often in an attempt to throw them off. Twice in the afternoon, the trail blanked out entirely and it was only after long searching that Sipar picked it up again—in one instance, a mile away from where it had vanished in thin air.

That vanishing bothered Duncan more than he would admit. Trails do not disappear entirely, not when the terrain remains the same, not when the weather is unchanged. Something was going on, something, perhaps, that Sipar knew far more about than it was willing to divulge.

He watched the native closely and there seemed nothing suspicious. It continued at its work. It was, for all to see, the good and faithful hound.

Late in the afternoon, the plain on which they had been traveling suddenly dropped away. They stood poised on the brink of a great escarpment and looked far out to great tangled forests and a flowing river.

It was like suddenly coming into another and beautiful room that one had not expected.

This was new land, never seen before by any Earthman. For no one had ever mentioned that somewhere to the west a forest lay beyond the bush. Men coming in from space had seen it, probably, but only as a different color-marking on the planet. To them, it made no difference.

But to the men who lived on Layard, to the planter and the trader, the prospector and the hunter, it was important. And I, thought Duncan with a sense of triumph, am the man who found it.

"Mister!"

"Now what?"

"Out there. *Skun*!"

"I don't—"

"Out there, mister. Across the river."

Duncan saw it then—a haze in the blueness of the rift—a puff of copper moving very fast, and as he watched, he heard the far-off keening of the storm, a shiver in the air rather than a sound.

He watched in fascination as it moved along the river and saw the boiling fury it made out of the forest. It struck and crossed the river, and the river for a moment seemed to stand on end, with a sheet of silvery water splashed toward the sky.

Then it was gone as quickly as it had happened, but there was a tumbled slash across the forest where the churning winds had traveled.

Back at the farm, Zikkara had warned him of the *skun*. This was the season for them, it had said, and a man caught in one wouldn't have a chance.

Duncan let his breath out slowly.

"Bad," said Sipar.

"Yes, very bad."

"Hit fast. No warning."

"What about the trail?" asked Duncan. "Did the Cytha—"

Sipar nodded downward.

"Can we make it before nightfall?"

"I think so," Sipar answered.

It was rougher than they had thought. Twice they went down

blind trails that pinched off, with sheer rock faces opening out into drops of hundreds of feet, and were forced to climb again and find another way.

They reached the bottom of the escarpment as the brief twilight closed in and they hurried to gather firewood. There was no water, but a little was still left in their canteens and they made do with that.

After their scant meal of rockahominy, Sipar rolled himself into a ball and went to sleep immediately.

Duncan sat with his back against a boulder which one day, long ago, had fallen from the slope above them, but was now half buried in the soil that through the ages had kept sifting down.

Two days gone, he told himself.

Was there, after all, some truth in the whispered tales that made the rounds back at the settlements—that no one should waste his time in tracking down a Cytha, since a Cytha was unkillable?

Nonsense, he told himself. And yet the hunt had toughened, the trail become more difficult, the Cytha a much more cunning and elusive quarry. Where it had run from them the day before, now it fought to shake them off. And if it did that the second day, why had it not tried to throw them off the first? And what about the third day—tomorrow?

He shook his head. It seemed incredible that an animal would become more formidable as the hunt progressed. But that seemed to be exactly what had happened. More spooked, perhaps, more frightened—only the Cytha did not act like a frightened beast. It was acting like an animal that was gaining savvy and determination, and that was somehow frightening.

From far off to the west, toward the forest and the river, came the laughter and the howling of a pack of screamers. Duncan leaned his rifle against the boulder and got up to pile more wood on the fire. He stared out into the western darkness, listening to the racket. He made a wry face and pushed a hand absent-mindedly through his hair. He put out a silent hope that the screamers would decide to keep their distance. They were something a man could do without.

Behind him, a pebble came bumping down the slope. It thudded to a rest just short of the fire.

Duncan spun around. Foolish thing to do, he thought, to camp so near the slope. If something big should start to move, they'd be out of luck.

He stood and listened. The night was quiet. Even the screamers had shut up for the moment. Just one rolling rock and he had his hackles up. He'd have to get himself in hand.

He went back to the boulder, and as he stooped to pick up the rifle, he heard the faint beginning of a rumble. He straightened swiftly to face the scarp that blotted out the star-strewn sky—and the rumble grew!

In one leap, he was at Sipar's side. He reached down and grasped the native by an arm, jerked it erect, held it on its feet. Sipar's eyes snapped open, blinking in the firelight.

The rumble had grown to a roar and there were thumping noises, as of heavy boulders bouncing, and beneath the roar the silky, ominous rustle of sliding soil and rock.

Sipar jerked its arm free of Duncan's grip and plunged into the darkness. Duncan whirled and followed.

They ran, stumbling in the dark, and behind them the roar of the sliding, bouncing rock became a throaty roll of thunder that filled the night from brim to brim. As he ran, Duncan could feel, in dread anticipation, the gusty breath of hurtling debris blowing on his neck, the crushing impact of a boulder smashing into him, the engulfing flood of tumbling talus snatching at his legs.

A puff of billowing dust came out and caught them and they ran choking as well as stumbling. Off to the left of them, a mighty chunk of rock chugged along the ground in jerky, almost reluctant fashion.

Then the thunder stopped and all one could hear was the small slitherings of the lesser debris as it trickled down the slope.

Duncan stopped running and slowly turned around. The campfire was gone, buried, no doubt, beneath tons of overlay, and the stars had paled because of the great cloud of dust which still billowed up into the sky.

He heard Sipar moving near him and reached out a hand, searching for the tracker, not knowing exactly where it was. He found the native, grasped it by the shoulder and pulled it up beside him.

Sipar was shivering.

"It's all right," said Duncan.

And it was all right, he reassured himself. He still had the rifle. The extra drum of ammunition and the knife were on his belt, the bag of rockahominy in his pocket. The canteens were all they had lost—the canteens and the fire.

"We'll have to hole up somewhere for the night," Duncan said. "There are screamers on the loose."

He didn't like what he was thinking, nor the sharp edge of fear that was beginning to crowd in upon him. He tried to shrug it off, but it still stayed with him, just out of reach.

Sipar plucked at his elbow.

"Thorn thicket, mister. Over there. We could crawl inside. We would be safe from screamers."

It was torture, but they made it.

"Screamers and you are taboo," said Duncan, suddenly remembering. "How come you are afraid of them?"

"Afraid for you, mister, mostly. Afraid for myself just a little. Screamers could forget. They might not recognize me until too late. Safer here."

"I agree with you," said Duncan.

The screamers came and padded all about the thicket. The beasts sniffed and clawed at the thorns to reach them, but finally went away.

When morning came, Duncan and Sipar climbed the scarp, clambering over the boulders and the tons of soil and rock that covered their camping place. Following the gash cut by the slide, they clambered up the slope and finally reached the point of the slide's beginning.

There they found the depression in which the poised slab of rock had rested and where the supporting soil had been dug away so that it could be started, with a push, down the slope above the campfire.

And all about were the deeply sunken pug marks of the Cytha!

IV

Now it was more than just a hunt. It was knife against the throat, kill or be killed. Now there was no stopping, when before there might have been. It was no longer sport and there was no mercy.

"And that's the way I like it," Duncan told himself.

He rubbed his hand along the rifle barrel and saw the metallic glints shine in the noonday sun. One more shot, he prayed. Just give me one more shot at it. This time there will be no slip-up. This time there will be more than three sodden hunks of flesh and fur lying in the grass to mock me.

He squinted his eyes against the heat shimmer rising from the river, watching Sipar hunkered beside the water's edge.

The native rose to its feet and trotted back to him.

"It crossed," said Sipar. "It walked out as far as it could go and it must have swum."

"Are you sure? It might have waded out to make us think it crossed, then doubled back again."

He stared at the purple-green of the trees across the river. Inside that forest, it would be hellish going.

"We can look," said Sipar.

"Good. You go downstream. I'll go up."

An hour later, they were back. They had found no tracks. There seemed little doubt the Cytha had really crossed the river.

They stood side by side, looking at the forest.

"Mister, we have come far. You are brave to hunt the Cytha. You have no fear of death."

"The fear of death," Duncan said, "is entirely infantile. And it's beside the point as well. I do not intend to die."

They waded out into the stream. The bottom shelved gradually and they had to swim no more than a hundred yards or so.

They reached the forest bank and threw themselves flat to rest.

Duncan looked back the way that they had come. To the east, the escarpment was a dark-blue smudge against the pale-blue burnished sky. And two days back of that lay the farm and the *vua* field, but they seemed much farther off than that. They were lost in time and distance; they belonged to another existence and another world.

All his life, it seemed to him, had faded and become inconsequential and forgotten, as if this moment in his life were the only one that counted; as if all the minutes and the hours, all the breaths and heartbeats, wake and sleep, had pointed toward this certain hour upon this certain stream, with the rifle molded to his hand and the cool, calculated bloodlust of a killer riding in his brain.

Sipar finally got up and began to range along the stream. Duncan sat up and watched.

Scared to death, he thought, and yet it stayed with me. At the campfire that first night, it had said it would stick to the death and apparently it had meant exactly what it said. It's hard, he thought, to figure out these jokers, hard to know what kind of mental operation, what seethings of emotion, what brand of ethics and what variety of belief and faith go to make them and their way of life.

It would have been so easy for Sipar to have missed the trail and swear it could not find it. Even from the start, it could have refused to go. Yet, fearing, it had gone. Reluctant, it had trailed. Without any need for faithfulness and loyalty, it had been loyal and faithful. But loyal to what, Duncan wondered, to him, the outlander and intruder? Loyal to itself? Or perhaps, although that seemed impossible, faithful to the Cytha?

What does Sipar think of me, he asked himself, and maybe more to the point, what do I think of Sipar? Is there a common meeting ground? Or are we, despite our humanoid forms, condemned forever to be alien and apart?

He held the rifle across his knees and stroked it, polishing it, petting it, making it even more closely a part of him, an instrument of his deadliness, an expression of his determination to track and kill the Cytha.

Just another chance, he begged. Just one second, or even less, to draw a steady bead. That is all I want, all I need, all I'll ask.

Then he could go back across the days that he had left behind him, back to the farm and field, back into that misty other life from which he had been so mysteriously divorced, but which in time undoubtedly would become real and meaningful again.

Sipar came back. "I found the trail."

Duncan heaved himself to his feet. "Good."

They left the river and plunged into the forest and there the heat closed in more mercilessly than ever—humid, stifling heat that felt like a soggy blanket wrapped tightly round the body.

The trail lay plain and clear. The Cytha now, it seemed, was intent upon piling up a lead without recourse to evasive tactics. Perhaps it had reasoned that its pursuers would lose some time at the river and it may have been trying to stretch out that margin even further. Perhaps it needed that extra time, he speculated, to set up the necessary machinery for another dirty trick.

Sipar stopped and waited for Duncan to catch up. "Your knife, mister?"

Duncan hesitated. "What for?"

"I have a thorn in my foot," the native said. "I have to get it out."

Duncan pulled the knife from his belt and tossed it. Sipar caught it deftly.

Looking straight at Duncan, with the flicker of a smile upon its lips, the native cut its throat.

V

He should go back, he knew. Without the tracker, he didn't have a chance. The odds were now with the Cytha—if, indeed, they had not been with it from the very start.

Unkillable? Unkillable because it grew in intelligence to meet emergencies? Unkillable because, pressed, it could fashion a bow and arrow, however crude? Unkillable because it had a sense of tactics, like rolling rocks at night upon its enemy? Unkillable because a native tracker would cheerfully kill itself to protect the Cytha?

A sort of crisis-beast, perhaps? One able to develop intelligence and abilities to meet each new situation and then lapsing back to the level of non-intelligent contentment? That, thought Duncan, would be a sensible way for anything to live. It would do away with the inconvenience and the irritability and the discontentment of intelligence when intelligence was unneeded. But the intelligence, and the abilities which went with it, would be there, safely tucked away where one could reach in and get them, like a necklace or a gun—something to be used or to be put away as the case might be.

Duncan hunched forward and with a stick of wood pushed the fire together. The flames blazed up anew and sent sparks flying up into the whispering darkness of the trees. The night had cooled off a little, but the humidity still hung on and a man felt uncomfortable—a little frightened, too.

Duncan lifted his head and stared up into the fire-flecked darkness. There were no stars because the heavy foliage shut them out. He missed the stars. He'd feel better if he could look up and see them.

When morning came, he should go back. He should quit this hunt which now had become impossible and even slightly foolish.

But he knew he wouldn't. Somewhere along the three-day trail, he had become committed to a purpose and a challenge, and he knew that when morning came, he would go on again. It was not hatred that drove him, nor vengeance, nor even the trophy-urge—the hunter-lust that prodded men to kill something strange or harder to kill or bigger than any man had ever killed before. It was something more than that, some weird entangling of the Cytha's meaning with his own.

He reached out and picked up the rifle and laid it in his lap. Its barrel gleamed dully in the flickering campfire light and he rubbed his hand along the stock as another man might stroke a woman's throat.

"Mister," said a voice.

It did not startle him, for the word was softly spoken and for a moment he had forgotten that Sipar was dead—dead with a half-smile fixed upon its face and with its throat laid wide open.

"Mister?"

Duncan stiffened.

Sipar was dead and there was no one else—and yet someone had spoken to him, and there could be only one thing in all this wilderness that might speak to him.

"Yes," he said.

He did not move. He simply sat there, with the rifle in his lap.

"You know who I am?"

"I suppose you are the Cytha."

"You have done well," the Cytha said. "You've made a splendid hunt. There is no dishonor if you should decide to quit. Why don't you go back? I promise you no harm."

It was over there, somewhere in front of him, somewhere in the brush beyond the fire, almost straight across the fire from him, Duncan told himself. If he could keep it talking, perhaps even lure it out—

"Why should I?" he asked. "The hunt is never done until one gets the thing one is after."

"I can kill you," the Cytha told him. "But I do not want to kill. It hurts to kill."

"That's right," said Duncan. "You are most perceptive."

For he had it pegged now. He knew exactly where it was. He could afford a little mockery.

His thumb slid up the metal and nudged the fire control to automatic and he flexed his legs beneath him so that he could rise and fire in one single motion.

"Why did you hunt me?" the Cytha asked. "You are a stranger on my world and you had no right to hunt me. Not that I mind, of course. In fact, I found it stimulating. We must do it again. When I am ready to be hunted, I shall come and tell you and we can spend a day or two at it."

"Sure we can," said Duncan, rising. And as he rose into his crouch, he held the trigger down and the gun danced in insane fury, the muzzle flare a flicking tongue of hatred and the hail of death hissing spitefully in the underbrush.

"Anytime you want to," yelled Duncan gleefully, "I'll come and hunt you! You just say the word and I'll be on your tail. I might even kill you. How do you like it, chump!"

And he held the trigger tight and kept his crouch so the slugs would not fly high, but would cut their swath just above the ground, and he moved the muzzle back and forth a lot so that he covered extra ground to compensate for any miscalculations he might have made.

The magazine ran out and the gun clicked empty and the vicious chatter stopped. Powder smoke drifted softly in the camp-fire light and the smell of it was perfume in the nostrils and in the underbrush many little feet were running, as if a thousand frightened mice were scurrying from catastrophe.

Duncan unhooked the extra magazine from where it hung upon his belt and replaced the empty one. Then he snatched a burning length of wood from the fire and waved it frantically until it burst into a blaze and became a torch. Rifle grasped in one hand and the torch in the other, he plunged into the underbrush. Little chittering things fled to escape him.

He did not find the Cytha. He found chewed-up bushes and soil churned by flying metal, and he found five lumps of flesh and fur, and these he brought back to the fire.

Now the fear that had been stalking him, keeping just beyond his reach, walked out from the shadows and hunkered by the campfire with him.

He placed the rifle within easy reach and arranged the five bloody chunks on the ground close to the fire and he tried with trembling fingers to restore them to the shape they'd been before the bullets struck them. And that was a good one, he thought with grim irony, because they had no shape. They had been part of the Cytha and you killed a Cytha inch by inch, not with a single shot. You knocked a pound of meat off it the first time, and the next time you shot off another pound or two, and if you got enough shots at it, you finally carved it down to size and maybe you could kill it then, although he wasn't sure.

He was afraid. He admitted that he was and he squatted there and watched his fingers shake and he kept his jaws clamped tight to stop the chatter of his teeth.

The fear had been getting closer all the time; he knew it had moved in by a step or two when Sipar cut its throat, and why in the name of God had the damn fool done it? It made no sense at all. He had wondered about Sipar's loyalties, and the very loyalties that he had dismissed as a sheer impossibility had been the answer, after all. In the end, for some obscure reason—obscure to humans, that is—Sipar's loyalty had been to the Cytha.

But then what was the use of searching for any reason in it? Nothing that had happened made any sense. It made no sense that a beast one was pursuing should up and talk to one—although it did fit in with the theory of the crisis-beast he had fashioned in his mind.

Progressive adaptation, he told himself. Carry adaptation far enough and you'd reach communication. But might not the Cytha's power of adaptation be running down? Had the Cytha gone about as far as it could force itself to go? Maybe so, he thought. It might be worth a gamble. Sipar's suicide, for all its casualness, bore the overtones of last-notch desperation. And the Cytha's speaking to Duncan, its attempt to parley with him, contained a note of weakness.

The arrow had failed and the rockslide had failed and so had Sipar's death. What next would the Cytha try? Had it anything to try?

Tomorrow he'd find out. Tomorrow he'd go on. He couldn't turn back now.

He was too deeply involved. He'd always wonder, if he turned back now, whether another hour or two might not have seen the end of it. There were too many questions, too much mystery—there was now far more at stake than ten rows of *vua*.

Another day might make some sense of it, might banish the dread walker that trod upon his heels, might bring some peace of mind.

As it stood right at the moment, none of it made sense.

But even as he thought it, suddenly one of the bits of bloody flesh and mangled fur made sense.

Beneath the punching and prodding of his fingers, it had assumed a shape.

Breathlessly, Duncan bent above it, not believing, not even wanting to believe, hoping frantically that it should prove completely wrong.

But there was nothing wrong with it. The shape was there and could not be denied. It had somehow fitted back into its natural shape and it was a baby screamer—well, maybe not a baby, but at least a tiny screamer.

Duncan sat back on his heels and sweated. He wiped his bloody hands upon the ground. He wondered what other shapes he'd find if he put back into proper place the other hunks of limpness that lay beside the fire.

He tried and failed. They were too smashed and torn.

He picked them up and tossed them in the fire. He took up his rifle and walked around the fire, sat down with his back against a tree, cradling the gun across his knees.

Those little scurrying feet, he wondered—like the scampering of a thousand busy mice. He had heard them twice, that first night in the thicket by the waterhole and again tonight.

And what could the Cytha be? Certainly not the simple, uncomplicated, marauding animal he had thought to start with.

A hive-beast? A host animal? A thing masquerading in many different forms?

Shotwell, trained in such deductions, might make a fairly accurate guess, but Shotwell was not here. He was at the farm, fretting, more than likely, over Duncan's failure to return.

Finally the first light of morning began to filter through the forest and it was not the glaring, clean white light of the open plain and bush, but a softened, diluted, fuzzy green light to match the smothering vegetation.

The night noises died away and the noises of the day took up—the sawings of unseen insects, the screechings of hidden birds, and something far away began to make a noise that sounded like an empty barrel falling slowly down a stairway.

What little coolness the night had brought dissipated swiftly and the heat clamped down, a breathless, relentless heat that quivered in the air.

Circling, Duncan picked up the Cytha trail not more than a hundred yards from camp.

The beast had been traveling fast. The pug marks were deeply sunk and widely spaced. Duncan followed as rapidly as he dared. It was a temptation to follow at a run, to match the Cytha's speed, for the trail was plain and fresh and it fairly beckoned.

And that was wrong, Duncan told himself. It was too fresh, too plain—almost as if the animal had gone to endless trouble so that the human could not miss the trail.

He stopped his trailing and crouched beside a tree and studied the tracks ahead. His hands were too tense upon the gun, his body keyed too high and fine. He forced himself to take slow, deep breaths. He had to calm himself. He had to loosen up.

He studied the tracks ahead—four bunched pug marks, then a long leap interval, then four more bunched tracks, and between the sets of marks the forest floor was innocent and smooth.

Too smooth, perhaps. Especially the third one from him. Too smooth and somehow artificial, as if someone had patted it with gentle hands to make it unsuspicious.

Duncan sucked his breath in slowly.

Trap?

Or was his imagination playing tricks on him?

And if it were a trap, he would have fallen into it if he had kept on following as he had started out.

Now there was something else, a strange uneasiness, and he stirred uncomfortably, casting frantically for some clue to what it was.

He rose and stepped out from the tree, with the gun at ready. What a perfect place to set a trap, he thought. One would be looking at the pug marks, never at the space between them, for the space between would be neutral ground, safe to stride out upon.

Oh, clever Cytha, he said to himself. Oh, clever, clever Cytha!

And now he knew what the other trouble was—the great uneasiness. It was the sense of being watched.

Somewhere up ahead, the Cytha was crouched, watching and waiting—anxious or exultant, maybe even with laughter rumbling in its throat.

He walked slowly forward until he reached the third set of tracks and he saw that he had been right. The little area ahead was smoother than it should be.

"Cytha!" he called.

His voice was far louder than he had meant it to be and he stood astonished and a bit abashed.

Then he realized why it was so loud.

It was the only sound there was!

The forest suddenly had fallen silent. The insects and birds were quiet and the thing in the distance had quit falling down the stairs. Even the leaves were silent. There was no rustle in them and they hung limp upon their stems.

There was a feeling of doom and the green light had changed to a copper light and everything was still.

And the light was *copper!*

Duncan spun around in panic. There was no place for him to hide.

Before he could take another step, the *skun* came and the winds rushed out of nowhere. The air was clogged with flying leaves and debris. Trees snapped and popped and tumbled in the air.

The wind hurled Duncan to his knees, and as he fought to regain his feet, he remembered, in a blinding flash of total recall, how it had looked from atop the escarpment—the boiling fury of the winds and the mad swirling of the coppery mist and how the trees had whipped in whirlpool fashion.

He came half erect and stumbled, clawing at the ground in an attempt to get up again, while inside his brain an insistent, clicking voice cried out for him to run, and somewhere another voice said to lie flat upon the ground, to dig in as best he could.

Something struck him from behind and he went down, pinned flat, with his rifle wedged beneath him. He cracked his head upon the ground and the world whirled sickeningly and plastered his face with a handful of mud and tattered leaves.

He tried to crawl and couldn't, for something had grabbed him by the ankle and was hanging on.

With a frantic hand, he clawed the mess out of his eyes, spat it from his mouth.

Across the spinning ground, something black and angular tumbled rapidly. It was coming straight toward him and he saw it was the Cytha and that in another second it would be on top of him.

He threw up an arm across his face, with the elbow crooked, to take the impact of the wind-blown Cytha and to ward it off.

But it never reached him. Less than a yard away, the ground opened up to take the Cytha and it was no longer there.

Suddenly the wind cut off and the leaves once more hung motionless and the heat clamped down again and that was the end of it. The *skun* had come and struck and gone.

Minutes, Duncan wondered, or perhaps no more than seconds. But in those seconds, the forest had been flattened and the trees lay in shattered heaps.

He raised himself on an elbow and looked to see what was the matter with his foot and he saw that a fallen tree had trapped his foot beneath it.

He tugged a few times, experimentally. It was no use. Two close-set limbs, branching almost at right angles from the bole, had been driven deep into the ground and his foot, he saw, had been caught at the ankle in the fork of the buried branches.

The foot didn't hurt—not yet. It didn't seem to be there at all. He tried wiggling his toes and felt none.

He wiped the sweat off his face with a shirt sleeve and fought to force down the panic that was rising in him. Getting panicky was the worst thing a man could do in a spot like this. The thing to do was to take stock of the situation, figure out the best approach, then go ahead and try it.

The tree looked heavy, but perhaps he could handle it if he had to, although there was the danger that if he shifted it, the bole might settle more solidly and crush his foot beneath it. At the moment, the two heavy branches, thrust into the ground on either side of his ankle, were holding most of the tree's weight off his foot.

The best thing to do, he decided, was to dig the ground away beneath his foot until he could pull it out.

He twisted around and started digging with the fingers of one hand. Beneath the thin covering of humus, he struck a solid surface and his fingers slid along it.

With mounting alarm, he explored the ground, scratching at the humus. There was nothing but rock—some long-buried boulder, the top of which lay just beneath the ground.

His foot was trapped between a heavy tree and a massive boulder, held securely in place by forked branches that had forced their splintering way down along the boulder's sides.

He lay back, propped on an elbow. It was evident that he could do nothing about the buried boulder. If he was going to do anything, his problem was the tree.

To move the tree, he would need a lever and he had a good, stout lever in his rifle. It would be a shame, he thought a little wryly, to use a gun for such a purpose, but he had no choice.

He worked for an hour and it was no good. Even with the rifle as a pry, he could not budge the tree.

He lay back, defeated, breathing hard, wringing wet with perspiration.

He grimaced at the sky.

All right, Cytha, he thought, you won out in the end. But it took a *skun* to do it. With all your tricks, you couldn't do the job until. . . .

Then he remembered.

He sat up hurriedly.

"Cytha!" he called.

The Cytha had fallen into a hole that had opened in the ground. The hole was less than an arm's length away from him, with a little debris around its edges still trickling into it.

Duncan stretched out his body, lying flat upon the ground, and looked into the hole. There, at the bottom of it, was the Cytha.

It was the first time he'd gotten a good look at the Cytha and it was a crazily put-together thing. It seemed to have nothing functional about it and it looked more like a heap of something, just thrown on the ground, than it did an animal.

The hole, he saw, was more than an ordinary hole. It was a pit and very cleverly constructed. The mouth was about four feet in diameter and it widened to roughly twice that at the bottom. It was, in general, bottle-shaped, with an incurving shoulder at the top so that anything that fell in could not climb out. Anything falling into that pit was in to stay.

This, Duncan knew, was what had lain beneath that too-smooth interval between the two sets of Cytha tracks. The Cytha had worked all night to dig it, then had carried away the dirt dug out of the pit and had built a flimsy camouflage cover over it. Then it had gone back and made the trail that was so loud and clear, so easy to make out and follow. And having done all that, having labored hard and stealthily, the Cytha had settled down to watch, to make sure the following human had fallen in the pit.

"Hi, pal," said Duncan. "How are you making out?"

The Cytha did not answer.

"Classy pit," said Duncan. "Do you always den up in luxury like this?"

But the Cytha didn't answer.

Something queer was happening to the Cytha. It was coming all apart.

Duncan watched with fascinated horror as the Cytha broke down into a thousand lumps of motion that scurried in the pit and tried to scramble up its sides, only to fall back in tiny showers of sand.

Amid the scurrying lumps, one thing remained intact, a fragile object that resembled nothing quite so much as the stripped skeleton of a Thanksgiving turkey. But it was a most extraordinary Thanksgiving skeleton, for it throbbed with pulsing life and glowed with a steady violet light.

Chitterings and squeakings came out of the pit and the soft patter of tiny running feet, and as Duncan's eyes became accustomed to the darkness of the pit, he began to make out the forms of some of the scurrying shapes. There were tiny screamers and some donovans and sawmill birds and a bevy of kill-devils and something else as well.

Duncan raised a hand and pressed it against his eyes, then took it quickly away. The little faces still were there, looking up as if beseeching him, with the white shine of their teeth and the white rolling of their eyes.

He felt horror wrenching at his stomach and the sour, bitter taste of revulsion welled into his throat, but he fought it down, harking back to that day at the farm before they had started on the hunt.

"I can track down anything but screamers, stilt-birds, longhorns and donovans," Sipar had told him solemnly. "These are my taboos."

And Sipar was also their taboo, for he had not feared the donovan. Sipar had been, however, somewhat fearful of the screamers in the dead of night because, the native had told him reasonably, screamers were forgetful.

Forgetful of what!

Forgetful of the Cytha-mother? Forgetful of the motley brood in which they had spent their childhood?

For that was the only answer to what was running in the pit and the whole, unsuspected answer to the enigma against which men like Shotwell had frustratedly banged their heads for years.

Strange, he told himself. All right, it might be strange, but if it worked, what difference did it make? So the planet's denizens were sexless because there was no need of sex—what was wrong with that? It might, in fact, Duncan admitted to himself, head off a lot of trouble. No family spats, no triangle trouble, no fighting over mates. While it might be unexciting, it did seem downright peaceful.

And since there was no sex, the Cytha species was the planetary mother—but more than just a mother. The Cytha, more than likely, was mother-father, incubator, nursery, teacher and perhaps many other things besides, all rolled into one.

In many ways, he thought, it might make a lot of sense. Here natural selection would be ruled out and ecology could be controlled in considerable degree and mutation might even be a matter of deliberate choice rather than random happenstance.

And it would make for a potential planetary unity such as no other world had ever known. Everything here was kin to everything else. Here was a planet where Man, or any other alien, must learn to tread most softly. For it was not inconceivable that, in a crisis or a clash of interests, one might find himself faced suddenly with a unified and cooperating planet, with every form of life making common cause against the interloper.

The little scurrying things had given up; they'd gone back to their places, clustered around the pulsing violet of the Thanksgiving skeleton, each one fitting into place until the Cytha had taken shape again. As if, Duncan told himself, blood and nerve and muscle had come back from a brief vacation to form the beast anew.

"Mister," asked the Cytha, "what do we do now?"

"You should know," Duncan told it. "You were the one who dug the pit."

"I split myself," the Cytha said. "A part of me dug the pit and the other part that stayed on the surface got me out when the job was done."

"Convenient," grunted Duncan.

And it was convenient. That was what had happened to the Cytha when he had shot at it—it had split into all its component parts and had got away. And that night beside the waterhole, it had spied on him, again in the form of all its separate parts, from the safety of the thicket.

"You are caught and so am I," the Cytha said. "Both of us will die here. It seems a fitting end to our association. Do you not agree with me?"

"I'll get you out," said Duncan wearily. "I have no quarrel with children."

He dragged the rifle toward him and unhooked the sling from the stock. Carefully he lowered the gun by the sling, still attached to the barrel, down into the pit.

The Cytha reared up and grasped it with its forepaws.

"Easy now," Duncan cautioned. "You're heavy. I don't know if I can hold you."

But he needn't have worried. The little ones were detaching themselves and scrambling up the rifle and the sling. They reached his extended arms and ran up them with scrabbling claws. Little sneering screamers and the comic stilt-birds and the mouse-size kill-devils that snarled at him as they climbed. And the little grinning natives—not babies, scarcely children, but small editions of full-grown humanoids. And the weird donovans scampering happily.

They came climbing up his arms and across his shoulders and milled about on the ground beside him, waiting for the others.

And finally the Cytha, not skinned down to the bare bones of its Thanksgiving-turkey-size, but far smaller than it had been, climbed awkwardly up the rifle and the sling to safety.

Duncan hauled the rifle up and twisted himself into a sitting position.

The Cytha, he saw, was reassembling.

He watched in fascination as the restless miniatures of the planet's life swarmed and seethed like a hive of bees, each one clicking into place to form the entire beast.

And now the Cytha was complete. Yet small—still small—no more than lion-size.

"But it is such a little one," Zikkara had argued with him that morning at the farm. "It is such a young one."

Just a young brood, no more than suckling infants—if suckling was the word, or even some kind of wild approximation. And through the months and years, the Cytha would grow, with the growing of its diverse children, until it became a monstrous thing.

It stood there looking at Duncan and the tree.

"Now," said Duncan, "if you'll push on the tree, I think that between the two of us—"

"It is too bad," the Cytha said, and wheeled itself about.

He watched it go loping off.

"Hey!" he yelled.

But it didn't stop.

He grabbed up the rifle and had it halfway to his shoulder before he remembered how absolutely futile it was to shoot at the Cytha.

He let the rifle down.

"The dirty, ungrateful, double-crossing—"

He stopped himself. There was no profit in rage. When you were in a jam, you did the best you could. You figured out the problem and you picked the course that seemed best and you didn't panic at the odds.

He laid the rifle in his lap and started to hook up the sling and it was not till then that he saw the barrel was packed with sand and dirt.

He sat numbly for a moment, thinking back to how close he had been to firing at the Cytha, and if that barrel was packed hard enough or deep enough, he might have had an exploding weapon in his hands.

He had used the rifle as a crowbar, which was no way to use a gun. That was one way, he told himself, that was guaranteed to ruin it.

Duncan hunted around and found a twig and dug at the clogged muzzle, but the dirt was jammed too firmly in it and he made little progress.

He dropped the twig and was hunting for another, stronger one when he caught the motion in a nearby clump of brush.

He watched closely for a moment and there was nothing, so he resumed the hunt for a stronger twig. He found one and started poking at the muzzle and there was another flash of motion.

He twisted around. Not more than twenty feet away, a screamer sat easily on its haunches. Its tongue was lolling out and it had what looked like a grin upon its face.

And there was another, just at the edge of the clump of brush where he had caught the motion first.

There were others as well, he knew. He could hear them sliding through the tangle of fallen trees, could sense the soft padding of their feet.

The executioners, he thought.

The Cytha certainly had not wasted any time.

He raised the rifle and rapped the barrel smartly on the fallen tree, trying to dislodge the obstruction in the bore. But it didn't budge; the barrel still was packed with sand.

But no matter—he'd have to fire anyhow and take whatever chance there was.

He shoved the control to automatic, and tilted up the muzzle.

There were six of them now, sitting in a ragged row, grinning at him, not in any hurry. They were sure of him and there was no hurry. He'd still be there when they decided to move in.

And there were others—on all sides of him.

Once it started, he wouldn't have a chance.

"It'll be expensive, gents," he told them.

And he was astonished at how calm, how coldly objective he could be, now that the chips were down. But that was the way it was, he realized.

He'd thought, a while ago, how a man might suddenly find himself face to face with an aroused and cooperating planet. Maybe this was it in miniature.

The Cytha had obviously passed the word along: *Man back there needs killing. Go and get him.*

Just like that, for a Cytha would be the power here. A life force, the giver of life, the decider of life, the repository of all animal life on the entire planet.

There was more than one of them, of course. Probably they had home districts, spheres of influence and responsibility mapped out. And each one would be a power supreme in its own district.

Momism, he thought with a sour grin. Momism at its absolute peak.

Nevertheless, he told himself, it wasn't too bad a system if you wanted to consider it objectively.

But he was in a poor position to be objective about that or anything else.

The screamers were inching closer, hitching themselves forward slowly on their bottoms.

"I'm going to set up a deadline for you critters," Duncan called out. "Just two feet farther, up to that rock, and I let you have it."

He'd get all six of them, of course, but the shots would be the signal for the general rush by all those other animals slinking in the brush.

If he were free, if he were on his feet, possibly he could beat them off. But pinned as he was, he didn't have a chance. It would be all over less than a minute after he opened fire. He might, he figured, last as long as that.

The six inched closer and he raised the rifle.

But they stopped and moved no farther. Their ears lifted just a little, as if they might be listening, and the grins dropped from their faces. They squirmed uneasily and assumed a look of guilt and, like shadows, they were gone, melting away so swiftly that he scarcely saw them go.

Duncan sat quietly, listening, but he could hear no sound.

Reprieve, he thought. But for how long? Something had scared them off, but in a while they might be back. He had to get out of here and he had to make it fast.

If he could find a longer lever, he could move the tree. There was a branch slanting up from the topside of the fallen tree. It was almost four inches at the butt and it carried its diameter well.

He slid the knife from his belt and looked at it. Too small, too thin, he thought, to chisel through a four-inch branch, but it was all he had. When a man was desperate enough, though, when his very life depended on it, he would do anything.

He hitched himself along, sliding toward the point where the branch protruded from the tree. His pinned leg protested with stabs of pain as his body wrenched it around. He gritted his teeth and pushed himself closer. Pain slashed through his leg again and he was still long inches from the branch.

He tried once more, then gave up. He lay panting on the ground.

There was just one thing left.

He'd have to try to hack out a notch in the trunk just above his leg. No, that would be next to impossible, for he'd be cutting into the whorled and twisted grain at the base of the supporting fork.

Either that or cut off his foot, and that was even more impossible. A man would faint before he got the job done.

It was useless, he knew. He could do neither one. There was nothing he could do.

For the first time, he admitted to himself: He would stay here and die. Shotwell, back at the farm, in a day or two might set out hunting for him. But Shotwell would never find him. And anyhow, by nightfall, if not sooner, the screamers would be back.

He laughed gruffly in his throat—laughing at himself.

The Cytha had won the hunt hands down. It had used a human weakness to win and then had used that same human weakness to achieve a viciously poetic vengeance.

After all, what could one expect? One could not equate human ethics with the ethics of the Cytha. Might not human ethics, in certain cases, seem as weird and illogical, as infamous and ungrateful, to an alien?

He hunted for a twig and began working again to clean the rifle bore.

A crashing behind him twisted him around and he saw the Cytha. Behind the Cytha stalked a donovan.

He tossed away the twig and raised the gun.

"No," said the Cytha sharply.

The donovan tramped purposefully forward and Duncan felt the prickling of the skin along his back. It was a frightful thing. Nothing could stand before a donovan. The screamers had turned tail and run when they had heard it a couple of miles or more away.

The donovan was named for the first known human to be killed by one. That first was only one of many. The roll of donovan-victims ran long, and no wonder, Duncan thought. It was the closest he had ever been to one of the beasts and he felt a coldness creeping over him. It was like an elephant and a tiger and a grizzly bear wrapped in the selfsame hide. It was the most vicious fighting machine that ever had been spawned.

He lowered the rifle. There would be no point in shooting. In two quick strides, the beast could be upon him.

The donovan almost stepped on him and he flinched away. Then the great head lowered and gave the fallen tree a butt and the tree bounced for a yard or two. The donovan kept on walking. Its powerfully muscled stern moved into the brush and out of sight.

"Now we are even," said the Cytha. "I had to get some help."

Duncan grunted. He flexed the leg that had been trapped and he could not feel the foot. Using his rifle as a cane, he pulled himself erect. He tried putting weight on the injured foot and it screamed with pain.

He braced himself with the rifle and rotated so that he faced the Cytha.

"Thanks, pal," he said. "I didn't think you'd do it."

"You will not hunt me now?"

Duncan shook his head. "I'm in no shape for hunting. I am heading home."

"It was the *vua,* wasn't it? That was why you hunted me?"

"The *vua* is my livelihood," said Duncan. "I cannot let you eat it."

The Cytha stood silently and Duncan watched it for a moment. Then he wheeled. Using the rifle for a crutch, he started hobbling away.

The Cytha hurried to catch up with him.

"Let us make a bargain, mister. I will not eat the *vua* and you will not hunt me. Is that fair enough?"

"That is fine with me," said Duncan. "Let us shake on it."

He put down a hand and the Cytha lifted up a paw. They shook, somewhat awkwardly, but very solemnly.

"Now," the Cytha said, "I will see you home. The screamers would have you before you got out of the woods."

VI

They halted on a knoll. Below them lay the farm, with the *vua* rows straight and green in the red soil of the fields.

"You can make it from here," the Cytha said. "I am wearing thin. It is an awful effort to keep on being smart. I want to go back to ignorance and comfort."

"It was nice knowing you," Duncan told it politely. "And thanks for sticking with me."

He started down the hill, leaning heavily on the rifle-crutch. Then he frowned troubledly and turned back.

"Look," he said, "you'll go back to animal again. Then you will forget. One of these days, you'll see all that nice, tender *vua* and—"

"Very simple," said the Cytha. "If you find me in the *vua,* just begin hunting me. With you after me, I will quickly get smart and remember once again and it will be all right."

"Sure," agreed Duncan. "I guess that will work."

The Cytha watched him go stumping down the hill.

Admirable, it thought. Next time I have a brood, I think I'll raise a dozen like him.

It turned around and headed for the deeper brush.

It felt intelligence slipping from it, felt the old, uncaring comfort coming back again. But it glowed with anticipation, seethed with happiness at the big surprise it had in store for its new-found friend.

Won't he be happy and surprised when I drop them at his door, it thought.

Will he be ever pleased!

CLIFFORD D. SIMAK, during his fifty-five-year career, produced some of the most iconic science fiction stories ever written. Born in 1904 on a farm in southwestern Wisconsin, Simak got a job at a small-town newspaper in 1929 and eventually became news editor of the *Minneapolis Star-Tribune*, writing fiction in his spare time. Simak was best known for the book *City*, a reaction to the horrors of World War II, and for his novel *Way Station*. In 1953 *City* was awarded the International Fantasy Award, and in following years, Simak won three Hugo Awards and a Nebula Award. In 1977 he became the third Grand Master of the Science Fiction and Fantasy Writers of America, and before his death in 1988, he was named one of three inaugural winners of the Horror Writers Association's Bram Stoker Award for Lifetime Achievement.

DAVID W. WIXON was a close friend of Clifford D. Simak's. As Simak's health declined, Wixon, already familiar with science fiction publishing, began more and more to handle such things as his friend's business correspondence and contract matters. Named literary executor of the estate after Simak's death, Wixon began a long-term project to secure the rights to all of Simak's stories and find a way to make them available to readers who, given the fifty-five-year span of Simak's writing career, might never have gotten the chance to enjoy all of his short fiction. Along the way, Wixon also read the author's surviving journals and rejected manuscripts, which made him uniquely able to provide Simak's readers with interesting and thought-provoking commentary that sheds new light on the work and thought of a great writer.

THE COMPLETE SHORT FICTION OF CLIFFORD D. SIMAK

FROM OPEN ROAD MEDIA

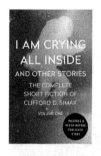

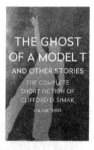
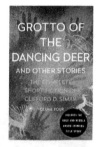

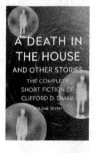
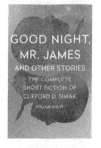

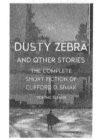

OPEN ROAD

INTEGRATED MEDIA

INTEGRATED MEDIA

CPSIA information can be obtained
at www.ICGtesting.com
Printed in the USA
JSHW081924050623
42734JS00001B/1